The Deceit of Riches

by V M Karren

FLY-BY-NIGHT PRESS

Today is a little worse than yesterday, but a bit better than tomorrow.
- *Russian proverb*

The following is a work of fiction,
as was most of official Soviet history.

FOREWORD

Dear Reader,

As husband and wife living and working in Nizhny Novgorod, Russia during the same tumultuous time period as the author, we so identify with this gripping novel. Though Peter Turner might be fictional, the chaos, the explosion of crime and the mafia, and the struggle for basic necessities were not. This was a dangerous, yet exciting, time to be in Russia but also deeply sad to see how the Russia people suffered due to all the changes enveloping their country—criminal and otherwise.

Val Karren brings to life this crazy, unsettling time during the fall of the Soviet Union by telling us the compelling story of Peter Turner, an American university student in Nizhny Novgorod, who inadvertently gets caught up in the local power struggles. He experiences first hand many of the day-to-day struggles facing the common man and woman; describing some of the repercussions of what Russia's new-found freedoms brought to the Russian people and their culture. Through the eyes of Peter Turner, the author is also able to give us a glimpse of the difficulty of moral choices when circumstances become dire, and nearly everyone seems corrupted, either through need or greed.

A positive thing that does come through the author's words is his love for the country of Russia itself; its beauties and the paradoxes of the Russian culture and its people.

This story will be entertaining and enlightening for anyone interested in this period of Russia, especially as seen through the eyes of someone who was actually there. For those who experienced Russia, while all this tumultuous change was happening, this will be a particularly great read. It is a glimpse of life that most outside of Russia and the Soviet Bloc know very little about; it shows hardship and how it can change people—for good or bad. Also, and perhaps most importantly, it shows that there are people who will fight for what is morally right—even when the outcome is in doubt.

We are looking forward to many other stories about the "Motherland" and Peter Turner's adventures from author Val Karren!

Mike and Bonnie Ramsdell
Best-selling Author of *A Train to Potevka*

0. Obituary

PRESS RELEASE: RUSSIAN AVIONICS HERO IVAN
SERGEYEVICH S. FOUND MURDERED

November 14, 1994 / Union News Services
Moscow / Bishkek

A spokesman for the Ministry of Defense of the Russian Federation this morning expressed his condolences to the family members of Ivan Sergeyevich S. who was found dead in his Bishkek hotel room in the late evening of Sunday, November 13, 1994. The Kremlin, it was stated, is committed to a full investigation into the death of S., which has been classified as an act of terrorism against the Russian Federation. The authorities in the former Soviet republic of Kyrgyzstan have committed their full cooperation to solve the crime and bring his murderer to justice.

Ivan Sergeyevich S. was a decorated veteran of the armed forces of both the Soviet Union and Russian Federation. S. was awarded the medal "Hero of the Red Army" in 1978 for his contributions to the advancement of both Soviet and Russian military aviation.

S. served in the Red Army in the German Democratic Republic in the 1950s after the liberation of Europe from fascism, helping to restore peace and security on the borders of the Motherland after the Great Patriotic War.

A graduate of Moscow State University with an advanced scientific degree in radar and radio sciences, S. served his country heroically in the research and development of aviation supremacy of the Soviet military, successfully protecting our homeland against the imperialist aggression of the United States & Great Britain for thirty-five years.

This morning the President of the Russian Federation, Boris N. Yeltsin, had awarded S. the highest civilian honor of our country for his selfless sacrifice in fulfilling his duty to the Motherland. S. was murdered while taking part in a security operation with the RF state security agencies against the theft and smuggling of Russian military technology through former Soviet republics in central Asia to Chechen separatists and terrorists.

S. is survived by his wife Natalya Federovna and his only son Igor Ivanovich, who live still in the Volga river city Nizhniy Novgorod. S. directed radar technology development at the Government Institute of Military Avionics in that provincial capital city since 1979 until his untimely death.

Glory to the Heroes of the Soviet Union and the Russian Federation!

06

1. Yulia

Up until the moment that the airplane touched down at Moscow's International Airport, nerves and doubts played in my mind on a repeating loop. It had been seven months since my last stay in Russia. I was unsure what would happen once I was again on the ground. Would I still be able to speak Russian? Surely, I'd forgotten too much already! Would I make it to my hotel without getting mugged? Why was I doing this again? As soon as the wheels touched the runway, all my insecurities scattered as quickly as cockroaches from the morning sun.

The only question from the stern-faced woman controlling my passport behind the thick, scratched glass was: "Do you speak Russian, Mr. Peter Turner?" she asked with disapproval in her voice.

"Yes, of course!" I answered with no hesitation but taken aback that she even addressed me.

"Where did you learn it?" she asked, looking up from her computer terminal without moving her head, her eyes on me with a glance of suspicion.

"On the Volga," I replied again, a wisp of nostalgia in my voice and a smile.

"On the Volga?" she asked surprised and looked me full in the face.

"Yes, on the Volga," I repeated with animation. "In the towns on the river like Yaroslavl, Plyos, and Nizhniy Novgorod."

"Very nice," she muttered with just a twinge of a smile in her eyes.

She stamped my student visa and my passport and slid both back to me under the glass with a lingering trace of curiosity on her face. I collected my documents and nodded my thanks to her.

Perhaps more unusual in this exchange than an American happily speaking Russian to the stern, khaki-clad immigration officer in Moscow, was the smile on the officer's face as I stepped away. Centuries old ingrained suspicion of foreigners in their country was melting quickly with the changes in the early 1990s. Russians expressed pleasant surprise when westerners spoke fluent Russian with them. Such exchanges perhaps went to validate a citizen's hope in the post-Soviet shift, as Russia lurched ideologically closer—with abrupt starts and stops— toward Europe and the United States. If foreigners were learning their language and coming to stay, they surely thought, perhaps it wasn't such desperate situation after all. Maybe the sun was just about to rise again.

Russia, in the early years after the rejection of the Soviet Union and its communist mandate, had embraced the ideals of free market reforms and the privatization of the country's entire infrastructure and economy. It was moving quickly to undo the almost seventy-five years of state control over almost all economic activity and personal choice. Unfortunately, most citizens were not ready for the rapid changes dictated from the top down which clashed with all they had known and learned from childhood. Groups of very clever, dishonest people in high places within Moscow's inner circles of power, and criminals who violently usurped it, were those who benefited the most. Those same people also accelerated the pace of reform where they could before their advantage evaporated with the re-education of the population. While foreign money poured into Russia to invest in newly privatized hotels, factories, and oil fields, which was being reported with glee in western newsrooms, the workers and pensioners were being swindled out of their shares and homes by con-men and gangsters who could more deftly adapt when the wind changed directions. Banks weren't just robbed—the banks were stolen and moved to Switzerland. What once belonged to everyone now belonged to only a few. Those who couldn't stand the motion sickness caused by the untempered gyrations towards capitalism and democracy were simply ground into the dust that covered the cars and buildings in the cities and villages across Russia.

Russia's potential in that time was intoxicating and irresistible to any entrepreneur, foreign or domestic. The present was latent with possibilities. The intelligence, the perseverance, the long suffering of its populace offered the children of Russia a future of prosperity and freedom unknown ever before to the children of the Motherland, if only Moscow would allow it.

Moscow for the last several years had been eating its own children. Mercy and decency were not to be found in circles where money and power were being consolidated. President Yeltsin, who was surrounded by self-seeking, opportunistic figures from circles of both politicians and criminals, seemed unaware or unable to control the wholesale theft of the country's future. The new laws of deregulation were strong with new ideology but void of a long-term perspective for Russia and her people. The ability for the country to correct its path before it was too late was slipping quickly away with each new assassination, car bomb, and back alley murder. The future was up for grabs and everybody was grabbing what they could before the music stopped.

On the numerous billboards along the Leningradskiy Highway, on our way into central Moscow, I read that Christmas had been officially rehabilitated and was once again in fashion. The taxi driver, a young man with small children who needed gifts from Dedya Moroz (Father Frost) in the morning, charged me an extortionate sixty dollars in cold hard American cash for a lift into town. It surely hadn't taken long for the principles of supply and demand to be understood on the streets of Moscow.

I sniffed the air in the cabin of the cramped car and looked with suspicion at my driver.

"What's that I smell?" I asked suspiciously.

"All is normal, all is normal," my driver responded without actually reassuring me that everything was fine. Seeing my continued distrust, the driver leaned across me, his left hand still on the steering wheel, and reached into the miniature glove compartment of this mud splattered Lada, and produced a glass flask of Vodka and showed it to me with a proud smile.

"Thanks.... but no," I held up my hands to refuse his hospitality with even more concern on my face.

"It's for the windshield!" he insisted as he waved the bottle in the air motioning to the dirty glass we were both squinting to see through.

Right on cue, a large freight truck passed us on the left spraying the windows with thick mud from the slushy street. For a second or two we could see nothing but brown sludge out of the front windows. The smell of strong alcohol filled the cabin of the car again as the windshield wipers worked frantically to rinse away the mud and snow. Another shot of vodka from the lever on the steering column and we could see the dim street lights again as we hurled down Leningradskoe Boulevard passing the northern river station on our right.

"It never freezes, and it's cheaper than the real stuff, and I can get it anywhere!" the driver continued to explain his enterprising use of Russia's magic elixir.

"Clever!" I snorted with irony.

With a gleeful smile, he closed the glove box before swerving to exit Leningradskiy Prospect just before Belorusskiy Train Station; he then swung on to the northern bend of Moscow's outer ring road towards Prospect Mira, and my waiting bed.

"Nope! Nothing has changed since I left," I said to myself and settled into my seat as we careened through the slushy roads and falling snow, just as Moscow's skyscrapers came into view through the Christmas snow and urban twilight. Ruby-lit stars burned visibly in a halo above the old city center. It was good to be back.

"Wah wah wah — wah wah wah wah?"" That was all I understood from the ticket window at the Kazanskiy Train Station after announcing my destination.

"The cheaper the better," I replied and waited for the large, gray woman behind the glass to tell me a price for the lowest class ticket for the overnight train to Nizhniy Novgorod.

As I moved slowly with my luggage to the train platforms, an older police man in his blue shapka and muddy boots lazing at the side of the gate, eyeing a foreigner, stood up right.

He asked gruffly, "What are you?"

"American," I answered a bit annoyed.

"Where are you going?" he inquired, holding out his hand to signal to inspect my travel authorization.

"To Nizhniy," I answered. I glanced upward to the departure board displaying the same destination.

"You? To Nizhniy? We'll see about that." He took my passport, visa, and train ticket and inspected them all with a suspicious surprise. "What is your program?"

"Linguistics and Literature," was my official reply.

"Show me your invitation letter," he demanded.

I produced a faxed copy of my acceptance letter from the Nizhgorodskiy State University stating I was expected on the tenth of January to begin lectures and readings in Russian linguistics and literature.

After a check and recheck of my documents, he handed all the items back to me. He eyed me up one last time looking for any reason to refuse me. Finding nothing out of place, he relented. With a flick of his head, he waved me on to the platform to my waiting third class sleeper car, wherein I hardly slept a wink of the four-hundred-kilometer train ride to Nizhniy Novgorod.

Both the surprise and suspicion of the police officer about my intention to travel to Nizhniy Novgorod was expected. Nizhniy Novgorod was until just two years ago a "NO GO" city for all foreigners. During the Cold War, the city was a hotbed of research and development of Soviet military technology and was therefore off limits to all without express permission to be there. When the leadership of the Soviet Union wanted to make Andrey Sakharov unreachable to the outside world for his peace activism around the world they exiled him to this closed bastion under house arrest, where the foreign press and Nobel committee couldn't reach him. To meet an American traveling unaccompanied to this city just a few years earlier was unheard of in the USSR. All requests to visit would have been summarily refused, and any credentials stating the opposite would have been highly suspect and most likely forged.

Nizhniy Novgorod has been a Russian manufacturing base of both military and civilian machinery since before the Second World War and the revolution of 1917. Renamed Gorkiy during the communist period, to honor a socialist author from the city, the engineers here produced Russia's greatest technological developments. The SOKOL aircraft factory has been designing and assembling fighter planes since the Great Patriotic War in the 1940s and more recently the MIG fighter aircraft during the Cold War. The ubiquitous black Volga sedan that mid-level apparatchiks and their staff drive around Moscow, as well as the light blue versions for taxis, are all assembled in Nizhniy Novgorod in the Avtozavod (car factory) region of the city. The massive GAZ trucks, born here, roll constantly over the streets of the town, cruising up and down Prospect Lenina on the western bank of the Oka River making deliveries to the plethora of factories. Through the decades Gorkiy developed into Russia's third city, after Moscow and Leningrad, due to its strategic location on the Volga River which flows through the heart of Russia's interior. Students in the province could receive top rated education in aeronautics, mechanical engineering or classical music without having to relocate to either Moscow or Leningrad. In the skies, streets, and waterways around Nizhniy Novgorod, Russia's latest technologies were being tested and unveiled well out of sight of curious onlookers, benign or otherwise, until the early 1990s.

When the Soviet Union came apart at the seams politically and economically in the mid-1980s, the orders which kept the factories of Gorkiy producing at full steam started to falter. As

Russia focused on reforming its failed economic system, its military and industrial orders slowed to a trickle and many factories were shuttered and fell into disuse. Viable factories that could find foreign markets for their products were privatized and turned into Joint Stock Companies, and the directors traveled abroad to market their wares. Simple laborers suddenly became clueless stock holders in their factories. Smelling an opportunity through others' ignorance, gangsters quickly resorted to violence to gain control of the newly privatized factories. A select few became very wealthy by any standard, while many lost their jobs and started driving mini-cabs to try to make ends meet. A degree in radio technology became useless. Learning to sell Snickers bars, Wrigley's chewing gum, pantyhose and cheap alcohol among a huddle of similar kiosks near the train and metro stations was how youth of Nizhniy Novgorod were earning their bread and salt. Then came the protection rackets.

It was still dark in Nizhniy Novgorod when the train pulled into the Moscovskiy Station at seven-thirty in the morning. In January at these latitudes, the sun doesn't break the gravity of the horizon until nine-thirty, and by late afternoon the street lights turn on again. Luckily, winter days, although bitter cold, are usually bright and sunny, except when it's snowing, which is too often in January.

I watched from the windows in the carriage's corridor as the train pulled up to the platform of the station. I waved through the frozen window to Yulia, waiting for me on the platform, as the train cars came to a gradual stop and jolted softly forward in a slow chain reaction collision. The conductor's shrill whistle broke the quiet reverence of the moment of arrival. The crowds piled out the doors and into the cold morning. Steam filled the platform.

I had met Yulia the summer prior. I was working as a tour guide and interpreter for American tourists who were seeing Russia for the first time from the deck of a cruise boat, visiting one-horse villages and industrial cities up and down the Volga River. When we first met, there was friction. The friction, though, had created a curious spark that kept the both of us coming back to check what that spark might possibly become. It was a happy moment of trepidation and anticipation to see her again waiting for me. She greeted me with a warm hug on the icy platform.

"Peter, I am so happy you have arrived! Welcome back to Nizhniy Novgorod." Yulia greeted me with the pageantry of a tour guide meeting jet lagged tourists for the first time.

Ladend like a camel with my bags, dressed in fur and wool, I trundled through the station behind Yulia and down the escalators to the metro platforms.

"My, it is very cold here." I commented as my chin began to stiffen in the frozen air.

"Yes, it's not sailing weather anymore! I'm glad you still have your shapka. You'll need that in Russia. Ukrainian winters just aren't the same"," she boasted of Russia's northern extremes. "Are you hungry? We have a breakfast waiting for you at home"."

"Yes, thank you. Didn't get a chance to have any dinner last night," I apologized.

"Did you see anything in Moscow this time?" she asked, not knowing yet what to talk with me about.

"No, not really. It was Christmas day so only the biggest attractions and restaurants were open. I showed some acquaintances from the hostel around Red Square and the Kremlin."

"Did you bring other shoes than those?" she said, glancing at my feet.

"Yes, I have my winter boots in this large bag," I replied, slapping my luggage with two good thuds.

"That's good because your feet will freeze in those." she said laughing at my folly.

"Yes, I was not very comfortable yesterday in Moscow. Luckily, I have good socks," I said with an entertained smile at her concern for this naive foreigner experiencing his first Russian winter. The temperature was negative seventeen Celsius.

If the tea hadn't warmed me, the five flights of stairs carrying my luggage would have. I was sweating in my long underwear in the warm apartment. Inside, I shed my wool and fur as quickly as possible. Not having slept on the train I involuntarily drooped off to sleep in my chair.

When I woke up the apartment had been flooded by bright winter sunlight and the ladies were already preparing lunch. I was rather embarrassed and begged their pardon.

"Please excuse me. I don't know what happened. I was here and then I was asleep," I bumbled, still a bit disoriented.

"It's not a problem. You've had a long journey." Yulia's gracious mother replied. "You're awake just in time for lunch."

"Peter, after lunch we'll walk over to Mikhail's apartment before it gets dark again and you can take an early bedtime. We have arranged for you to sleep there for the weekend until Monday when your room in the student hall will be ready," Yulia explained.

"Very kind of you to arrange all this for me, Yulia, thank you very much," I thanked her sincerely.

"I hope you will be comfortable there," she replied politely. "We have an appointment for you with Valentina Petrovna at the university on Monday morning at ten-thirty. I don't have lectures on Monday, so I will take you there to make sure you get introduced there"."

"Thank you again," I offered with a smile.

We ate bread and pickled cucumbers and sipped warm tea politely as we tried to get reacquainted after seven months.

Yulia, a feisty, persistent student of journalism seemed to me one the most resourceful people in all of Russia. She carried a self-confidence in her which seemed to make it difficult for anybody to tell her no. Her face, while very pretty, most times had a look of intensity and determination that would wear her opponents down with reasoning, questioning and just a pinch of sugar. She had a fair complexion next to her strawberry blonde hair and deep round brown eyes that made her memorable to even casual acquaintances. With the typical long legs of young eastern European women, she struck an elegant, long, slender figure. She was a free thinker, ignoring perceived limitations to her goals and dreams, yet she was as pragmatic as a popular politician. When she was sweet, she was as sweet as wild honey. When she was irritated her wrath could lay waste to the city. She beguiled and frightened me at the same time. She was Russia embodied in a beautiful young woman.

My decision to return specifically to Nizhniy Novgorod, and not to Moscow or St. Petersburg to study after an intense summer on the riverboats, was greatly due to her influence and her facilitating communication, and ultimately my acceptance at the university. Understanding the politics of bureaucrats, she lobbied my independent application with the needed professors, vouching for me and promising great results. She was relentless in search of needed approvals for my admission and ultimately succeeded despite all the red tape and delays. When she set her mind to something it was nearly impossible to exorcise her of it until she was fully satisfied. She was a researcher, a detective, and a prosecutor. Her opinions once formed were as hard as granite. Her good grace once lost was never to be granted again. She judged quickly on first impressions and was rarely wrong.

My initial meeting with Valentina Petrovna on Monday morning at the University's foreign student's office on Gagarin Street was not a pleasant nor comforting experience. In the place of a cordial greeting, I was chided and scolded for one thing or another, from my muddy shoes to wearing my coat and shapka in the building. There was a wardrobe at the entrance of the building for such things and I should learn to use them. Yulia was livid at Valentina's condescending attitude and excused herself halfway through the interview before she said something she shouldn't have.

Valentina Petrovna would not speak Russian to me although I answered all her questions quickly in the local language. I sat across from her over her pressboard desk while she questioned me.

"Mr. Turner, where have you been sleeping since your arrival?" was her first line of interrogation.

"With acquaintances nearby," I replied, expecting some polite conversation.

"Why have you not yet reported to the local police station to register?" she demanded.

"Because I do not know where my dormitory is located," I answered truthfully.

"How do you plan to pay for your studies?" She was making notes as she questioned me.

"In cash as instructed." I tried to see what she was writing as I answered her random questions.

"Peter, are you carrying that money with you in town?" She looked up at me with a startled face from her writing.

"No, I will use a credit card to withdraw money from my account in the USA at the right time," I said, sitting back in my chair looking her in the eyes.

After my interrogation and instruction from the directress, I was introduced to Pasha and Marina, a cute couple who were co-presidents of the school's new English Club. They were very enthusiastic to have a native English speaker join the department and had volunteered to show me around the dormitories and the Gagarin Street complex. Pasha, a handsome, well-dressed and groomed young man who spoke with reserve, was juxtaposed with Marina, a very bubbly bright-eyed girl with an infectious smile and pale blue eyes. She was very excited to speak English with me.

The two showed me and Yulia the way to the dormitories and gave a brief tour of the ground floor. There was a cold, bare cafeteria, a sterile medical station, void of any nurse that morning, and a wardrobe for coats and shapkas from where the superintendent kept tabs on everybody as they came and went, making notes of the times students arrived or departed. I was begrudgingly given a key by the middle-aged woman from her office next to the wardrobe. As we climbed the stairs to the student rooms, Marina whispered some advice to me about our less than friendly superintendent.

"She never had a husband. He is dead in the big war. She no likes our boys. I think you reminds of her dead lover," she explained in her best English possible. "Don't talk to her. Just say thank you and go away quickly."

Pasha commented in Russian, "She is always watching us and tries to make problems for us if we have had too much beer. She makes notes of everything you do so don't try to do things against the rules. She knows everything! She must work for the secret police," he said, rolling his eyes.

Marina hissed back at him, "Pasha, you must speak English!"

He rolled his eyes again behind her back as we climbed up two flights of stairs. Yulia thought this was a rather funny exchange and laughed aloud, causing everybody to chuckle.

Pasha showed me to my room while the ladies lingered in the stairwell and chatted with each other like hens. The bedroom, empty of roommates still to return from the winter break, looked itself like a cheerful jail cell, or a clean Russian hospital room. The walls were jarring bright green and there were matching green and white fuzzy wool blankets on the bunk beds. The room screamed "Gulag" at me, except for the large window with sheers and curtains. The chunky radiator hidden under the window sheers was fully opened, warming the room to near suffocation levels. The hot air in the room caused the residual odors of the occupants in a closed terrarium to rush into the cold hallway through the open door: garlic, onions, alcohol, body odor, and tea all mixed into a pungent eastern blend. There was a samovar station in the corner of the room on a triangular table that fit snuggly in the corner. Assorted unwashed utensils and plates in a washing-up box and washed clothing lay at the foot of beds to dry. At first look, my stomach turned upside down.

"Do you share this room as well, Pasha?" I asked him with caution.

"No. I sleep in a different room," he answered slowly and deliberately in English.

Holding my nose in exaggeration I asked, "Does your room smell better?"

Pasha looked at me as if I was completely crazy. "Do you think this room smells bad?" he asked as he took in a deep breath through wide nostrils. "Smells like everybody's room. It's normal." He shrugged. I was immediately conscious that I would not be able to handle such conditions for more than two weeks, if that.

Marina proposed that the four of us meet for dinner that night and spend some more time speaking English. For Russians to speak English now, more than ever, was a requisite for success. To speak English well-improved one's chances of getting noticed by a new joint venture business moving into Russia to work locally as an interpreter, or even eventually to be asked to work abroad. We agreed to meet on Minin Square at six o'clock that evening for dinner in a Stubbe inside one of the city's kremlin towers.

Dinner with Marina and Pasha was a half game of charades and laughing. Marina refused to speak Russian and was searching for English words in the smoky air hanging above our table. This spectacle drew the attention of the entire café to our corner table.

"Why did you choose your study in Nizhniy?" Marina asked me after drinks had been brought to the table.

"I have heard that in Nizhniy the governor is helping to grow private businesses by making good new laws. I want to study how he is doing that," I answered slowly for her and Pasha to understand.

"Not because you have a beautiful girlfriend here?" Marina asked smiling and winking at Yulia.

"That helped my decision," I admitted bashfully. "I want to understand how Russia is changing on the inside, not just in Moscow. Maybe I came more to live the changes than studying it from books," I added regarding my motivations.

"But why? Why come to our country when it's falling apart?" Pasha challenged me.

"Is it falling apart? I think maybe it's just getting a new life. Don't you maybe think?" I countered.

"Oh no! In four years I have been student we have so less opportunity now for job than at beginning. My certificate will not get me engineer job. I will have to look to work for foreign company to earn money," he said with some urgency and regret.

"Then we had better speak English to give you lots of practice," I offered, hoping to soothe the sting of his situation.

"But you have come here to learn to speak Russian," Pasha returned my offer.

"But he already speaks Russian!" Marina interrupted. Turning to me, she continued, "I heard you talk with Valentina Petrovna. You speak very good Russian already. We need to learn English like you speak Russian."

"Really, Marina, it takes immersion in a language to learn to speak it fluently. You can't learn to think in a language from a book, no matter how much you read," I explained as she pouted.

"Yes, but Peter sound as if he is Russian. Maybe like he's come from Estonia," she moaned again to Pasha who seemed less concerned.

"When you study abroad, Masha, you can sound like English girl, too," Pasha said deliberately to his disheartened girlfriend.

"Peter? Did you work with a private company in America? Do they like you to speak Russian?" Marina asked me directly.

"Yes, in fact, Yulia and I met when I worked for an American company in Russia. We know the people in Moscow who hire interpreters. If you want we can introduce you to them," I offered, reassuring her distress that she was figuratively missing her ship of opportunity as Russia sailed further with only the bilingual.

"Oy! That will be ...wonder...very nice of you." She looked to Yulia for confirmation.

"I have Irina's telephone number in Moscow, we can tell her about you." Yulia's spoken English was awkward but always very correct. She understood far more quickly the spoken word than she could speak it back, but when she did it was always the right word with the right grammar.

"Will I speak to Americans the whole day through?" she asked excitedly.

"Yes, many Americans with many different accents. All day long, and sometimes in the middle of the night too," I warned her.

After we had eaten a bit of our dinners, two tall young men in their late twenties came over and introduced themselves in very sophisticated English accents and shook hands. Their clothes looked a bit shabby and their hair a bit wayward creating an obvious mismatch between accent and appearance.

"Good evening, I am Richard, this is Andrew," the first one spoke for both, while both leaned in for a proper handshake. I stood to meet their handshakes.

"Hallo. Peter Turner. This is Pasha, Marina, and Yulia," I replied, motioning to each of them in turn.

"Nice to meet you all," Richard said to all three, looking them politely in their faces. "So sorry for intruding but we don't hear many American accents in this town, or spoken English here for that matter. We just had to find out about you as we know probably all the westerners here."

"Just arrived over the holiday weekend. I've come for a master's program here at the university for the next year," I revealed. "What brings you both here? You've been here a little while I can see" ." I pinched my still stiff collar on my shirt.

Richard rolled his eyes with a bit of knowing disgust and pinched his collar to help it stand a bit taller. "We are here with the World Bank outreach," he replied.

"Really!?" I was immediately pleased to meet them for the research connections that they represented.

"That's right," Andrew replied just behind Richard's shoulder in the cramped corner space of the Stubbe.

"How long has that been going on?" I inquired.

"About fourteen months now, but we've only arrived maybe four months ago and will stay another two," Andrew confirmed.

"Would you like to join us?" I asked. I made a scooting motion with my hands to those sitting in the corner booth bench to see if we could make room for two more backsides.

"You are very welcome!" Marina bubbled as she moved closer to Pasha to further compress her already small size.

Richard replied politely, "No, no, please, we were just leaving, but please stop by our office for a chat. It's just around the corner next to the new pizza restaurant 'New York's Best.'" This term 'New York's Best' was spoken with some irony between the three westerners.

"I certainly will. Our history lectures are here at the square on Mondays and Wednesdays," I mentioned.

Marina nodded to confirm the information.

"Very nice to meet you, Peter," Richard said, holding out his hand again for a second shake.

After seeing Yulia onto her bus that would take her back across the Oka River, the three of us rode the bus back to the dormitories on Gagarin Street. Pasha helped me carry my bags that we had retrieved from Yulia's apartment earlier in the afternoon. Marina kept talking and asking questions, half in English and half in Russian while we rode through the cold dark night.

We wished Marina a good evening and climbed the stairs with my bags, after paying homage to the superintendent who noted our arrival. Pasha kindly introduced me to my roommates, now present, and in different half states of being dressed, the radiator still open and pumping waves of rising heat at full force.

Standing in the open door surveying my new colleagues, Vitaly, the only Russian in the room, dressed in Adidas training pants, tapochki with no socks, and a sleeveless undershirt yelled, "Current!"

Hearing this I reflexively flung my backpack onto my bed and kicked the door closed with my left foot.

Most cultures in eastern Europe have a paranoid fear of drafts or cross winds in a room. If a window is open and a door is left ajar at the same time, those in the room will yell, "Current!" This translates loosely into English as, "Close the door before you make us all sick!"

Vitaly was immediately very curious. "You are American? Why do you come to Russia? We all want to go to America or Europe."

"I have lived in America, I have lived in England and now it's time to visit Russia," I replied without guile.

"You are crazy! How did you learn to speak Russian?" he demanded to know.

"I spent last summer working on the Volga boats as a translator for American tourists, and that is where I learned to speak real RUSSIAN," I emphasized the word 'Russian' with a local Volga accent —very heavy and very round on the vowels.

"Where did you visit?" His questions were rapid fire.

"Almost every little village between Moscow and Volgograd. I really like Yaroslavl and Nizhniy the best, but Volgograd is something special!"

"Did you visit the little town Ilyanovsk nearby Saratov? I am from Ilyanovsk," he proudly proclaimed.

"No, we sailed past Ilyankovsk but stopped in Samara and Saratov," I consoled him.

"You speak very good Russian," Vitaly remarked while jabbing my chest with an index finger in a friendly gesture of approval. "I think you might be a spy, maybe CIA?" He joked from one side of his mouth while suspicion rummaged around in his thoughts.

"That's all past tense now. Russia and America are friends now," I rebutted.

"No, Russia is being a lap dog, and America the boss, not friends. One day, Russia will bite back for sure," Vitaly proclaimed with a big of arrogance.

"I don't know. I don't think that one can stop the progress that has come, and the changes already made will be very hard to turn back," I commented as I started unpacking one of my backpacks.

"America is happy now about Gorbachev and Yeltsin, letting them do whatever they like around the world, but America needs to worry about when the mafia takes over. That is when the real fighting begins! When the big mafia bosses want something, they'll kill anybody to get it. Nothing matters to them except control and money. Did you not see the TV exposé special last week about it? We hardly know who is mafia and who is for Russia," he blathered on.

"Don't you think democracy will fix that problem?" I remarked, trying to brush him off.

"Hallo, American boy!" Vitaly spoke in good spirit but was serious. "Russians don't know yet how democracy works. Russian workers don't know what capitalism is. We were taught that profits were for criminals until five years ago. Do you think everything has changed because we voted for Yeltsin? It will take too much time to fix. But do you know who already understands these situations? The criminals, because they lived outside the Soviet laws already for many years. They know how the world works and will be the first to figure out how to take over Russia, and maybe with lots of blood. Russians aren't afraid of blood in the streets," he continued on, obviously already drunk.

"C'mon, Vitaly," I rebutted, a bit annoyed at his pointless rambling. "Ivan the Terrible has been dead a long time. The modern world doesn't work like that any longer!"

"You tell that to Stalin! He is dead now only forty years. He killed more people that Ivan Groznovo. Stalin could come back. Some say he never died"." Vitaly raised his eyebrows for suspense. "Did you hear about what is going on in Moscow? The gangs are killing each other every day. One group wants to control the aluminum factories in Siberia, another wants the nickel mines in Murmansk, one group is fighting to control the ports and customs duties. The government isn't able to do anything about it. Business men are being killed every day in Moscow! The government doesn't do anything about it because they are all part of a secret group, too, helping make it all legal by privatizing Russia's black gold into their own hands. I stay out of politics and business. It's too dangerous. I'll be an engineer and build bridges and keep myself alive."

Another roommate spoke up, Murat from Kazakstan. "He's been drinking too much! Don't listen to him. He always drinks too much. It's the Chechens and Uzbeks we all have to watch out for. They'll cut your throat while you sleep and drink your blood."

"Ohh!" Vitaly cried foul. "How can a good Russian share a room with all foreigners and not tell them how the world is? Russia may be down right now, but that's because we let in too many foreigners. Russia will come back strong again, just like after the war. We just have to get it together. We need a strong man, one who doesn't drink vodka and can speak without drooling in the microphone. That drunk Yeltsin will get us all killed!"

We all looked at each other, a bit unsure what to say. Criticizing the sitting president was not a good way for a student in Russia to start the year and hope to keep his scholarship. Seeing our discomfort, Vitaly grinned the toothy grin of a patient and visionary avenger and then offered me a very warm bottle of beer and toasted me. "But for now, we will be friends! Na zdaroviya!" And he then chugged the rest of his oversized bottle in one breath.

Just a few minutes later Vitaly was snoring on his bottom bunk across from me, stinking of beer and body odor. I turned to the wall and tried my best to sleep.

06

2. Valentina & Karamzin

Early the following morning after a less than satisfying shower and a light breakfast of borrowed tea and dry bread from the breakfast nook in my room, I went to meet Valentina Petrovna and Arkadiy, her secretary. They were to accompany me to the university's accounting office to hand over my tuition fees in hard currency. I had been instructed to pay this money in cash on arrival because a wire transfer to a local account was not a possibility. Money, when sent via wire to or from Russia, seemed to disappear more often than not. Banks were no longer safe places to put one's money as nobody was quite sure when the next bank would collapse under bad debt or large-scale embezzlements. Hard currency in hand is what the people trusted. To get that much cash required an advance from the Inkombank on Varavara Street where Visa and MasterCard were an honored foreign currency.

The morning was cold and still. Steam rose straight up into the frozen morning's stratosphere. My breath crystallized as I exhaled. A fresh carpet of midnight snow hid the muddy imperfections of urban living and hushed the traffic on the wide boulevard in front of the campus. We shuffled through the fresh ankle-deep powder to the alley behind the administration building and climbed into the back of a waiting gray mini-bus with large knobby tires. There were no windows nor seats, only hard wooden benches along the walls with handgrips in place of seat belts. The bus hurdled violently over the ruts and bumps of frozen potholes or snow and ice. The three of us in the back braced ourselves with hands and legs to keep our heads from hitting the roof of the bus. The trolleybus would have been more comfortable, but Valentina Petrovna insisted that we take the university's van and driver out of "an abundance of caution" because of the amount of cash I needed to carry back to the school. It seemed to me that everybody was over-concerned about the local propensity for street crime. In hindsight though, perhaps it was the bankers, not the hooligans, that made the locals so nervous—and for good reason!

Confusion reigned when our small party of three entered the accounting offices at the school's administration building. The clerks looked like startled sloths when we walked in. Nobody acknowledged us as we quietly closed the door behind us. There was no more than a glance and certainly no movement or knowing looks in our direction. After half a minute went by in near silence, a tension began to rise in the room. One could sense a concerted effort to be as nonchalant as possible. Something seemed very wrong.

"Young man!" Valentina blurted dramatically as if reading lines from a play. "As arranged we are here to pay this student's study fees in foreign valuta."

After some glancing around and shifting in his chair he replied, "That's not possible, ma'am."

Valentina insisted again. "I was told we could deposit this money here today." She seemed to be putting on an act.

The clerk reaffirmed his position with an argument. "The university cannot deposit cash. We have no way to receive foreign currency," he explained.

Valentina Petrovna turned to me and said in English, assuming I didn't understand her conversation with the clerk, "Please give him your money and show him your receipt from the bank from this morning. He is afraid to accept the money not knowing its source."

I reached for my passport and wallet from inside my coat while looking questioningly at the impotent accountant, looking for an approving nod or a step forward that didn't come. His face was blank. He stood looking at Valentina as I slowly walked to his desk and gave him my documents and the receipt, but not yet the money. He obviously couldn't read them. He quickly glanced over them and handed the items back to me with a shrug and a blank expression as if to say 'What is going on here?' I stepped away without producing the fifteen bank notes in my other pocket.

"Valentina, he doesn't know what to do with the money," I stated the obvious.

She looked frustrated and flustered like an actor who had forgotten her lines.

I turned and addressed the clerk directly. "Tell me, please, if we exchanged these dollars into rubles, could the university accept the cash then?"

"Nyet, our office does not have access to a bank account. We transfer credits given to us by the administration and the government. Nobody pays with cash for education in Russia," the clerk explained further.

"Mr. Turner please stay out of this matter. I will arrange this," Valentina huffed again in English.

"Well, it seems we should be doing this differently, isn't this so my friend?" I turned again to the statuesque clerk, hoping for a suggestion of alternate solution from him.

"Mr. Turner, please give me the money and the receipt and I will work this out."

I gave the envelope and receipt to Valentina who then placed it deliberately on the clerk's desk.

"Please put this money in the safe, young man, and I will work out the acceptance of this money with the university's director later this afternoon," she instructed.

I watched as my tuition money was locked in a thick cast iron box with a large jagged key which the clerk took from an unlocked desk drawer.

"So much for an abundance of precaution," I commented to Valentina, mocking her with sarcasm which she didn't grasp at that moment. I had my doubts that my money would ever be seen in the accounts of the university.

I was quiet for the ten-minute ride back to the Gagarin Street building and dormitories trying to take in just exactly what had happened, but Valentina interrupted my thoughts to chide me again. "Mr. Turner. Please remember that you are a foreigner. People in our city are not used to dealing with foreigners. There are ways to do things in Russia and ways NOT to do things. To exchange so much money would draw attention and you could become a target. Please just focus on your studies and let the university take care of such matters."

"Very well then, Valentina. I trust my money will be received and I can study then?" I poked the proverbial bear to hear her response, as my suspicions had been piqued by the act in the accounting office.

"Arkadiy is our witness that your money was deposited with the university," she motioned to Arkadiy, who was already nodding with a docile smile on his face.

Arkadiy was an interesting character; He was a former Soviet air force intelligence officer who spoke and wrote English like no other Russian I had ever met, yet so subservient to Valentina Petrovna. He must have been stationed abroad in a Soviet embassy in an English-speaking country. Was this the fate of ex-Soviet military officers: to be clerks in the newly organized foreign students' offices around Russia? Whatever his story, he was my witness.

With my tuition paid, that morning I was introduced to the heads of the two departments in which I would be studying: Dean Roman Sergeyevich Karamzin, the head of the History Faculty, and Professor Lyudmila Ivanovna Dashkova of the School of Pedagogy.

Professor Dashkova, a plump middle-aged woman with thick curly black hair was a warm and encouraging mentor who corrected mistakes without chiding. Self-correction of grammar, mis-enunciation or an incorrect stress on a changing adjectival form would be congratulated with a warm smile from her round, rosy cheeks. She was a doting mother over her students, who absolutely loved reading and teaching the Russian classics—Pushkin, in particular, was her specialty and she evangelized the world with the virtues of his tales and poetry. For her, there was only one version of the Russian lexicon that was acceptable, and that was Pushkin's! Street slang and foreign cognates were to her as abhorrent as margarine to a French pastry chef. Only the best ingredients went into our essays.

In our initial meeting, Professor Dashkova spoke only Russian with me and asked open questions to make me speak and explain myself.

"Young man, please tell me what motivated you to study Russian and Russian literature," Lyudmila began.

"Well, I think it all started because I was afraid of war between our countries." My reply startled the professor.

"So you are here to study the language of the enemy?" she asked suspiciously.

"No, just the opposite," I gave a startled return to her accusation, "so that we don't remain enemies!"

"Oh, yes, I understand." She seemed relieved yet a bit ruffled.

"I started teaching myself how to read the Russian alphabet when I was sixteen years old. For several years, I taught myself vocabulary and phrases and started trying to read lexicons—but that was too advanced for me to do on my own. Once I reached university level and could take proper courses from a Russian-born professor I really started to love this language. I find it very expressive. I wish English had so many adjectives."

"Have you done much reading in the classics in your study?" she inquired.

"Sorry, I only know the stereotypical Russian authors. Tolstoy, Dostoyevsky, and Pushkin. I can understand Tolstoy's writing if I really concentrate, but then I have to read a paragraph twice. I can't follow Dostoyevskiy in English or Russian, but I love Pushkin's short stories! They are so Russian and timeless. I feel I understand Russia so much better through Pushkin," I expounded.

"I too love Pushkin very much. I feel he was the true Russian writer who not only observed Russia, like Tolstoy but who accurately interpreted Russia and Russians. Tolstoy was too caught up in Russia's relation to and with France and other European countries. Pushkin was focused fully on Russian matters. He was the original Russian writer," she said with a sparkle in her eyes.

"I look forward to reading more of his works. I only know a very few," I admitted.

"And so we shall, and so we shall," Ludmilla confirmed.

"Your Russian skills seem to be excellent. Your grammar is very careful and accurate, your accent is very good, and your vocabulary seems to have good depth. But I notice you do not use idioms and expressions. You speak very literally." Her analysis intrigued me. "You don't think or dream in Russian yet, do you?"

"No, not yet," I conceded.

"Well, if we put your nose into Pushkin a few hours every day, we can change that." She smiled and made some notes in her notebook. "The more you read Pushkin, the more you will speak and write like Pushkin. So we will focus heavily on reading the classics and essay writing. Your conversation skills are excellent, you don't seem to miss many details. Much of this work will be self-study, so you will have to motivate and discipline yourself. Try to speak with people of all different kinds while you're here. Old people speak differently than students. Lawyers speak differently than a worker from one of the automobile factories. You will do well to speak more than listen to lectures." She rattled these instructions off like a pharmacist giving instructions for the careful use of dispensed medicines. "And in April we will do a pre-test for the entrance exams to the Moscow State University, the MGU, and in June I expect that you will pass that proficiency exam. When you do that you will be eligible to study in Moscow if you wish," she explained with proxy excitement.

Dean Karamzin was a man larger than life. A life-loving Russian academic with a head of thick dark hair and endless historical facts, dates, and allusions to historical events. His booming voice from his barrel chest could be heard through the entire lecture hall without a microphone. This was the case when speaking to sheepish students in history lectures or with a hall filled with arguing intellectuals. The dean was in a very good mood when I met him for the first time in his office on Minin Square.

"It is exciting to have a foreign student come to earn a master's degree in history and not to study just poems and grammar!" The dean seemed to frown on the touchy feely disciplines and expressed his preference for dates and facts.

"Thank you, sir. It is surely a unique chance for me as well to be here, learning first hand instead of just reading other people's research from the other side of the ocean," I remarked.

"Indeed, indeed! So, what part of Russia's history interests you? Do you have a proposal for a thesis yet?" he asked with what seemed to be a tinge of glee.

"Well, current events are what truly interest me. As you know, history is being rewritten from the Soviet version to Russian version right now, and I wouldn't know what is acceptable or even real to research. Current events seem to be the only thing a student can see is really true."

"You speak the truth about our bad habit of changing our histories to suit our politics, but remember that nothing in Russia is ever as it looks on the surface, even what you read tomorrow in the newspaper. You will need to research for yourself to get to the truth," he warned me with a chiding voice.

"Yes sir, even in the USA nothing is really as it seems. There is always a hidden agenda in everything a politician does and says. I learned that after four years of studying my country's politics and policies," I commented with some exasperation.

"Ah yes! This is a new discipline here at our university and we're just starting to publish papers and journals with the study of the current political happenings. In the Soviet Union, we didn't have politics, we had only policy. With a one-party system, all politics were party politics and writing about that only got journalists arrested and sent to Siberia."

Dean Karamzin's face then lit up and his tone changed from resignation to excitement. "With your academic experience would you like to sponsor an article in our political journal at the end of the spring term? That would really set you apart academically to publish articles before you write and defend your thesis," the dean suggested, already wound up with the prospect of making his journal an international collaboration.

"I think it would be a great challenge. Who do I need to speak with?" I asked in my own excitement.

"Me! I am the head of the History and Politics faculty and the publisher and editor of the journal." He looked very proud of himself to tell this fact to other people.

Dean Karamzin not only went on to agree with all my proposals for my academic agenda in Nizhniy Novgorod but was stacking up resource upon resource for me that would make it almost easy and certainly a source of rich materials for researchers that would follow after me.

"Would you like to interview Nemtsov?" he said, referring to the current governor of the province, Boris Nemtsov. "He is old friend of mine."

"I sure would. I've heard great things about him." I replied like a little boy getting to sit in a fire truck for the first time with wide eyes.

"I know people in Moscow, too. We could travel to Moscow and interview Yeltsin's people."

"Tii-Shto!" (Get out!) I blurted in street slang.

"Yes, I know them, too," he boasted again.

"Did you already receive access to the university's American Library from Valentina Petrovna?" he asked off hand.

"The what? An American library here in Nizhniy?" I nearly jumped out of my chair on hearing this.

"Yes, it was gift from American Ambassador Pickering in November last year. There is much data and computers to use for research, in English, Russian, and other languages, too," he said as a matter of fact.

"That would be wonderful if I could get access and an account there," I agreed.

"I will ask Professor Strelyenko to go with you tomorrow and enrol you there, to open an account, etc." He waved his hand as if he was commanding an unseen aide de camp who would execute his whims.

He then stopped and looked at me as if surprised I was the only person in the room with him. "Strelyenko will also be your tutor for the term. He is very involved in the current political events and has written many books now being published in St. Petersburg. We have a free press now you know. He is a bit radical, but it would be good for you to speak with him regularly and balance your western views with his pro-Slavic views. You will then together see the truth in the middle."

"Should I limit my focus at all? Is there something I should be careful about?" "I asked with a prompting caution in my intonation.

"Why? What for? I am not Stalin. Stalin is dead already many years," he recoiled at my naive idea that the thought police were still knocking on doors in the dark of night.

"Is there anything you would like me to research that could be published in the journal?" I was feeling out the possibilities and his tolerance, but he didn't restrict me at all.

"I just want you to use the data and information from MY library to contribute to the journal. It will be great!"

"Well, I am very interested in this whole transition from state owned to privately owned businesses. I know here in Nizhniy they are pioneering this process the right way, at least that is what the press says. With some local interviews and case studies and some nationwide data to compare, I think it could make an interesting mix of economics with politics. What is your opinion?"

"It sounds to me like you just formulated your thesis, Mr. Turner. Please consider using this opportunity to refine it and we can publish the first version of it in June! Agreed?" the Dean seemed pleased.

He stood up to dismiss me from his office with a handshake. I left him as his telephone buzzed on his desk. "HAALOH?" he bellowed as I pulled the door closed behind me.

Vitaly was folding his clothes when I returned to our dorm room after a full day. I flopped on to my bed exhausted still from jet-lag and a culture shock. My stomach grumbled disapprovingly from my neglect of it.

"Vitaly, can ask you something?" I asked sitting half way up on the bed. My roommate, sober this time, nodded silently with his back still to me.

"Isn't it illegal from the start of this year to use dollars or German marks to pay in Russia, except when exchanging money for rubles of course?" I asked him a bit puzzled and concerned.

"Yes, but nobody cares. Everybody still wants dollars," he commented, unconcerned.

"Who? Who still wants dollars?" I asked.

"Everybody. Everybody wants to exchange their salaries for dollars as quickly as possible," he commented without drama or excitement.

"To preserve their buying power." I understood quickly what my new friend was telling me.

He explained further, "Nobody has faith in the ruble anymore. You lose your savings as soon as you put it on your account. Poof! it disappears! Can't even buy bread. You should talk to my grandma. Her pension is worthless."

"Why would I have to pay for my tuition in dollars then do you think?" I asked with caution as I admitted to the morning's drama.

"Your dollars will go right to the bankers who are the ones who run the exchange kiosks. No doubt about it! Are you paying for your room and board in dollars too?" He saw right through my agreement with the university.

"Yes, exactly. So, you don't think that money will go to the university, eh? So, tell me, what's the deal there?" I asked unassumingly.

"From what I've heard the university has a patron saint in Nizhniy Novgorod who takes his payoff in dollars," he said with without any irony in his voice.

"A patron saint?" I asked, confused.

"A patron saint of protection from accidents, arson, and other man-made mishaps. Protection from another patron saint even," he explained in his mysterious code.

"So, because the university has a source of hard currency, some mafia boss is muscling in to take a share?" I postulated.

"You'll need to be careful not to say it that way. Just a little warning to you because you're new." Vitaly turned to look at me with a serious look in his eyes.

"What about what you told me last night, even though you were a bit drunk, about the mafia bosses taking over the government?" I asked carefully.

"Oh, it's real. We see it everywhere, but there is a very popular journalist in Moscow, a communist journalist, but a very good investigator. He broke a huge story last weekend just before the New Year. He isn't afraid of anybody. He named names and gave figures. He must have a source in the parliament, maybe an old communist, an enemy of Yeltsin, who must have given him some real documents. He showed that government ministers are selling Russia's assets, to turn them over to private hands, but for ten percent their real values. The gangsters are paying them big amounts of cash to do it this way. It's crazy. Completely crazy. If the ministers say no, the gangsters kill their families, blow them up. It is too crazy for words!"

"What is the name of the journalist?" I asked, wanting to research his articles.

"Bolshakov. Dmitri Bolshakov."

The next afternoon I met Professor Strelyenko on Minin Street just up the river embankment from the history department at the School of Linguistics. The American library was on the ground floor behind very sternly barred windows, hung nicely with white sheers on the inside.

Strelyenko, a junior professor of Dean Karamzin's faculty, was a stern looking young man in his early thirties. He was known for being a very vocal Russian nationalist. Some suspected him of and labeled him as an extremist. Strelyenko seemed to make everybody at the university—except the dean himself—rather nervous. I held my breath in his lectures at the foreign students' faculty as he had no problem ruffling feathers and offending those from the former Soviet republics. The tension was at times as thick as the ice on the Volga River in January when he was lecturing. He spoke English very well and didn't find that to be in conflict with his political leanings. He dressed like the avant-guard academic and intellectual that he was: black high-necked sweater and Russian made blue jeans. We all wore the same looking coats boots and hats in the winter.

The library was everything that the dean said it would be: new, sleek, and bright, and it had a wall of CDROMs filled with data from journals, periodicals, magazines, and Russian government reports covering at least the last ten years. The computers weren't state of the art, but they were definitely the best collection of computing power in the university.

With Strelyneko looking over my shoulder I entered a few search words: privatization, economic reform, private enterprises, finance, and finally the name of the Moscow journalist who Vitaly told me about: Bolshakov. Tens of references to recent articles from dozens of magazines and journals filled the screen. I commented to Strelyenko that it would be difficult to get me to ever leave once I started a serious research topic. He slapped me on the back in a manly way to show his pleasure of having another political junky come to study under his tutorage, even if I was a foreigner.

Strelyenko introduced me to the head librarian, Olga. She took my student card and copied my name and student number into a ledger and returned it to me together with hand written paper with my user name and password and a nervous smile.

Stelyenko and I stood outside waiting for the trolleybus in snow and cold. We spoke in English. He smoked a cigarette with indifference.

"What is your interest in the economic reforms, Pyotr?" Strenlyenko asked with smoke coming out his nostrils. "Are you hoping to invest?"

"No, I am very interested to watch how a country rebuilds itself," I replied sincerely. "I hope that Yeltsin learns from what the Soviet system did wrong and makes good changes. I think that privatization is a great step forward."

"Boris Yeltsin was only good in opposition. He is not a ruler. He was a good Russian conscience but since he took power, he only blew up the parliament with his tanks and let the criminals run Moscow. So, I would say that he has been slow to learn from the mistakes of the Soviet system. He needs to go back to the opposition and let real Russians run Russia," was Strelyenko's commentary to my idealism.

"Yeltsin is not a real Russian?" I asked, curious to understand his point of view.

"No, he is not. He's from Siberia, probably descended from Imperial period criminals," he sneered. "'We need to have the true Russian bloodline ruling Russia again, looking out for both Russia and her children!"

"Are you a Tsarist then?" I asked with certainty of his answer.

"Yes, my position is that the Bolsheviks' actions were fully unconstitutional, and Kerensky should have been shot for treason for deposing the Tsar," he said politely, as if he was in one of the fashionable parlors of St. Petersburg discussing politics in 1917.

"I have read some articles that say the same thing. Revolutions though are always unconstitutional, by definition, so it's a weak argument to use the definition of the word to brand it as criminal." I parried his swipe at the modern situation.

"True, but it still didn't make it legal," he shot back.

"Did the Tsar abdicate or was he truly under duress?" I asked in my advance.

"It is not legal nor moral for a Tsar to abdicate his God given duty. Just like God says in the Bible, 'what God has put together let no man put asunder.' Just because Kerensky said it was legal for the Tsar to abdicate makes it about as acceptable for man and woman to divorce. Man's laws cannot override God's words!" he said well rehearsed.

"Are you a believing Orthodox man then?" I jabbed at him.

"Every real Russian man is." He smiled and took a drag from his cigarette.

"What is your opinion of Mr. Zhilenskiy in the modern political arena?" I asked, slightly changing the subject.

"Still too soon to know. He has conviction. I just don't know yet where it will lead to. It could go one of two ways: one, restoring a strong Russian nobility and the virtues that go with it, or two, ethnic cleansing due to lack of virtues. He's a loose cannon that could help win the battle or burn down our own house." He answered while he exhaled tobacco smoke into the still frozen afternoon air. "We can talk about it further next week during our first session, yes?"

The walk between the two faculties where I studied was about three kilometers. When history lectures let out on Wednesday morning at lunch time at Minin Square, the walk up the sloping pedestrian district, Bolshaya Pokrovka, was always a fun stroll past shops, flea markets, and cafés. The city's most interesting and historic architecture is found along this walking street. A historic, very Teutonic looking bank, looks like it's straight out of Bavaria, made of gray stone and rounded turrets. There is a classical drama theatre in happy yellow with a small square spread out under the entrance staircase, an old mansion of Boyars from centuries earlier brightly painted in the St Petersburg neo-classical style. All this history seamlessly blended with the food busses and currency exchange kiosks to create a relaxed aura of leisurely doing one's daily chores and shopping.

It was here on Bolshaya Pokrovka that I discovered the bread called lavash done in the Georgian style, round and thick. This bread would become my staple of existence in a world where most meat was questionable and the cheeses were less than tempting. One bought this heavenly bread, literally, from a hole in the wall on "Pokrovka." One knocks. The hatch is slid open. One presents three one-hundred ruble notes, one gets three round discs of warm lavash. No words. No faces. Just soft, warm delicious bread at lunch time for a bargain price. The only drawback was the line at lunch time was long and it wasn't a well-kept secret.

At the top of Pakrovka stands a monolithic square gray stone building hewn by muscled socialist-realist sculptors: The Post, Telephone and Telegraph building, or the PTT as the locals called it. Here, those without telephones in their homes could reserve a phone booth on a given day at a given hour to make long distance telephone calls all over the world. One would only need to write down the number to be called and hand it to an operator. An operator would then usher the caller to a sound proof, numbered booth with a big cushy chair to sit in while talking. After a few minutes, the telephone would ring—and through the wonders of modern technology, my mother would always be on the other end of the line in America. It made making a telephone call into a lavish production similar to going to an opera or an old-time cinema where folks would dress in their Sunday best to watch a "movie." All that was missing was warm cocoa with marshmallows and an admission charge.

From this gray stone building, local agents of the Federal Security Bureau (FSB) spy on the residents and visitors of the city and listen in comfort to all the international phone calls coming into and going out from the city. It was an unspoken rule in Russia that conversations over the telephone were limited to the weather and one's health and not much more. My mother just needed a proof of life by hearing my voice once a month. The other details I wrote in letters.

One afternoon after a group literature lecture for the foreign students with Professor Dashkova, I was introduced to Hans from East Germany. An economics student from Leipzig, he spoke English very well but was struggling to be understood in Russian due to his thick German accent. He was a tough looking fellow, broad, muscular, and fit with a nearly bald head with a fuzzy shadow of hair which he kept almost shaved.

"Hans, why haven't we met in the dormitories yet?" I asked him curiously.

"Oh, I don't stay in the student rooms. I have my own apartment in the old city," he revealed.

"Can you do that?" I asked with an exciting start.

"Yes, anybody can I believe. I have been living there since October last year," he confirmed.

"Did you have to ask for special permission?" I pushed for details.

"No, the police don't mind. I paid six months in advance so the owner was happy. I receive my own post in the letter box. It is very cozy." Hans was very pleased with himself.

"Are the apartments expensive? Do you pay a lot for a place in the old town?" I was desperate to leave the dorms.

"It's okay. I pay one hundred Deutsch Marks per month, but the German government gives me one hundred fifty per month for a room in Leipzig, so I buy my food with that money, too. It's a big apartment and I can almost see the river from my balcony." He seemed to be recalculating the deal he had while we spoke.

"Well, I've got to look into that! Just a week now in the dormitory and I feel like I'm a pickled beet," I moaned.

Before our weekly support group broke up, Valentina Petrovna asked me to step into her office. I braced myself for another chiding. What could it be now?

Valentina handed me a folded paper across her desk. I unfolded it and read the name and telephone number. It didn't mean anything to me. I gave Valentina an inquisitive look.

"It is the name and telephone number of an American businessman here in Nizhniy who lives in the city center," she explained. "Maybe you would like to meet him. You have many interests in common. He asked me to pass you his number."

I didn't know what to say. I was speechless. An American businessman in Nizhniy Novgorod? That couldn't be right.

"What more can you tell me about him? Which company is he working for? How long has he been here?" I peppered her with questions.

"Telephone him. He is not traveling this week and would like to meet you," she said, amused at my excitement.

"Thank you. I will call him tonight." I was stunned to learn that another American was in the city, and maybe a bit disappointed at the same time that I was not the first American to set up an outpost in Nizhniy Novgorod. I was also very curious. Maybe he could be my step into the business world that was a constantly moving target. Deep down that is why I came to Russia—to make my fortune and become an unmissable part of a western corporation setting up its operations. I was no different from the other students I had already met who were dreaming of their financial success by helping bridge the linguistic divide between those with money and those with local connections and local know-how.

After lectures, I met Yulia at the river station in the lower old city for a light dinner in a traditional café there on the waterfront. Even though darkness falls around mid-afternoon in January, the white snow illuminated dark corners in the city's alleys and the opaque ice on the Volga lit up the vast expanse of the night so that black silhouetted ice fisherman in the middle of the frozen river were visible in the twilight at four o'clock.

"You look very tired!" Yulia said concerned as we took a corner table waited for soup and bread to be served.

"I am very tired. Haven't slept well for almost a week and can't get enough to eat. I am not feeling too chipper tonight," I admitted.

"Why can't you sleep?" she asked like a concerned mother.

"Jet-lag, roommates who stink and snore, and my goodness you'd never believe how warm it is in that room," I complained like an over tired child. Everything annoyed and irritated.

"Can you change rooms maybe?" she suggested, setting aside her menu.

"I have a better idea! I met another student today from Germany who is renting his own apartment in the city center, says he almost has a view of the Volga." I perked up a bit when a warm bowl of borscht and black bread was put under my nose.

"It's very expensive to live the city center," Yulia commented from her financial perspective.

"Maybe I could get a room on your side of the river where it's less expensive. Maybe a room, not an apartment?" I ventured.

"You need permission from the university and the police to do that," Yulia cautioned.

"So, I'll ask permission. And I'm pretty sure I can live anywhere in Nizhegorodskiy Province according to the stamp on my visa." I had pulled out my passport and was reading the back of the yellow tri-fold paper with my picture on it.

"Really, can I read it please?" Yulia reached out her hand. "I don't believe it, but you're right. It says you can live anywhere in Nizhniy Novgorod. We used to have our identity documents with our home addresses on it. I wonder why they changed?"

"Everything is changing, my dear." I smiled the smile of a robber baron sensing an opportunity for exploit.

After filling bread and warming borscht, the frozen evening felt a bit more hospitable. We strolled out to the land's edge overlooking the frozen river, reminiscing about the time when we met on the river in the summer. We snapped a photo of the two of us 'for old time's sake,' the dark abyss of the wide Volga behind us, our faces pale white from the flash.

"It sure would be fun to take another voyage this summer," Yulia commented wistfully as we turned to walk back to the river station and the bus stop that would take her home.

I interrupted the nostalgic moment to tell her about my new contact in town. "Hey, you'll never guess what. Valentina Petrovna handed a name and telephone number to me today of an American businessman living here in Nizhniy. He has invited me for dinner on Friday night. Wouldn't it be great if I could get good work with him and stay on here for a few years after my degree, and well, just see what happens?"

"Peter, keep your feet on the ground. You should be very careful when people speak about business in Russia. It is not always what it seems and there is usually something darker behind it," Yulia cautioned me.

"What could be so bad about it?" I scoffed at her caution.

"Just be careful, Peter. You never know who is behind it. There must always be a Russian partner to set up a company in Russia, and the laws in Russia right now make these things sketchy. Somebody is dancing with the devil in order to get permits and stay protected from criminals if their partners aren't the criminal types," she said as we paced through the shin high snow in tandem.

I listened to her warning but didn't question her any further. I remarked to myself that she was too cautious, too worried, but let her comments go unchallenged. She bade me goodnight with a peck on the cheek and boarded her bus in front of the river station. I watched as her bus disappeared down the quay into the remnants of a pale pink winter dusk.

06

3. Del Sanning

Friday afternoons in the old town center of Nizhniy Novgorod were always flooded with the youth of the city. Lectures ended on Friday afternoon at lunch time and with the pending weekend, nobody was in a rush to head home, or back to a cramped dorm room. Hans invited me for lunch with him at a new fried chicken restaurant on the upper river embankment not far from his apartment. My mouth salivated at the thought of fried chicken and a cold Pepsi. My belt, already a notch tighter, pleaded at me daily to fill my belly properly. I was truly grateful for Hans' suggestion and invitation. Between the two of us, we bought and ate more chicken pieces than I could count. The bones piled high on the table. We sat for fifteen minutes, blurry eyed and satiated before we could stand to leave. I had to fight falling asleep where I sat.

"Peter, I think we should do this every week!" Hans commented as I picked the last scraps of oily meat from the bones on my plate.

"Hans, that's the best idea I've heard since I arrived in town. Hey, by the way, I am trying to move out of the dorms. Do you need a roommate by any chance?" I asked sheepishly.

"No room for that. It's a one-bedroom apartment and well, let's say on the weekends it's a busy bedroom." He left the details unsaid as he wiped his greasy mouth and fingers with a napkin and wiggled his eyebrows at me to confirm my assumptions about his meaning.

"Wouldn't want to get in the way. It's just that your apartment is so perfectly located between the history department and the American library, and this fine eating establishment that I thought I should at least ask," I said disappointedly.

"Sorry, Peter, a man must have his priorities straight," Hans said with a sheepish grin on his face.

"Understood, my friend. Say, I'm on way now to the American Library on Minin Street. I'm headed right past your apartment. Are you going that way?"

"Why are you going to study on Friday afternoon? The girls are waiting, Peter," Hans said, alarmed at my over studious ambition.

"Ah yes, but the library is not open tomorrow, and the girls will still be in the city on Saturday. I want to start to narrow my field for a thesis topic already and I'm curious to see what type of data I can access here. Just gotta go check it out." I smiled and waved him goodbye and headed toward the door. "See you next week, same place, same time?"

"Ja sicher, mein Herr!" Hans shouted to me as I pulled the door open to a blast of freezing air in my face.

On my way toward Minim Street I passed the Rossiya Hotel, just a stone's throw from the chicken restaurant, and stepped inside purely out of curiosity. As I pushed through the revolving doors of the street level lobby I spotted immediately on the concierge's desk a display with a stack of several copies of *The Economist* magazine. It was a week late but included everything I had missed in the news cycle of the last two weeks. I eagerly bought a copy from the receptionist and started for the door, but turned and spoke again with the concierge on a whim.

"Does this magazine come every week?" I queried.

"Da, it is delivered each Thursday morning," was the concierge's uninterested answer.

I handed him a twenty-dollar bill from my wallet. "Can you always reserve one for me each week? I will come by to pick it up each Friday afternoon."

"Of course!" he said, this time with great interest and slipped the bill effortlessly into the breast pocket of his shirt.

"Yes, my dear, everything is a changin'!" I repeated to myself, recalling my discussion with Yulia earlier that week as I pushed the door around letting me out again on to the cold street.

When I arrived at Del Sanning's apartment block on Frunze Street for our dinner appointment that evening, the snow was coming down hard. I rode the lift to the top floor and was still brushing snow off my shapka while I knocked on door 26 and waited. I sensed someone looking through the peephole. There was no noise, just a blinking eye. I sensed a nervousness behind the door.

I called out in English through the door, "Hello, is this the Sanning's' home?"

The latches instantly began clapping and the door swung open quickly. In the doorway, inviting me in, stood what looked to be a middle-aged cowboy, sans cowboy hat, with flashy white teeth, broad shoulders and chest and rugged face with sandy brown hair and blue eyes, dressed in Wrangler blue jeans and an ugly Christmas sweater.

"It sure is! Are you Peter?" Mr. Sanning bellowed with enthusiasm.

"Who else would it be?" I asked sarcastically.

"Well, you sure as hell don't look like what I was expecting. You looked like a Russian knocking on my door!" he continued in his cowboy manner.

"Well, that could very well be as we are in Russia," I said very logically, a bit flustered by his bombastic reception.

"I'm Del! C'mon in and take off your boots and coat. Is it snowing outside?" he asked seeing the cover of snow on my fur hat.

"When isn't it?" I huffed.

The Sanning's' apartment was a typical Russian apartment with a small rectangular living room looking out to a glassed-in balcony, overlooking the next apartment block which overlooked the next apartment block. There were two small bedrooms, one converted into a home office with a computer, telephone and a fax machine and one for the pair to sleep in. The kitchen was long and narrow tiled in white ceramics. The water closet and shower shared the wall of the kitchen sink with water pipes exposed on either side. Hot water was heated in the building's boiler in the basement. The only real difference to a local citizen's apartment was that it wasn't stuffed full of the souvenirs of a full life: photographs of children or parents on the walls, sets or books, the good china. Obviously missing was the clutter of common Russian families who have to hoard a bit, keeping a cupboard of home preserved fruits and vegetables from a garden plot, old clothing, extra blankets and whatnot as one doesn't know when they might get a chance to purchase them again.

The Sannings obviously hadn't been in the apartment long and from what I could gather weren't planning on staying for years. This was a temporary home. It was spacious enough for the two and a guest, tastefully furnished in a Scandinavian style, well lit and clean. I hung my wool and fur at the door and removed my boots and slipped into the house slippers for guests, and Del then led me into the living room.

"So how do you know Valentina Petrovna from the university?" was my attempt to break the thin ice.

"Well, the mayor introduced us to her when we first arrived a few months ago. Thought maybe we could use her as an interpreter for our project," Del answered, hiding nothing.

"Oh, so she is working for you on the side?" I hoped to hear that she was. It wouldn't have surprised me.

"No, couldn't use her. She didn't want to travel, and I already had a young local fellow who does my books, taxes, and whatnot who does the local stuff. Valentina now just sends us video tapes of CNN. She has a satellite dish at the university that catches the signal. That way at least we catch the highlights of the world news from last week." He chattered on like a ranch hand who hadn't seen anybody but the cows for a week.

"Clever," I remarked.

"So what brings you to Nizhniy? We don't see many Americans here at all, let alone one who moves in and sets up camp," Del asked.

"I've come for a master's program for the next twelve months, but not anxious to leave after that," I said, as a matter of fact, hoping he would read between the lines.

"You sure looked Russian at the door. Do you speak the language as well?" he continued his tirade of questions.

"Yes, sir. Spent some time here last summer working on the riverboats, turning my book Russian into real world experience," I said with a twinge of pride.

"Were you here when Yeltsin blew up the White House?" Del sounded so 'cowboy' it was distracting my thoughts.

"No, that was the summer before. I was in Moscow for the first time just last summer. The building looked to be in good repair when I saw it in May," I remarked.

"That's because they hired a Turkish construction company to repair it after Boris put a few tank shells into it. You know that Russia is the only real estate market that deals in NEW second-hand buildings, right? You ever seen a building site here? The place is half broken before it's finished," he was waxing philosophical.

"Yes, I've noticed that everything modern looks like it was built for a Gulag camp, inside and out," I mentioned, thinking of my dorm room.

"Exactly!" he hollered and nearly jumped out of his chair at me.

After a signal from his wife, Els, who was busy cooking in the kitchen, Del looked at me with a serious face. "Soup's on."

Del Sanning was a true blue, dyed in the wool American from the heart of the prairie land. He looked it, he talked it, and his wife sure cooked it. After ten days of watery Russian cabbage or over salted beet soup and meat dumplings of questionable origins, and too much garlic, a home cooked cowboy stew was a true comfort. Els Sanning was a studious and intelligent woman who didn't show her hand quickly. She was hospitable and generous and full of questions of a different sort. She knew how to ask questions that opened a discussion up quickly to the heart of the matter.

"So, why did you choose to study in Nizhniy? Why not Moscow or St. Petersburg? It would seem that you would have more resources and a bit more comfort than out here in the boondocks," Els asked.

"I wanted to go where the others had yet to see. Told Del just now that I spent last summer working on the river and saw so much of the country and realized that there was much more to Russia than Moscow," I said thoughtfully.

"What's your major then? Or are you just here for language training?" was her follow-up.

"Funny you should ask; I just came from the research library and I think I'm going to write my thesis about the privatization of state companies to find the secret to success and figure out why one succeeds and another doesn't," I replied resolutely.

"Sounds very academic," Del said and glanced over at Els.

"...and very ambitious," Els said gravely, setting down her fork and folding her hands above her steaming bowl.

"Well, we'll see where it takes me..." I brushed off their obvious cautiousness and concern for my academic project and took another chunk of beef with a potato.

"Peter, Del and I have been in Russia about four years now," Els was trying to be tactful but was dead serious. "The people who you will need to research for these topics don't like to be asked too many questions. What you might think is a transparent, orderly process is nothing but a free-for-all. Businessmen and journalists are being murdered on a weekly or monthly basis. Rules don't apply here. Be very, very careful about the type of questions you ask. You might live to regret a number of them if you are not very tactful and very careful. It's not what you read in the American press. Take some time and observe...."

44

Del interrupted, "You'll need connections! The business people here are not typical managers or CEOs. They usually have something to hide and don't trust people with their life stories. Doing any due diligence is like pulling teeth. They give you the official books and you play along for a few days and then you have to ask for the shadow bookkeeping before you know the true health of a modern Russian enterprise. They play the shell game with assets and cash better than anybody I've ever played with. The truth is a slippery pig, my young friend." It seemed both Del and Els were trying to dissuade me from taking up this line of research.

"Yes, I've heard about the shadow accountants," I commented as I chewed a chunk of beef.

"Really, from who?" Del reacted surprised.

"A bookshop keeper in St. Petersburg. Selling books, paintings, postcards, Kodak film." I didn't think anything of it.

"Really, he just told you about it?" Del seemed put out. I couldn't understand why.

"No, we asked him. I was translating for one of my tourists who was an accountant. He asked him straight up about how he can make a profit in the mess of communist and capitalist rules. The fellow knew what he was talking about. The owner of the place just opened up and told us about his shadow books. Look I'm not making this stuff up! I was just translating," I said defensively.

"Kid, everybody here has a shadow life or a shadow operation and they keep it very close; sometimes they don't even tell their spouses what they're up to! And this shopkeeper in Petersburg just tells you this in the middle of his shop, right as he's ringing up the till, like he's talking about the weather?"

Els chimed in, "Del, maybe you should take him to your next meeting with your contractors. Maybe he has a trustworthy face..." Els smiled a play pity smile to tease her husband.

"I'm pretty sure that even the university has a shadow administration. I saw it in action earlier this week. I understand that my tuition, paid in cash, won't make it on the university's balance sheet," I said between bites. On saying this I knew I probably shouldn't have and moved quickly to change the topic. "So, what brings the two of you to Nizhniy?" I tried to mask the embarrassment caused by my big mouth.

"Del is the project manager for the planning of a new hotel here in the old town," Els answered for him.

"A decent hotel I hope, because the one down the street near Minin Square looks like it is filled with roaches and the other types of bugs—the ones with microphones. It reminded me of the Intourist on Red Square," I chuckled as I remembered the horrid, dirty hotel in Moscow.

"You stayed in the Intourist? You are a brave lad aren't you?" Del chuckled with me.

"When I was there it was all thugs and hookers. Nothing too dangerous," I remarked.

"Haaah! The thugs AND the hookers were all probably KGB. That's what they do these days," Del pointed out.

"So what hotel is it going to be? Something American or are you working for a European group?" I asked, truly interested.

"We don't know what the marquis will say yet. We're more the ground workers who get the permissions, the land, and set up organizations to build for the most interested hotel chain. We have our hopeful buyers of course, but right now we're just putting in the ground work," Del explained in a serious voice. "It will be a good one though, at least four stars with a state-of-the-art business center where a guy can make a call, check emails, and send faxes without having somebody read his notes over his shoulder. A place with some privacy. We succeeded in Moscow a few years back and so now they sent me here because Nizhniy has become interesting for foreign investors, and they'll all need some place to sleep while they're here."

"I did find this today at the roach hotel." I pulled the new copy of *The Economist* out of my school bag and showed it with pride.

Del looked delighted at my revelation. "Can you get us one, too?"

"I paid the concierge twenty dollars to reserve me one each week, on top of the cover price of course. I can pick it up each Friday afternoon," I said gloating a bit.

"Do you think he'll set two of those aside?" Del reached for his wallet and handed me another Andrew Jackson.

"And when you deliver it, you can come for dinner and keep us up to date with your research," Els kindly invited.

4. Babushka & Raiya

It took me another week to convince Valentina Petrovna to allow me to move out of the student accommodations and into a privately rented room. During the back and forth with her I was suspicious that somebody behind the scenes didn't want to let go of my monthly fee paid in dollars for room and board. In the end, the local police department settled the argument and confirmed it was legal for me to live wherever I wished.

Yulia placed an advertisement in a local newspaper where she was interning and within a few days had a telephone call from a landlord offering a room in a communal apartment on the other side of the Oka river in the Lenninskiy district. Yulia joined me and Hans for our fried chicken Friday ritual in the old city. She had just come from viewing the apartment which was not far from her own.

"It's right on the metro line and a bus line so getting to school won't be a problem, and then you're just two metro stops from my place. Nice and easy to get together!" She seemed pleased her new-found talent as a real-estate agent.

She continued, "It's on the ground floor, it's rather dirty inside, we'll have to clean it. It hasn't any furniture, but the owner will bring some. The cost is twenty dollars, cash, each month. I think it is the best we will find. You can always move if you don't like it after one month." She was already convinced I would live there happily, close to her.

"It couldn't be any worse than what I am suffering through right now, that's for sure!" I replied enthusiastically. "I can't take another night of drunken snoring and that infernal radiator. It's like trying to sleep in a sauna."

Hans was washing down a chicken thigh with the locally brewed lemonade. He screwed up his face as if he had bitten into a concentrated lemon. "It's great to have your own space!" he said, rasping as he battled the strong after effect of the homemade soft drink.

Yulia picked up a chicken bone and threw it at him in jest, but also in disgust of his manners. She demanded manners from the men around her and never hid her disapproval.

"It's settled then!" I said, glancing back and forth between my two friends looking for moral support and getting none. "I'll take the room. When can I move in?"

"Tomorrow at two o'clock," Yulia said, turning her shoulder and looking away from Frank who continued to inhale the chicken on his plate.

The next morning early, I shook hands with my roommates sober enough to be awake and headed for the trolley-bus stop on Gagarin Street carrying my bags like a pack mule. I felt like a convict walking away from the jail house after a long incarceration.

The bus took a sharp dive down the river bluff switchbacks down to the bridge over the Oka River and into the Zarechniy and Leninskiy districts, where the factory workers of the city lived, void of the old and ancient. Built up after the Great Patriotic War in the 1940s and 1950s for the mass production needed for the victorious Soviet war machine, it was a centrally planned neighborhood with identical five story apartment blocks street after street, with groves of birch trees, benches, and playgrounds between them. Now cars parked haphazardly between the trees, on curbs and sidewalks and in front of doors taking up the planned natural spaces for rest and repose after a hard day at the factory. Gone was the worker's paradise.

"You should leave your money, passport and plane ticket with us here. This apartment is much safer than where you will be living. You'll be on the ground floor with windows on the street. Anybody could break in and take all your things. Here on the fifth floor, it would be the last place a thief would think to break in, if he's sober enough to climb the stairs," was Yulia's mother's advice to me about living alone.

"Ok, but I must have my passport and visa with me at all times, but maybe you are right about the money stash and the plane ticket. Those would be impossible to replace," I conceded.

"Will you have a telephone in your apartment?" Olya asked further.

"No, I don't think so." I looked to Yulia who shook her head no.

"If not, you will have to use the public phones at the metro station. You should not hold long conversations on the telephone. Keep your calls short and maybe even speak English when you can so nobody understands what you're saying. Somebody is always listening, and you never know what they will do," she babbled on.

"No, he shouldn't speak English because that will call too much attention. People will hear he is a foreigner and then target him," Yulia contradicted her mother's advice.

"No, I am talking about the people on the telephone line listening to him talk. People in the metro station won't be able to hear what he is saying in Russian or English," she rebutted her daughter. Turning back to me she continued, "You'll want to use code words, like, 'the usual place,' 'the usual time,' etc., but never actually talk about specifics."

I sat dumbfounded as I listened to this conversation between mother and daughter go on longer and longer and actually get quieter and quieter the more animated it got. Olga was looking suspiciously around her own living room to make sure nobody else was there hearing this subversive information to the unwitting foreigner. At one point, she stood up and turned on the kitchen radio to create some background noise and static so she couldn't be overheard. The state radio station was chiming eleven o'clock. It was all just a bit surreal.

"Also, don't talk to people on the bus or the metro. People around here are not used to having foreigners in the neighborhood. You might get unwanted attention from people who don't like foreigners—and worse, Americans!" Olga was bordering on paranoia.

"I've never had a problem in any part of Russia being seen and known as a foreigner. Everybody can hear it in my accent," I said, hoping to defuse the rhetoric going around the room.

"Yes, but don't forget that the Soviet Union has many accents of Russian. You look and sound like you could be from one of the Baltic republics, Estonia maybe? And that's okay for people, but to hear that you are a westerner, and American, could cause you some trouble," she said adamantly.

Leaving my money belt and my return plane ticket with Olga for safe keeping, Yulia and I headed down the five flights stairs to the bus stop for the short ride from Zarachenaya to Proletarskaya for our one o'clock appointment with my new landlord.

"It's really just a simple room." The landlord apologized as he opened the room from the corridor, fumbling with the keys he obviously hadn't used much himself.

The room was empty except for a rickety cot with a musty mattress, a wooden table with two chairs and a filthy free-standing cabinet, table top height, with drawers. My heart sank on seeing the filthy, naked state of the room.

"Of course, we will bring back the furniture that belongs in the room," he continued after a dramatic pause. "After some cleaning, it should be livable again."

"How soon can the furniture be brought?" Yulia asked in a confrontational voice, feeling somewhat mislead from the conversation on the telephone a few days earlier.

"We can bring a sofa-bed and a coat and hat rack, a wardrobe and a large cupboard, and a larger table and two more chairs in three weeks, because we have to borrow my brother's delivery bus and he is driving with it on a job now," he replied with apology in his voice.

"It's good enough," I said with some doubt in my head. "I can camp here for a few weeks. It will be alright. I will work to fix it up."

"It's an inexpensive room without a landlady to clean or cook. The kitchen and bathrooms are shared with the others that live here," was his justification for offering a dusty, empty room to rent.

"I don't see any problem with that," I said off hand.

"Yes, but the neighbors are Tatars. That's why nobody else wants to rent the room," he added cautiously.

The apartment was on the ground floor of the building and my window looked out on to Prospect Lenina, a four-lane highway leading to and from the factories on its southern extremity. Gratefully there was a pleasant strip of snow-covered grass and a grove of frosted birch trees that buffered the view from my window and the sounds and smells of the broad avenue. The entrance to the apartment was dark and cavernous as the light bulbs in the lamps in the stairwell were stolen one by one within two days of being replaced. In short order, I learned how to lock and unlock my doors by touch after I had memorized every step, chip, and uneven slope on the concrete floor. I just had to hope that nobody was lurking in the dark waiting for me.

The corridor, kitchen, bathroom, and WC were shared facilities. The bathroom was just that, a small room just big enough for a bathtub, the gas heater for the water, a washbasin with a scratchy mirror hanging above it, and one dim light bulb hanging from its cord. The kitchen was very basic; it had a sink, a hot water heater, and a gas oven and range. I found out quickly that the oven was a gas leak danger so I bought a pot, a frying pan, one kitchen knife and cutting board for cooking on the gas range. The others in the flat had a small half-size refrigerator with a small ice box, which doubled as a preparation counter. There were no cupboards or drawers so I hung my pans and utensils on nails high on the kitchen wall.

With some good sweeping, scrubbing, well-hung curtains and a light shade over the bare light bulb dangling from the ceiling, the room started to become a home. A cold home, but nonetheless, it was my space. I discovered that the space between the two window panes was cold enough to keep foods frozen for over a week and so I had no need for a refrigerator. For the first three weeks, I slept on the floor next to the radiator with the mattress and blankets from the rickety old cot. Most nights I slept with my big wool coat wrapped around my feet and my black mink shapka on my head to stay warm enough. Some nights in February were cold enough in my room that by morning a thin layer of ice would form on a pot of boiling water I would place under my bed to help get warm enough to drift off to sleep.

My new neighbors and flat mates were two women, an aunt and niece combination. The aunt, Natasha, who I simply called Babushka (Grandma) was nearly seventy years old, and her niece, Raiya, was in her early forties. These women were indeed both Tatars, not Russians. Babushka's parents settled in Nizhniy before the communist revolution, from Kazan, the cultural center of the Muslim Tatar nation just down river from Nizhniy. The two ladies shared one room that was the same size as the one I lived in alone.

When I first moved into my room my neighbors were very distrustful of me and each evening they each made a point of closing their door with a slam and very loud and obvious turn of the deadbolt, once, twice, thrice. This went on for about two weeks before they realized that I was not a threat. It took about three weeks of living around each other before they were willing to open up and have any type of 'get to know you' conversation.

"A few years ago, I had my own two-bedroom apartment and lived in the old city where I worked as a secretary at a trading company, but now my salary doesn't even pay for a room by myself," Raiya complained to me as we prepared our separate dinners in the kitchen. "All the prices went up about three years ago. In three months, my entire savings was used just to feed myself! No more holidays, no more birthday presents for the nephew and niece, and don't even talk about Babushka's pension. She can hardly buy a loaf of bread with it since Yeltsin raised all the prices. With Gorbachev, we were all hungry together. With Yeltsin, we see the others eating while we scrape crumbs off the table now."

Babushka pouted on her stool in the corner of the kitchen looking sour and bitter mulling, "...and the factory used to give me new boots every winter as part of my pension, but now they don't even do that. The army doctors all want a bribe and then we have to pay for the medicines they prescribe to us. What is fifty years of service to the Red Army good for anymore? Nothing! My pension buys me one week of food. If I didn't own my room, I'd be on the streets already like Raiya."

By mid-February, I started recognizing the locals: faces in shops, at the bus and metro stations. I knew where a few of them lived specifically, knew who their families were and their free roaming pets. One of the faces and routines that I came to notice most often was that of a woman who always walked her dog at the oddest times, but usually around the same time every day—twice a day no matter how cold or hard the snow was falling. She was very devoted to the care of her dog. Several times a week I would see her outside my window in the stretch of snow and trees between my ground floor window and the street.

Some bus drivers and shop keepers even started recognizing me, too. When the fellow at the newspaper kiosk at the metro station saw me at the window, he would have my preferred newspaper ready and I paid him usually just once a week. Despite the ever-freezing temperatures I was slowly warming up to the neighborhood and life in the workers' district.

5. When the Shark Bites

"Yulia, what's wrong? Why are you crying? What's happened?" I whispered into the telephone hanging in the metro station.

Yulia had missed our lunch date that Sunday morning, bright and bone chilling cold. I called to hear if she had fallen ill or if something else had come up. Not having a telephone, I seemed to always need to call around to hear the details when plans changed.

"He's dead, Peter. They killed him!" she whimpered on her side of the line. "They killed him in front of his children and wife right on the street. It's just horrible." She sobbed and hung up the phone.

I rode the metro to the Zarachenaya Station to Yulia's apartment and found her there alone, curled up on the sofa with the television on. The serious and shocked tones of the newscasters coupled with the gruesome camera footage of a corpse under a blanket laying on top of a crimson ice pack on a frozen Moscow street chilled my blood.

"Yulia, who is that? Who is dead there under that blanket?" I asked quietly, not taking my eyes from the television screen.

"Bolshakov, Dmitri Bolshakov," she replied with the voice of a mouse, nearly catatonic.

"You mean the journalist Bolshakov?" I asked, shocked. She nodded again and tears rolled down her cheeks. She held her face in her hands. I tried my best to comfort her but could only put my arm around her shoulders and sit with her quietly on the sofa.

"I read some of his articles at the library this week. He is a brazen reporter, that is for sure," I commented in praise of his fearless reporting on corruption and criminals.

After nearly an hour of saying very little and watching the same footage play on a loop, Yulia turned off the television set and tried to collect herself.

"Please excuse me. I don't like people to see me this way. I will go clean myself up," she apologized.

"Yulia, sit down. You don't need to apologize. Tell me more about Bolshakov. Tell me why you think he was murdered. I am very interested to understand what has happened," I said quietly inviting her to sit down again and talk about it.

Yulia sat down again on the sofa and pulled her blanket up over her legs and up around her neck, leaving only her face and hair exposed to the afternoon sun, which poured in from the frozen outside.

"Bolshakov was the most important investigative journalist in the whole country. He was working to expose the corruption that Gorbachev was working to root out of the government before Yeltsin took over. So many other journalists and newspapers are too afraid to report on the things he reports on and now for sure, nobody else will go after the corrupt ministers and criminals when they see this on the television and in the newspapers today. They control us with fear, Peter, and they get away with it because they can kill anybody, anywhere and keep stealing from us and the government doesn't do anything about it." The fire in her eyes began to burn again as she talked.

"Who do you think did it?" I asked to keep her talking.

"The government, the criminals. They're all the same. Does it matter who actually shot the man?" she ranted. "The gangsters pay the civil servants, the civil servants protect the criminals, and they all get rich together while they rob us all blind!" Yulia's feisty spark was warming up her pale cheeks.

"I heard that Bolshakov broadcast a very damning news report in late December. Vitaly from the dorms was telling me about it before I moved out. Wasn't it about how the government ministers were giving away very valuable state assets, like oil fields to the criminal groups in Moscow and Siberia?" I prompted.

"Yes. It was a masterpiece. A wonderful piece of journalism. He proved everything with government documents and witnesses. There was no second guessing what he had compiled. How he got all his materials is a mystery, but we all know the real thing when we see it. Bolshakov really exposed a lot of people, in and out of the government who have become very rich by scamming the new programs for privatizing the country's natural resources and factories," she explained in increasing detail and anger.

"What are Bolshakov's politics? Who is he trying to expose?" I asked, only having read a few of his articles to date.

"He is a communist. He was always against the corruption in the Communist Party and he wrote a lot during Perestroika that helped Gorbachev clean up the back handed deals within the Communist Party; you know the nepotism and people scratching each other's backs, in general, the abuse of their office for personal gain," Yulia explained further. "But ever since Yeltsin started giving away oil companies and selling the mines with precious metals for ten percent their value, Bolshakov has become even more important because he was the only one telling us the real story behind the headlines."

"A communist who loves a free press...that's ironic don't you think?" I muttered to myself.

"Why not? A free press means that even a communist today can write what he chooses. It's the principle, Peter. Besides all that, it's possible to have an honest communist who is for treating the people fairly. It's the corruption that he is fighting against." Yulia stopped herself and corrected her description of Bolshakov to the past tense, "It's the corruption and the criminals he *was* working against."

"What effect do you think this will have on journalists going forward?" I asked with concern for her and her studies in particular.

"I really don't know. Bolshakov had developed a cult of personality at our school. There are many of us who are very inspired by his use of the press to expose the scams and back-handed deals in Moscow. I really don't know what my class is going to do with this news. We read his pieces every week and debated them." Her thoughts trailed off as she stared outside into the bright afternoon sunshine.

"What types of deals was he exposing recently? Who would have wanted him dead?" I queried further to keep her talking.

"He had just uncovered a huge deal between the government and a number of bankers, and of course behind the money in the bank were some very, very bad people who are career criminals since even before Gorbachev started his reform program. It turns out that the government has leased the rights to our most valuable natural resources for about ten percent their real value! For all the talk they do about market reforms, they certainly didn't let the market work on these deals. It was all rigged. It was just a show for the public and the western newspapers. Somebody certainly got a very nice back scratch!" she exclaimed as her thoughts focused on the swindles the Bolshakov had exposed. "They call this type of deal a 'shock reform.' Yes! it is a shock to us all that they are giving away our country!"

"Makes you wonder who really has the power in Moscow, doesn't it?" I muttered again.

"Just as long as the old communists aren't calling the shots, the western governments don't care and they just keep supporting Yeltsin, even though they are making these types of corrupt and illegal deals," Yulia said with some exasperation.

"Is Yeltsin in control, do you think? Or is he just a figurehead, the acceptable face to the world right now?" I asked with skepticism as I listened to Yulia explain the most recent events that we were not even yet in the archives I was searching in at the university.

"The public in Moscow loves him. They voted for him again even after he blew up the parliament with his tanks. People in Moscow are very happy with the new freedoms they have in their personal lives, but they are looking only at the short-term effect. Yeltsin's advisors are selling all of our futures away to the crime bosses. They will get richer and richer and keep all the money from the oil while we can't get medicines here in the provinces," she moaned.

"Don't you think Bolshakov's television exposé will help people see that? I heard it was very specific," I questioned.

"Maybe. Only maybe! Russians only believe when they want to believe something, nothing can change their minds. If they believe in Yeltsin and Chubais then they'll believe them while they are being buried alive that it is for their own good." She was spitting fire now at this point. "They all need to wake up!"

"Yes, I did read some statement from Chubais that he thought that mafia money being used to buy legitimate businesses from the government was a good thing. He liked the idea of being able to tax their illegally earned money. Ridiculous!" I added, "They need to confiscate it and stop the joyriding, not legitimize their status and give them a seat at the table. Makes me wonder who is really being served here."

"What, does Chubais think that they'll just stop doing what they're doing, earning lots and lots of money by exploiting and hurting other people because they are waiting to do an 'honest day's work'? He is crazy." Yulia was pacing around the room now. "They'll just keep doing what they're doing but with more money and influence just to grind us down further as their slaves."

"What can we do to fix this?" I asked, seeing the downward spiral in front of me, opening up on the floor under the sofa ready to swallow us all up.

"What can we do to fix it? Ha ha ha. There is nothing that you or I, or my entire class of future journalists can do! They'll just shoot us on Sunday evening after a family outing, or blow up the bus we ride to work every day. Peter, there is nothing we can do about it." She looked at me as if I was a complete idiot, a naive American idiot.

"You can't just let Bolshakov be buried and forget about what he's done. You've got to fight on!" I said in my best inspirational voice.

"Peter, if you think it's so horrible, you do something about it! As for me, I think I'm going to become an entertainment critic and write glowing reviews about this year's upcoming Victory Day concerts in May and keep myself from getting shot. It's not a time to go sticking your head up. If they'll kill somebody as visible as Bolshkov, it means that they can and will kill anybody that they want to." She refused to speak with me any further on the topic.

I was very saddened to hear and see how defeated Yulia was. The young idealist I knew had also been shot, it seemed, and killed next to the famous journalist that horrible Saturday night in Moscow. I didn't press the matter with her any further and, sensing her wanting to be alone again, I excused myself and headed home before it got too dark on the street.

Outside on the square across the street from the Zarechnaya Metro Station, the weekend bazaar was just wrapping up with the setting sun. Merchants lugging their goods in huge plastic sacks were standing together at the bus stops to head home for the night. I climbed aboard for the short ride back to my apartment and quickly took a seat behind the driver.

As the bus pulled away from the curb, a middle-aged woman began demanding something from me that I didn't understand. Her stern approach led me to believe she was a transit controller who was asking to see my bus ticket.

The transit systems in Russia are systematically abused because one can board the bus without buying a ticket first, and without paying the fare if you get off quick enough. Many times, during very crowded bus rides one is requested to pass money forward to the driver's cabin while the bus is moving so that a ticket can be purchased for you and passed back. It happens often that passengers must get off the bus before their tickets are able to find them. On the night buses, from where the money comes and to whom the tickets belong can sometimes remain a mystery.

Taking this babbling woman for a plain clothes transit controller, I quickly reached for my monthly bus pass along with my student card and flashed it confidently at her with a slightly defiant attitude. She apologized in a very humble voice and turned to grab a hand-rail as the bus lurched from the curb. She did not go on to ask anybody else for proof of payment. Her quiet apology was also very odd as most controllers usually just look and move on to the next passenger, who is usually hurrying to get out his money to look as if he is passing it forward to buy a ticket by proxy.

It became evident to me that I had misunderstood this woman and what it was that she was asking of me. Wanting to know what had just happened, I leaned over to the white haired older woman sitting next to me and spoke in a low voice, "Excuse me please, Babushka, I am a foreigner. Can you help me understand why the controller was so angry at me?"

"She's not a controller. She just didn't want to stand with her groceries. She's healthy enough. She can stand for five minutes." The grandma smirked as she looked the other woman, in her mid-forties, up and down with a dismissive eye.

Still puzzled, I followed up, "Then why did she stop yelling at me when I showed her my bus pass and student card?" I held up my documents to show her what I had in my hand.

"She must have mistaken your student card as an invalid's pass," she assumed and dismissed my question.

This explanation puzzled me even more and I just couldn't let it go. "Excuse me, Babushka, I look twice as healthy and strong as she does, why would she think I would be carrying an invalid's pass?"

"Oh, young man, our boys from Nizhniy are now starting to come home from the fighting in Chechnya, some of them dead, God rest their souls, and many of them are badly wounded and have been given invalid papers and an army pension. She must have mistaken you for one our boys," the grandmother said in a grave tone.

"Oh, well, I will give her my seat then!" I said, determined to clear up the misunderstanding.

"No, no, you just sit here." She took my hand and held it the rest of the ride until my stop.

"My youngest grandson has just been drafted into the army and he will soon go fight in Grozny. We said goodbye to him ten days ago and I fear that this was the last time that I will see him alive. My father died in Stalingrad. I understand that sacrifice against the Nazi fascists; we all did then, it was a matter of life and death for us, for Russia and our children and grandchildren. Nobody understands why we are sending our boys to fight our own people. Why should we fight each other? I can't understand it. It will be the end of us when we send our own boys to kill the boys of our neighbors. Young, man, leave Russia before it's too late! Don't stay here. Nothing good will come of this."

Between my afternoon discussion with Yulia and this encounter with a shriveled gray grandmother on the bus, I started thinking that perhaps it was better to leave Russia and go home while the going was still good. Once inside I collapsed on my bed a mess of emotions and worries. Bolshakov's body in the blood-stained snow and Chechen soldiers filled my dreams that night.

6. Strelyenko

Strelyenko, a junior professor, had only a cramped, poorly furnished room for an office that was eternally hazy with the cigarette smoke of an anxious and pensive chain smoking intellectual that he certainly embodied. The smell conveyed a sense of troubled thoughts. His ash trays seemed not to have been emptied since the last October. His desk was made of cheap pressboard as well as his bookshelves, which were overflowing with books in many different languages. His desk top was not visible, covered in exercise booklets filled with students' essays, his own notepads and hand scribbled thoughts, and an ancient typewriter. On the wall behind him hung a historic imperial Russian flag and by the door and a framed photo of the late Tsar Nicholas II, the last of the Romanovs to sit on Russia's throne. It seemed he wanted nothing to do with the modern era. I was startled to spy a telephone in the room. It seemed very out of place.

"Russia is indivisible and not even the Chechens should doubt that!" Strelyenko proclaimed at my questions about the Chechen rebellion and hope for an independent nation from Russia.

"Why shouldn't Chechnya also ask for its independence just like Russia and Kazakhstan did a few years ago, leaving the USSR?" I asked inquisitively.

The professor retorted, "Because, Russia and Ukraine and Belarus were in fact different republics making a union. Constitutionally these were sovereign republics and could decide their own fate. Chechnya is not a sovereign province, not even an autonomous province like Tatarstan, you know, around Kazan. Chechnya is an inseparable part of the Russian Federation and has no constitutional prerogative to secede."

"So the only way to do that then is by armed struggle," I concluded.

"Which they will lose! They can't take on the whole of the Russian army with a thousand guerrillas driving Ferraris and hope to win," Strelyenko predicted with resentment in his voice. "Russia will never let itself be divided again, and the world needs to understand that what was also once Russia will be reclaimed. It may take some time, but what the Soviet Union took from Russia will be restored, through armed conflict if necessary."

"And how far back do you propose to go in history for your definition of greater Russia?" I asked, alarmed.

"From 1917 of course, when our last rightful monarch was deposed, as we discussed already last week," he stated with no hesitation.

"That's a lot of territory to take back," I said with surprise on my face.

"Well, my friend, Rome wasn't built in a day. Kiev won't be regained in a year, but we will be patient and rebuild what was lost to the republicans and then to the communists," he calmly assured me.

"And Poland then?" I feared his answer.

"That is an interesting question. One should answer that first by answering the question of whether or not Poland has a historical right to exist as an independent country. When did it really come into existence and how? To whom does Danzig belong?" the professor postulated.

"Danzig?" I queried unsure of the geography he was referencing.

"You would know it as Gdansk in Poland, but under the Prussian Keiser it was called Danzig," he clarified.

"So, eighty years of existence since the end of the first world war for you isn't historical enough?" The hair on the back of my neck began to stand up.

"Neither Stalin nor Hitler recognized this in 1939 after only thirty short years of its existence. Everybody could see that they couldn't remain an independent nation and had to be taken into protection."

"Protection?" I gasped. "You call that protection?"

"It's all how you look at it, my American friend," he said haughtily.

"Let's agree to disagree then," I proposed, "because what the Nazis and the Communists did in Poland cannot be called protection from my perspective."

"Fair enough, but for the record, I have not decided my position on Poland personally. It's a difficult question," Strelyenko clarified.

"For some of us, maybe," I remarked with a sneer.

"Yes, and that's why we have dialogue," he replied to my youthful disgust.

"Oh, yes, dialogue, like the kind going on now in Grozny with rocket launchers and artillery?" I rebuked him.

"It was the Chechens who refused to talk and took up arms and blockaded the province. They are violating the rights of Russian citizens enforcing their Islamic traditions on people who are not Muslims. Those people have the right to be Christians if they choose and this must be protected. The president will clean this up quickly with a strong police action and bring law and order back to Chechnya after too many years of letting the criminals and mafia take over the local economy there." Strelyenko's reply made me rethink my position.

"So, this is a fight against criminality in your mind, and not the suppression of national and ethnic identity?" I asked with some unsureness.

"Yes, and the president would do good to use the army to clean up Moscow as well when he is done. The criminals from Grozny have moved into Moscow trying to secure their position to control different industries and trade. A gang war has erupted in Moscow and the Chechens are in the middle of it, but the government needs to act now against all the mafia groups in Russia, not just the Chechen thieves. These groups are the single most dangerous threat to Russia's future. The people must get together now and demand the president takes action against the profiteers and thieves who are robbing our country blind of our God-granted resources and territory!" he said while slapping his table with his open palm, rather worked up.

Somehow, from between the lines of Strelyenko's extreme nationalistic rhetoric I concluded that his call to action for the long-term health of Russia and its citizens, whether it was in Chechnya, Moscow, or Siberia, wasn't too far off the mark.

Stelyenko didn't stop; he continued slapping his desk top. "Law and order has to be restored! If not, then those ready to use violence to trump the rule of law could stunt the future of our entire country for good. It must be stamped out."

On leaving Strenlyenko's office I bumped into Dean Karamzin in the hallway and he asked me to walk with him to his office. He took his chair behind his desk while I stood at attention across the desk from him.

"Mr. Turner, as you are a student, an observer of politics, can I invite you to the first plenum of The Left Front party of Nizhniy Novgorod? Purely as a guest and observer of course," the dean proclaimed in his usual blustery manner.

"A new party?" I asked, intrigued.

"Oh yes, new parties in Russia are forming every day. Mostly they are unprofessional, built on demagoguery and those wanting to throw out all Jews, create the Soviet Union again but without the black republics," he said off hand.

"The black republics?" I asked, unsure of the reference.

"Yes, Georgia, Armenia, Azerbaijan," he explained.

"Funny because in English we call that area the Caucasian republics, which means white," I explained from a linguistic perspective.

"Well, they're not my words, they're the words of that nut in Moscow, Zhilanskiy. You know of him?'

I nodded my head solemnly.

"He says anything to get his votes for the new Russian Duma." The dean showed his disgust with a brush of his hand through the air. "But the Left Front Party of Nizhniy Novgorod is a group of real thinkers."

"Oh, we have the nouveau bourgouise and the nouveau intelligentsia coming back?" I smiled at the irony.

"Mr. Turner, you surprise me with your knowledge of the communist rhetoric," the dean suddenly said very seriously.

"Sorry, I will try to be less skeptical of today's Russia," I replied humbly.

"Being skeptical in Russia keeps you healthy and alive!" he declared with an amused look on his face.

"So, the new intelligentsia?" I said, bringing us back on point.

"The Left Front is a group of local academics who want to have an influence in the local and provincial government. This is not a national party; well, maybe not yet," he explained.

"Left Front? Are they specifically liberal, like the Yeltsin and Gaidar camps?" I inquired.

"No, they are not particularly politically oriented. The Left Front is a reference to a famous battle during the war in defense of the Volga region. No right- or left-wing politics involved."

"Are you a member of it too then?" I pushed for more details.

"No, but I am advising the party how to create a meaningful manifesto and will be the chairman at the plenum. You are very welcome to attend and listen as my guest." From his perspective, he was bestowing on me a great honor.

"Thank you, I would be honored," I said politely.

The dean gave me a mono-colored flyer printed on rough grey paper that looked as if it could have been from the promoters of the 1917 communists' traveling revival show. It seemed to me that so much of the administration and records keeping could have been the same before the revolution, with the exception of the fax machine in Arkadiy's office at Gagarin Street. The dean's telephone buzzed on his desk as we shook hands. He bellowed "'Halloah'" into the handset as I pulled the door closed behind me and made a mental note for Friday afternoon's event.

After a few days had passed since the assassination of Dmitri Bolshakov, Yulia had mostly recovered her composure and started going to classes again, but something still wasn't quite the same. A spark in her eyes had gone out or was just very dim, so I was surprised when she accepted my invitation to come with me to observe the plenum meeting of the Left Front Party. When we arrived at the city administration offices in the kremlin for the party conference, the banquet room was already filled with more than fifty men and a few women. We had to find a place to sit in the left back of the room. There was nobody to take our coats and hats at the wardrobe, so we carried our shapkas and coats over our arms and laid them over the back of a free chair next to us. The inlaid wooden floor of the banquet hall creaked and shifted under our boots and chairs as we took our seats.

"Very unusual that nobody greeted us at the door and nobody to take coats and hats?" Yulia commented slightly annoyed.

"It's not a ball tonight. It's a debate," I said carefully as she was a bit fragile still. Yulia gave me an annoyed look.

"It's still the city administration office," she insisted.

"And so it is," I said, folding my arms and settling into my chair and taking in the scene.

The dean spotted me and gave me a wave over the crowd from the raised podium, acknowledging that I had arrived. I didn't feel free to introduce Yulia as she hadn't been invited and was there as the press incognito. Luckily, he didn't come over to great us.

"That's it? He's just going to wave and not shake hands?" Yulia huffed again.

"He's busy, can't you see that?" I said defensively.

"He should at least shake your hand. He invited us," she pouted.

"What's the problem, Yulia? Do you not want to stay?" I asked, trying to feel out her mood. She didn't reply but looked straight ahead, ignoring my question.

I rolled my eyes while looking away. I was thrilled just to have been invited and was satisfied to be able to watch the organization of a new party, in a region of the country that had top talent and was becoming a case study for restructuring and reform. Forget the greetings and handshakes, politics was in the air! For all we knew the tent could come down tonight in a proper brawl with fists and chairs being thrown.

Dean Karamzin stood up to call the meeting to order. The din of the crowd died down and wispy gray-haired men, already hot in debate with each other, took their seats. I noticed Strelyenko in the front row, his full, young head of hair waving without any wind, and thought to myself, "this could get interesting." I wondered if he was a party member or just here helping the dean with the administration of the meeting.

The first order of business was the agenda, which was read with only one amendment requested from the front row: adopted. Second order of business was to confirm the first party leader. The intellect behind the formation of the party was unanimously elected as party leader: Sergey Nicholievich T. This seemed to be a foregone conclusion as it was his influence that brought the different academics across the various faculties together under one flag. He himself was a professor of economics and had spent some time in both Moscow and Sverdlovsk consulting Mr. Yeltsin's cabinet about economic policy. He looked to be fifty years old.

The third matter of business was to agree the manifesto. We were to hear the reports of the three committees that were tasked to each create a manifesto chapter on the three pillars of the party. These would then be voted on, to either accept or send the proposed sections of the manifesto back to the committee for revision and improvement. The first two pillars of the party were predictable—economic and political reform—but my ears perked up when the third pillar was announced: Law and Order, and the Rule of Law.

While the first two draft articles for the manifesto passed without significant debate, as they were mostly idealistic statements without policy proposals, the third article caused a massive rift in the room. It read:

"We the LFPNN call on the city, provincial, and national governments to fight organized crime wherever it may be found corrupting the rule of law, fairness, and transparency, and to combat the influence of illegal activities in our communities, places of employment and in government."

All hell broke loose at this point. Debates suddenly broke out in small groups around the room. Who had proposed something so dangerous and so irresponsible? All the academics were exasperated. People were overheard shouting to the chairman and leader, "Something so direct and accusatory should never be allowed to be published," and, "Who was the head of this committee? It should never have left the committee with such strong words," and, "We will all be shot!" A few people headed for the door and slammed it behind them, fleeing before their names could be recorded as official party members.

The dean called the room to order again and a proper debate ensued regarding the proposed article. Many of the speakers were all very much against the article as it was written. Several younger members were for it, but the crowd seemed spooked. Then, something electric happened. Strelyenko stood up to speak. The room quieted down to listen.

"Brothers, brothers. Why are we here tonight? Why did you come here tonight? Was it not to make a difference and save Mother Russia from the current thieves and hooligans that are running our country into the ground? You are all smart men, scientific men! Surely you can predict the end if we do not protect ourselves from the gangsters that are quickly now taking over our economy and government, making themselves rich and our children poor. There won't be affordable bread for your children and grandchildren if we continue to sell our resources to foreign investors and let gangsters sell them back to us for double the price.

"We must have complete accountability and complete transparency in order to save Russia. Our leaders must be first Russians, then fathers, then governors and mayors. They cannot have hidden agendas and secret fortunes in foreign banks. Their dachas must be next to ours. We must know them and in which schools their children study and from which shop they buy their meat and vegetables and if they drive a car how they paid for it. We do not call for hot actions but for clever thinkers to help us think our way out of this mess created by Yeltsin and Gaidar and the United States before it's too late!"

The mood turned from low energy to electric in a crescendo that grew with each of Strelyenko's words, starting at the repeating of the word 'brothers.' Somehow this young professor, this young idealist had tapped into the popular mood, the common man's frustration and released their imaginations for a better, a fairer, a safer Russia. The plenum had just been hijacked. Strelyenko brought the crowd to a fevered pitch as he continued.

"Why do we sit on our hands while our government sells our homes, shops, and factories to the highest bidders? Who are they trying to please? Who are they taking care of? The western financiers or the home-grown criminals? Who, I ask you, who is ready to stand up and defend our mothers, wives and daughters from these profiteers? If this continues much longer, we will have wished we had let the fascists win fifty years ago and kill us quickly, instead of being slowly enslaved by our own people who murder us one by one in the streets. Who has been arrested yet for the murder last week of Dmitri Bolshakov? No one! Why does the Prosecutor General still sit in the Kremlin? Brothers, we must hold our leaders accountable for the crimes they commit against us and against Russia!"

Sergey Nicholeivich, the newly elected party leader, was beside himself. This type of speech was not supposed to happen at his party rally. They were to be the guardians of policy, a united think-tank, the brains behind the governor—not on the front line of politics, taking names and holding politicians and gangsters accountable. Sergey Nicholaevich trembled with rage and fear in his chair as he stood to intervene in this unsanctioned turn of events. He shouted over the clamor of the party members and called the room to order. His voice quivered with emotion, but not the kind that motivates the masses.

"Ladies and gentlemen," his follow up to Strelyenko's appeal to his brothers neutralized whatever else followed, "this party was organized to bring academic quality into our political discussion and policy ch-ch-choices." The chairman stuttered nervously as he slowly realized from the body language and faces of his party members that he had lost rank and file. He looked from side to side looking for a friendly face in the audience.

"Vote, vote, vote!" a low chant from a chorus came from the front left of the room.

"Please! Ladies and gentlemen, do not let your emotions carry you away from our plans," the party chairman stammered, feeling his hold on the reins was already lost and chiding them for their rash change of mind.

"Vote, vote, vote!" the chorus was growing.

Feeling he had no more choice, Sergey Nicholaevich gave a nod to Dean Karamzin to conduct a vote in his capacity as chairman of the meeting.

Above the low chatter and excitement, Karamzin's voice boomed through the hall.

"All in favor of the adoption of the third article of the manifesto as recommended by the committee to the members of the LFPNN, say 'aye.'"

The hall bloomed with a synchronized voice of contempt for the current system. There was no question that the majority was behind Strelyenko's proposed manifesto.

"And all those against, please," Karamzin boomed.

Only silence followed. I heard myself blink in the two seconds it took to count five contrary votes, one of which was Sergey Nicholaevich's who meekly held his hand above his head.

The third article passed. Sergey Nicholvaevich sat sullen with his head in hands, the victim of his own ambitions as the newly formed LFPNN set itself on a collision course for the rocks against which many Russian reformers had been smashed to pieces: corruption and criminals.

"Peter, we really need to leave now!" Yulia stood up quickly to gather her coat and handbag.

"Why? What's the matter!" I whispered with some irritation.

"You shouldn't be here. I shouldn't be here. We could be expelled from school for being here and taking part in this," she answered with a flash of fear in her eyes.

"Yulia, I was invited by my professor. Of course I should be here," I stammered in confusion.

"What's just happened here is very dangerous. Remember Peter, that it never is what it seems." Yulia sat down again, but only on the edge of her chair ready still to leave without me if I wouldn't go with her. "The party was allowed to organize but not for this reason. Didn't you hear him say that? Look at him shaking there in his chair. He knows he's in trouble. Russia may have elected a president, but the rest of the system is still rigged, Peter. Opposition is a sanctioned position in Russia. Opposition party leaders are hand picked to be irrelevant. It's a show, a production. Look what Yeltsin did to his challengers when they really decided to be an opposition."

"I think you're going a bit far, Yulia. Please, you're just still shook up from Bolshakov's murder." I tried to reason with her. She stood up and looked at me with daggers in her eyes and stormed out of the hall, slamming the door behind her.

I found Yulia outside on Minin Square alone at the bus stop in the snow but she would not speak to me.

"What did I do to make you so mad at me?" I pleaded for an explanation. She would not reply. Her bus pulled up to the curb but she didn't board it. She stood frozen as the bus pulled away toward the train station.

We stood silent for a few moments and then she began a tirade that stung like a hot poker. "Do you think this is some sort of fun spectacle, Peter? Something for you to digest after dinner and something to write about for people back in America? This is the real thing, Peter. People are dying everyday while trying to live with dignity. What are you doing to help this besides watching with amusement? Why are you even here? What do you think you can do about it, or are you even going to try? You go back to your meeting of intellectuals and academics and go write your thesis about how horrible Russia is. Then you'll disappear back to America like the dog who has eaten his fill and what good will it do us here? Nothing!"

I stood shocked and speechless. A retort was pointless. She was beyond reasoning. Another bus heading someplace pulled up and she climbed on board and turned her back to me as she sat against the frosty window. I watched helplessly as the bus pulled away.

Els greeted me at the door excusing her husband who could be overheard in his study talking animatedly on the telephone. Els discreetly pulled his door closed to prevent any eves dropping of a curious student's ears and showed me into the living room. I took a seat on the couch and felt the weight of the world fall on my shoulders.

"You look like you need a week on the Black Sea!" Els began.

"Anyplace I could see the sun would be welcome at this point," I said with a disheartened sigh.

"Are you finding the studies more difficult than you thought they would be in Russian?" she suggested.

"No, actually. The language is not a problem. What is really tough is an article I've committed to with the dean of the department." I sat up straight at the prospect of having a sympathetic ear listen to my problems.

Els sympathized, "I was a bit skeptical, when you first mentioned it, that you wouldn't find the needed materials here in Nizhniy. It may only be three hundred kilometers from Moscow, but it's the provinces, and as we all know that all power in this country is centered in Moscow."

"Oh no, finding material is not my problem! What's discouraging is what I am learning about Russia and the corruption that goes so high and so deep. The entire country is being hoodwinked by the politicians and the nouveau riche that there is going to be nothing left in ten more years. The party apparatchiks just changed the color of their ties from red to blue and now are rolling in the money and making themselves and their new friends richer than yours and my wildest dreams!" I was a bit worked up now especially after Yulia's damning accusations about me doing nothing and also just profiteering from the situation in my own way.

"One of the most frustrating things that Del and I came up against working in Moscow for a few years was that the people in public service who were supposed to be neutral, those supposed to be there for helping to support the transition and development, were the first with their hands in the cookie jar. Everybody had a hidden agenda. We didn't know who we could trust." Els was calm and philosophical about it, tempered by experience and exposure.

"Yes! Every decision made on the national level about the privatization process has a back alley pay-off for a bureaucrat who is just in it for himself. There is no transparency...no justice..." I was feeling even more discouraged than when I started.

"Peter, why did you come here? You're not here to have fun as a student, are you? It seems to me that you are on a quest, like some sort of modern Don Quixote quest, to protect the Russians from themselves. Where does that come from?"

"I don't know," I admitted.

Just then Del, in all his bravado, burst from his study with a bow-legged gate, stepped into the living room interrupting the train of discussion and thought.

"Peter, welcome! How the hell are ya?" His cheerfulness was amusing and lightened the mood in the room. "It's been a few weeks, huh? What have you been keeping busy with?" Sitting down in a chair opposite me he continued without pausing. "We had a great visit in Germany last week and I think we'll be able to break through some red tape and get the project moving forward again."

Dinner with Del and Els was a welcome distraction from the unpleasant exchange with Yulia earlier. As every trip abroad means moving through Moscow, when he visited Del made it a point to bully the little hooligans that hang around in hotel lobbies, looking tough but are toothless. His stories not only entertained but left me more and more curious about the man. He was either fearless or able to discern who was truly dangerous and then was not afraid too and had no problem letting another alpha-male, who was lower on the pecking list, know where he stood in Del's rankings.

"...and then the punk nearly swallowed his cigarette right there in the elevator of the hotel, still lit!" Del rehearsed in his cowboy drawl. I couldn't help but lighten up a bit.

After we wiped away the tears of laughter and the crumbs from the table, Del went on to tell me about the problems that he experienced in his last project in Moscow, also a hotel, as the local politicians began to interfere to try to control the hotel.

"Even though we had all the needed permits and permissions and had greased the right hands at the time, somebody else wanted to muscle in on the operation as everybody began to see that we were going to make it! It was a miracle...but we had turned the corner. As Moscow was opening up more and more to foreigners, and more importantly foreign investors and businessmen, they needed a trusted name and a trusted hotel to meet in where they would not have hookers sent to their rooms in the middle of the night and then have compromising photos presented to them the next morning, or pretty girls letting themselves into their rooms. We provided security and privacy for negotiations. So anyway, some mafia goons wanted in on it and we wouldn't sell them any share of the operation. No way! So what happens? The mayor starts getting involved and is demanding that we take on a local partner. We already had a local partner in the joint venture. None of it made sense. Anyhow that turned into quite a stand-off which the US Embassy got involved with. The whole thing is frozen now with little change...but, yeah, you just never know from which direction these things will come from in this crazy country. People's intentions are hidden and their actions even more unpredictable when money is dangled in their faces. You've got to be very careful here not to get too deep into it that you can't walk away at the last minute. You just never know when it's going to go south on you!"

"Don't you want to help change things, though? Russia has such a potential and it just seems to be sinking further since all the reforms started. Instead of taking wings like we all expected, it took a nose dive. It all seems preventable if," I asked trying to feel out his motivations.

"...if what? How do you think you could change this? You can't stop a moving train by jumping in front of it, kid; it will just roll right over you. Nobody will even notice. You won't even be a speed bump on the rail. You'll be a moth on the windshield. You'll only annoy the engineer and he will just wash you off with the windshield wipers. You need to be able to walk away when it's time to walk away," Del pontificated in his prairie philosophy. "Don't try to be a hero, Peter. You didn't make this mess. You are not obligated to help clean it up."

"Oh, I almost forgot!" I stood up to find my bag and from it produced three weeks of *The Economist* that Del had missed being away.

Els saw me to the door and said with a bit of motherly concern, "Peter, be sure to have some fun too! Remember that you can't change the world on your own!"

Outside, snow was still falling and piling up on the pavement. I rode the bus across the river to the Moscovskiy Train Station. When I stepped off the bus there was a smoldering kiosk, charred black and shattered glass, that had recently been extinguished by fire fighters. I didn't linger and look or ask the last fire fighters what had happened. Everybody knew what had happened. Somebody hadn't paid their protection money.

06

7. Valentine's Day

After a few days of not seeing each other and not speaking, I phoned Yulia to invite her out for a real sit-down dinner, in a real restaurant on the Bolshaya Pokrovka, to celebrate Valentine's Day. Like Christmas, western holidays were in vogue with the students but in the city, there was very little observance. To my surprise, Yulia accepted my invitation to reconciliation very graciously.

A few days before my invitation to Yulia, while walking between classes together, Marina pointed out to me that an acquaintance of hers had recently bought a newly privatized restaurant and it was open for customers. This, of course, piqued my interest. Marina and I stopped to look at the menu of traditional Russian foods. I noticed immediately that there were no listed prices on the menu. I stepped inside to ask for a reservation for the evening of St. Valentine's Day. Marina was all starry eyed at how romantic it was going to be, and she wasn't even invited. She was like that.

When Yulia and I arrived for dinner we were met, greeted, and seated promptly by a well-dressed and well-mannered waiter. Yulia approved immediately. The dining room was in a sous-terrain, basement with a vaulted brick ceiling. There was a shabby-chic feeling as the basement had been decorated to feel as if the diners were eating in the wine cellar. The white paint peeling off the red bricks of the faux vaulting added to the feeling of being someplace other than snowy, frozen, pickled Russia.

The tables were covered in proper linen table cloths and napkins. The silverware was shiny and heavy in the hand. The lighting low and focused creating an intimate and private atmosphere. Yuila thought she was Sophia Lauren and that diamonds were to be served as the appetizer and couldn't stop smiling. Everybody was so polite and chivalrous as professional waiters and services should be. Menus were brought and aperitifs presented. This boded well to help patch things up between us.

"It all looks so good!" Yulia beamed as she inspected the menu offerings.

"I haven't had chicken Kiev since I was in Kiev a few years ago," I said with some wonder. "I think I will try that tonight."

"I've never had it. I hear it's really good when it's cooked right," she said with stars in her eyes.

We both ordered the chicken Kiev but enjoyed a five-course presentation with starters, both warm and cold, an in-between chef's surprise, a buttery chicken Kiev with a gourmet potato puree with fresh green vegetables, and ended with a traditional Russian jam of berries in an unsweetened cream. We drank chilled sparkling mineral water from Austria. The waiter took a photo of us. I was curious but didn't speak about it with Yulia, but noticed that still there was no mention of a charge or a single price on the menu for the royal treatment of this gourmet dinner.

"Peter, I feel really horrible for the things I said to you that night at the bus stop. I don't know what came over me. I think you were right that my nerves were still raw from, well, you know what. I don't want to speak of such things in such a nice place." It was the first time I ever heard her apologize. It made me uncomfortable.

"Listen, don't worry about. We all say things sometimes that we don't mean. Please just let it go." I reached out and held her hand across the table for a few moments before dessert was served.

As the evening grew later the dining room filled to capacity, not with elegant diners or couples celebrating Valentine's Day together, but with groups of young men in their twenties in purple suits. For every table of four or five young men in flashy shoes and ties, short hair buzzed off, there were one or two girls, about the same age at the table hanging on the arm of one of the diners. The ladies were not dressed for dinner.

Yulia finally noticed the other diners and gave me a concerned look across the table, and in a low voice commented in English, "Peter, do you see the people here? They all are criminals. Look at their clothes. Normal people cannot buy these clothes."

"Yes, I've noticed. I like the purple suits!" I said with a grin.

Yulia screwed up her face and looked away.

"This a private restaurant," I said to her in coded language. She understood.

"What private?" she gasped.

"Meaning that this restaurant is privately owned. I wanted to come here to see what a private restaurant meant. The food has been excellent. The service has been great. Don't you think so?" I asked innocently.

"Peter, the only people who can pay for a restaurant are criminals. I can't believe you brought me here," she huffed and tried not to be too conspicuous about not looking around her.

As Yulia was becoming very uncomfortable I politely asked for the check. The waiter told us that the charge would be forty dollars and retreated to his service station. Yulia was shocked!

"Peter, forty dollars? That is two month's rent for your apartment! How many rubles is that? My mother and I can feed ourselves for a whole month for that amount! How are you going to pay for that?" she was genuinely concerned that we were in trouble with the wrong people.

"Shhh," I hushed my date's growing hysteria. "I expected this and came prepared. You don't have to worry. I have plenty of money."

I signalled the waiter again. "Do you accept payment in rubles?" I asked him.

"No, unfortunately only in hard currency, dollars or marks."

I cheerfully paid the waiter with two twenty-dollar bills from my billfold with one hundred dollars in it. The waiter retreated again to his station.

"Peter, that is illegal in Russia. Everybody must accept payment in rubles. You can't pay in dollars anymore since the beginning of the year," Yulia hissed into my ear.

"Yes, I understand that, but do you want to tell that to him and him and him?" I whispered back, looking at each thug with a nod of my head.

She looked confused as she turned to look around the dining room filled with thugs and their girls.

"Yulia, this is a mafia restaurant. You don't argue with the waiter in a mafia restaurant. You pay. You smile. You compliment the chef. You leave," I said as I stood up slowly from my chair.

The waiter came with our coats and handed us our hats to be put on outside. He helped Yulia into her long winter coat, this time to her great disapproval.

As we moved up the stairs from the sous-terrain, with the waiter following up behind us, we were confronted immediately with the blue flashing lights of a city police car that had just come to a skidding stop in front of the entrance to the restaurant. Yulia looked at me with panic in her eyes and a look of disdain that I had brought her once again into danger. I too stood frozen in place thinking about the forty-dollars I had just handed to the waiter, complicit in an illegal transaction.

The two police men bounded from their car, but instead of moving directly to the entrance of the restaurant, they moved to open the back doors of their patrol car. From the back seat, they removed two young men in handcuffs and bloody noses. They looked like they had taken a good beating at the hands of the police officers. The four men came through the restaurant's main entrance and moved directly through a service door into and through the kitchen. Not a word was said, no polite excuses were given for the disruptions. It was as if they hadn't even been seen by anybody around them. Yulia and I looked at each other in disbelief.

Before we could make any further movement towards the door, another car came sliding to a stop outside the restaurant on the snowy cobblestones. The headlights shined directly into the restaurant, blinding us. Before we could make a step towards the door, in walked three men who obviously were not going to yield the right of way nor hold the door open for us. We stood aside as three angry faces passed us, glaring and sizing us up for any potential threat; two identical-looking bodyguards walked in front of and directly behind a shorter, stouter man with a clean shaven bald head dressed in the latest fashions from Paris. The bald one looked directly at me, and his eyes stayed on me as his entourage passed us, trying to be as flat as possible against the wall. His eyes looked black against his bright white open collar and the concentrated fury in them frightened me, turning my gut into jelly.

After a slight pause in the lobby and some discreet instructions to the waiter who was seeing us out, these three men joined now by two younger cadets from the dining room disappeared through the same service door as the police officers and their prisoners. As they vanished from the lobby Yulia and I both scrambled for the door and exited in tandem, bumping shoulders over the threshold as we rushed out on to the street.

"You there, stand still!" a voice came from behind the precariously parked cars on the restaurant's sidewalk. The blue lights from the police car twirled around, revealing and concealing a third police officer standing in the open driver's door. "What's your business here?"

Yulia was tongue tied and looked to me to explain our way out of the situation.

"I am very sorry. I do not speak Russian" I said calmly in English to the policeman. "Angliskiy?" I asked putting on a stupid American face as I approached him slowly, putting a hand to my ear. This seemed to defuse the officer's suspicion and he spoke again without questioning.

"Please leave here immediately. This is an official police action," he commanded while using sign language to move us on. Yulia didn't speak. I nodded and waved in a friendly manner to the cop to acknowledge our understanding and we slipped away into Pokrovka Street towards Gorkiy Square.

Once we were out of sight and ear shot of the police cars, Yulia held nothing back and let into me in another tirade. "How could you, Peter? How could you do this to me again? Why do you think that you can play with fire and not get burned? You shouldn't tempt fate like this, Peter...and certainly not with me around. They will figure out very quickly who you are, who I am. We just saw them kidnapping people with the help of the police. If those two guys show up dead tomorrow they'll remember that there were witnesses. Do you think that they are just going to forget about that? Do you think this is normal? And then that stupid foreigner act? They'll grab you before you know it. We warned you about speaking English with people you don't know. You don't know who they are or what they might do to you later, or at that very moment! How could you do this?" She was genuinely frightened.

Yulia stomped off ahead of me with a brisk, angry pace. I called after her, trying to calm her down, but she wouldn't yield. I trudged up the street after her and finally caught up and reached out to touch her arm and ask her to stop for a moment and listen to an apology. Instead, she turned and hissed, "I think it's better that you and I aren't seen together for a while for safety reasons, and until you get these stupid ideas out of your head. Remember that if things go wrong, you can always leave. I have to live here. Don't drag me down with your curiosity crusade, Peter!"

I didn't see Yulia again until the ice on the Volga had melted.

06

8. The World Bank

By early March the weather started becoming a bit more unsettled and the air less frozen. Large patches of water began to appear in the middle of the river's flow between the receding ice sheets on either bank of the river. The snow fell wetter, streets were filled more with slush instead of compacted snow, and where potholes in the gutters were once frozen solid, they now were filled with icy slush water and became a hazard to be avoided for those stepping off buses. The wind coming off the rivers filled with growing humidity would create a chill to my core and the sky was regularly gray with clouds.

Being outside during the thaw was not pleasant, so I spent long days and evenings indoors researching and translating, taking notes and building the outline of my term paper, and waiting for the spring to come. I kept my head down and out of sight...at least for a few weeks.

As I scrolled through articles and skimmed reports, the data began to take some form. It clearly said that nobody had any idea what the future would bring to Russia. To find some answers I ventured out of my corner of the library and reemerged into the city from which I was hiding.

The doors to the World Bank office on the corner of Minin Square were locked but all the lights were still on. I was curious if everybody was next door already at four o'clock for "tea-time" with one of New York's best platters. I was immediately conscious that I had also stood up Hans for fried chicken the last three weeks and wondered how he was.

As I walked a few doors further up the street, I noticed a number of flashy cars parked straddling the curbs and one directly on the sidewalk in front of the pizza parlor. They were anything but inconspicuous. The restaurant was empty, though, except for my acquaintances seated in the corner of the pizzeria on plastic patio furniture wrapped in wool coats and scarves, both nursing bottles of soft drinks while waiting patiently for a Russian pizza. I approached their table with a bit of irony in my voice.

"Funny to meet you here," I removed my black shapka and shook hands with both of them.

"I thought that your office was next to the pizza place. . ."

"Well, we've all got to eat at least once a day," was Andrew's guilty confession.

"Come for the grand tour then?" Richard motioned around the empty restaurant acting like a proud owner of a country estate.

"Have a seat. I guess we all got hungry at the same time." Andrew offered an empty plastic patio chair.

"Naaah, I actually came to talk shop with you," I replied taking the chair.

"About what then?" Richard queried.

"I have to put together a thesis for the term. I figured the two of you were probably the ones with the best oversight in the entire city about the reforms happening," I was embellishing in sarcasm but speaking the truth at the same time.

"Oh, so you've chosen the light study courses!" Andrew replied with a stuttering chuckle.

"The never-ending rabbit hole of economic reform...," was Richard's reaction.

The thuggish character from behind the service counter called to Andrew to collect his hot pizza with indescribable indifference.

"We certainly shouldn't talk shop on an empty stomach," Andrew remarked, standing to collect his prize. "Would you join us for a slice or two?"

"I would be honored." We continued our misplaced formality in the middle of the draughty, whitewashed fluorescent-lit pizza palace.

After a few triangles of soggy crust and hot cheese had been inhaled, Andrew sat back in his patio chair and made a dry comment: "That pizza crust was about as thin and soggy as the cover that this pizza joint presents for their other activities, wouldn't you say?" He threw his napkin onto the empty platter.

"Yes, I don't think that those Mercedes parked out front are the delivery boys'..." Richard commented, leering out the window to the makeshift parking lot. "So, what can we help you with, Peter?"

"I'm having trouble finding real data about companies that have already been sold to private investors, or entrepreneurs, or in general about new private start-ups. You being the local bankers, I thought you could point me in the right direction. What can you recommend?" I asked.

"Don't believe any of the data. That's what we recommend. Nobody is reporting their real incomes and profits. On paper, every private company in Russia is failing," Richard stated emphatically.

"That doesn't add up," I muttered, scratching my chin.

"Exactly. Somebody is making money somehow and then turning that into something else, and then taking over a factory and then selling the goods abroad and keeping the profits for himself and not reinvesting. Where the seed money is coming from and where the profits are going, as two economists in a shady pizza joint, we have our suspicions, but nobody is talking about that," Richard speculated.

"Foreign investors?" I postulated.

"Yes, but it hardly accounts for half of the shadow deals going around," Andrew stated.

"Funny money then. Off the books. Black money?" I concluded with a question mark.

"Yes, from one source or another," Andrew confirmed.

"My advice for a thesis is to keep it local and keep it narrow. Use local sources and examples. Otherwise, you will get lost in data that you won't know whether it is true or not. Nobody knows what's going on. It's a huge mess on the national level. But if you stay focused on local efforts and start-up enterprises, you might be able to put something interesting together, maybe even academic if you can cite your sources from interviews and whatnot," Richard counselled.

"OK, I can chew on that for a while," I replied

"Are you talking about the crust... or the advice?" Andrew remarked and we all laughed aloud in our common pizza poverty.

"So, what's the World Bank's role in all this? You can't decide who owns assets can you?" I asked in a different vein.

"No, of course not. We are more or less consulting the lawmakers about what type of transparency and governance the World Bank needs in order to extend loans and credits. The rest is up to them to bring those elements in an application. The biggest problem with this is that even though the rules are more or less acceptable, every Tom, Dick, and Harry thinks he can run a successful business; but there is no track record, no assets to mortgage for a loan, no contracts for production, no guarantee the lent money could ever be repaid or recovered. So, in the end, we are very conservative and very creative. It's really the question of 'which comes first: the chicken or the egg?' It's not a traditional lending market," Richard explained.

"So, what are the new local banks doing?" I asked again.

"Well, perhaps that's a discussion for another time in another venue," Richard commented as he cautiously looked around the empty pizzeria indicating that it would not be prudent to go into such discussions in places where the walls have ears . . . and guns.

"Have you maybe heard of the local privatization auctions being held in Nizhniy?" Andrew asked.

"No. How does that work?" my curiosity was peaked.

"The local government is auctioning off small businesses, like grocery stores, restaurants, and retail shops in the cities. They simply sell to the highest bidders. Sometimes the workers get together to buy it, sometimes an investor buys it up and keeps everybody working there. It's been going on now for about two years. They haven't auctioned the factories yet in this way, as that's a bit more complex, but they are planning to do it in the next phase. Yegor Gaidar, Yeltsin's economics guru, is a real fan of the process. The World Bank has been assisting via-via with that locally. Perhaps we could get you close enough to the auction process to give you a taste of the action," Andrew suggested.

Del was in fine form after dinner and seemed to have forgotten about any prudence as he was venting his frustrations.

"It's true, Peter. Yes, it's true. Everything is on hold. Getting needed financing in this day and age in Russia has become nearly impossible in the last six months, and nobody has the liquidity in a currency that is worth its weight in paper. The laws are changing so quickly that nobody dares take collateral except in the form of cold hard cash parked in a numbered Swiss bank account. With new reforms and new laws coming out every three months, it just keeps everything frozen. Why agree today when in just a few months the terms could be all the better? And those with the influence over the timing of the policies, they know what is coming and when, so they just stall with the expectation that they will simply take over our projects and ideas as the restrictions on foreign owners continue to pile up."

"Are there no regulations from even the Soviet period that help to stabilize the situation?" I appealed.

"Maybe, but nobody believes they will be in place in three more months. Everything is shifting, it's all on sandy ground.

Nobody can put down a foundation in sandy soil," he explained in his cowboy common sense.

"So how are the newer local businesses going forward?" I inquired.

"Well, the types running the new private businesses with success are those that don't rely on their financing to be above board, come with standard interest rates, or even from a bank... and they certainly don't rely on local lawmen to enforce their contracts," Del explained.

"Are you referring then to trust and a hand shake, or do you mean breaking the knees of those who break an agreement?" The situation was starting to become clear to me.

"Broken knees, arson, intimidation of family members, and the likes," Del confirmed. "The biggest risk right now is that the groups that are starting out this way, taking the spoils while the sheriff has his hands tied, is that once they get strong enough and the dust all settles, these same criminals will control so much that it will be impossible to separate their lawful, legitimate money from the shadow money made in the illegal activities. They'll have their own built in money laundering facilities in their business groups. It will be impossible to untangle them all when the laws catch up with the business men."

"As we all know, it's the businessmen who run the politicians in any country," I blurted skeptically. "So the laws will rarely catch up to the businessmen."

"Are you familiar with the current situation where the criminal gangs are hiring local bureaucrats to consult them, as well as sort out disputes about territory and product control?" Del asked me straight faced.

"What? Are you joking?" My jaw dropped. "How does that all work?"

"The criminal groups have figured out that they can go on fighting each other and all wind up dead, or they can coordinate their efforts to build their own specific criminal enterprises and fight the government together. They actually have a pool of money that everybody contributes to that goes to pay the politicians to sort out their disagreements so that it doesn't come to cutting each other's throats," Del said dryly.

I sat with nothing more to say. I stared at him with a blank face from across the room.

"It's true, kid." Del continued to lay it all out for me, "The gangs will simply latch onto a competent entrepreneur and make him their slave. If anybody shows a bit of talent for making a bit of money, they'll bleed him dry like leeches. If he refuses he is shot in a back alley, his car is bombed, his wife is kidnapped, his mother raped and murdered. Much of their own infighting now is about whose businessman is whose. So, they hire a local official to decide for them who gets to exploit which sectors. The government man then makes sure that laws and regulations support his decisions that benefit the gangs. They call this guy 'the roof' or 'krisha' in Russian."

"How deep do you suppose it all goes?" I asked Del, referring to the political corruption.

"Well Peter, I think you might be looking at it with just a touch of naivete. We Americans, in general, have a simple view of the world and how it ought to be: never tell a lie, Honest Abe, checks and balances. That's unique in the world outside the USA except in countries like England and France. Hell, even Spain and Portugal were fascist dictatorships up until maybe twenty years ago. People do what they have to do just to get by in most of the world. The system is stacked against them and so they find a work around.

"Power in Moscow is used in a totally different way than in Washington. For them, it's the perks of the job. We're the ones who call it 'corruption' when we can't figure it all out and get a share of it. That's the way it's been for a very long time and four years of reforms ain't gonna pull it out of the gutter. The whole culture runs this way."

"Doesn't this frustrate you as a business man?" I complained.

"Sure does, but it's not my money, and they want me to play by 'the rules.' I tell them how we could get it done and then they tell me something else. So, I do what they want. Listen, I'm being paid so much money that I'll never have to work again when I'm done here. They've got me in golden handcuffs right now, so I'll do what they want and how they want, but I tell it to them as it is. They make the decisions," Del explained in his own defense.

"Fair enough," I snorted.

9. Midterm

Professor Dashkova was very pleased with the results of my first attempt at the Russian language assessment exam from the Moscow State University. We had a few months to go before June's final exams, but I had already passed with just the minimum score on the practice round held during the midterm period. It could only get better, in theory.

"Mr. Turner, if you pass with a higher score in June, you could go to study in Moscow in September instead of here in Nizhniy," Lyudmila said proudly.

"I am very satisfied to stay here in Nizhniy. I've seen Moscow and I am not too interested to go live there," I remarked modestly.

"Young man, if you are invited to study in Moscow, you cannot refuse it! It's the honor that all the students are hoping to achieve. The best of the best study in Moscow," Lyudmila pressed.

"I understand, professor, but I am busy with projects here in Nizhniy and wouldn't want to give those up," I insisted.

"I am so amazed at your dedication to your studies. Our Russian students are never as serious as you and don't apply themselves to make so much progress. It would be a shame if you did not go to Moscow if you can," she pleaded.

"Thanks again, but I speak Russian now like a Nizhniy local, with Ukrainian parents, and they'll only laugh at my accent in Moscow like they did last summer! Moscovites are rather snobbish that way," I accentuated it by putting on a high-pitched whine like a Muscovite.

"Yes, you are correct, but it should not stop you. And that's that." Lyudmila closed her binder and rested her folded hands over the cover of her portfolio and wouldn't discuss the matter any further. If it was up to her I would be in Moscow already.

Valentina Petrovna was brought up to speed on my midterm scores and also gave me compliments for the quality of my studies and test results. What was more surprising was that now she would only speak Russian with me!

"I also have a note from the American library that you spend too much time there, Peter. Olga is concerned that you are not healthy and are not being social." Valentina sounded like a doctor diagnosing a patient.

"Is that all she said? That I don't seem to have friends? That's funny." I chuckled.

"This Saturday night, there is a student event at The Monastery, a local night club, I assume you know of it, which is held every quarter by the owner for the students after their exams. If you show your student card entrance is free. You are required to attend!" Valentina ordered.

Just then Hans walked past the open door of Valentina Petrovna's office. I hadn't seen him for about a month during my self-internment at the research library.

"Outstanding, Valentina Petrovna, thanks! I'll sleep over at Hans's Saturday night. He lives close. I promise to have some fun!" I darted from her office to catch Hans before he disappeared. The mood in the office was festive, almost jolly as the exams were all but over for the most of us. Relief was palpable in the halls.

My final mid-term evaluation was with Dean Karamzin in his office on Friday afternoon to review the direction and progress of the article that he was demanding in June from me. I explained in depth to the dean what I had been reading about and documenting.

"The evidence is damning. The documentation is fuzzy and misleading and the effects that these deals are having on the government's budgets are dramatic! Industries that the central government once controlled and funded the country with have been sold off to sketchy groups with no track record in the industries. In fact, some didn't exist weeks before the sales. Company assets have been systematically stripped and sold to the highest bidders and the directors of the new companies have disappeared with the proceeds from those sales! No more taxes, no more export duties, no more jobs.

"The government sold the companies for a song and a dance, in several instances for about ten percent of their market value, and now no tax revenues and lot of unemployed people needing assistance. It's like the companies just evaporated into thin air after selling their equipment and infrastructures. It's been one huge liquidation and carpet bagging exercise for those who pushed the sales through."

The dean mulled over this information with a surprised look.

"And then there are the banks!" I was ready to continue my monologue. The dean stopped me.

"You found all this documentation in my library?" was his first puzzled question.

"Uhhh, yes. Why? Is this a problem?" I asked like a mouse caught in a trap with cheese in its mouth.

"A problem? No! This is wonderful that our library has this information!" he exclaimed. "You know I don't believe many people use the database because we don't speak English well enough. But to have you extract this information in an academic way from our library is a great step forward for the university! Mr. Turner this is outstanding news," the dean said solemnly with excitement.

I continued to explain my hope for the paper, but the dean interrupted my monologue.

"Mr. Turner, I would like you to now focus on the local effects of the corrupt privatization activities instead of continuing to research this on the national level. We need to produce something that has a direct local effect and leave Moscow to sort out Moscow's problems."

"But Moscow's problems, Moscow's abuses will have a bad long-term effect on Nizhniy as well and people need to know the country is being robbed blind!" I protested.

"We will survive to face those problems in the future, I am sure. We survived Brezhnev, didn't we? I will arrange a number of interviews with my contacts in the city and in the Nizhegorodskiy leadership for your questions and proposals about how to stop this from happening here. I want to have concrete, academically researched policy proposals that we as the university can publish to push this agenda forward," he instructed.

"That's going to be difficult because the mention of Nizhniy Novgorod in the articles really is minimal up until now, except to praise Nemtsov for his support of privatization efforts," I explained.

"And that is why you need to do your local research." The Dean was adamant.

We paused and looked at each other intently. The wheels were spinning in both of our heads. We had caught a thought wave together and we watched it break. I broke the silence and spoke rapidly before he changed his mind.

"Through the six or seven case studies of the biggest swindles there was always a small start...and always through a deception...whether harmful or not, undeclared money becomes the seed of a banking or industrial empire. So, somebody earned some decent seed money working in the black market, and then they buy some party hacks who are now leftover civil servants from the Soviet period, who have no personal prospects for the future, who wouldn't know what to do with a smelting factory in the wider world, but they do know what to do with two hundred fifty million dollars between the four of them! Then somehow, no big mystery, Yeltsin has given the businessman a franchise or he becomes, low and behold, a deputy prime minister making decisions that have HUGE conflicts of interest—in their own favor of course, and then move their money to Switzerland out of the hands of any future regulators, or the next mafioso who takes the office after he is sunning himself in Cyprus.

"So, if I am going to do my own research here locally, and put a provincial spin on it, I need to locate a little shark. Even a petty shark who is trying to become a bigger shark— you know? Shark eat shark—and who is trying to make the next step up by trying to ingratiate himself with the politicians and business class, or trying to become an elected official himself."

Dean Karamzin scratched his face somewhat dumbfounded and shocked with no words.

"You learned all this in my library?" he asked again with a befuddled expression I had never seen on his face before.

"Yes, and more." I sat tight lipped and waited.

The dean leaned back in his chair and whistled a low thoughtful whistle, which to do indoors in Russia is akin to throwing money, but perhaps in this case, caution, right out the window. He sat up straight in his chair, leaning over his desk and looked me straight in the eyes. "Will you be attending the university event at night club tomorrow night?" he asked, assuming I would attend.

"Yes, why?" I inquired.

"Keep your eyes open there and come see me on Monday after our history lecture."

"Why, what am I looking for?" I asked, still wound up and on high receive.

"How did you say it? A small shark who is swimming with some big daddies..." The dean smiled a mysterious smile.

"Say what? You're sending me into the shark tank to take photographs?" I was quickly sobering up.

"I would leave the camera at home, but certainly go and take mental notes. We'll talk in depth about it and I'll fill in the details that you haven't already figured out. You're a sharp student. I think you'll be able to figure it all out rather quickly."

He stood up to bid me goodbye. We shook hands over his desk as the telephone there started to buzz. He shouted, "Halloah" into the handset as I pulled the door carefully closed behind me. The man was always in demand.

As I emerged from the dark tunnel from the inner courtyard onto the street in front of the history faculty, the sky was surprisingly bright and blue and the air was...warm! I stopped in my tracks and looked about to make sure I was really on Minin Square. Somehow, I had missed the fact that almost all the snow on the pavement and street had melted away into the gutters and sewers. What used to be fields of dirty grey snow were now pavements, muddy flower beds, and dark green, trampled grass.

A warm wind from the south had come up the river the night before, and the early afternoon was bright. The mercury had risen to six degrees on the digital thermometer on the front of the Sberbank branch at the bottom of Pokrovka. I wandered in wonder like a man who had just regained his vision after months of blindness, in awe of the colors that the sunlight contained. What was dirty and grey was now all shades and subtitles of red, blue, and yellow. A freshly washed candy-apple red Volkswagen Passat with clean alloy rims passed in front of me as I waited under the shadow of the kremlin wall to cross the street. How it danced, how it glided in slow motion over the asphalt, quiet, luxurious! I removed my wool overcoat to feel the sunshine.

As I strolled onto Pokrovka, an odd sensation overcame me. Liberated from the fur shapka and the wool overcoat with the sunshine on my face, I turned my green felt cap backwards and put a pen behind my ear. In just my blazer for warmth, I bulldozed my way up through the shopping throngs to the snack bar and movie theatre where I met Hans to take in a film at the Kino-house.

I was told several times that when I was dressed in my own winter coat, black mink hat and boots, that I surprisingly resembled Mikhail Gorbechev in his own winter get-up. For me these types of comments and observations were as good as gold in my quest to blend in and be considered as just part of the scenery. I had never before tried to make a scene or reveal myself to a group that I was anything but Russian. The wrong comment though at the wrong moment can create a reaction deep down inside, an irrational panic with the possibility that perhaps one has come too close to the edge of "going native" and perhaps has become too much like the locals.

After months of hard studying and research, and especially after the last month of being a hermit in the library, today with the sun on my back I needed to break free from being Russian for the afternoon. As I moved purposefully up Pokrovka I looked straight ahead, not at the ground in front of my feet like the throngs. I looked people in the eyes and smiled and even waved at a few particularly pretty girls who had also shed the heavy coats and bulky snow boots. They looked better than ever today: tall lean, shapely with bright smiles! I refused to speak Russian with the teller behind the window at the currency exchange bureau as I exchanged forty dollars for rubles. A number of the street vendors tried their best to speak broken English with me; one of them tried to communicate with me in German, but I just blinked at him incredulously. I bought a bottle of Pepsi and drank it as I walked, just like in the TV commercials with my head tipped way back and the bottle straight up in the air, guzzling the soda-pop in one breath.

I became immediately self-conscious of my bravado and remembered with a start and a shock that just a month earlier I had run through the snow away from corrupt cops and gangsters who knew that I had seen their handiwork. Despite the sun and blue sky, I put my coat and scarf on again and resumed the afternoon as a local face. I wondered if Yulia was ready to speak to me again. I needed to be more careful.

06

10. The Monastery

On Saturday evening, after a day of sleeping in, watching TV, and fried chicken, Hans and I put on our cleanest casuals and ventured out to the upper embankment to the night club called The Monastery. It had been hyped up to be one of the best events for the university students for a number of years already. Everybody was excited. Big act names from Moscow and St. Petersburg were usually on the stage; groups or artists that would otherwise never perform in the provinces.

Neither Hans nor I had been to the club yet and so it took us a bit of looking to find the right street. It wasn't where I had imagined it would be from the descriptions of the other students.

"Any idea why it's called the The Monastery, Hans?" I puzzled.

"No, because I hope zat zere vill be lots of girlz zhere. No girlz? No Hans!" he proclaimed with a put-on over-zealous German accent.

I stood still to click my heels in and shouted his proclamation to all the passersby. "Achtung! Keine Meidschen, Keine Hans!"

"I did not know that you can speak German, Peter." He looked so shocked and surprised.

"Eh! A little bit of this, a little bit of that," I replied, shrugging my shoulders.

As we were coming to the end of the street and very near the edge of the bluff overlooking the Volga, there was nothing to see but a large old church with three green domes sitting in a church yard surrounded by several outbuildings. There was still some snow in the shade of the trees as twilight turned to dusk.

"That can't be it, can it?" we asked each other simultaneously and then laughed at ourselves.

Then a door to the church opened and some stage hands dressed in black moved some crates into the building. Out of the door poured a stream of deep electronic bass drum thuds and other sounds of electronic dance music. As we approached we could hear the music coming from inside the church and heard a group milling out behind in a courtyard between the chapel and the outbuildings. Yes, this was the place.

"Now I know why it's called The Monastery," Hans said, slapping me in the chest with a backhand.

"This can't be real! This is wrong on so many levels." I stood mute and glued to my place on the ground looking around with disgust and disapproval.

Throughout the church yard were parked several very gaudy automobiles, with their drivers milling around smoking, some wiping mud and dust off of fenders and doors with damp rags. The cars were mostly German with a long, chunky Mercedes being the model of choice from different years. There were some older BMW 5 series each with random body damage in an unfinished state of repair, but also what looked to be there in the dark, a pristine stretch 7 series BMW with all the trimmings and its parking lights on. Its paint shined even in the dark.

There were Range Rovers and other luxury sport utility trucks, but they looked Asian, not European. The drivers were dressed like models from a BOSS commercial with the hair to match. These were no sloughs taking on a driving job at night. They looked more like bodyguards the closer I tried not to look. I wouldn't have been surprised to find out they were all armed, packing heat of one sort or another in a belt or a holster under the arm, as many of the Mercedes were the bullet-proof kind. The license plates were all from Moscow. As I took all this in, I remembered the instructions of the dean on Friday afternoon, "keep your eyes open...." A little shark was holding an open house for all to see.

Hans and I made our way to the courtyard where the students were gathering under a suspended awning with heat lamps. There were stand tables where drinks were being served for the reception. As we came closer, a bouncer appeared from the shadows and asked to see our student cards. With no further questions, we joined the reception and were served drinks of our choice by skinny waitresses in black short skirts and heels as tall as their own tibulas were long, each with hair pulled back into a tight, slick ponytail. They walked like they were on stilts made of toothpicks.

The group was already near one hundred, maybe more. Many of the faces I recognized but certainly not by how they were dressed. Being used to seeing them in bulky sweaters, scarves, and boots, tussled hair in the thralls of winter weather, I barely recognized many of them as they looked so formal and professional with little black dresses or dark suits on, hair beautifully done in feminine curls or slicked back with oil. The atmosphere was light, but also felt false. These didn't look like the same people I studied with, as if they were actors on a set. The night was getting a bit cold, even under the awning and heat lamps. This was still Russia and it wasn't April yet!

After a short speech by somebody I didn't recognize from the university's administration, thanking this person and that, a short, stocky man dressed in a very fine suit and shoes, head shaved smooth, was introduced: Mr. P., the proprietor of The Monastery and tonight's host. A round of polite applause came up from the crowd. I recognized him immediately.

"Ladies and gents, I welcome you to The Monastery as my guests tonight. You are very welcome. Please come and dance and drink with me and my friends and none of you can go home earlier than three o'clock! Your exams are done. You have no lessons to finish before Monday. Tonight, we have a lot of fun!" A round of barbaric cheers swelled up from the crowd of students, like heathens who had just been given the order to fall on their foes and pull them from limb to limb until the sun came up.

With the host leading the chorus, the crowd chanted, "one... two...three!" On three, the doors of the chapel-club were pulled open by thuggish bouncers in gaudy, what looked to be iridescent suits that shimmered in the disco lights like in some sort of perverted theme park way. The sight was so surreal and unexpected that I laughed out loud at the sheer folly of what seemed to be the purposefully overdone effects. There was no frivolity in this pageant. Everybody was taking themselves very seriously, almost solemnly, as the students rushed in to their own Pleasure Island for a night of uninhibited, unsupervised vice.

The interior of the chapel had not been renovated much at all. The ceiling paintings were still visible, in poor repair after seventy-five years of communism's neglect, but even in the black lights of the disco floor one could see the saints and patriarchs looking down giving a scornful scowl at the revelers below. In the center of the church, directly under the church's central dome crowned with three onion shaped copulas, the DJ had set up his tools of the trade. The crowd was already encircling the raised stage set up with mixing tables and blaring speakers and bobbing up and down. Behind the stage into the apse where an altar would have been, another stage was ready for a live performance of a mystery guest yet to be announced. It was a tradition to leave that a secret until performance , leaving the guests in suspense until the last minute.

The bars were set up in the side aisles and the music worshipers were left to dance and frolic in the space where the pews for the faithful had once stood now void of prayer books and sacraments. I didn't even want to know what happened inside the confessionals.

As I pushed my way through the crowd from the narthex into the nave, I bumped into Pasha's back and pushed him into Marina who was already dancing up a small storm. When I turned to apologize to Pasha for having bumped into him and he recognized my face, his eyes lit up as well as Marina's and we laughed off the collision in the dark. After some spoken greetings, Marina took my hand and said that she would like to introduce me to somebody. I let her guide me through the crowd to one of the side chapels which had been filled with tables and benches along the curved walls. Sitting at these tables, drinking their drinks surrounded by very well-dressed women of exceptional figures and faces, were undoubtedly the owners of the fleet of luxury cars parked in the church yard. Marina, almost skipping through the crowd, brought me directly to the host of the night, Mr. P., and introduced me as her 'American friend'.

In the split second that I realized who I was standing with and just about to shake hands, I remembered the fury in his black eyes I had seen that frightening evening at his restaurant on Valentine's Day. Not being able to help myself when I came face to face with him once more, I looked again into his eyes. This time there was no blackness, just glazed over blurry eyeballs. He was already drunk. The relief quickly spread through my system.

"Very pleased. You are very welcome tonight. You are a student in Nizhniy?" Mr. P. asked.

"Yes, I study with Dean Karamzin," I replied.

"Ah, my good friend....how is Roman Sergeiyevich?" he inquired.

"He is certainly healthy." I replied.

"You are American? You speak very good Russian," he said, over-complimenting me as drunks regularly do.

"Thank you, I have studied it for years," I informed him.

Turning to his comrades in crime still sitting at the table and yelling louder than needed, "Guys, we have a spy with us tonight from USA. Maybe he is FBI or CIA?"

Marina came to my defense with a pout at Mr. P., "Da Nyet, Peter is a very good boy! Very kind!"

"Maybe we talk later together, Peter. Maybe you come see me another day for lunch and you can tell me about yourself, why you come to Russia," Mr. P. proposed.

"That would be ...cool," was my purposefully dumbed down answer.

We clasped hands in a brutish manner, like how I imagine kick-boxers greet each other, but we didn't shake, just slapped.

Mr. P. turned back to his guests and I quickly disappeared into the crowd with Marina before his brain cells, slowed by alcohol, made the connection with me and where I'd been seen earlier.

After we were a safe distance to be out of sight, I leaned down to Marina's ear. "How do you know Mr. P?"

"He is friend of my uncle. They do biznis together," she happily chirped, flipping her head and hair to the techno beats.

"Really? Is this what we call 'biznis' in Russia?" I asked ironically, indicating everything unholy going on around us in a house of worship.

"Da, Nyet, Peter. He runs private 'biznises' in Nizhniy. Restaurants, shops, kiosks. He buys and sells lots of import products from Germany and Korea, you know, cars and TVs," she told me.

"Yes, I'll bet he buys and sells the girls too from the looks of it. What else does he import? Anything from Afghanistan or Columbia?" I was sarcastic bordering on a bit angry.

"I don't know what you are talking about..." Marina looked c   o   n   f   u   s   e   d   .

Just then I saw a very skanky-looking, overdone young woman in fish net stockings and heels pull a young man into the confessional booth by his tie and pull the door closed behind her. His friends stood in the corner gawking and jabbing each other, already half drunk. Were they seeking privacy for blowing a line of cocaine or was she providing another service? I stepped outside to the courtyard to get some air after my unexpected and undesired brush with the past I was trying to avoid. The heat lamps were still warm and a number of students were outside smoking cigarettes in the cold, hanging around the stand tables in groups of two and three. A familiar voice called to me.

"Peter. Hello. Come join us." An acquaintance of mine from the English Club, Olya, was summoning me to her table and offered me a cigarette. I politely refused with an upheld hand of temperance.

"Olya, I hardly recognized you dressed all fancy," I commented with a smile and an intended compliment as she looked very attractive.

Olya was an interesting young lady who I had become acquainted with through the English Club. She seemed a bit older than the other students and not an academic at all. She seemed to have more street smarts than book smarts. She wasn't in any of my other lectures and I had never seen her anywhere but at English Club, but she wasn't the only one who fell into that category. The university had a wide range of schools under its umbrella. Even though I had never asked her what she studied, apart from English, I had figured that she was in an engineering focus of some sort, being more practical than studious.

As I approached the table to stand opposite Olya, her friend gave me a polite smile, and touching Olya's arm took her leave and went back into the church as she extinguished her cigarette in the ash tray on the table, dropping ashes on the deep purple velvet table wrap. When we were alone Olya replied, "You didn't recognize me? It is me who did not recognize you yesterday on Prokovka."

"Oh, I didn't even see you yesterday. I'm sorry I didn't notice you," I apologized.

"That's okay. You did not see me on the street. It was many moments before I recognized you, dressed in the funny way, and then you were very far away to call to you. You looked different," she mentioned.

"Hmmm...yes, Friday afternoon I had a bit of a, well, let's just say I had to stop being Russian for an afternoon, and be more myself. With my exams done and my research paper approved and with the good weather, I just felt like running through a grassy park and kissing all the pretty girls."

Olya laughed. "You are a funny boy, Peter."

"And you are a mysterious girl, Olya," I replied with a mysterious voice.

"Mysterious? What means mysterious?" she asked for translation.

"In Russian?" I offered.

"No, explain me in English, please, for practice," she requested.

"It means I don't know very much about you, but yet you seem to be somebody who knows a lot but never says anything about what you know. You keep secrets, maybe," I offered.

"Hmmm, very good thoughts about me," she said pensively.

"So, do you study somewhere on Pokrovka? I didn't know there were university buildings on that street." I was sincerely interested.

"No, I was working," she replied shortly.

"Working? I didn't think students were allowed to have jobs. Oh, are you working in a private shop there on the street?" I was excited to meet somebody who worked in one of the newly privatized retails shops.

"No, I was ..." she tried to explain before I stopped her short.

"Let me guess, you were selling your rubbish at the flea market in front of the creative arts museum?" I was teasing her.

At this remark, she became very perturbed and denied being a gypsy girl in some very unambiguous and un-ladylike terms.

"Then tell me what you do. Maybe I could stop by on some days and say hello while you're working," I suggested.

"That would not be possible," she answered quickly and resolutely.

"Why not? I could always buy something from you," I proposed.

"No, it's not like that." She turned and looked behind her and continued in a hushed voice. "Can you keep a secret?"

"Secrets are dangerous things to have in Russia, I understand," I whispered back.

"Can you keep a secret?" she asked again, emphatically raising the tone of her hushed voice.

"Yes, yes, I can keep a secret," I mumbled back. I wondered if she was drunk already, too.

"I work in the TT building at the top of Pokrovka," she revealed with shifting eyes.

"Really? I've been in there a few times to call my mother in the USA. What do you do there?" I asked naively.

She switched into Russian to quickly explain her vocation. "I'm not a telephone operator, Peter, I work for the FSB. l listen to telephone calls in and out of the city," she said, looking over my shoulder this time.

I found this such a preposterous idea that I laughed out loud a deep belly laugh and couldn't stop for a few moments. When I finally got my composure back I started poking fun at her.

"Did you hear my last call to my mother? That was a funny conversation!"

"Nyet, but I know somebody listened and there is a transcript of that call. All foreigners are recorded and reviewed, and especially the Americans are watched very carefully."

"Well, y'all must not be doing a very good job because there is definitely nobody watching me, except for maybe Valentina

Petronva," I said in English in a lazy, casual way. I thought for a few seconds, but then swatted this idea out of the air. "Naah, I hardly even talk to her anymore."

"No, I know you are watched and they must do good job if you are not knowing you are being listened to and watched," Olya affirmed.

"C'mon. That's all in the past now. The communists are all gone now. Nobody's watching me or listening to my phone calls," I replied again in English.

"Peter, what do you think happened to KGB on the day Soviet Union went away? Do you think they go to home and said, 'Hey, dorogaya maya, communist party collapsed today, so now we are all good guys and they don't need me anymore?' You don't think new Russian government don't have need for secret police? You think that all departments of KGB just stopped existing? They changed the name to FSB and everybody keep their jobs. That's it. We do the same thing, Peter. Listen, I like you. You are a nice guy and you like living in Russia. You go to classes, you study a lot, you aren't involved with the mafia—well maybe tonight you are—and you don't call anybody but your mother, but be careful who you talk to, what you say, what you do. You don't want anybody to misunderstand you." Her tone was professional, not drunk.

"You're serious, aren't you?" I asked, flabbergasted.

"Yes, and you promised to keep a secret." She smiled and took a sip of her cocktail.

"I didn't think it would be that kind of secret. Okay, if you really are who you say you are, what was the last conversation you listened to on the telephone?" I had begun to be curious.

"Medical student from Turkey called his father," she answered with clarity.

"Do you speak Turkish, too?" I was surprised.

"No, I almost fell asleep for forty minutes. I recorded it and interpreter made Russian transcript on same day. There is transcripts of your calls, too," she reported.

"I would love to have that for posterity!" I commented sarcastically.

"Sorry, I cannot give those to you." She was dead serious.

"You're really serious, aren't you? You're not even a student, are you? You just come to the English Club to watch everybody and hear what people are thinking. Do you write reports about that, too?" I asked, somewhat offended.

"Da, of course," she answered without apology.

"Geez, c'mon Olya. Is Olya your real name?" I asked, expecting a denial.

"No, it's not," she said, taking a drag from her cigarette.

"Wow, I just don't know what to say." I sighed. An awkward pause hung in the air between us.

"Do you want to dance with me?" Olya asked switching into Russian, "I'm still a girl, and you are still a boy and I have a job at FSB. It's nothing bad. It's Russia."

"Sure, let's go dance. The night couldn't get any more surreal!" And off we went back into the club and joined the moshing crowd of very drunk students dancing to techno-trash Russian tracks that all sounded the same. Exams were over and nobody had use for their brains until Monday morning, so why not? My mind was already blown by the revelations of the evening so what else did I have to lose? My colleagues were family of the local mafia boss, and my acquaintances were KGB operatives. What else could go wrong?

At eleven o'clock the music stopped; the spotlights swiveled in unison and turned to light up the stage in the nave. The big act was about to start. Mr. P. took to the stage and riled up the crowd, wanting to hear how excited they were to know who was playing in the club tonight. The crowd responded with increasingly louder shouts of "DAAAAAAAA!" when asked if they were excited three different times—a spectacle not seen since high school pep rallies.

Behind Mr. P. the spotlights had lit up the backdrop of the act to come. There was a ruby red outline of the Moscow kremlin towers with three red flags on poles displayed on either side of the closed gate of the Spaskiy Tower. The laurel branches of the Soviet Union's seal extended to either side of the stages in an upward bending fashion, all against a backdrop of a city night scape of apartment buildings. It had a very nationalistic feel to it. I was intrigued about what we might see here. I was severely disappointed.

After a drunken introduction and Mr. P.'s stumbling from the stage, the members of the band came skipping out from under the Spaskiy gate tower cut-out dressed all in black leather, with leather cowboy hats. They took up their positions on the stage with a keyboard, drums, and a single electric guitar. They didn't look young, and they did not look cool. One had a beer belly! The lead singer came skipping out as well from behind the Kremlin cut-outs dressed like a feminine, overweight pirate with a scruffy beard and long brown hair, gyrating his hips in a way that made me cringe. He was wearing black spandex, a flowing white blouse with a gold embroidered black vest, and black knee-high boots. The crowd of students knew who the group was and cheered as if Bruce Springsteen had just taken the stage. The music of the first number sounded just like what the DJ had been playing. I couldn't stay and watch. I think they were lip-synching as well, but who would really know, being so inebriated. When you're that drunk nobodies' words match the mouth movements, not even your own.

I found Hans at one of the bars listing a bit on a bar stool, smiling with a glazed over look. He had a glass of something in his hand, half gone. I took a stool next to him and leaned my back up against the bar and faced the dance floor and joined Hans's gaze at all the 'girlz.' As I settled onto my bar stool and propped my dazed friend up by the shoulder, a very tall and curvy woman walked past us in very tight pants and a sheer blouse with her bra fully visible through the gauzy material in front and back. I'm sure she was a trophy of one gangster in the room, but she was eye candy for the rest of us. Trying to move through the crowd, she had to pause directly in front of Hans and turn her back, with her backside to him to let others pass through the narrow side aisles.

I saw it in slow motion, like a train wreck about to happen, but I could do nothing to stop it. Hans's drunken arm slowly rose, and his hand reached for the underside of her leather clad buns and squeezed with vigor and intent.

In his German accented Russian he said, "Syadeese, dyevuchka, Syadeese!" (Please, girl, sit down here!)

The slap came so fast that it made my head spin. Hans dropped his drink and fell off his bar stool and everybody around us laughed uncontrollably. The woman was so incensed that she kicked him a few times and spat on him while he was trying to get back onto his wobbly legs. With the last kick, he fell again and hit his head against another bar stool. Before another kick or slap could come I jumped between the two of them, holding my hands in front of me, facing her with my hands visible to sign "enough is enough." Hans stood up behind me completely dazed, but a bit more sober. The woman had fire in her eyes and Gucci platform shoes on her feet. Over her shoulder I could see a beefy body guard making his way through the crowd to her.

"Oh, Hans! You had better run!" I muttered to him in English from the side of my mouth with my eyes fixed on Brutus moving quickly towards us.

As Hans tried to get out of the bar, he stumbled on his drunk legs, was collared by the bouncer and thrown out of the club on his face by both of the thugs with a violent shove. He was lucky not to have gotten a beating before he was ejected.

11. Hangover

I helped Hans stagger home. He wasn't moving very swiftly after being kicked and hitting his head, as well as being wasted from vodka. It was eleven-thirty on Saturday night and I wish I had brought a hat with me to the club. The wind was sharp and cold again after two warmish days. My ears were burning with the night's wind chill.

Sitting at Hans's kitchen table under a dim light with a mug of hot Nescafe and some 'tabletki' for his aching head, we sat in silence and listened to the pendulum on the living room wall swing and click, swing and click.

"It vas vorth it!" Hans smiled. "It felt so good in my hand . . ." He held out the offending hand and squeezed the air slowly.

"Shut up you idiot," I quipped. "You could have gotten us both pretty badly beat up."

"Yes, maybe you are right. I heard Mr. P. had been in jail for beating somebody dead in somebody else's night club," Hans commented through his drunken slurring.

"Really!?" I asked, intrigued.

"This iz what ze students say," he confirmed.

I looked away from Hans's stupid expression in disgust and also to avoid his rank breath. Why did Russian alcohol have to smell so bad?

Hans was snoring and sweating at two in the morning. I could hear him and smell him; it made me think back to Vitaly, my roommate from the dorms. Why did it have to smell so bad? Between the clock hanging over the couch above me, Hans snoring in the next room and my mind swimming in everything I learned that evening before at The Monastery, certainly a place I would never want to return to, there was little chance of me sleeping for at least another hour.

I tossed and turned as I mulled over Olya's revelation that she knew I was being watched. What concerned me more was her warning not to do things that would be misunderstood by those watching me. Was Mr. P. really an ex-convict or just a wannabe? What had the dean wanted me to pay attention to in particular last night? What had I missed that I should have been looking for? Who was my personal tail, my perverse guardian angel, from the city secret police? What had I really said to mother on the telephone the last time I spoke to her? Would Mr. P. beat me to death if was to learn what the dean was suggesting I do? What was the dean suggesting I do, expose him and his thug friends in a university publication? Why? Why would the dean ask me to do that? Maybe Mr. P. can't read? What specifically was his racket anyway? Why should I be interested in a local thug anyway? I was more interested in exposing the swindles with the privatization process more than the rise of a local crime boss. What influence was Mr. P. trying to build up locally? It seemed to me he was just an overgrown pimp. Just an alpha hooligan with a protection racket in town. Probably didn't even control the drugs being used in his own club.

Trying to sleep I could only see all those 'girlz' behind my eyelids dancing and twirling their dresses on the dance floor. They all had looked very pretty tonight! Indeed, all of them.

I returned home on Sunday afternoon after brunch at Hans's place. He hadn't remembered much of the night and he cringed when I told him what had happened. He rubbed the back of his head as perhaps some of the more poignant moments were coming back to him. What a fool.

Babushka was up and busy in the early afternoon in our apartment when I turned the locks and shuffled in from the dark stairwell. The hall light was on. She could see that I had slept about as well as Hans had looked that morning and offered to make me some tea.

"Nu shto?" was Babushka's only question as we sat silently around her stunted refrigerator in the kitchen.

"Nothing, really nothing. I slept very poorly that's all," I tried to justify my ashen face.

"Drank too much did you?" she accused.

"Baba, you know I don't drink." I puffed my breath at her for her to smell.

"Good boy, golden boy." She nodded and rubbed her hands on her apron.

I smiled warmly at this woman who had assumed the role of my real grandmother.

"Yulia came to visit last night," Baba commented.

"Yulia, she was here?" I asked, pleased, hoping that the ice had thawed.

"Pretty girl! I had to tell her that you were away for the night. She seemed sad that you weren't home. Been a long time since she has been here. You should be careful," was the matchmaker's advice, "said she would come back today sometime to find you, but today our family is coming to visit. My niece and her children, Raiya's older sister."

"I will be very quiet in my room. I promise," I said accommodatingly.

"Da, nyet. The children will have to be quiet. Children should be quiet and obedient," she said as she twirled her hands continually through her apron hem.

Moments later the bell on the door rang and Babushka shuffled to the door in her tapochki. With the door open I heard the voices of children greeting their great-aunt. Kisses on the cheeks and the youngest, a girl, maybe six years old could be heard squirming away from the old lady's kisses with a giggle. The nephew, nine years old, was a bit more formal and respectful, being the only man in the group.

Everybody was dressed in their Sunday best and the children brought flowers, not a bouquet, but a few scrawny flowers for Aunt Natasha and Aunt Raiya. The conversation between the three ladies didn't have a single pause in it. I couldn't understand a word of it. Were they speaking Tatar?

I put on some soft music to drown out the chatter of the Tatar trio next door, found a clean page in my writing block behind my other research notes, dug through my school bag for a pen, and started to sketch out what I had learned about Mr. P. the night before. I wrote down every detail I could remember about the club, the cars, the appearance of the drivers, the bars, those in attendance who were not from the student body of the university. The woman Hans groped was certainly not from the school! Who was she? Imports from Germany and Korea, the body guards, the bouncers, the drugs, the booze, and the young prostitutes. I wrote it all down in as much detail as I could remember. When I finished I had about three pages filled with scribbles of handwriting. On rereading it and reflecting on it I started asking questions. "Why open the night club up for free, free drinks, free drugs, free girls? Why?"

Deep in thought and a bit parched, I reached for a bottle behind the curtains in my window sill, chilling nicely next to the window. As I swatted the curtains open to reach my bottle without having to stand up, I could see the bright afternoon sunshine, and for the first time, grass in front of my window. I stood up to look at it. While I could still see the breath of people passing by my ground floor window, and there were still patches of snow on the ground outside in the trees, I was so thrilled to see that indeed there was green grass showing from under the snow! Much to my annoyance, too, there also was the neighborhood dog there doing his business on the grass and his owner standing between the birches, looking the other direction while smoking.

It always annoyed me in Russia how nobody understood the practice of conservation. It seemed that as soon as the grass showed the people thought: Quick. Let a dog leave a pile on it! As soon as there were new light bulbs installed in the stairwells, somebody had already nicked them before night fall. The examples went on and on. As the lady with the stupid expression saw what must have been my disapproving look regarding her dog, she threw her cigarette away and whistled to her dog and walked off out of sight toward the metro station.

As I turned from the window there was a quiet knock on my door and two children poking their curious heads in to look. They had never seen this room in the apartment, as the room had been closed and locked for years.

"Come in, come in." I waved them into the room with my free hand. They stood at the open door and gazed around the room.

"Babushka says you talk funny," was the introduction from the young girl.

"Well, what do you think?" Both of the kids giggled. "I think that is yes." I put on a clown's false frown and hung my head.

"Neecheevooah!" the girl shouted, laughing, saying in one word, "It's okay, it's not important."

The smile jumped back on to my face. More giggles.

"I come from a faraway place across the ocean, where we speak a different language. Different from Russian and different from Tatar."

We introduced ourselves. Murat the boy and Nelya the girl both introduced themselves in Russian and then in Tatar, and I introduced myself in Russian and then in English. How they giggled. How exotic! As it goes with little children, a little grown-up talk goes a long way and they retreated to the kitchen where they drew pictures with crayons for the rest of the afternoon.

I went back to brooding over my notes from the night before. The doorbell rang again. It was Yulia.

"Come in, please!" I greeted her warmly. We sat down at my table facing each other on the corner. I didn't touch her at all.

"How are you? It's been a long time," she said awkwardly.

"Yes, about five weeks," I remarked with remorse. "Are you still angry with me?"

"The reason I was angry at you was justified, but I shouldn't have stayed away so long. I'm sorry. I know you didn't mean to cause me grief. You just didn't know any better being new here. I should have thought more about it. The food, the setting, the service. It's not typical. I should have warned you when we arrived...but I guess I wanted to be treated like a lady for a night. It was a very nice dinner and you paid so much for it and I was so ungrateful," was her apology.

"What have you been doing for five weeks then?" I asked, trying to change the subject that I was still ashamed of.

"Lots of writing for our newspaper column. I am trying to write something more about Bolshakov, of course, and try to slip something into our newspaper about the issues he wrote about, but of course I am being censored by the editor. He says he doesn't want anymore dead journalists, especially himself. But I keep trying and arguing with him anyhow."

"What about all that talk about staying away from these dangerous matters that you lectured me about? It seems rather unfair that you'd not talk to me for five weeks and then still try to get an article about the same topics into the newspaper," I pointed out her the hypocrisy.

"I know, that's why I am here tonight. I realized that, too," she said, ashamed of herself.

There was a long awkward silence. Yulia broke the silence.

"What have you been up to since we saw each other last?" she asked me.

"I've been buried in the research library hiding from the weather, as well as Mr. P. as you warned me I needed to," I told her honestly.

"Who is Mr. P.?" Yulia asked.

"You remember the bald man who came into the restaurant after the police officers went into the back room? That is Mr. P. He's the boss." I was surprised that Yulia didn't know who he was.

"How did you learn his name?" she asked curiously.

"I was dancing at his club last night," I said without thinking of the implications.

"Dancing? Dancing with who?" she asked with her ears pointing straight up with a stunned face.

"Hans, I went dancing with Hans," I replied innocently.

"You danced the whole night with Hans? I don't think so. Who did you dance with?" she demanded to know.

"Woah! Calm yourself. We hadn't seen each other for five weeks. Why do you think I can't dance with anybody I choose?" I said defensively.

"Did you dance with one girl the whole night, or just skip around the dance floor dancing with any pretty face?" Her jealousy was rising and I was desperate to cool it off.

"I was there on assignment from the dean! I didn't go to go dancing, and you know I didn't go there to drink," I said, trying to give the evening perspective.

"Why would the dean send you dancing to a club for an academic assignment? And you had better be very careful with you answer, Peter, very careful," she warned me with a upheld finger.

"I was there to see Mr. P. in his element," I admitted, "and it was quite a show."

"Why would your professor tell you to do that?" she demanded to know the answer to such a ridiculous idea.

"He wants me to write my article about Mr. P. and his activities," I said carefully.

"What?!? How....what are you...are you mad? Are you completely out of your head?" she exploded.

She stood up and paced the room.

"Are you trying to get yourself killed? You don't write about the local neighborhood mafia boss, certainly not somebody who already knows your face! Are you so foolish?" she ranted.

"And you're trying to have articles printed to carry on the work of Bolshakov? What's the difference, Yulia? Tell me, what is the difference? We both see injustice, abuse and we both want to do something about it. Can't you see you're just as crazy as me?" I blurted out.

"Yes, but I can take care of myself. I can't protect you, though, if you keep doing stupid things like this!" she screamed at me and then burst into tears.

"Can't we do this together then?" I proposed.

12. The Shark Cage

By Monday morning I had to put my snow boots on again as well as my wool overcoat and shapka to make my way to the history faculty for a fateful meeting with the dean in his office. I wondered that morning if Russia had a similar tradition to the American Ground Hog's Day, a day on which winter and spring would battle for pole position before the spring equinox. If it had, I concluded that in Russia there would always be six more weeks of winter. The weather was miserably wet and humid with slush everywhere.

The history lecture that morning seemed to last forever with wet snowing falling outside, streaking the classroom windows. I huffed at the weather. The battles of old Muscovy were not relevant to the contemporary issues I was pondering. I stopped listening after fifteen minutes. I was very agitated and restless.

Sitting down behind his desk, Dean Karamzin cleared away a number of papers and folders, stacking them in a hurried fashion onto an already leaning stack of other folders and papers. He put his arms in front of him on the desk.

"So, Mr. Turner, did you enjoy the party on Saturday evening?"

"Yes, it was very educational. I learned a lot about a number of different people. It's amazing what people will tell you when they have a few drinks in them," I postulated.

"Did you get a chance to see Mr. P.?" he asked excitedly.

"Yes. In fact, we shook hands and were introduced by Marina Karlovna; you'll know her from our lectures. Cute, short girl, always smiling," I mentioned.

"Oh yes, Marina. So, you met him. Did you speak at all?" He was wanting the play by play account.

"Well, he speculated that I am a CIA or FBI agent, and then he invited me to lunch one day so I could tell him why I came to Russia," I reported.

"That's perfect. That means he doesn't suspect you at all," the dean exclaimed with glee.

"Suspect me of what?" I was puzzled.

"That you are watching him, trying to learn about him and what he does," the Dean clarified.

"It's not that he was hiding very well. The drugs, the booze, the girls, the cars, the other hooligans he was hosting on Saturday makes it very obvious what he is doing," I proclaimed.

"Oh yes, and what is that and what proof do you have of it? Is it obvious how he does it? Did he tell you how he has earned his money?" the dean remarked and grilled me sarcastically.

"Well, when you look at it like that no, but..." I stammered.

"And this is why Russia, Yeltsin, and Nemtsov are unable to put these guys in jail. Nobody is willing to prove it in court. Everybody knows it, but nobody is willing to talk about it, and they continue to build their wealth through illegal and violent means. Then they become powerful enough, with just enough of a reputation, that nobody dares to open their mouths or lift a hand to stop them," Karamzin stated.

"Dean, listen, I am not a public prosecutor, nor am I am detective. I can't put these guys in jail. I'm a student," I pleaded.

"Yes, a highly visible student who is very dedicated to his work in history and economics and is very good with the Russian language. Your reputation is very well-known at the school. Everybody knows you and knows you to be a dedicated academic. That is why Mr. P. would never suspect you. Academics are harmless. They write meaningless articles that nobody reads, and if they do read them the articles are neutral, so they don't rock the boat and nobody cares as long as something academic was published. We have a chance to change that now with you. You can write an entry that means something. If you need to, you can always leave and go back to USA. If I write it and make the wrong people angry then I could get into big trouble with the university and with others with less patience. You can just fly away." Karamzin was dreaming of the chance to advance the visibility and usefulness of his department and field with ground-breaking work written by a disposable student.

Just then the telephone on his desk starting belching its sickly buzz, instead of a ring. The dean ripped the handset from the console and yelled, "We are very busy. Don't call back," and slammed it down again.

"I'm not researching criminal law, I'm researching how to improve the privatization process of state companies so that Russia doesn't lose any more of its wealth to a few robber-barrons," I protested.

"Mr. Turner, tell me about your observations on Saturday and then I will tell you what I know that you don't know," the dean said, slightly annoyed with me.

"Fine then, I will start with a question that has been in my mind since Saturday: Why would Mr. P. open up his night club for free and provide the drinks, drugs, and girls for free? What motivation does he have? With these actions, he is not earning money. In fact, it is costing him big money. Mr. P., even though he is a buffoon, in my opinion, with no education, he has street smarts, the street smarts of a capitalist, a marketeer, a PR manager. He knows how to make people like him and how to win their tolerance of what he is doing.

'True, I have no proof that he runs the kiosk protection rackets in town. True, I have no proof that he is pimping all the girls at his club offering free services on Saturday. True, I have no proof that he is trafficking the drugs being snorted and smoked at the club. So, if he throws great parties for the university students he can slowly pull them into his world. He shows them that he is a nice guy who likes the city and can contribute to the city. Maybe some of the people start working in his import business of TVs and home electronics from Korea. Seems legit enough. In fact, it probably is. He gives free tickets to journalists to see great concerts at The Monastery and then they don't write bad things about him or they will lose the fun perks that they can't afford on a provincial journalist's salary. A fellow has to have some fun, maybe he even gets a free girl that night too. Mr. P. is using his money and people's own vices to ingratiate himself to the city's citizens. No bad press, nobody writing bad things about him. Who doesn't love him, right? I can imagine on any other given night we'll find the chief of Nizhniy police there as well with two very pretty young girls on each knee with his hand up one skirt and another under the other's blouse thinking he's the most attractive fat, hairy, bald guy in all of Russia. So, Saturday night, and other nights like it, are a big pubic relations expense.

"What's the end game, though? I saw other thugs in prettier cars with prettier girls than Mr. P.'s there from Moscow. Drivers dressed like supermodels carrying guns under their suits, I believe, and everybody drinking imported beers and Russian vodka. It was quite brash and obvious. But OK, everybody is paying off a police chief or two. Is Mr. P. trying to get to swim with the big sharks by showing off at these types of events? At what point will the big sharks let a provincial shark into the feeding frenzy? Is Mr. P. just picking from the floating carcasses that come down the river from Moscow, or is he able to get his jaws full of something real, something that is still flailing and bleeding? What can he bring to the table to share? What are his dues for admission to the big sharks' club? I don't know. This is far as my thinking takes me."

"You have lots of fact finding to do, young man. You have more questions than facts. An academic paper is written on facts, documented facts." The look on Dean K's face was one of 'checkmate'! He leaned back in his chair and began to tell me his story.

"Mr. P., or Igor Ivanovich was his name when I knew him as a school mate of mine. You understand that P. is not his birth name. He changed his name after he was released from prison. I'm sure that you have heard the rumors. He likes everybody to know he is a killer, even though it was an accident.

"A few weeks ago, Igor Ivanovich and I bumped into each other in Moscow at a new hotel in the center. It was pure coincidence. He invited me for a drink and so we had a few hundred grams of vodka at the bar. Nothing horrible. Igor goes on tell me that he wants to be a candidate in the next provincial elections for governor. Further, he wants to form a political party with a platform of law and order. He was perhaps a bit drunk, but then again he always is, and he went on tell me how the criminals were taking over Russia and stealing from the good people of the motherland. These may have been the first honest words I ever heard him speak in his life, but there they were. He went on to say that he wanted to become a benevolent dictator in order to stop the crime and return the money to the people and live in peace and happiness the rest of his days. That was his plan: to be the new Stalin with the heart of Robin Hood," was the dean's revelation.

"Do you believe him?" I asked.

"What's the difference? He's such a small player that he wouldn't be able to survive on a provincial platform, let alone the national stage. He may be a big fish in a small pond here in Nizhniy, but he is not hard enough to take on the system. He doesn't have enough money to buy off so many people. He would have to discover an oil well under his Monastery to make the next step up... but none the less, he is making his move now and wants to enter politics," was the dean's follow-up.

"You just said he doesn't have a chance, so how could he make that a reality?" I pouted.

"True, but that doesn't mean he can't put together a party and get something started with some help," Karamzin speculated.

"Who could help him?" I asked, half knowing the answer already.

"He wants to pay me to consult on how to set up and start a party here in Nizhniy Novgorod." The dean beamed with honor.

I sat still in my chair, incredulous at what the dean had just admitted. I blinked at him, hesitated, screwed up my face, and shook my head back and forth. "I'm sorry. I misunderstood you. Did you say you, Dean Karamzin, would be helping him to establish a party of his own?"

"Yes. Who else is going to?" he conjectured.

"Why? Why would you help such a figure make a step into government office?" I asked in repulsion.

"He won't make it ,of course, but this way I can make sure he doesn't get competent help to make him into something he is not...and he is paying a big fee for my services." The dean chuckled victoriously.

"Aren't you already consulting on a political party, The Left Front Party?" I reminded him.

"Yes, of course, but that is finished now and they have their platform. Now we'll put together a manifesto for 'The Right Front Party'. We must create balance! There must always be an opposition party to check the other. Right?" He was searching for my approval.

"In theory, yes, but it's better if an opposition party has a moral compass," I grumbled.

"In theory, yes, but all politicians are dirty liars anyway," Karamzin rebutted.

"Touché!"

"Listen, Peter, I will set up an interview for you with Mr. P., Igor Ivanovich. You have already met, you said, so it will be a natural step. I will tell him that you are an eager student of economics and politics. Talk about the privatization if you want because he took over a restaurant recently that was state owned, but also talk about his trading company that imports goods. You'll be surprised at all the legitimate sources of income that he has; that's why he is a slippery eel. Talk about his political aspirations. You can tell him that I told you about forming a party. If you pretend to think he's clever, he will try to prove it to you. Play to his ego. Challenge him a bit and he will tell you everything! You are a smart young man. Don't talk about the organized crime aspect of his business. That will only cause you and me both trouble. I will let you know when you can meet him," the dean proposed.

"Dean, wait, wait! I have to think about this. This is really risky. I don't know if I could keep my knees from going weak while I'm there talking to him while also trying to trick him. What if he sees through me? What if he gets a sense of what we are really trying to do?" I pleaded.

"He's in idiot," Karamzin said, dismissing my anxiety.

"An idiot with a gun and thugs to throw me in the river!" I reminded him.

"He wouldn't do it to a foreigner. He couldn't escape a real investigation with the US Embassy behind it," was the Dean's convenient conclusion.

"That's comforting, thanks!" I muttered under my breath.

"OK, Peter, you think about it for one week, and then we'll talk next week at the same time. If you don't want to finally, I will tell Mr. P. that your focus is changing to International investment or something else that doesn't matter to us in Nizhniy. Then you're off the hook. Yes, fine?" was the dean's offer.

"Yes, fine. I'll consider it—but I know I won't like it," I mumbled even further under my breath.

I left the dean's office without a congenial handshake over his desk as there was no deal to shake on this time. I was greatly flustered of doing what the dean was suggesting I do. I stumbled down the stairs to the courtyard, through the tunnel and on to the square. I took a deep breath. I wandered over to the Chkalov monument and stood above the grand staircase that lead down the bluff's steep slope to the river front.

The view was always one of great comfort. Whatever temporary problem or stress a person could be facing when standing over this river—the view gave one a great perspective.

If the Volga, the life force of Mother Russia, could keep flowing through the heartlands in both the good and bad times, through all the decades of horrible bloody history that Russia has known, with even more murderous and corrupt men in power than today, why should I care so much to even consider doing what the dean is asking me to do? Why don't I just say 'Hell no!' and walk away? Was it because I wanted to save Russians from themselves as Els had suggested? Was I really another Don Quixote trying to restore a gallantry and honor code that had never even existed in Russia at the public level? Was I in it for myself? What was I looking for by going on a crazy quest, and would I realistically be able to attain it?

I walked along the embankment above the Volga and through the kremlin gates to the park inside. Deep in thought, I walked

112

the interior perimeter of the fortress, tracing the thick red walls and turrets with my fingers. I took a peek over the parapets every now and then, watching out for invaders of a modern type. What was to be done?

06

13. Auction House

With little incentive to be outdoors again, after a few warmer days of reprieve, I buried myself again in my research corner on Minin Street, searching for additional documentation on the local privatization efforts of the government. I was hoping to manufacture a way to appease the dean's wish for a thesis about the local situation, with local consequences using something and somebody other than the town mob boss as my study specimen. I would work to keep my dream intact, but also my knees and face. I had one week to find an alternate thesis topic.

While skimming the databases I was reminded about the offer from Richard and Andrew at the World Bank mission to let me attend one of the monthly auctions in town; these were administered by the provincial government, who was divesting real-estate and business licenses for retail shops. I checked my watch.

"Where would they be at three o'clock on a Thursday afternoon?" I asked myself. I gathered up my notebooks and new print-outs and headed for the bus stop. I waved Olga good evening and slipped out the door quickly.

I found both Richard and Andrew in their office this time, instead of at a local mafia establishment next door eating pizza, and rang the bell while I waved through the street window to them. Richard stood and came to the door to let me in and locked the door behind us. We stood between their desks, in an uneasy casual position half sitting, half leaning while I tried to remove scarves and hats without looking like I was setting up camp.

"We thought you had left town. Thought maybe you'd seen enough after six weeks and left without saying goodbye," Richard broke the ice.

114

"Very sorry about that. I've been very busy with my research. I realized as well that I didn't call my mother either on the first Saturday of the month. Can't believe it's April already," I said, concerned about my own memory.

"So how are you getting on? You look thinner," Richard noticed.

"Thanks for your concern but I have a grandmother already," I grinned and looked them up and down. "Speaking of thinner, you're both looking like you're ready to go home soon. Is New York Pizza serving dieters' pizzas these days?"

"Ghastly, that place. You would think they would at least try to hide their real intentions next door. The cars that come and go from there. The clothes! They must be drug dealers!" Andrew chuckled.

"Ahhh, yes. I've learned some very interesting things about the goings-on in this town. Maybe too much," I commiserated.

"So, you came and ate our pizza, picked our brains, and then you never came back," Richard brought us back to point.

"Sorry, I've been so deep in research and writing and with midterm exams, I really lost track of time. When did we have pizza together? Must have been mid-February. Sorry about that," I apologized.

"Look, don't worry, I am only having a go at you. Truth is we've been traveling quite a bit and just got back last week from visiting cities less attractive than this. We're just finishing up a big report as well," Richard said as he took a chair.

"Alright, I won't take up more of your time, but we had talked about me maybe attending a government auction when the chance came up. I could really use that chance now as I am trying to...well let's just say my options are narrowing and I don't like one of the options. I need to manufacture another good option to make my thesis work. Otherwise, I may miss the opportunity to publish in June," I explained.

Andrew leaned back in his swivel desk chair and spoke to me and the ceiling at the time. "Coincidently, it's a good thing you came by right now, as we are leaving at four-thirty, because tomorrow mid-morning in the Yarkmarka...do you know where the Yarmarka is, there just across the first Oka river bridge?" He paused as I nodded my admission. "...the provincial and city governments will be selling off their grocery store holdings."

"Well now, must have had an angel on my shoulder today!" I beamed.

"Maybe it was a devil! This one is going to be controversial as Yegor Gaidar himself will be there with Governor Nemtsov. But that's not the kicker. The kicker is that the bidders had to preregister beforehand to be vetted and somehow a local mob boss has made the list next to a number of groups of employees hoping to stage some 'management buyouts,' as we are calling them in our reports to the mother ship," Richard added.

"A local mob-boss? Would that happen to be Mr. P.?" I asked, already knowing the answer.

"Oh, I can't remember all these Russian names from the Chinese ones, let me check." Andrew turned his chair around to open a dossier on his desk. "Let's see now," he muttered as he scanned his lists. "A one Mr. P. indeed. Why, do you know him?"

"Met him. Don't know him," I qualified my comments.

"Do tell. How did you come to meet him? We understand he is not the most accessible fellow," Andrew revealed.

"Don't know what you mean by that. He was showing off like a peacock last weekend at his Monastery here just up the road. It was a disgusting display if you ask me," I said with disdain.

"Well, he doesn't take appointments is what we understood from the mayor's office. He evidently put down a deposit of cash for the auction instead of having his books or credit examined to be sure he could purchase what he may bid on. We understand it was quite a bit of money," Andrew continued.

"Did anybody ask where the money came from?" I queried.

"It's in escrow at INKOMBank—solid enough bank being the national reserve bank and all," Andrew confirmed.

"Sorry, I meant, did anybody go over his tax returns to understand where the money came from?" I clarified my question.

"Import business. He evidently already owns a few stores where he sells home electronics and a car lot where he deals in used cars from—Japan was it?" Andrew looked to Richard.

"Korea," I interjected.

"You seem to know him well," Richard mused.

"Sounds like we know only what Mr. P. wants us to know about him. I learned what I know on the dance floor at his holy house of disco. You learned yours from the mayor's office, I guess?" I concluded.

"Spot on." Andrew made a motion of poking a dot in the air with his pen.

We all hummed and hawed for a few minutes taking in the revelations.

"Can I attend the auctions as an observer? An academic observer from the university?" I requested.

"Anybody with the stomach for it can attend. It's a public auction to keep in line with transparency and whatnot, keep the officials accountable, etc., etc." Richard explained.

"Will you both be there?" I asked.

"Occupational hazard, I'm afraid," said Andrew, turning back to his word processing.

I gave a searching look to Richard to understand Andrew's reluctance.

"The communists always protest in large numbers. It's a bit unnerving," he explained.

"Communists? Weren't they outlawed by Yeltsin in 1992?" I was puzzled.

"The party was outlawed, that is correct, but these are mostly the younger pensioners waving the Soviet flag and holding pictures of Lenin and Marx and getting up in people's faces. It's a bit bothersome. Because Mr. Gaidar will be there tomorrow the demonstration we understand is getting some national flavor and support from other regions. It's supposed to be rather large tomorrow," Richard explained while Andrew avoided the topic.

"OK, I'll be there. What time does it begin?"

On Friday morning, I caught the metro from Proletarskaya and rode it until Moscovskaya, the train station. The metro from there crossed east over the Oka and into the lower old city where I hadn't spent much time, as the river had been frozen, and the walk up and down the steep bluff was not the for faint of heart for one wearing wool and fur. The ice from the river was all but gone now at the beginning of April. The first boats were moving up and down river: flat barges, mostly, nothing too tall yet for fear of not slipping under the bridges as the tributaries were over full of melting snow packs and the Volga was swelling. The hydrofoils, or as the locals called them 'Rockyetiy,' would soon be running up and down and crisscross, connecting river villages to the cities. Then would come some larger container vessels as soon as the water table fell a bit. At the end of April would come the fleet of river cruisers carrying tourists and holiday makers from Moscow to Volgograd and back. The Volga was slowly waking up from its winter hibernation.

From the Moscow Train Station, I walked up the west bank of the Oka River, parallel to Soviet Street, to the exhibition hall, passing a five-story tall statue of Vladimir Lenin so courteously pointing the way for me. As I approached the broad square in front of the Yarmarka, I saw a fleet of black Volga and Chaika limousines, a hoard of police vans and black clad riot police and a large group of civilians in a semi-circle, surrounded by the riot police. The civilians were waving red and yellow flags with different years commemorated on them. Some had the hammer and sickle and others the letters of CPSU (Communist Party

Soviet Union) embroidered on them. The group wasn't chanting as much as they were screaming and yelling, making an uncoordinated ruckus. I supposed that Russians had yet to learn how to effectively use their new freedom to protest. It appeared that the riot police had corralled the group of protestors and weren't letting them go much further or cause much disruption to the events. I could not get close to them without having to push police out of my way or politely ask to be let through.

The Yarmarka is an impressive building from outside and in. On the outside, it is an architectural piece that one would expect to see on Moscow's beautiful Red Square. It is an old building that was built by the merchant community of Nizhniy Novgorod in the 19th Century as an exhibition hall for their manufactured goods. A long, noble building with a thick fortress feel, perhaps mirroring the kremlin opposite it across the river on the bluff. The red brick facade is filled with windows, letting natural light pour in. The exhibition hall is behind that and taller by another story with a line of long, tall arches enclosed with glass, much like in English or French railway station, but with a very Russian style. I wondered why they didn't make this building the train station as it would truly impress the visitor as they arrived in Nizhniy.

I stood in the main entrance hall looking for a directional board that would tell me in which room today's auction would be held. There was no information being volunteered for the unfamiliar visitor to find. Except for the protestors and limousines out front, I wouldn't have thought that anything was going on in the building at all that Friday morning. I tried to open a few doors in a long corridor on the left and right, but all the doors were locked. The office windows were dark. I stepped out again on to the square to see if there was a less obvious entrance being used. As I stepped out in front of the fountains on the square to view the facade better, I watched a motorcade approach: two black Volga sedans, one in front and one in back of a dark burgundy colored Mercedes stretch sedan with black tinted windows, including the windshield. Completely bullet proof. They drove almost right over my feet. If I hadn't stepped back along the flank of the fountain they very well would have driven right over me.

Two body guards stepped out of the car and scoped the square. They looked directly at me and I stood and blinked at them like a possum caught in the headlights of a speeding car. Then the back door of the Mercedes swung open and out stepped the bald head of a man I met not a week ago at his night club. Mr. P. himself had just arrived. I stood and watched as he and his entourage pushed themselves deftly into and through the crowd of police men and protesters and thru a smaller door where the protesters had gathered.

As Mr. P. and his thugs disappeared into the building amid shouts and raised fists from the protesters, I headed into the line of police men behind them, pushing just as I saw Mr. P.'s guards do. It worked. As I passed the last layer of police officers, stepping in front of their shields, I entered in the thick of the protestors who turned out to be very un-intimidating. The group was made of older women in head scarves and older men without teeth in shabby overcoats holding handmade photos and placards of the old communist guard. I smiled at them all meekly and motioned toward the doors behind them, and they let me pass without shouts of blood and brimstone on my head. Without a limousine or bodyguards, I must have appeared harmless to both the police and the protestors.

I slipped into the room unnoticed and took a seat in the back. Richard and Andrew were present but were working closely with an interpreter and staffers, trying to keep up themselves with what was going on and hastily giving orders and scribbling in their notepads. The auction was held in a cramped conference room set up with the auctioneer at the head of the room and the bidders in the first two rows, twelve people in total. Next to the auctioneer was a stack of files on a low table, each containing a property and license representing a retail store somewhere in the city that were all for auction. Each file had a number on it which corresponded to the program given to the bidders with detailed descriptions of what was on offer. The session started after a delay from the official observers sitting front left at a long table draped in a green cloth. They pointed into the crowd and whispered frantically.

I did not see Mr. Gaidar nor Mr. Nemtsov in the room, much to my disappointment. Of course, they were present just for the photo opportunity and sound bites that had happened just before I arrived. They hadn't come to actually run the auction. I felt rather foolish that I had expected the governor himself, gavel in hand, would be personally selling off unwanted stores and warehouses.

As the bidding was opened after a long-winded reading of the rules and technicalities of the process, it didn't take long for the tension in the room to rise as the prices for the properties rose. The grand prize of the day was a run-down grocer directly opposite the Moscovskiy Train Station on Filchenkova Street at Revolution Square. The amount of foot traffic, bus traffic, and automobile traffic and the parking spaces in front of it made it perfectly positioned for visibility and accessibility. I knew the location well. It was perfectly located for any retail sales. There were three primary groups in the contest for win this location with the needed permits: a group of the current store's management team, a consortium of the store's employees represented by their chairwoman and a lawyer, and Mr. P. The split between manager and workers of the store was palpable in the front row as both groups continued to up the ante and price for the property. Mr. P. sat silently as the two rivals scowled at each other and whispered amongst themselves with every extra hundred-thousand rubles being committed. The observers were breathless as the price spiraled higher and higher.

Neither group, the managers or the staff consortium, would have the money to purchase the store and its operations outright. It would require a mortgage and then the staffs' entire wages for several years to be able to pay the debt of acquisition. Would they be able to turn a profit? Nobody really knew. The banks behind the offered mortgages perhaps didn't know either but at least they would have a valuable property in their hands should the owners fail to pay the mortgage. The only person who could purchase the lot outright was Mr. P., but he wasn't lifting his paddle to signal his interest. He sat idly by while the managers and workers battled it out. Only after the price rose above two million rubles did Mr. P. even start to twitch.

"Two-million ten thousand, two-million twenty thousand, two-million twenty-five thousand, two-million twenty-seven thousand rubles..." and the bidding started losing steam.

The price stopped rising by ten thousands and was now clawing higher at smaller and smaller increments. The auctioneer looked at the workers' representatives and asked if there was any higher bid from their side. After a quick consultation between the lawyer and the chairwoman from the workers' group, she shook her head and then bowed it, defeated and deflated. The managers' group was now on the line for close to forty thousand dollars. The room held its collective breath. Just before the gavel was dropped, Mr. P. finally put his hand and offered two million twenty-eight thousand rubles . . .and the bidding found a second wind. The price finally settled at two million thirty-three thousand rubles. It was no surprise who had the longest breath. Mr. P. wouldn't even have to sell his Mercedes to be able to front forty thousand dollars. The bank would simply book the escrow over to the city's account and the property would change hands without anybody even handling the cash.

The bidders were furious. The workers' chairwoman stood up and berated the auctioneer. The lawyer accompanying the managers' delegation said that they would file an appeal and then both turned and started shouting at Mr. P., who didn't show any emotion except to check his wrist watch, his Rolex wrist watch to be exact. Arrogance oozed out of him and left rings under the armpits in his crisp white Swiss made shirt. Would either the managers or the workers still have a job tomorrow? Doubtful. They would probably be replaced with Mr. P.'s hangers-on and friends and family aligned with his current enterprises. All the current managers and staff could do was protest and shout and insult Mr. P., but everybody knew the way this auction system worked. The highest bidder had won.

The exasperation from the observers' table was visible as well, but they had to admit just like everybody else in the room that the bidding process was fair and transparent and that the auctioneer followed all the rules as they had been explained at the beginning. There was no irregularity to appeal. With this ruling from the neutral observers, the managers' delegation stood and left in a flurry of accusation and finger pointing. The chairwoman from the workers' group looked directly at Mr. P. and told him that they would find a way to stop him from taking over their store. She then gathered her handbag and departed with her lawyer as well. I suppose it wasn't the fact that Mr. P. had won the bidding, but it was the contempt that he showed everybody in the room by waiting until the very end, after driving up everybody's hopes, and then simply outbidding them by one thousand rubles each time, just baiting them. He could have easily started the bidding at two million rubles, but instead, he tried to get it for less by waiting to understand the competition's highest threshold. He allowed the others to feel the dream so close; the dream of working for themselves, making a good living, taking pride in their enterprise, and be rewarded financially for their labor and sacrifices; and then smashed them in an offhand fashion for just another cold investment. He then went on to buy up three smaller properties in the city for almost nothing as the other parties had all left the event in disgust, leaving him to purchase what he wished at will for prices far below fair market values.

It was a disgusting display of how wealth can manipulate a system being lauded in the press and around the world as being so open, fair, and transparent. The closer one looked, the less this was the reality in Nizhniy's successes. Businesses were being privatized for the highest prices the government could earn, but at what cost? Was there not a more just way of reaching the same goal? Did the swing from communism to capitalism require rubbing the noses of the law-abiding citizens in the disdain of the illegally wealthy? Surely there was a more just way. Surely there was a way to plan for a better long-term perspective than just jettisoning assets to the highest bidders regardless of the origin of the funds. What was to be done?

It was becoming apparent to me that through some mishap of destiny, the different options I had for writing a thesis this term were narrowing and merging. The conclusions would be one and the same, regardless of the starting point. The only way that the national and regional governments could obtain the results they had promised to international money lenders, who were keeping Russia from falling into a deeper economic pit, was that they would have to accept that elements of the corrupt shadow economy be incorporated into the official economy; and the bosses of the crime syndicates would have to be given a seat at the table of government in exchange for providing the stashed cash to keep the home fires burning. Through some sick twist of fate, Russia had become a hostage to its criminal organizations. The price of liberation was granting legitimacy to their practices by adapting the laws of the country to help them preserve their ill-gotten gains for posterity. Were the people properly informed of the decisions the President and the Duma were making in Moscow that had led to this compromise of integrity? What led to it? How did it get so far?

14. Into the Shadows

"Del, I need some good advice before Monday morning." I sighed.

"Well, you are probably in the wrong place for that. Hell, I think if we both had any good sense we would leave this place and head for the Bahamas or Puerto Vallarta and sell cold drinks on a beach for the rest of our lives," Del said, zipping up his sweater.

"Yes, that would be good advice!" I replied with no argument.

"What's eating at you, kid?" he asked as he sat down.

"You know I am busy with research for a thesis, and that if it turns out to be worth its weight in paper, could be published in June in the university's new periodical of economics and politics. My problem is this: the theme that grabs my interest and for which I am gathering incredible data and documentation is the privatization process of state companies. The method, the system is really bad and the people are getting ripped off, hoodwinked, and robbed. The national government, and I suppose the local governments to some extent, are not being transparent about it and are privatizing everything at a huge cost to the country purely for the sake of privatizing. It's like the ideology has taken over rational thinking; they will drive at full speed over a cliff rather than hit the brakes and reevaluate the situation before more damage is done. It's economic suicide what is happening right now," I forwarded.

"Are you thinking of running for office?" Del asked, mocking me.

"If only I could, eh? The problem is this, no matter where I start this paper it is going to have the same ending. That ending will have to name the illegal activities of some local actors in order to prove that even the much-loved privatization process, yes, right here in 'River City,' is also falling victim to the developments out of the shadow economy. It needs to be revised to prevent entrenching the 'mafia goons'—borrowing your description by the way—and their families into quasi-legal positions which will be nearly impossible to dislodge. It's critical now! Without a complete collapse of the economy—and I mean a complete collapse—or legal precedence being suspended to confiscate them of their assets, they will achieve complete legitimacy and continue to wield their corrupt influences." I ranted.

"Who is the local fellow and what is he into?" Del asked curiously.

"Mr. P. I imagine he started in common thuggery years ago, but now I am pretty sure he is running protection rackets all over the city, pimping, drugs, and other contraband without paying the taxes. I wouldn't be surprised to find that he is importing with protection through big payoffs to inspectors to avoid customs duties because the laws are so that you can't make a profit importing cars legally. Now he is branching out in retail outlets for home electronics. And this morning he bought Nizhniy's best-placed grocery store, so I suppose he going into consumables now," I explained.

"You seem to know a lot about him," Del remarked.

"In just the last week he has become a wall in my research. Every way I turn I come up against him. He is certainly a force to reckon with in the city. I think he may be in business with the mayor, but I have no evidence of that," I speculated.

"What makes you think that?" Del continued to ask short, clear questions.

"The mayor's office is vouching for him. I think protecting him from audits and other scrutiny because he is a good citizen on some levels. He has money to make things in Nizhniy happen, the things that politicians usually get good press for," I remarked.

"Has he moved into real estate do you know?" was Del's only interest.

"I don't know, but my clever dean is somehow friends enough with him that he wants to arrange for me to do a full interview with him, so I can ask him about all his private ventures and learn how a modern businessman gets the job done in post-soviet Russia. I don't know if I have the guts to go through with the interview and use it in my paper. I'd get my knees broken, that's for sure!" I predicted.

Els interrupted to offer good advice. "Maybe you have a bit of common sense that is stopping you from doing it, instead of not having the guts. Maybe it's your mother's voice you are hearing in your head."

Del brushed her off as over cautious. "Kid, remember, never get too deep into this place that you can't walk away. Don't let it matter so much that your good judgment gets overridden by your ego. That's a recipe for disaster. Gotta be able to walk away."

"So are you saying that I should do the interview..."

Del finished my sentence for me, "...and then yes, if it goes south, be ready to cut and run. Don't wait around and hide and think you can just go back to life as normal after everybody calms down and moves on, because these types have a very long memory."

"This is not how I saw things happening when I left home in January. I had really wanted to stay a few years and make myself a good start here, not blow the ceiling off the place and have to high-tail it out of here, burning the bridges as I go. I had really hoped to stick around and watch things change, be a neutral observer of sorts, not get involved up to my neck and then...cut and run," I moaned.

Els tried to bring some perspective to the discussion again. "Peter, just drop the project. There is nothing that says you need to publish in this magazine. Don't let the dean push you into a corner, a potentially deadly corner. I'm sure there is plenty you could write about without the dean taking advantage of you. Have you asked yourself why your dean would want so badly for you to go forward? What does he have to gain from it? Where are his interests? I know Del has said this to you before, but remember that everybody in Russia these days has a shadow life, the darkness of which can really surprise even spouses. So, what does the dean have to gain?"

"I haven't looked into that at all, honestly. I figured the dean is an academic and is looking for the truth like me," I guessed.

"Not everybody is as sincere and altruistic as you are being in this situation. Everybody has something they're hiding. Don't be misled into a situation that can have serious consequences for yourself while somebody else exploits your misfortune for their gain," Els warned again.

With the bowls empty and the bread consumed, Els began clearing the table. On that cue Del invited me into the living room with something special to discuss with me. We sat facing each other in the swivel chairs, a coffee table between each other.

"I have an offer for you that I want you to consider," Del stated.

I was sincerely surprised as our relationship for the last three months was purely one of camaraderie, nothing official and certainly nothing binding.

"I mentioned to you a few weeks ago when we came back from Germany that we had cut through some red tape and my employer was ready to take the next step. Well, that is now going forward and we're ready to make preparations for the next step. I won't bore you with the details, but this next step will open up some opportunities that I would like your help with," he said frankly.

"You would like my help? I don't know what I could possibly offer you."

"Just listen, it's not as difficult as you might first think. My employer is now putting together a project team that will eventually replace me and I will move on. I'm not an architect or a builder, and I do not run hotels. I'm a wedge that pushes the door open for the rest of the organization. Once they have a foothold, a legal standing, and are correctly connected, I move onto the next project. So, now that the project team is being picked and I have already submitted their documents for their work and residency permits, the next step is to find them a place to live during their term here in Nizhniy. As you have discovered, and the reason I am here, is that there are no decent hotels that could safely and securely house a group of professionals. The organization is not authorized to purchase real estate to house the staff, and the staff ain't gonna invest for themselves in a Russian home when nobody really knows who will have a right to it in two years' time That is where you come in," he explained.

I sat up straight in my easy chair and leaned in to catch the details.

"Els and I see a chance to exploit this hole in the business plan and set up a rental agency. We will then rent apartments for the expats coming to town, which they can expense to the company. The company itself may not sign the leases. Red tape. So, we will set up a new company, rent apartments from the current owners for two years at a time, and then rent those out for more than double the rental price... well, I think you get the picture," Del was getting excited by his own explanation.

"Do you realize that I pay all of twenty-dollars for my room, and could probably rent the whole thing for sixty dollars if I wanted to and have all the room I could possibly need? Nobody would pay five or six hundred dollars for what they could get for one hundred," I commented skeptically.

"Ah yes, but you are a student on a student's budget. Do you have a telephone in your apartment?" Del challenged me.

"No," I replied.

"No telephone line means no fax and no email service, and you're cut off from the world. Do you have any security at your place?" he pushed again.

"No, I have my babushka and that's about it," I replied.

"Do you have a kitchen?" He was really touching the sore places.

"Good point," I conceded.

"Do you have a shower, a lift, good shopping, and restaurants or a theatre or museum nearby?" He was going for the kill.

"No, I live in the workers' neighborhood," I admitted.

"How long does it take you into the old town?" He was mocking me now.

"Thirty to forty minutes on the commuter bus or metro," I confessed.

"Exactly! Expats expect a certain standard and ease of living or they won't, can't even be enticed to go abroad for even two months and live like a student, not even if somebody else is paying for it. Being asked to go to Russia to start with already hikes the hardship surcharge up to the armpits, so if you get an employee so far that they will accept an offer to staff a Russian operation, and then outside of Moscow or Petersburg!? Well you had better be ready to pamper them, or your staff won't stay." Del seemed to know what he was talking about.

"OK, so where do I come into this?" I asked curiously.

"I would like you to work with Misha, my local office manager and bookkeeper to scout out apartments, advertise, whatever it takes. Evaluate what is being offered as if you were a western expat from the USA, France, Germany, or England and give us a thumb up or down. It's that simple. Misha will take care of setting up a little real estate agency registration in Nizhniy that has a license to broker the renting of apartments and other property. You could consider yourself a type of quality control manager of the properties offered. Does that sound like something you could manage between your studies?" he asked.

"Yeah, that doesn't sound too difficult or complicated. Maybe I could even find myself something better to live in, closer to town!" I answered.

"Listen, I will pay you a running commission for every apartment you and Misha secure and are able to rent to the expats. It will take some weeks to find the right sort of property, but then it will pay off eventually," Del offered.

"I don't have permission to work. I'm here on a student visa," I stated cautiously.

"Peter, don't try to be holier than the Pope. Nobody cares. You're here and that's all that matters. It's Russia. Half the taxi drivers in Moscow are here illegally from Tbilisi. If you hesitate because of technicalities you'll miss your boat," he scolded.

"Agreed," I said firmly.

"Great, I'll get you Misha's telephone number and ask you to meet up with him at your first chance to set up a regular schedule for viewing apartments," Del instructed.

"Sounds like a good way to earn my tuition for the fall term."

Del invited me into his office where on the wall were technical maps of the old city and conceptual sketches from an architect showing what the hotel would look like and the master planning for a parcel of land for which Del was negotiating with the city and provincial councils to be allowed to develop. To my surprise and my unexpressed concern, this planned hotel was on the upper embankment walk just past Gordost and a stone's throw from The Monastery. The site would have a great view of the river, perched on the bluff, and have great proximity to the city's best attractions and restaurants. It would certainly be a prestigious location for any new project.

On leaving the Sannings' I called Yulia from a telephone booth on the corner of Minin Square before catching a bus across the river to the Moscovskiy Train Station to catch the metro line, which ran directly past her apartment and then on to mine.

The telephone booths, like most telephone booths in the world, were not meant to be free of cost, yet they were all free for calls in the city. The pay phones had of course been designed to work on coins, and probably for fifty years or more, a five-kopek coin. Now that the Russian ruble was fifty-eight to the dollar, and a small loaf of white bread, a baton, cost two hundred rubles, the kopek was no longer circulated and the telephones were always active for whoever, whenever, without charge. If you dared to speak in length about anything other than the weather or a train time table, the line was yours.

Yulia answered, "Halloah"

"Hi, it's me," I said without saying who I was.

"It's late. Where are you?" she asked.

"I have some good news."

"Not over the phone. Where are you?"

"In the old town."

"Come by on your way home and tell us," she ordered.

"OK, see you soon," I agreed and hung up the handset.

When I finally arrived at Yulia's apartment she was full of news. "Do you know who phoned me earlier tonight? Irina Ivanovna," Yulia beamed.

"Do you mean Irina the cruise director from the Giorgiy Zhukov last summer?" I asked excitedly.

"Yes, exactly. The spring sailing schedule starts in two weeks and they called to invite me to sail with them again to Moscow and back at the end of the month," she said. grinning.

"Excellent!" I remarked.

"I told them that you were here as well, and they invited us both to travel with them as guests on the cruise." She was nearly bouncing in her chair.

"That would be heavenly, but I will have to ask for permission to travel. My visa only permits me to be in Nizhniy and Moscow," I said cautiously.

"Nobody checks your papers on the cruise because you won't sleep in hotels. If you sleep on the boat and stay with the tour group, nobody will look at you." She sounded annoyed that something might disrupt her new summer plans.

"I will just ask Valentina Petrovna how I can obtain permission to travel. Shouldn't be a big problem as I did it last summer, too." I tried to sound reassuring.

"It would be so romantic to take that trip again!" Yulia pined. "So, what good news do you have?"

"I've been offered a job. It won't make me rich, but it's a start," I said cautiously.

"Peter, you aren't going to work for the American businessman, are you?" Yulia knew how to start with the third degree. "You don't know him well enough to trust him. You don't know what kind of trouble this could get you into."

"Why are you so against it? You don't even know the guy," I protested, annoyed.

"And you have done your research on him, have you? If you know about him, who is funding him? Who is he working for? Would you even be working legally?" Her skepticism annoyed me but I knew she was right.

"Yulia, you have to trust somebody in this life, or you won't get anywhere! Sometimes you have to take risks," I offered a weak defense.

"Peter, wake up! This is Russia. Trusting people you don't know gets you killed. You can't forget that. For all you know he could be a criminal, too. He could be a spy. He could be anything and you're just going to go work for him? Where does he work? Out of his home? Have you ever seen anything he has produced?" Yulia the journalist wanted cold hard facts and trusted nobody that couldn't produce them.

"OK fine! You win. I'll turn down the offer. It was just a chance to work and earn some money and stay longer, maybe see where this all....never mind," I muttered, defeated.

Even though I verbalized my acquiescence in the face of Yulia and her mother's objections to me working for Del, my heart chose a different path of defiance and I decided to trust that Del was what he said he was. I chose then to deceive my friends and pursue what I came to Russia to pursue, not assume their wishes, desire, and fears. I decided I would not tell Yulia anymore about my research topic or anything I was writing. I would not tell her that I was working for Del. I would not tell Del about Yulia, I would not tell my professor about Del.

I drew a curtain, a wall between the different compartments of my life in Nizhniy and was determined that they would not intersect. With Yulia, I would talk about the weather and the river boats and go strolling on the waterfront but not let her any further into my other dealings and activities. With that discussion and that split decision on a late Friday evening in early April, my own shadow life was born.

Saturday was spent brooding with Hans and a pile of fried chicken overlooking the Volga together. The landscape had slowly taken on a light green tint in the trees and hillside on top of the bluff. Small buds were starting to appear on the hedges and branches. I had left my wool coat at home that day. The river was well over its normal banks and the lower embankment was completely under water. The sky was filled with dark threatening clouds juxtaposed against dark blue patches. It was a great day to be sitting out of the wind overlooking the old city, the river, and God's wider creations, with a stack of chicken on one plate and chicken bones on the other. Spring was definitely in the air. We kept going back for drumsticks and thighs much to the annoyance of the plump middle-aged woman in the kitchen. I drank Pepsi while Hans tried again to choke down the local lemonade.

I explained my several dilemmas of opportunity to my German friend, who knew nobody in my circle of influence except for Valentina Petrovna, and he disliked her about as much as I did. I needed an independent opinion detached from Dean Karamzin, the Sannings, and Yulia and her mother. We spoke English no louder than a whisper in the corner of the dining room to avoid being overheard.

More for my sake, than for his understanding, I explained to Hans the focus of my research and how it kept leading me head long into the operations of the local mafia boss, and about my decision deadline on Monday morning about whether or not I would interview Mr. P. I recounted the property auction, the cash escrow deposits of forty and fifty thousand dollars at the INKOM Bank. Hans, an economics major, having studied how Germany handled its own transition from state-owned companies to private ownership, assured me of what I already had concluded: black money should not be allowed to enter the official economy through privatization.

"You see, Peter, East Germany had Vest Germany to help viz its own transition from communism to a free society. Legally, zere was no difference between the East and Vest Germanies once unification vas finished and the federal government vent into heavy debt to finance the rebuilding of old communist controlled regionz. Russia has nobody to throw it a lifeline, to show zem how to properly transition zeir laws to protect ze public interest. Now Russia has to look for cash and knowhow on its own from wherever it can find it, and that is why the shadow economy iz being allowed to knowingly flow into the visible economy."

"That is very insightful, Mein Freund. Thanks for that," I said with appreciation, surprised that he had really intelligent thoughts, something I hadn't yet heard from him earlier.

"Zo, do you sink I can ask ze fat lady for more again, or vill she throw us out?" Hans asked stupidly.

"C'mon Hans, we already can't go back to The Monastery, where all the pretty girls live. I don't want to be persona-non-grata at my favorite restaurant in all of Russia as well. I think we've already eaten a murder of crows here. Let's pack it in," I suggested.

"Okey, okey." He threw his napkin on to his plate and we nursed our bottles of soda until about four o'clock.

"Zo, are you going to verk with ze Amerikan? Do you sink it vill lead to somezing bigger?" he asked me pensively.

"I would hope so, but I get the feeling that nothing is for sure in this country. Maybe I'll work for a few months for him, but there is so much uncertainty in it all that I can't imagine it being a long- term thing. We'll just have to see," I said, taking another swig from my bottle.

"Vill you vant to stay if he asks you to do somezing bigger?" he asked again.

"If I do this interview and the research paper and if it gets published, I may not live that long. But I just don't feel, knowing what I know now, that I could rest until I put in on paper and at least try to tell the people what is going on," I said, somewhat defeated by inevitability.

"Why do you sink that zey don't already know it? Russians are not stupid people," Hans truthfully pointed out.

"Stupid no, but this is all so new to everybody," I said defensively.

"Corruption is nothing new to Russians. The communists exported it to East Germany, Czechoslovakia, and Poland, and you sink the Russians don't know it when they smell it? The Germans knew it but it took a long time to push away the communists because of ze Russian tanks and soldiers. Oh, Peter, zey know it's all corrupt, but zey know as vell zat zey are powerless to change it. If the wider world condones it as a legitimate system then nothing will change. It was zo in East Germany, Poland, Romania. If somebody with bigger tanks isn't ready to help, then we all just kept our heads down instead of getting smashed in by the secret police. The Russians know it. Zey just don't want to have their families hurt by doing somesing about it. No mistake about it."

"Maybe then all the more reason to do it..." I decided to throw caution to the wind and follow my sense of justice.

Before lectures on Monday morning I went straight to the dean's office before class. Before he was able to take his chair and with me still standing and leaning over the desk, I blurted at him, "Let's do it!"

06

15. The Zhukov

It was a brilliant Friday, April afternoon without a cloud in the sky. The air was warm and fresh and one could smell the sunshine in the air. All seemed bright and clean. To stand still in the sunlight next to the surging river, eyes closed tight, pointing directly into the prodigal sun, sparked rejoicing and mourning in one deeply mixed up emotion: where had it been hiding? Will it leave us again soon? I wanted nothing more than to stand right there at the edge of the water, rooted like a sunflower, and follow every degree of the sun's progress towards the Tropic of Cancer. Oh, how much I would miss it when it's gone again! The joy of the warm sun today juxtaposed against the despair of cold snow showers from the week before was the discouraging mania that made this one moment so beautiful.

The rechniy flot, or river fleet, based in Nizhniy Novgorod which plies the waterways of Russia for pleasure, was coming out of its winter hibernation in mid-April. It was flushing the water tanks, tuning up the diesel turbines, painting the decks and cleaning the passengers' cabins, and taking on supplies and fuel. Even though the river was too high still to sail the largest of these holiday boats under a number of the bridges upstream, towards the Volga-Moscow canal and ultimately Moscow, the crew was bustling on the decks making the boats shine and getting ready for five months of vagabonding all over Russia, from St. Petersburg to Astrakhan, and Moscow to Volgograd. It was a thrill to see the boats again as they came one by one and moored at the Nizhniy Novgorod River Station to show off their colors and flags before the holiday makers boarded for the year's first sailings. In high summer, one usually walks down the gang plank to board a river cruiser. As the water had refused to recede, we had to walk up to reach the first railings from the docks. It was a fine feeling to be back onboard the Georgiy Zhukov! It felt to me like arriving home after a long absence.

We were all one year older but almost all the same happy faces were there on board already to greet me and Yulia as we stepped onboard for an impromptu reunion with our friends, and my former colleagues, with whom I had worked the summer prior. Even the captain remembered me and stopped to shake hands and greet us as he passed by, clipboard in hand, barking instructions to a deck hand.

Irina, a tall lanky older woman with long gray hair, greeted us as we stepped over the threshold. An outdoor enthusiast, she was the senior of the tour guides of the group and spoke English with a proper English accent and perfect Russian with a warm literary accent. When she spoke, or retold a story, one could easily think that she was reading one of Russia's folk tales filled with fantastic verbs and adjectives. Life always seemed enchanting when she shared her adventures or even issued a warning.

Nikolai, my good friend, was the complete opposite of Irina. This dark skinned, sunglasses clad Georgian from Tbilisi was in anything but in a hurry, and spoke Russian with an accent reminiscent of Josef Stalin's, also a Georgian, with a cigarette never too far from his lips. He was maybe in his mid-forties and a father of two older children. Our friendship was built mostly in the bar drinking vodka and Pepsi, in between sailings when we were waiting for the next tourists from America. Somehow all his brown, white, and yellow polyester shirts were missing the top two or three buttons and were always showing off his thick chest hair and gold chains with tiny icons hanging off them. If one didn't know his good-natured heart and intense interest in people, one might mistake him for a Georgian gangster or pimp. His command of English, as well, was unimpeachable.

Olga was a truly professional tour guide. Despite the weather or the destination, she was always dressed in a navy blue blazer and knee length skirt with a white collared blouse, white stockings, and dark pumps. She was in her mid-fifties with dirty blond hair down to her shoulders but kept in wavy full curls. It didn't move in the wind, not even on deck on a windy afternoon. She spoke English exactly and was a history master. She had obviously traveled the river for tens of years with tourists and knew every bend of the Volga, every village, and every monument. She was the epitome of order and punctuality.

Matvei was a youth prodigy of maybe seventeen years when we met the year before. In 1994 his exposure to western pop-culture, Russian history, the English language, and the courage that being seventeen gives a young man to do anything that enters his mind, made him a favorite among the American tourists. He had also become my right-hand man for tracking down lost tourists in Moscow and greasing the palms of local harbor masters who needed a little extra incentive to help them look the other way at times. His mother was an English instructor, his father a history professor in Moscow. He was indispensable on our voyages.

"Peter, we thought maybe you were dead after what happened last summer. Nobody knew that you were flying back to Moscow from Volgograd that day and we thought we had left you behind half way to Saratov," Nikolai muttered from one side of his mouth with a passive cigarette hanging out of the other corner of his mouth, the smoke blowing behind us in the sunny river breeze.

"Sorry about that. I wasn't in my best form when I departed," was my apologetic reply. "Sorry to have caused you worry."

"And can you imagine my reaction when Nikolai told me that you weren't on board? Nobody knew what had happened to you," Yulia chimed in.

"Oh Nikolai, do you still have my gray overcoat?" I asked between the discussion.

"I am sorry, but my brother needed a good coat last fall. I gave it to him," Nikolai apologized.

"Not a problem, my friend, not a problem," I waved it off.

"The last I saw you, we were sitting on the river bank watching all the pretty girls' legs in short sun dresses, and then you were gone a few hours later!" Nikolai continued.

Yulia gave me an elbow in the ribs and a disapproving look. I gave an apologetic gesture and a glance toward Nikolai to blame him and absolve myself of the accusation in her eyes.

"Yes, I was told there was an extra seat on the flight and the ship's doctor thought it best I departed rather than sail again after what happened in Kazan," I explained dryly. Everybody nodded as they remembered watching medics and an ambulance drive me away in front all the worried tourists.

"What did happen in Kazan?" Matvei asked.

"Things that I don't want to remember. Maybe on a different day I'll tell you all, but with the sun shining and weather so beautiful..." I rummaged in my book bag and pulled out a squat two-liter bottle of Pepsi-Cola "...I think it's time for a drink on deck!" I winked at Nikolai.

"Oiy, Oiy, Oiy! Americans." They all sighed in unison looking exasperated at each other while Yulia laughed at me and told me to put it away.

"I'll find some glasses!" was Nikolai's reply. "And a bottle of vodka!"

Sitting just out of the breeze but still in the sunshine, it felt like it could have been June. The sky was as azure as any tropical sea. The temperature was perfect. We smoked and drank and reminisced about the challenges and the scares of the last summer when we were working on the river.

"What ever happened to Rocky? You remember the big man who broke his leg at the Kremlin in Moscow?" Matvei inquired.

"You know, I had a letter from him in November just before the winter holidays. He told me he had made a full recovery and thanked us all again for our quick action," I informed the group. "He said it could have been a lot worse if we hadn't done all we did to help him."

Yulia hadn't been with us on that voyage and she asked to hear the story.

"Ok, but let me tell it in English. Otherwise, it won't be as good in Russian," I demanded.

Everybody nodded to indicate no problem as everybody in the group spoke English better than I did Russian, except for Yulia.

"Rocky, Rocky....Rocky..." I was trying to remember his last name.

"Balboa!" came a reply from Matvei.

"You and all your movie references, Matvei, it's amazing. Did you spend your ENTIRE childhood watching bootleg movies from the USA?" I asked in a mocking tone.

"Almost!" he grinned.

"Rocky Balzano, that was it, Balzano! A very large man. Had worked as a meat packer his whole life in Philadelphia. Big fellow. Tall but also broad. Not in the shoulders, but like a barrel. The man had circumference!" I motioned in a large circle around my own non-existent belly. "He came to Russia because he was a big fan of some actor from Moscow, can't remember who now. How he would have known the actor, being a meat packer in Philly, I never could figure out. He really liked acting and films though. I guess everybody has a hobby, right? But he talked with all the Russians on the boat about him and they thought him the most cultured American they ever met. Anyhow, he sprained his knee in St. Petersburg on one of our first days of the entire trip, and so he did nothing really except sit on deck and in the bar drinking with the other Russians who didn't care to see the little Volga villages."

Irina chimed in, "Yes, I remember him too now. Very charming man. His stories were always so colorful and unbelievable, but he told them with such detail that they could not have been made up."

"That's him! Exactly!" I confirmed. "And when he had some drink in him, you couldn't get him to stop talking. So anyhow, on our last day in Moscow before everybody flew home, of course, we always ended with the tour of the Kremlin cathedrals. Well, Rocky wasn't going to miss this! He was in Russia and he was going to see the Kremlin, hurt knee or not! Only, the night before we had also had an older fellow in the group who thought he had had a heart attack after dinner. His wife was all worked up about it, but there was no way in hell that he was going to miss the Kremlin tour. He said to me, 'we've finally beat those damn Rooskies and I want them to see my face in the kremlin.' Something very belligerent like that. It was so personal to him.

"Anyhow, I was assigned to this fellow with the heart attack. We couldn't persuade him to rest that day so I was assigned to be his shadow for the day in case something happened. I wrote all the emergency numbers up my left arm of the US Embassy, the American and British medical clinics, etcetera." I pulled up my shirt sleeve and motioned like I was writing over my veins showing through my white underarm. "So, we're on Cathedral Square inside the Kremlin, just in front of the huge cannon and stack of cannon balls, and everybody is getting a lecture from the official tour guide about the height of the towers, the golden copulas, and the boring stuff that they all memorize in English. So, the tour guide invites us all to go into the cathedral now and I can't see anything in the shadows on the ground after staring at those white cathedral walls and the shining domes in the sunshine. I don't know where my charge has wandered off to and I panic a bit.

"Just then I heard somebody behind me give a yelp of pain and maybe stumble? So, I turn around but my eyes couldn't see anything yet. It takes me a second just standing there looking dumb while Rocky is falling over." I turned to the others at the table and asked, "Do you all remember his wife Alice? Skinny, frail woman? Well, there she was trying to hold up this huge man and looks like he is about to crush her as he is falling."

"How horrible!" gasped Yulia.

The others were just laughing.

"So, as soon as I could see again I jumped under his arm and sent Alice off to find some help from, well, you all," I said, motioning to my colleagues around the table, "who disappeared so quickly, to help me keep Rocky from falling over and hurting himself more. Well, Alice didn't come back. So, there I am with Rocky in the middle of cathedral square hugging while he is moaning and asking for help so sit down; says his other leg is just about to give out. Remember, very big fellow, early sixties. Not in very good shape to be hopscotching around Cathedral Square on one leg."

"Did he actually break his leg then?" Olga asked.

"No, he later had x-rays taken at the hospital. It wasn't broken. It was just his weight, the sprain, walking on cobblestone probably, but anyway he thought he had really damaged his leg and was in lots of pain!" I clarified.

I continued. "Rocky needs to sit down before he falls over and hits his head. So, were standing not far from the Kremlin Palace and there were two soldiers, two guards standing in front of the ceremonial entrance. It's all for show of course. I whistled to them and asked them to come help. They hesitated and wouldn't come. So, I whistled at them again and then yelled at them for help. POMOGIY, POMOGIY! They came running with their rifles on their shoulders. I told them that Rocky's knee was broken and we needed to call an ambulance. The soldiers each got under one of Rocky's arms and they just stood there. He was too big and heavy to carry. It was a great sight and I wish I had a picture of it, but I didn't think of it at the time. It was like a proud father with his Russian boys in honor guard uniforms." I was laughing as I recalled the details.

"You have to be making this up!" Yulia couldn't believe the story.

"Every word is true. Every word is true!" Nikolai confirmed the story. Yulia was flabbergasted and laughed in disbelief.

"But wait, it gets better! I ask the guards where I could find a telephone. Remember that we couldn't take our walkie-talkie radios into the Kremlin? We had to leave them on the coach so there was no way I could call our coach driver to meet us at the gates or something, and I needed to call an ambulance. So, one of the guards pointed out that the security office was just around a corner and there I could speak to the chief of Kremlin security. Instead of asking one of the soldiers to do it, I take off like lightning. The office was behind these tall wooden doors and I pull it open and find a startled guard sitting behind a metal detector, 'I need your chair, it's an emergency!' I commanded and walked right through the metal detector, grabbed his metal folding chair, and ran out the door. The metal detector, of course, is going off, alarm bells ringing because of the metal chair and all. Poor guy didn't even know what hit him." I was on a roll.

"This can't be real, in the Kremlin? And nobody is trying to stop you?" Yulia had her hand to her forehead. "Why do they even have guards there?"

"I know what you mean. When I look back on this I just think, I hope that their nuclear codes aren't stored in that place. It's so easy to manipulate the guards. I can't imagine they get many urgencies like this one. Everybody must be so well behaved that they don't expect this type of thing. So, Rocky is now sitting on a flimsy metal chair, but he is so big that he has to straddle the chair, you know, like on a horse, and he has his walking stick on one side to lean on while his injured leg has to be held straight. It looked so uncomfortable!

"I still needed to call an ambulance and so I run back to the security office. The guard this time was on the telephone in his office. I walked straight through the metal detector again, alarms go off again, and tell this fellow directly that I need to use the telephone to call an ambulance. He puts the handset down and steps back. I'm rolling up my left sleeve to read all the emergency numbers I wrote there that morning. I must have looked like some junkie rolling up his sleeve to find a vein." I was flicking my lower arm to accentuate the drugs allusion. Olga was laughing quite heavily at this.

"I called the American and the British medical clinics but because it was Sunday only the Brits would accept the patient, but he had to pay two hundred dollars cash on arrival. If we could be there before four o'clock they would treat him. Great! So, I ran out the door again back to Rocky and told him the details. And what do you think happened? He got angry! He started yelling about being blackmailed and exploited and completely refused to cooperate. He said even if he had the cash, which he didn't because it was all in travelers' checks, he wouldn't pay such scandalous ransoms!" I was hollering to imitate Rocky's anger.

Yulia gasped. "Where were the palace guards at this point?"

"They were standing there with Rocky smoking, just like on the boat, and he was just chatting the boys up. One of them, I guess, could speak a few words of English and Rocky was smoking with them telling them stories!" I couldn't help but get animated for the dramatic effect.

"No way! This is getting absurd!" Yulia was beyond laughter and was waiting to hear how this ended.

"So, I said to Rocky, 'Rocky, you will not like the alternative. Soviet hospitals are where people go to die, not get better!'"

Both Olga and Nikolai started clapping their hands in amusement and Olga inquired, "And where did a young

American boy learn that idiom about Soviet hospitals? It's so true!"

"I've been around the Soyuz," so as to say, I had traveled the Soviet Union, was my reply to Olga, and I continued with the story. "Rocky's reply was 'Damn the consequences, take me to a hospital of the people!' Somehow, he thought he had become one of the proletariat after eight days on the Volga. He must have drunk the river water. So off I went again to the security office. As I pulled open the big wooden doors I saw a different fellow standing there this time in a full-dress uniform, shiny boots, hat, ribbons. Must have been a war hero," I speculated.

"Peter, no! Don't tell me you did the same thing to this officer!" Yulia was truly scared for me now, a full year later.

"I simply said there was an emergency and I needed to use the telephone again. I was very polite, but he said very firmly to me, 'Nyet! That phone is for Kremlin security matters only!' Did I tell you all that it was a red telephone? Does that make you all just a bit more uneasy?" I asked poking the bear.

Nikolai was shaking his head in disbelief at my brazen reveling in what could have been a very unfortunate situation for an American in the kremlin.

I continued. "So, I get up in this guy's face and say, 'I understand that this the office of the Chief of Kremlin security. I demand to speak to him, RIGHT NOW!' and he replied just as heated back to me, 'I AM the chief of Kremlin security, and I said NO!' At that point, I did realize that maybe I had gone a bit too far and I got this horrible feeling in my chest and belly and my legs went a bit numb, and thought for a second that I might wet my pants if he made a move toward me. He looked very angry."

"So how did you get Rocky off of Cathedral Square?" Yulia thought the story was over.

"Oh, the ambulance came right into the Kremlin!" Olga confirmed again.

"But how?" Yulia pleaded.

"I don't really know why I did it, but I didn't back down. I just started yelling at him louder and louder about how heavy and big Rocky was and that moving him without an ambulance would be dangerous for his leg. The Chief of Security told me I was out of luck and that no ambulance would be allowed into the Kremlin compound for security reasons. It was not permitted. No way! So, now I was really worked up and I told the Chief to follow me outside by using my finger, like this." I motioned with my index finger to show the group how condescending such a movement could look to an authority figure.

"Horrible!" huffed Yulia. "In Russia that is almost a vulgar gesture!"

"I know, I know! I've learned since not to use it. I guess I hadn't been around too much, eh, Olga? I still have some things to learn," I confessed.

"Didn't he arrest you?" Yulia was hoping I had been thoroughly punished for insubordination.

"I can imagine he wanted to, but he followed me outside and was yelling something at me, but I think the adrenaline in my blood was too much to understand him at this point. So, we rounded the corner that opened up onto Cathedral Square and I stopped and pointed to Rocky so the chief could take in the size of the man. Even from that distance, it was clear to see how large this man was. Now, by this time, you all—" and I motioned around the table again to my colleagues, "—had come out of the cathedrals and had gathered around Rocky on this little chair and there was a lot of flurry. The guards were still mixed with the group taking pictures at attention with their rifles and just having a grand old time with the tourists. Remember that these guards had bayonets and everything on their rifles, and one of the soldiers was pointing his rifle right at somebody's camera for a great souvenir photo. I just hope the guns weren't loaded!" I said, feigning caution.

"Crazy, crazy, crazy! Was everybody out of their minds?" Yulia was speechless.

"So, I was standing with the chief of Kremlin security taking in the three-ring circus happening in the middle of Cathedral Square. I kept pointing with an outstretched arm while I looked at him. His eyes were getting larger and larger and his face redder and redder; he was gritting his teeth and seething with anger! Then I said to him, right or not I said it: 'You see how large he is? He is a Russian bear! You can move him yourself, but I am going to go call an ambulance!' I started back toward the security office and the telephone. And what happened? He turned on his shiny boots and caught up to me and said, '...and I will authorize it.' So, he called for the ambulance in the end and we shook hands. I returned to the group on the Square to wait for a city ambulance."

"Incredible! Why aren't you in jail?" Olga questioned. "If I had done something like that being Russian, they would have put me in Lyubyanka and then off to Siberia with me! You just can't do that inside the Kremlin. To get our tour guide license we had a whole security training course and were told that there were strict consequences for stepping out of line while leading a tour."

"And they let me back into the country too!" I said, holding out my arms like a circus performer who just finished a death defying stunt with a hungry tiger, with a toothy grin on my face.

"Bozhe moy! (My God!)" Olga muttered. "You are crazy!"

"After all that though, Rocky realized he had made a mistake when we got to the hospital there in central Moscow, and he didn't talk back to me again and just listened to me like a lap dog." I was winding down the story. "It was also my first time in a Russian hospital and it was traumatic for him, his wife, and for me. What I remember most was seeing an old man on a gurney, you know a roller table. He must have been hit by a car, or fallen down a long staircase. His face was battered and he was bleeding from his head. His leg was turned in a very unnatural position, his ankle was turned in the opposite direction of his leg etcetera..."

Yulia gasped and cringed and Irina, who had taken in the whole story at the Kremlin with an entertained smile of amusement also looked a bit saddened to hear of this.

"...and everybody was ignoring the man!" I still felt traumatized by the sight. "All he wanted was a pillow for his head and he kept muttering it to everybody who passed him in the hallway. So, I finally got him one without asking. When we were done with Rocky's x-rays and all the old man was gone. I figured out later that they had given him morphine and were just waiting for him to die. He was so badly injured and so old that I am pretty sure they just gave up on him; triage had given up hope and they took Rocky first, but they had left him there in the hallway with no dignity, no care, no comfort. It was a very traumatic experience. I was completely wasted when we finally got back to the ship at the River Station that evening."

"How did you get Rocky back to the boat?" Irina asked me in English.

"We paid the ambulance driver twenty dollars to take the three of us," I stated without irony.

"Unbelievable what people will do for a few dollars these days. Using a city ambulance to make some extra money." Irina turned her head and made a quick, mock spitting action with her pursed lips, a gesture of disgust.

Matvei chimed in to tell his own adventure from last summer. "Do you remember, Peter, when we lost that one lady with the funny eye and the funny hair when we were at the Sparrow Hills with the group? One minute she was there and the next she was gone. I remember you handing me dollar bills between the seats for the taxi driver as we went from place to place looking for her.

Do you remember that eventually we found her at McDonald's on Pushkin Square?"

"Yes, I remember that. Very scary moment!" I replied.

"How did she get from the Sparrow Hills to Pushkin Square?" Olga asked, unaware of this event.

"On the metro." Matvei grinned. "Somebody helped her take the metro and dropped her off at McDonald's on Pushkin Square because she thought the group would be going to McDonald's that afternoon. Problem was, it was the other McDonald's we visited on Tverskaya Street, not Pushkin Square. But we found her and brought her back to the boat before dinner."

"She was so shaken up that she didn't want to leave the boat again. She said that some hooligans tried to mug her at Sparrow Hills and she ran away and then couldn't find her way back. Somebody helped her buy a metro ticket and delivered her to 'the other American embassy' was my addition to the story.

Everybody laughed at the thought of the US Embassy being a McDonald's. Nikolai toasted the irony with another hundred grams of Vodka. I raised my shot of Pepsi and downed it one gulp with him.

"Do you remember that foolish woman who threw her open suitcase at the customs officer at Sheremetyevo airport during their departure inspection?" Olga put her hand over her eyes and shook her head in disbelief. "It took me ninety minutes to get her out of custody and onto her airplane! You Americans just don't understand that in Russia, you are nobody special and you just can't do this to officers and soldiers! Who is going to tell them that this year?"

"And the guy who kept his passport in his sock!? I kept finding it on the upper deck of the ship and gave it back to him three or four times!" Matvei added as he joined in our chorus of disbelief.

It was so good to be among old friends. It felt like we had been members of an elite espionage squad getting back together to remember good old times and drink our troubles away. We had worked through so many crises together the last summer that we trusted each other with life and limb, literally. I felt sad that I wouldn't be working with them again and wished I could drop my studies and work and sail the river with them one more time. What a wonderful summer that had been! So much experience. So much learned.

As the afternoon came to a chilly close, as it was still only mid-April, Yulia and I gathered up our things and headed for the gang plank. Irina had invited us again to join a cruise during the summer holidays. We could earn our room and board by translating and telling great stories to the new batch of tourists about to arrive from the USA. We were very enthusiastic about the invitation and agreed to come on board in mid-July when the boat would be docked at Nizhniy's River Station overnight for a crew rotation. It was a great thought to have that opportunity waiting after school was out for the summer. We waved goodbye and the ladies gave each other kisses and Yulia and I headed down the gang plank to terra firma, turned again into the setting sun and waved again to our friends, then scurried up the embankment stairs to the street and the bus stop. It had been a wonderful, sunny afternoon aboard the Zhukov.

16. Misha

I had received instructions from Del to phone Mikhail, or Misha, as his friends and comrades called him, to set up a work schedule with the young project manager for Del's business activities in Nizhniy Novgorod. Was this a private enterprise on the side that Del was putting together, or was it integral to the success of the hotel project? I wasn't quite sure of either answer, nor was I completely sure of the questions. I was hoping a meeting with Misha would help to clear up some of the questions. I had resolved to phone him on Saturday morning but found all the public telephones to be out of service at the metro station, so I waited until later in the afternoon in hopes of finding them operational again. They were.

After some struggle to dial the right number, the crank damaged by overuse and vandalism, I heard the line buzz, crack, and finally settle into the normal clicks and beeps before finding the right telephone line. Then the scratchy, wobbly ringing tone of an open line repeated over and over in the ear piece, for what seemed like two or three minutes before the telephone was answered.

"Halloah?" a groggy man's voice demanded an answer.

"Good day. My name is Pyotr," I used the Russian pronunciation of my name to avoid the constant question of WHO? WHO? WHO? when people didn't understand the English pronunciation of my name.

"Who are you calling?" Again very gruff and hostile. I must have woken him with the telephone call.

"Is this the number of Mikhail Porashevsvkiy?" I asked with doubt in my question.

"Who are you?"

"My name is Pyotr. Do you know Del?" I asked skeptically.

"No names please," the voice commanded.

"We are supposed to meet today," I stated timidly.

"Yes, why so late?" the voice grumbled.

"Where and when can I meet you?" I asked with a bit of relief that I'd reached the right person.

"Do you know Kulibin Park on Byelinskovo Street?" he demanded to know.

"No," I admitted my ignorance.

"Find it. Meet me at the little white church in the park at four o'clock," he demanded.

Without waiting for an agreement or a question from me the line went dead. I looked curiously at the hand set, looking to see if my ears had deceived me. I put it again to my ear to double check that he had really hung up. "Halloah? Misha?" Nobody was there.

It was already two o'clock so after buying a handful of piroshki from the old lady selling food in the dark metro tunnel I bounded up the stairs to the daylight, and crossed Prospect Lenina just in time to catch the autobus, a long articulated, yellow stinky diesel engine bus. As it climbed the switchbacks of the bluff it felt like the bus would come apart, like an over-stretched accordion before we made it up the hill into the old town. As the bus crested the peak and emerged onto Lyadova Square on its way toward Gorkiy Square, I spotted the street name Byelinksovo and moved quickly to the exit, tapping people on the shoulder and asking, "Are you getting off?" With every question, the other passengers would turn their shoulders and let me pass until I was standing directly in front of the doors. I exited at the next stop and started trekking up Byelinskovo Street.

I came quickly to a park on the right side and crossed the road, dodging the passing street car. Walking along the pavement of the street I was peering into the park looking for a little white Orthodox chapel. As the spring foliage had yet to fill in I could see through the entire park and saw nothing that even closely resembled a small white church. The park was filled with lines of birch trees, a children's playground, a café, and restaurant, but no white chapel. As I passed the main entrance to the park, I found a map of the grounds and discovered that this park was not Park Kulibin, but Park Pushkin. I scratched my head and looked about.

"Excuse me, please?" I turned and addressed an older woman leaving the park. "Can you tell me please where Park Kulibin is?"

"Further that way on the other side of the street." She was motioning further up the street in the direction I had already been walking.

"And do you know if there is a little white church in that park?" I queried.

"Yes! Two of them!" She put her head down and trudged on, towing her small dog behind her on a leash.

After fifteen minutes more, I came to what turned out to be to Park Kulibin. To my relief, both white churches were visible through the naked birch groves as their spires poked above the tree lines. It was rather obvious which was the smaller one.

I had still an hour to wait. I found a small café in the middle of the park and waited. As I sat and nursed a wretched, over-bitter mug of cacao, I couldn't imagine why there had to be so much melodrama around meeting Misha. What an odd character he was. His demeanor and commands on the telephone reminded me of Yulia's paranoid attitude toward talking on the telephone. I thought back to Olya's revelation that the telephones were all bugged and everybody was still listened to by the secret police. It was no wonder that nobody wanted to speak more than needed over the telephone, but certainly people could be more polite about it!

At four o'clock sharp, Misha appeared from the woods in front of the chapel and approached me directly. "Are you Pytor?"

Without answering his question directly, I asked back, "Are you Misha?"

With my question, he thrust his hand forward to shake hands with me. "Come, let's walk this way." He led me deeper into the park away from the encircling streets.

Mikhail, or Misha, was a nondescript man of average height, average weight, dark hair and dark eyes with a light beard and was in his late twenties or early thirties. He dressed in gray. He would match any police description except that of a tall bald mafia enforcer with gold teeth. He wore wire rimmed spectacles. He wasn't bold, but neither was he a mouse of a man. He walked with purpose.

"Why all the cloak and dagger?" I asked him with a bit of relief in my voice.

"Del's business is always under investigation from one police or tax inspector or another. I never discuss on the telephone about where I am or will be. This is to keep Del's paperwork and records safe. Otherwise, the next thing you know the place has been burgled. It's happened twice since I started working for Del only one year ago," Misha explained.

"What are the investigations for?" I queried.

"Jealousy, espionage, trying to steal his information in order to steal the business plans. So, when you call me, we will always meet in a new place to discuss our assignments, but never in my home or my office. We've had so many setbacks in one year that we can't take any risks," he apologized.

"What about Del's place? He doesn't seem too concerned," I pointed out.

"No, that's because that is his official home and those working in the shadows would never risk attacking his home because he is in the good circle with the mayor, you know? To be that brazen would mean that Del would have reason to close up shop and leave, which nobody wants because of the foreign investment he represents. The word is out that nobody can touch Del in his home. They try backhanded ways that don't look overtly suspicious." Misha talked as quickly as he walked.

"Why not just keep everything in Del's apartment?" I thought I was asking an obvious question.

"That's like leaving honey for the bear! It's too tempting. Sooner or later when there is a frustration, somebody will go take everything and bump off Del, literally or figuratively, so we keep things moving around so Del can't be forced out of the project." Misha seemed to know what he was up against.

We walked further into the park and eventually right out the other side. We crossed Gorkiy Street and straight down Osharskaya Street. I was following Misha thinking that we were heading to his office or apartment for a briefing and to give me a list of apartments to visit and view.

"I am supposed to be inspecting apartments that Del is going to rent. Are there already any apartments to visit?" I asked my guide.

"Yes, we have had seven people interested to rent or sell their apartments to us, but because we aren't sure of the ownership of the apartments at this point, we will only visit those for rent. If in the end we get thrown out of these places by the rightful or new owners, then we haven't lost any real money. Do you understand?" It seemed Misha had thought the whole thing through and was ready for any contingency.

"Yes, of course. Seems wise to me," I stammered, trying not to seem to clueless.

"Do you have time right now to go and view the apartments?" he asked me abruptly.

"Sure, but don't we have to make an appointment?" I said, trying to stall due to my unsettled nerves.

"No, these people are so eager to rent the places we could arrive at ten o'clock tonight and they would serve us tea and take us on a grand tour," Misha said with some arrogance.

"I have no further appointments tonight, so let's go," I said, trying to muster up my courage.

"Very good, then. We're there!" Misha stopped walking and pointed upwards.

I stopped and looked around me to see a small park on our right, boxed in on three sides by a mix of squat three story buildings from the turn of the century in bold colors in a folk architecture style. On the left was a well-kept apartment building from the 1960s with some interesting modern architectural elements. The standard block apartment buildings were nowhere to be seen. These apartments were obviously built for the intelligentsia of the city, not the working class. With the offices of the Atomic Energy Project around the corner on Svoboda Square, it was obvious that these apartments were a grade above what I was living in, meant for people a grade higher than who I was living with. It was a constant surprise to me to find these types of hidden, pleasant squares and nooks in the city. Here is where the city's middle class lived. I could imagine nuclear engineers and professors wandering around the memorial gardens dreaming about solutions to complex equations and reactions, and reading Tolstoy and Pasternak on weekends in the shade while enjoying a smoke from a pipe with a cravat around their throats.

Before we entered the five-story red and white brick building, Misha stopped me to give me some instructions.

"It would be very wise if you didn't say anything while we are viewing the apartments. Just take mental notes, write some things down if you want to. I don't know how people might respond to a foreigner asking questions." His face was cold and serious.

"OK, I will just smile and be polite." I nodded and pinched my lips closed with my thumb and index finger.

"Very good!" He was happy to be obeyed.

We rode the lift to the fifth and top floor in a narrow cabin lined with wood, a wrought iron grate protecting us from falling out as we passed upwards through each floor of thick concrete slabs and rebar. The cabin jolted to a halt on the fifth floor and Misha threw open the grating for us to step out onto the landing, a door on either side of us: numbers 51 and 52. On most floors of a workers' building there could be four or six different doors with small two room apartments behind each door. Standing on the landing these apartments promised to be large and spacious. Misha rang the bell at number 52.

Misha whispered to me as we waited for the door to open. "Del wants all the apartments to be at least five floors up, for security. We'll have to put steel doors on these as well, for security."

I nodded saying nothing, looking at the floor.

When the door opened we were met by a well-dressed older woman in her early sixties who obviously had been very attractive in her youth. She was in no way brash and trendy, but it was obvious from the way she carried herself and spoke that she had been well educated and well-heeled for her whole life, yet lacking the arrogance of the nouveau riche in Russia. The apartment was also well appointed, but dated. The furniture was obviously 1970s Russia and the television and other fixtures showed that little renovation had been done, but was in surprisingly good repair. The living room was as I had expected, spacious with lots of light. The kitchen was also well equipped with a large refrigerator, a full oven and cooking range, standard cabinets for a Russian home, but again kept very clean and crumb free. The floors were a mix of hardwood and tiles with the bathroom tiled in stylish art-deco mosaics in black and white. Very avant-garde! It was a dashing apartment with a view onto the tree-filled park below in the square with a pleasant view of the more traditional buildings surrounding the park.

To my surprise, this very proper woman, without seeing any credentials or asking for any identification, let us into her home to look around and ask all sorts of questions. She went so far as to tell us that her husband, who had been an engineer in the town, had died a few months earlier and that she was going to stay with her daughter in Samara. She planned to be away for a year as she was expecting her first grandchild, a girl, and needed to make an agreement quickly about renting the apartment. Misha left some paperwork for her to fill in and promised to call her after the weekend to let her know if 'our agency' would work to fill her apartment. We left with polite greetings. Once we were on the street walking toward Gorkiy Street, and out of earshot of any potential clients, I turned and questioned Misha.

"Misha, I don't understand any of this. I have to speak honestly! This woman doesn't know you or me from Ivan the Terrible, and she just lets us into her apartment without any assurance that we are who we say we are. We could have robbed her blind! We could have tied her up and carried her away after dark and just taken over her apartment. My friends tell me not to talk to anybody, not to let anybody I don't know into my apartment, and you won't even talk to me on the telephone, but yet we just walk right into a fancy apartment? Please explain this to me." I huffed in frustration.

"It's easy. Russians trust Russians," Misha said in a flippant expression.

"I'm sorry, can you please repeat that?" I said in disbelief.

"Russians .... trust ... Russians. Pyotr. If a Russian gives a billion rubles cash, in small notes, to a friend to guard for him while he goes on holiday to Cuba or Cyprus for three years, even if that friend loses his job, is evicted from his home and is starving in the streets, he would not touch his friend's money. Never! Friendship and trust between Russians are holy! You see, when somebody is from the government we do not trust the person because the government is only out to steal from the people. If you know that, you don't have to guess, and that person will never deceive you. They will walk in and tell you they are taking all your money and putting your grandmother in a hard labor camp. So, you stay away from that person and don't let them get into your business," he explained with surety.

"What about the Russian mafia? Isn't that Russians hurting Russians?" I challenged.

"Yes, but it's the same situation as with the government. They walk in with brass knuckles and knives, and you know exactly who you are dealing with. They don't hide themselves, you see them everywhere, and everybody knows who they are and what they do," he sketched without subtlety.

"What about the secret police, the KGB or FSB?" I continued to push.

"This is why we don't speak on the telephone, because we don't know who they are. But when a Russian looks into another Russian's eyes, they don't lie to each other. We don't deceive each other. Others don't get the same treatment. A Russian dealing with a foreigner is a dangerous and shadowy relationship. You will most likely never hear the truth from a Russian, you being a foreigner, unless you first become good friends," he said seriously.

"So that is why you asked me not to speak while we were visiting these apartments," I concluded.

"Yes, one word with your accent and the deal is over. It won't go any further because when a Russian gives his word to another Russian...well, Russians trust Russians," he said, again accepting this simple axiom.

"So, foreigners are not trusted in Russia?" I asked in a hurt tone.

"Always very suspect. Why are you and Del in Russia? Simply to get rich and then you will leave," he accused.

"Woah, hold on there. Please don't group me with the rest!" I stipulated.

"Why shouldn't I? Americans are always the first to come when they can make some money and the first to leave when things go wrong. The Brits follow right behind you. You cannot handle any moral ambiguity, and sacrifice is only good to a point until it hurts too much, then you run away, even if your cause is just," he said insultingly.

"You sure to do lay it on thick for a first date, my friend," I said with an uncomfortable laugh and a frustrated sigh.

"Do you know Stalingrad?" Misha asked quickly.

"Volgograd, yes I was there last summer," I replied.

"No, the battle of Stalingrad. Study that battle with the fascists and you will understand what it means to be Russian. Russians know what it means to suffer and sacrifice. They won't stop until they've won. They will throw their men, women, children and old men and old women at the enemy instead of surrendering their country to foreigners. They promised to protect their country, and with their backs to the Volga, they didn't let the Nazis cross. We all know we can trust Russians from Volgograd because their grandparents, every single one of their grandparents fought to beat the Germans, and we know that they have been taught to love Russia," he said proudly. "Do you know why a Russian woman who is beaten by her husband never leaves him?" Misha was treading on thin ice now with me. I didn't answer but gave him a very annoyed look.

"Because she's Russian," he said with no shame.

"Well, we Americans stuck it out to whoop your butts in the cold war," I said brazenly.

"Hah, nobody ever beats Russia. The Soviet Union lost to the United States, not Russia. Russia is still alive and will come right back now that the foreign leaders in Moscow are gone!" he said with some disgust in his voice.

"So why do you trust Del, a foreigner?" I challenged his hypocrisy.

"Trust? Who said I trust him? I work for him and I keep his business safe. He pays me. When he stops paying me, I won't protect his business any longer," he said with an emotional dryness that was believable.

"And what do you do precisely to protect Del?" I asked further.

"I keep the government from stealing from him," he said as we walked further.

"And you don't trust the government either," I concluded.

"Never will. Not until it stops stealing from its own people," he ruled.

"You are a bundle of contradictions, Misha, just like Russia herself. It's good to know you." I laughed aloud in disbelief.

"Please call me next Saturday morning and we will visit three more apartments," he said and held out his hand to shake mine.

"Where should I meet you?" I asked him, waiting to hear his wild instructions.

"I will tell you on Saturday morning."

06

17. Mr. P.

I stood opposite No. 11 on the Upper Embankment Street taking in the view of the flooded river below when I heard the resurrected church bells below chime eleven o'clock. With the chimes, I woke from my sun worship, cleared the blue and purple blotches from my vision, and turned to look at the three-story 19th-century mansion villa behind me. The house was in the design of perfect neo classical symmetry in its architecture and looked to be right out of St. Petersburg. The exterior was stripped of all color, only a mono-brown sandstone, speckled with plaster and dried concrete that greeted the passers-by. The gardens were surrounded by an old whitewashed stone wall. There was no view of the gardens at street level, but one could see the handsome grove of birch trees standing taller than the walls that shaded the house from the morning's searching sunlight. Except for the scaffolds and building materials visible on the porch a half story above the street, pedestrians would be forgiven for assuming that the house stood vacant and abandoned, a relic of the exterminated bourgeoisie, but the same would be mistaken. This was the new residence of Igor Ivanovich P. and it was being restored from the inside out at breakneck speed.

Dean Karamzin had been successful to entice his old friend into an interview with a foreign academic, but not without a carrot for Mr. P. It was intimated, without so many words by the dean, that the product of the research and the interview would be read by the governor, who would accept is as a policy recommendation concerning the future of entrepreneurial activities in the province. It was implied that Mr. P., by means of this independent academic research, could help to subtly influence public policy without creating any impression of impropriety between his business activities and the offices of the governor. I suppose the dean wasn't lying, but like the forked-tongue beast of old who ruined Eve's paradise, he spoke a deceiving truth.

It all seemed too easy for me to walk into the home of a mobster and ask him searching questions about his 'biznis' activities in the climate of the day. I began to be suspicious of the dean's motives. I hadn't heard the telephone call between the two; maybe I was being deceived in the same way as I thought Mr. P. was being deceived.

Els' words of warning rang in my ear as I stood on the pavement looking at this riverside mansion and debated walking away. Why would he agree to this so easily? Perhaps he felt his local notoriety made him untouchable. Maybe he was in his breakthrough phase from the shadows into the public eye, into government and immortality, and the more legitimate press he could get would only help him. Maybe I was too late and my interest in writing about him would only help his long-term goals. The doubts in my head swirled around as I stepped forward. The door was flush with the pavement at street level next to a driveway gated by two tall steel plates blocking any view of the curious pedestrian. I rang the bell half expecting a trapdoor to open up underneath me, dropping me into a basement dungeon where the bones of the local prosecutor were still chained to the wall. Instead, a loud buzzing came from the door frame signaling me to push it open and walk through as a welcome guest.

The street level floor of the house was dedicated to screening visitors and giving access to the driveway to the right of the house. Upon entering through the heavy, decorated steel door I came immediately into a brightly lit holding cell. As the heavy door closed with a clang behind me, I was startled and tried to open it again. It was held closed by electro-magnets and released from only behind the bars in front of me, where an older fellow in a proper security guard uniform was waiting for me. There were no bodyguards in Armani suits waiting to strip search me and beat me with rubber hoses. There was just a guard behind a barred window and another steel door.

After a brief explanation for my visit, a quick search of my book bag and a glance at my passport and student card, I was let through. On passing the inner barrier the guard asked me to stand still and ran a metal detector wand around me, between my legs, up the crotch of my pants, my ankles, under my arms, and around my back and belt. With nothing threatening found he wished me a good day and showed me to the staircase which led to the second floor. He sent me on my way without a further escort then returned to his chair and camera monitors over the sidewalk and curbs in front of the house and paid me no further attention as I ascended into the house.

Up the short staircase and through a swinging door I came to stand in front of a full-length glass window to my left, which looked out over a commanding view of the river and the countryside. I wondered to myself how the view looked from the third floor. On emerging from the dark ground-floor I was met by a very attractive woman with long legs and long black hair. She was dressed professionally without any gaudiness in a formal business suit with a fitted jacket and skirt. She informed me that she was the personal secretary of Mr. P., that I was expected but would have to wait maybe ten minutes for my host to finish his current telephone call. She offered me a glass of champagne while I waited but I politely refused. She offered me a chair to wait in and asked me not to smoke. I took a seat and glanced out the long window to take in the view of the river again, but felt my head turn to glimpse the other captivating view of the secretary walking back to her desk in the corner or the reception area. Russia's beauty in the spring time is certainly worth the wait!

The floors were a beautifully polished, newly inlaid birch wood in a very intricate traditional Russian pattern like one would see in a royal palace's ballroom. I felt as if I should have taken off my shoes and skated on the floor in my socks so as not to scuff it. I wondered how the secretary walked on it in high heels without gouging the floor with little pock marks. The interior was tastefully decorated with classical upholstered furniture in a tasteful Imperial style of the 18th century. The walls were painted a light yellow with moldings and door frames were painted in a stark plaster white. The columns on the porch outside cast long diagonal shadows across the floor and the furniture.

After perhaps fifteen minutes of waiting nervously, trying to look calm and collected, the secretary approached my chair in long graceful strides and asked if I would follow her to Mr. P's office. We ascended another staircase, but this time we swept upwards, instead of climbing, to the third floor over plush, red embroidered carpets pinned to white marble steps with brass bars at the base of each step up. The house was appointed inside like a miniature palace with no details spared to replicate the grandeur of what it once was. To my right over the railing now at eye level hung a crystal chandelier which cast faint, dispersed prisms on the yellow wall on my left as I followed the Cossack beauty up the staircase to the third floor. How did she walk on this thick rug in those heels without even wobbling? She must have gone to finishing school to learn that trick!

My mind seemed to be on anything but the interview that was about to start. I had to push out all the distractions of the environment and focus. I stopped watching the skirt and legs in front of me to get my thoughts together and watched my own dusty shoes shuffle over the shallow upward steps. I felt at once very underdressed seeing the frayed hem of my blue jeans, although they were clean, sort of. At least I was wearing a jacket with a clean shirt under it. What else was a poor student supposed to wear?

We had arrived. As I entered the palatial office on the third floor, Mr. P. rose from behind his large dark wooden desk and walked toward me with his stocky gate, his right hand extended to greet me in a very professional and warm way. As we shook hands he clasped his left hand on to my left shoulder, welcomed me to his home and invited me to sit down on a firm leather couch, one that might be found in the den of a British country gentleman. It was very comfortable. I set my book bag down, leaned up against the end of the couch. Notes would be taken later. His secretary who had been waiting at the door offered to serve drinks.

The floor in this office space was the same intricate, polished inlaid wood as downstairs and undoubtedly was the same in each room. The study was in the same classical style but the walls a dark gray with white highlights. A decorative column flanked both sides of the entrance to his open office. The window behind his desk looked south into the garden and the handsome grove of birch trees that grew there. A garden house could be seen but no garden furniture had yet been set out on account of the weather just having turned warm enough to do so.

Mr. P. was dressed in suit pants and a dress shirt but was not wearing a necktie. With his bright white collar open against his shaven bald head he was the epitome of sterile. His shoes, obviously not Russian, gleamed in the lamp light of the office. He sat opposite me on a matching couch with a glass-top coffee table between us whereon my water and his coffee sat slowing steaming.

"So, you are Mr. Peter Turner. We have met before, right?" he started. My heart stopped, remembering the night in his restaurant on Valentine's Day. I knew I couldn't just not answer him.

"Yes, we have. A few weeks ago, at The Monastery during the student event," I reminded him.

"Ah yes, Marina's American friend, but you did not stay too late, no?" he said, chiding me.

"I can only apologize for my colleague who misbehaved and was asked to leave," I said, trying to defuse the memory.

"He was drunk?" he asked in an accusatory tone.

"Who wasn't that night?" I replied with no guilt on my conscience.

"Yes, so was I, so was I!" he admitted.

"It was a great party and we had a fun time. Thanks for that," I said, telling a huge white lie.

"It was nothing. It gives me pleasure to give students some fun," Mr. P. said with fake humility.

"Well, I believe you succeeded," I said ironically.

"We have not met before in The Monastery?" he asked again, looking sideways at me.

"We had not been introduced before that night. Believe me, I would have remembered!" I said with a friendly smile, but inside I was ready to run for the door.

"So, you came to Russia to study the Russian language?" Mr. P. asked politely as he relaxed.

"Yes, in part, but also history and politics," I confirmed.

"In Russia, our history is politics. Who knows what the official political history is today? You must be careful about which history you read and write this year. Today maybe it's okay, but next year you might be deported to America again if they don't like your history and politics," he warned me, sitting up on the edge of his sofa.

"That is why I choose to mostly study the most recent history since 1992. When history is too new it is difficult to change it. When nobody remembers it any longer, or all who lived through it are dead, then it becomes easy to make it political," I parried his short lecture with a counter move.

"You speak very good Russian, Mr. Turner. Where do your people come from?" he asked.

"I have no Russian blood, if that is what you are asking," I replied vaguely.

"I thought maybe your parents were Jews from Russia twenty, thirty years ago when they left in the 1970s, maybe from Ukraine. You have a Ukrainian accent," he said, looking sideways at me.

"I spent some time there before I came to Nizhniy. I am told I have a Nizhniy accent as well when I speak to people from Moscow," I tried to push the discussion away from me.

"Da nyet, you sound like an American with a Ukrainian accent. Very unusual," he said and looked away.

"And where do your people come from?" I returned the interest in his genealogy.

"My grandparents are from the Volga village of Plyos. They were farmers on a kolkhoz. So I am more Russian than Mikhail Gorbachev and Boris Yeltsin combined. Real Russians come from the Volga," he said haughtily.

"As Dean Karamzin maybe explained to you, I am writing an academic paper about the current changes in the economic system and about the policy challenges to help the development of private business," I changed the subject.

"Yes, he explained this to me," he said somewhat disinterested in the intellectual.

"Will it be a problem if I ask you many, many questions about how you started your business activities, how you have grown them to what they are today, and what plans you have for the future?" I asked like a doctor examining a wounded pedestrian.

"Yes of course," he said with an arrogant manner, as if relishing being asked questions about himself.

"OK, thank you. But if there is anything I ask about that you cannot answer because it's confidential, I understand, so just tell me honestly if you cannot or do not want to answer a question. That will be no problem. I am just trying to gather as much data as possible, not trying to be intrusive," I said, hoping to convince him as I knew full well what I was up to.

"It won't be a problem. C'mon let's get started." Mr. P settled into his couch as if he was about to watch his favorite movie on the television. It looked like he was going to enjoy this.

"Can you describe your first entrepreneurial activities, and do you remember in which year these already started?" I asked him.

"It was 1986 when I started selling replacement and repair parts for the Volga sedans that are built here in Nizhniy Novgorod. Do you know those cars?" he asked me as he answered.

"Yes, my apartment is not far from the factory," I said, dismissing the point.

"I would deliver auto parts to the garages of the taxi companies. I kept the parts in my father's dacha and garden shed in the Avtozovodski district near the factory. I went to the mechanics and gave them my phone number. When they needed a part, they would call me. If I had it on hand I promised delivery within one hour anywhere in Nizhniy Novgorod," he said proudly, defying anybody else listening to do it better.

"So, you used Gorbachev's initiative Perestroika to start a business when you were in your late twenties," I helped to fill in the historical details.

"Correct. All of a sudden it was no longer a criminal act to make a profit for oneself. And because the factory only delivered parts on their own schedule, if at all, the mechanics couldn't wait any longer as the drivers were losing money by not making profits for themselves. Therefore, anybody who could provide the parts faster than the factory got the order. I had to make sure I had the most usual parts in my shed. There were always those that broke fastest or maybe were poorly made from the factory that had to be replaced faster than others," he explained.

"How did you get the parts?" I queried.

"I could buy them directly from the factory for cash but had to pick them up myself at night after closing, so I used my father's car once a week to load up the trunk and the seats and drive to our dacha and make the inventory." He painted a shady picture.

"Sounds very clever!" I swallowed my true reaction to sound harmless.

"It was effective and it was growing quickly as more people were driving their own cars as taxis. I had to find Lada parts and Chaika parts. Soon I bought GAZ truck parts for the delivery companies. Of course, I had to get a larger storage building. So, we rented a used warehouse for cash behind Prospect Lenina that wasn't being used, from a director of a parts maker for airplanes, and we grew and grew and grew," he said, spreading his arms wider and wider apart.

"What year was that?" I asked.

"Oh, that was right after Chernobyl, so it was... 1988," he counted years in the air.

"What kind of profits were you making? Was it just small margins and volume?" I asked clinically.

"We were charging big prices for quick delivery and what we called an 'inventory charge' on top of the official cost of the parts," he said, smiling.

"Were you wholesaling the parts for a discount?" I pushed for more details.

"We can say that I wasn't paying the full price for my parts. You must understand, it was a confusing time. Nobody understood how to price their materials and costs into a sale price. Factories were all producing at losses, but remember it was the volume of production that mattered in the old system, not the profits. Profit was a dirty word for the industrial managers. The quota was the goal. It was for quotas that they were rewarded. If they produced and could prove it—holiday on the Black Sea for the managers. What happened to the cars and parts after that wasn't important to anybody at the factory," he explained, justifying himself.

"Has that changed now, nine years later?" I asked not actually knowing the answer.

"Yes, as soon as the word 'privatniy' became known even those factory managers understood how to make profits. They made profits for themselves and not for their factories, but yes everybody understands it now. The difference between those who can and cannot make profits has to do with their position. Many people went out to find a position or a different job to make profits," he explained with a unique inside understanding.

"How did the business model change with the political environment?" I asked again like a scientist.

"When the director at GAZ figured out what we were doing with his car parts, he closed the gates and thought he could do it better than us. He tried, but it didn't work because he didn't have the market. We did." He was bragging now.

"What did you do then?" I egged him on.

"We started importing cars in 1990 from Germany. After the Berlin Wall, we could import Mercedes, BMWs, Opels, and Volkswagens. So instead of the car parts, we would sell the whole car to the young people driving taxis and to new businessmen in Russia," he said, reminiscing a bit.

"Do you speak German?" I asked, expecting him to answer in the negative.

"Yes, I had to study it in school, and my father lived in East Germany for many years and we would speak German at home—when nobody was listening of course. Nobody here likes Germans. He was an engineer so he helped me understand the difficult words and I sounded like I knew what I was talking about with those gypsies from Germany," he said, insulting the Turks in Germany.

"Sounds very clever!" I was starting to feel uneasy and tried to hide it by being agreeable.

"We even bought broken cars from Western Germany for parts. We would import broken cars and take them apart in our garage and make inventories. We started being specialists in German cars for all over Russia, not just in Nizhniy. Eventually, we were able to get our parts back from GAZ as they couldn't get our customers to order from them and so we did both," he added.

"Was it difficult to import in 1990 and 1991 before the Soviet Union was dissolved?" I was doing my best to sound academic and harmless by not asking deep questions about his operations.

"No, not really. If we came from Germany through Finland with our trucks with cars on them, we didn't have much trouble. In the Soviet years, we had to pay the borders guard with cigarettes and the colonel with a BMW so they wouldn't make problems for us. You see, they were in the wrong positions to make profits, and so they had to do what they had to do to get by, and we had to look after them. Remember that the stores were empty then. Even though the military had their own special stores for purchasing meat and vodka, the distribution system was terrible and they too would go many days without anything but cigarettes and tea at the border stations. The more cigarettes they could smoke the less they felt the hunger. We were importing with the right permissions, but they still had the guns. We had to do something to help the guards follow the law," he said without any apology.

"How is that today? Is it easier to import or more difficult?" I asked the best I could without prejudice.

"Relationships make all the difference. Like I already said, we looked after the border guards. A colonel only changes every three years. So even when the Union dissolved the same Russian colonel was watching the Finland border crossing for two more years. The changes have really been very little for importing for us. We even have Volvos now from Sweden," he boasted.

"Do you import form other places than Europe?" I asked, already knowing about his Korean connections.

"Yes, from Asia. We import electronics, mostly radios, televisions, and video tape players. Russian electronics are so poorly made that Russians won't buy those anymore. Usually, the drunks are employed at the radio and television factories. They can't build anything right!" he sneered.

"Did you start with radios in the same way you started with car parts?" I lead him on.

"Nyet, I had a license to import and I knew that radios and televisions from our factories were no good, so I made some connections through a taxi company I know in Vladivostok. They sent me a container filled with Korean radios and televisions. I wanted Japanese, SONY, but they were too expensive. So, we opened a shop in town and the people came and bought them so fast that we had to close the store after three days because we had nothing more to sell! Imagine that. We asked for more. And it just kept going like that for many months," he recalled.

"How did you start importing cars from Asia? It sounds like a different dynamic than in your early days," I asked.

"My contacts in Vladivostok were already importing Korean cars and the relationship moved from only electronics to include cars, too, and also spare parts. We are only importing second-hand cars. The new ones were still too expensive for the Russian taxi drivers. We are now the largest distributor of Hyundai parts on this side of the Ural Mountains. The Korean and Japanese cars are all you see in Vladivostok now. They're crazy out there," he said, holding his finger to his temple.

"From your history, I understand you are more an entrepreneur than a typical director of a factory or a farm or another organization that had experience with the new privatization process, so perhaps any questions I have about that maybe need to be for somebody else," I said, baiting the hook for him.

"Da nyet, I am also involved in privatization here in Nizhniy Novgorod. In fact, I have bought and run a restaurant now that was a state-owned enterprise, several shops that sell electronics that we import from Asia, and I am now investing in a number of grocery stores," he remarked.

"OK, that's an interesting step. Can you tell me about your experience with this process? Are you continuing the old operations with the same staff and suppliers or do you have your own network of suppliers and staff? Obviously, the imports from Korea are an additional supply chain, but do you continue to support the domestic producers?" I asked professionally.

"Understand that domestic production is so poor that nobody wants to buy it. Did you know that several people were killed in the late 1980s by exploding televisions? The circuits were so badly built that the tubes actually exploded with an overload and killed several old women. I am not joking.

"The people would only purchase the radios built in the second week of a month. Do you know why? Because it was the second week of the month that the managers were actually doing something to control quality. In the first week, they were still drunk or hungover from drinking their quota rewards for the month before. In the last week, they were too busy just pushing half built radios through the assembly line in order to reach quota by the end of the month. So, the women would demand the shop clerks to open the back of the radio to see the date of production, check the calendar, and then it had to be plugged in and the volume on as loud as it could go for a few minutes go before they would agree to buy it. So, do I support Russian factories? Not when gypsies, Tatars, and Kavkazi are building them in Russian factories," he said with disgust.

"So your sales of electronics are one hundred percent imported?" I confirmed.

"Yes, nobody wants Russian-made goods," he stated with fervor.

"When you purchased the shops from the government, did you keep the staff?" I tried to keep my questions sounding as if they were pre-planned, unswayed by his revelations.

"Anybody who has worked in a government shop does not know how to sell or how to treat customers. There were a few, some younger girls, who understood that you need to treat a customer correctly, but mostly it was older women working as shop clerks as the men were in the factories, so usually I replaced the staff with younger students who finished university and wanted to get involved with international businesses," he answered like a good business owner should.

"And in the restaurant?" I asked innocently.

"In the restaurant? The cooks are all Russian women because people do want Russian-made food. So, we kept the grandmothers cooking. It is good food! Do you know my restaurant on Bolshaya Pokrovka?" he asked with a flinch of pride.

"Yes, I ate there once in February. The food was good, but too expensive for a student to go again," I conceded.

"Yes, I must make a profit. The next time you want a special night out, you tell me, and I will make sure you get a good meal for a student's budget. Agreed?" He was being sincerely generous.

"That's very kind of you, thank you. Can you tell me about the grocery stores you are investing in? What is your business plan for these?" I continued to push through the details.

"These shops are to be made by Russians for Russians. Nothing imported. People want Russian food for their kitchens. I am busy now putting together the suppliers who can produce and package correctly so that these stores become convenient like shopping in Germany. We will hire mostly young women to work in the shop who understand customer service. I do not plan to make much money with these shops. I am doing this to help the local food producers in the Volga region and to provide the people with a modern shopping choice. I consider these stores to be my gift to the city and my people of the Volga," he said like a Tsar gifting his people with their very lives.

"What is your opinion about the government's initiatives to privatize these enterprises? Do you find it to be worthwhile? It sounds to me that you prefer to buy the property and not the enterprise. You replace staff, suppliers, etcetera. So, in fact, you aren't buying the enterprise at all." My question seemed accusatory and I braced myself for his reaction.

"It is true. I purchase the property and the license. After it is a private company and no longer a shop that belongs to one factory or another, then I am free to run that business as I choose. So, yes you are correct that I am not like the workers who buy a shop for themselves. I don't know how they think they can survive doing the same things, but then for themselves. These people don't know other suppliers, other producers. They know how to unload trucks, stock shelves and take people's money. They are not business managers. I have no faith in the workers' buyouts in Russia. I think the government makes a big mistake to think that a group of workers will know how to make their business successful. They pay lots of money to the government and then the bank and I expect that they will lose everything. We need entrepreneurs to run the businesses, not workers," he proclaimed.

"And the factories?" I didn't even know what I was asking with that remark but it was out there.

"That's different, of course. There you have technical people who can make, fix, design new things so they aren't helpless. What they lack is a commercial vision, a target market for their products, but I believe that the managers of most of the factories understand this. They have higher educations in economics, even if it was for a planned economy. But they are smart guys. If they can find some foreign investors and some foreign markets for the good Russian technology, after some time I believe they will do well," he said with some confidence in his compatriots.

"What about the privatization of natural resources and strategic infrastructure projects," I asked, poking the bear.

"Russia is being robbed!" he shouted.

"Excuse me?" I bumbled.

"Russia is being robbed by the communist apparatchiki and ministers in the Yeltsin government, and those men are making themselves rich! Somehow, they are doing this and getting away with it. They have not brought any new knowledge or efforts to improve the product. They are not improving Russia! They are just taking the money and putting it in Switzerland and Cyprus in their own accounts after they took the shares of their newly privatized ministries. It's the biggest crime being committed in Russia and somebody needs to stop it!" He was instantly angry.

"I agree completely!" I replied, truly in agreement.

"My private enterprises are giving things back to Russia and Russians. I make jobs, I sell products that people want and need, we provide parts and service to keep trucks and taxis moving, and people can earn their bread and salt. To just take the country's resources and sell them abroad to make a few men in the government rich is insulting to our homeland. Those men should be shot!" he demanded.

"Are you involved in the local politics or are you only interested in business and trade?" I asked, knowing the answer already.

"In Russia, business is politics. The economy is politics. The mayor consults with me on a regular basis about how to help private business thrive so they can get the votes and tax money of course. It's all mixed up. You can't keep it separate!" He waved his left hand in the air to signify confusion.

"Do you feel it should be kept separate like in the United States and Germany?" I asked with some superiority.

"Young man, don't be naive. American businesses run your government too and your CIA. How many times has your country overthrown a government in central America to make sure you kept access to cheap labor and have export markets? Remember that Marx and Lenin were not wrong about everything. You forget that Russia is still very good friends with Cuba," he said condescendingly.

"Good point," I conceded.

"Russia needs a real, God-fearing Russian in power. No more Ukrainians and Georgians and Siberians as President. It is time for the people of the Volga to lead Russia and care for the motherland. Russia was built on the Volga and by the Volga. The people of the Volga truly love the land and the history and suffered through the worst of our history. If we neglect the heart of our country, our country will die!" He was getting very worked up now.

"Do you have somebody in mind that could fill the role? Do you support a candidate?" I asked pushing him to talk about himself.

"Right now, there is nobody who loves Russia more than their own bank account. We need to start a new party of those who truly love Russia, a Volga Party that will stop the rape of this country by our own countrymen!" he declared.

"Sorry, I've gotten off track with my questions. Even though I agree with you one hundred percent, and I am glad to find somebody else who thinks like I do about it, can I ask you again about what kind of policies can help private businesses help Russia and Russians?" I interjected.

"The biggest problem are the government ministers, customs officers, and tax collectors who make it difficult to do anything without them all getting their kickbacks. They are lazy and have no imagination about how to work, and they suck the people dry after they work hard. We need to throw all those gypsies out of the government and let the people just work. The Russian knows how to work if he is left alone!" he said, pounding his fist into his own hand.

"It's government corruption then that holds your business back?" I asked for clarification.

"Yes, corrupt, self-serving bureaucrats that are robbing the people blind, laming private businesses like mine by giving rights and licenses to their friends and family and not allowing competition. They take every day and give nothing back of any value to Mother Russia," he restated more calmly this time.

"You also have a very popular night club in a unique setting. Can you tell me about that business and what plans you have for that in the future?" I asked going out on a limb a bit.

"Did you like The Monastery?" he asked with obvious pride in his voice.

"To be honest, it didn't feel good to me to be dancing like that in an old church. It lacks respect. But this is just my opinion," I said apologetically.

"OK, you can have your opinion. No problem," he said, brushing me off and protecting his pride.

"Can I ask how you purchased a church to make into a nightclub?" I queried, truly wanting to know the answer.

"It was easy. No more monks. Russian girls are too pretty. They were chasing girls when I bought it!" He laughed at his own joke.

"Yes, I agree. It would be difficult to be a monk in Russia," I truly agreed with that sentiment. "Do you have further plans to expand the night club operations, or are you satisfied with it?"

"It is a fun little club, but it does not make much money. It does not attract the people with the money. It is more for students to dance. It is not open every day, just weekends. So, I am planning to build a new one very close to it," he said with a bit a disappointment.

"How will the new one be different?" I was sincerely curious.

"Do you know Las Vegas?" He looked at me and winked his left eye, letting me in on a secret plan.

"Yes, of course..." I stammered, not understanding what he was telling me.

"To get people with money, you must have more than dancing. You need shows, a casino, buffets, and someplace for them to sleep." He paused, waiting for my acknowledgment. "Nizhniy has no good hotels. My friends, when they come from Moscow to The Monastery, they always complain to me that they need someplace to sleep that makes them comfortable. Nizhniy is a great town, a great Volga town, but it is not a modern city."

"So, you plan to make Nizhniy Novgorod the Las Vegas of Russia?" I asked with a pinch of repulsion.

"If God won't stop me, yes!" he replied, convinced of his crusade. "It will bring new construction, new hotels, new jobs, money from gambling, restaurants, airport. Just look at Macau! It's a great model for a city-state."

"Is this just a dream you have or are you working on plans already?" I swallowed my personal indifference to his plans to keep him talking.

"We are working on the plans already. Would you like to see the drawings? Maybe you can give some good tips about how to make it better, more American?" he said with enthusiasm.

Mr. P. retrieved some plastic tubes from behind his desk and rolled the technical drawings of a master plan on the glass coffee table. He secured the corners of the thin paper with heavy granite chess pieces and began to explain the specifics of the plan.

The drawings were impressive. The artist's sketches looked to give the hotel and the other buildings a unique, modern style but unmistakably with a rich Russian influence. It seemed almost to be a complimentary sort of architecture to the local kremlin and incorporated the architectural aspects of The Monastery as it now was. I studied it for some time as Mr. P. explained his favorite elements of the design and the layout and the architecture. There would indeed be a casino, fine dining, a hotel with three hundred and fifty rooms. The hotel, though, would not be a sky scraper like the monstrosities in Las Vegas, but a three-floor stone structure that would encircle the entertainment facilities, much like a fortress with a church and a village in the middle. The hotel rooms would all have a great view of the Volga, perched on and built into the panorama slope of the bluff. Somehow, the design of the hotel held true to Mr. P.'s belief and quasi-worship of the Volga River and the Russian aesthetic. It was ingenious, even to my eyes.

"And you see, here is The Monastery, so we will make sure that we keep the church and its buildings preserved. This was our agreement with the church and the city when they let us buy it. We will not keep it as a club forever. I promised if I could build my hotel on the land next to it that we would restore and preserve it for our history," he said with a bit of reverence and respect, which surprised me.

At once I recognized that this land for the Noviy Monastir, as Mr. P. was calling it, was very close to if not the same parcel of land that Del and his company were trying to receive permission to build on.

I chose my questions carefully now as I did not want to appear to know too much already. "When will the construction start? It looks like you are ready to start any day."

"We are waiting for the approval from the city council and the governor. This takes a long time now because there is a question about selling land for private use, for business," he remarked astutely.

"We've come back to the privatization process again," I pointed out.

"Yes, I suppose so." Mr. P. shrugged his shoulders. "We are waiting to know if we can lease the land or purchase it to own it."

"How long will this take?" I kept my questions short to not give insight into my insider knowledge.

"We expect to have a decision at the end of May, before the summer holidays. We would then start building maybe one year from now. One can't start construction in Russia in the autumn. The ground will freeze too soon and you can't lay a good foundation that won't sink in the spring. We have these problems all over Siberia with buildings that sink in the spring. Each year they sink another few centimeters." He was sounding more and more educated and knowledgeable.

"This is, of course, a huge project. Do you have partners or investors?" I knew I should not have asked this question as soon as it left my mouth.

"Yes, we have investors who are ready to help with the hotel building once the land is secure," he answered without giving details.

"Are you financing that land purchase yourself with the help of a bank?" What was I asking?

"No, no banks. Banks are criminals, too. They will find a way to rob me of my land if I borrow the money from them," he answered with the enthusiasm in his voice evaporating quickly.

"Well, your car imports and your electronics imports for Russian prices certainly have not been able to create profits enough to purchase this much land. You don't have any foreign investors who will help secure the financing?" For some reason, I could not stop asking these questions, I knew I was on thin ice now, but the adrenaline of the hunt had gone to my heart already. I almost had him in my net.

Mr. P. replied gruffly to my impertinent questioning, "No, I don't believe in foreign money. They will have too much control over Russia if we keep borrowing from them. I have some money my father left to me that I will use to pay for the land."

With that comment Mr. P. began to roll up the technical drawings, briskly without care, and slid them back into the plastic tubes and put them away behind his desk from where he had retrieved them. As he walked back towards me at the couches he did not sit down again, to signal that the interview was over. Getting the hint, I quickly gathered up my notebook and pen and put them in my book bag and stood up to meet Mr. P.'s eyes. He did not extend his hand for a farewell handshake as I extended mine. He kept his hands in the pockets of his slacks.

"I am sorry, but the interview must now be over. I am very busy and must get back to my work. Tatyana will show you out."

06

18. Shark Tank

It was the end of April and the evenings were becoming longer with daylight and twilight lasting until almost nine o'clock in the evening. Gone were the days of thick coats and double layers. I was so happy to hear my babushka say that shapkas after mid-April were not to be worn any longer. Evidently, it was bad for men's hairlines if they wore their fur hats in warm weather. She was full of those types of traditional wives' tales and I added this one to a list of them that I was keeping. The last snow showers had been in the second week of April but they were just passing flurries on a few cold, wet days when the wind and clouds came from the north. The wind was now blowing warm air up the river valley, making the days and evenings as pleasant as any I could remember.

As I strolled up Minin Street to Frunze Street to meet with Del and Els that Friday evening, I was deep in thought about what to do with the information that I gleaned from my discussions with Mr. P. He may have been an uneducated, maybe even dishonest businessman, but there was nothing that I could pinpoint from what I had learned about him that indicated that he was hurting the everyday Ivan Ivanovich on the street. In fact, he made a strong case for his ends justifying his means. Even if he had been getting his car parts off the back of somebody's truck, at the least he had been providing a service that benefited other entrepreneurs in the city, helping others make a living by being able to fix their cars quickly.

Perhaps Mr. P. was the wrong example on which to base my model of how the little shark becomes the big shark. He seemed rather adamant that those types of charlatans were only destroying Russia and looking out for themselves. Igor Ivanovich seemed to be, on the surface anyhow, building an enterprise that not only made him rich and influential but that helped move the local economy along in a very unsure time.

During this period of economic chaos in Russia, it was impossible for anybody to work completely within the law, and as Del rightly pointed out, the laws were changing every two or three months. What was perhaps illegal when it started was the catalyst for showing law makers that the laws had to change. I hoped that Del would be able to help me pick apart this new information and make some sense of it.

When the elevator doors opened on what I expected to be the fifth floor and the Sannings' apartment door, I had to double check that I had punched the right button. Perhaps I had mistakenly pressed 3 instead of 5? I punched the 5 again to see if the elevator would close and take me higher, but it didn't. I stood for a moment puzzled. I stepped back into the elevator and selected 0 to take me back to the ground floor. Perhaps I had entered the building through the wrong stairwell. Most Russian apartment buildings have multiple entrances on the ground floor along the length of the buildings, each entrance representing a stairwell or elevator shaft. I poked my head outside the ground floor entrance to check that there wasn't one more door to the left as the Sanning's apartment was on the fifth floor of the last stairwell from the street. As I looked left all I saw was a wall of cinder blocks about two and a half meters tall. On the other side of that low wall was Upper Embankment Street. I was in the right place. I rode the elevator again up to the fifth floor and deliberately knocked a measured three times on a newly installed, rust-colored steel security door. The knock echoed on the landing and up and down the stairwell. I waited.

From behind the doors, I heard the faint voice of Del asking in Russian, "Who is there?"

"It's the plumber, I've come to fix the sink," I replied in a put-on Brooklyn accent to make fun of the whole situation.

I rolled my eyes as I waited for Fort Sanning to open its doors. I half expected to see Del holding a double-barreled shotgun and chewing on a stubby cigar in the side of his mouth, wearing a cowboy hat and a patch over one eye. It all seemed very overdone. As I heard the bolt of the steel door finally release, I pulled the door toward me. Stepping out of its way and peering around the edge I said, "Open sesame?"

"Very funny, plumber man. Come on in," he bellowed. Del was in a good mood.

Without a coat, scarf, and shapka to hang up I walked straight into the living room through the dark hallway but bumped my

172

left arm on something protruding from the wall. That hadn't been there that last time I had visited the apartment.

"That's new, isn't it?" I asked as I stopped to inspect it and rub my arm that had bumped it. "What is it?" I stepped through the doorway into the living room. Els was in the kitchen off to the left.

"It's a panic button," Del said matter-of-factly, "It is an alarm that sets off bells and lights here in the apartment, the landing... and in the police station."

"Wow, you've got a burglar alarm wired to the police station? How far away is it from here?" I was puzzled.

"Minin Square, just a few minutes away, but we also have a police car stationed downstairs at night for the time being as well in case it happens again," he said distractedly.

"In case what happens again? Del, what happened?" I began to get a very worried feeling in my gut and waited for him to explain what was going on.

"A few nights ago, a group of three of four thugs forced their way into the apartment just before Els and I were going to bed," he said as if telling me a bedtime story.

"What!? Are you alright?" I looked around the door into the kitchen to see if Els had been beaten up. Seeing she was fine I looked Del up and down. Maybe I had missed a cast or a bandage on his arm or leg...

"Yes kid, we're fine. They didn't hurt us, they just smashed the place up a bit and that's all." Del seemed to want to brush it off. "It's nothing we haven't seen before in Moscow."

"Did they take anything?" I looked around and saw only the usual bookcases, television, and whatnot. Nothing even seemed out of place.

"No, it wasn't a robbery. They didn't even ask for our money or passports or anything," Del replied while he laid out silverware on the table. He just didn't seem too concerned about it.

"Okay, then, what am I missing and should I be concerned?" I was desperate to learn about what had happened.

Del stopped setting the table and stood pensively against the refrigerator. "You know, it was really amateurish the way it all went down, don't you think as well Els?"

"They certainly weren't professionals," was her input, and she continued adding vegetables to the cowboy stew.

"And how often have the two of you been attacked by professionals?" I asked sarcastically with a flip of my hand and arm into the air.

"What would you say, honey? Three or four times?" Del looked with a longing glance to his wife.

"This makes it four times now, sweetheart." She looked up from the soup and batted her eye lashes.

"You two are a real pair, you know that?" I laughed and took a seat at my usual seat at the table. "So, if they didn't beat you up, and they didn't steal anything from you...just knocked over some chairs..." I asked hoping to get more details.

"And a table!" Els added putting her knife into the air, her back still to me so as to be heard and seen.

"And a table," I continued. "Why did they even break in?"

"Pure intimidation, my friend, pure intimidation!" was Del's almost enthusiastic conclusion.

"Did they give you some sort of ultimatum to get out of town or something like that?" I interrogated further.

Del now took a chair and leaned towards me over the table. "No, they didn't demand a thing. In fact, they just yelled and hollered in Russian at us about how they could break our legs or bash in our skulls if they wanted to. Isn't that right, love?"

"You know I don't speak a word of this language, blue eyes." Els turned to me and said very matter of fact, "...but it's true, they seemed very threatening and intimidating, but they didn't lay a hand on us."

"The two of you are absolutely nuts!" I laughed. "So that panic button is because you're not worried they might come back? And that steel door is because..."

"Those, my friend, are a gift from the chief of police! He insisted." Del put on a voice to mock his high connections in the city.

"And the squad car downstairs I guess was his idea as well?" I challenged.

"Yep, he wants to make sure that we are safe and snug," Els said as she sat to wait for the stew to simmer.

Del did away with the acting and said in a serious tone, "Look, kid, whenever you do business in Russia, it's never what it seems. The goons that broke in here were wannabes. They couldn't have intimidated an old lady. They were scripted. They were obviously told not to hurt us but show us that we are vulnerable. They didn't even try to steal anything, didn't even ask if I had money in the house, which I don't. We didn't say anything. They did their thing and then they left and smashed a lamp and a glass or two on their way out. I almost laughed out loud at them."

"What's that all about then?" I was puzzled.

"It's so that the police can put a tail on me and watch everywhere I go. They create a threat, make a show of how they are protecting me, and insist that they send a squad car with me everywhere I go. Somebody is trying again to muscle in on the project and they think that if they know where I go in the daytime that they'll be able to eventually push me out and take over with my contacts. The goons in Moscow were much better at this than the provincial boys," he said, leaning back in his chair.

"Misha told me that you were being protected by the mayor, why has this changed all the sudden?" I spoke out of turn.

"Hmmm...he shouldn't have told you that." Del scowled. "Listen, things here are always changing. You can't ever get too comfortable. It's like I told you earlier, you need to be ready to walk away at any given moment. When it gets too dangerous, we will do the same. Don't ever trust anybody in business here, not even the mayor or the chief of police. Everybody has their price."

"Am I in danger?" I asked directly.

"I don't believe so. If it gets so far that I have any suspicions I will let you know and we will stop the project," he assured me.

"OK, agreed." I nodded in agreement, but felt an uneasy feeling come over me, making a knot in my stomach

"So, let's eat!"

After dinner, we sat in the living room and went over the notes of my interview with Mr. P. Del had obviously seen these types of characters in the past, up close and personal from the sounds of it, so I was counting on him being able to help me see this character in the full light of day.

With my notebook resting on the arm of the couch, my pen behind my ear and another in the corner of mouth to chew on, I started. "I have the impression that I have chosen the wrong man to prove my model of how illegal money influences government policies...in the new Russia."

"What makes you think he's legit?" Del never minced his words. He knew how to go right to the core of the question.

"It's not a matter of him being honest and moral. I saw the drugs and girls going around that club. I'm not trying to be the vice squad here. It's obvious a number of his current activities are obviously illegal, everybody thinks he runs the local protection rackets. But he seems to be against the idea of making himself richer at the cost of Russia's future. He's not out to rob the people or the land itself and move his wealth out of our Russia. He's set to keep it all right here, create jobs, he says." It sounded like I was advocating for Mr. P. I was a bit taken back by it.

"How did he get his start?" Del looked pensive, looking through me.

"He was a young man distributing car parts to taxi garages and mechanics in 1989, and then it grew into importing cars from Germany," I explained.

"Stolen car parts and stolen cars?" again Del went to the heart of the matter.

"He says he paid for them but admitted that he wasn't paying full value as nobody then knew how to price anything in those years," I apologized.

"You mean the car parts?" Del pushed.

"Yes, that's correct. He didn't say anything specifically about the imported cars from Germany." I was flipping through my first page of notes to perhaps jar my memory. I chewed hungrily on the pen in my mouth.

"I can assure you that he was part of a wider gang that was stealing cars in East and West Germany in the 1990s. They would put them in chop shops protected by the Red Army garrisons. The cars would be disassembled and smuggled through Poland as parts and reassembled in Russia in garages. The goons would then pay off the local traffic cops to get them Russian license plates and sell them for a huge profit here in Russia, and all over Eastern Europe. The Russians are very ingenious and industrious that way." Del was painting a grandiose picture for me.

"He told me about crossing the border from Finland and paying off the border and customs controllers. He said he had a license for importing, so it sounds half legal. What was his quote... 'It was all lawful, but they still had the guns, and so we had to help take care of them,' or something like that." I looked up puzzled from my notes.

"I wasn't aware of any smuggling going on at the Finnish border. The Finns have always been above board. They tried really hard to stay out of that mess," Del mumbled.

I moved the discussion along. "Anyhow, after a while their Russian car parts business got found out and the flow stopped from the local factory, but eventually he said they got it back because the factory director couldn't penetrate his market and his customers wouldn't buy from the factory manager."

"Kid, you know what that means right?" Del sat up in his chair like a prairie dog had just heard a hawk in the sky.

"I can only think that to mean he sent his thugs around to the garages and told them that if they ordered their parts from anyplace else the place would be burned down, fingers broken, and the like," I guessed.

"That's exactly what that means." He was almost sitting on the edge of his chair. "Oh yes, you've got a live one on the line, my friend."

"Del," I lowered my voice, "there is something else. You're not going to like it."

"C'mon boy out with it, what is there not to like?" He was getting really excited.

"I asked his plans to grow his current businesses. We talked about him buying up retails stores for electronics and groceries, and about the new supply chains he is building etcetera, etcetera. But then the topic of his night club came up, you know the one in the old church a ways up the road here?" I was pointing out toward the river, motioning eastward, waiting for Del to start to piece things together himself.

"You mean the old church out by our building site?" Del didn't have an idea of what was coming.

"Yes, that's the one. Mr. P. is also planning an expansion of his night club into a casino and hotel on nearly the same site..." I held my breath to see what his reaction would be.

"Really? We haven't discussed this at all at the city council meetings. There hasn't been any permit request or anything filed with the city hall or the governor's office. Are you sure it's not just a dream of his? Did he tell you a timeline on his plans?" Del was rather confident that this wasn't real.

"He showed me the master planning drawings, looked real to me but I'm not an architect nor engineer of course. He said they expected to have the question about the land title settled in June before the summer holidays and they would start digging in February or March next year. There was something about not being able to lay a foundation in the autumn..." I heard Del begin where I l left off.

"...Because the ground will freeze and thaw causing it to sink in the spring..." Del's voice trailed off. He was pensive and paused for a few moments. "Hmmm...he's obviously done his homework. What else can you tell me?"

I went over my notes again for a few minutes and did my best to recall the conversation behind each line of notes.

"What puzzled me the most was that he has no foreign investors nor domestic bank financing. He tells me that he is planning to finance it all with his own money and partner investors. He may make enough money to live like a local prince, but I can't imagine the sale of imported cars and radios to be enough to purchase and build such a palace of a place. Not even with the bit of pimping, drugs, and racketeering that he does," I ventured. "How much would it cost? You probably have a very good idea of that, Del."

"He would need at least one hundred twenty-five million US dollars to build a basic three-star hotel. Without him being invested in oil, coal, or other natural resources, he wouldn't have that type of liquidity. His partners would have to bring that to the table." Del was rubbing his chin thinking.

"I'm sorry, but we didn't discuss his partners, in fact, he tossed me out right after he showed me those master plans. It all ended very abruptly," I added to break the awkward silence.

Just then, Els who had been listening from the kitchen came into the living room and sat down across from me on the sofa. "Peter, what specifically did he say before the interview ended?"

"He said he was busy. He said he had to get back to his work and his secretary would show me out." I didn't understand what she was wanting to know.

"No, no. There must have been something he said that he didn't want any further questions about." Els spoke as she took the swivel chair next to Del and looked me in the face. "To tell all the information he told you about how he started, about his expansion plans and the rest, he must have seen you somehow immediately hostile and therefore ended the conversation quickly. Was it right after you were asking him questions about the financing that the interview ended?" Els had heard something in my story and had now honed in on what had not been said.

"Yes, that's where it ended and then I was shown out." I still wasn't able to put the pieces together.

Els turned to Del. "There must be something in the financing of the plans that he does not want anybody to know. He wouldn't go reading his biography to a curious foreign student and then just stop all of a sudden after a few more inquisitive questions. He could have made up a story about the financing and Peter wouldn't have been any the wiser for it and moved on. He stopped the interview and threw him out? There is something very sensitive that he is hiding in the financing of the hotel, something so personal that he doesn't dare discuss it with anybody."

I sat blinking at the both of them stunned and shocked. I felt a shadow agenda between them and the edge of the veil had been lifted for me to glimpse it but not understand it.

"You see, kid," Del said to me, "Els worked as a criminal psychologist. She worked for twelve years with the FBI before we met in San Francisco. Sorry to spook you like that. She is indispensable in this country for understanding people's behaviors and motives, especially when they are lying."

Els turned to me now. "Peter, there must have been something else he said, some tip that he let slip that made him realize he had just told you too much. He didn't mean to say it because he doesn't have a cover story. He's not good at thinking on his feet so he just threw you out of his office instead of trying to cover his tracks."

I looked back through to my notes again and chewed on my pen vigorously.

"It would have been just before he threw you out, not early in the meeting." She was coaching my memory like a hypnotist.

"I'm sorry. You have to remember that when I listen I translate right into English as I'm writing and sometimes I miss a sentence or two while I'm writing an important line. I miss lots of things still." I was a bit frantic as I felt I was being interrogated now.

Els's voice stayed calm and soothing. "It would have been about the financing of his project. What questions did you ask him? What questions would you still like to ask him to learn more?"

"OK." I took a deep breath to relax. "The question that remains in my mind is why he was so confident that he would get the building permit for that land when there is a competing, foreign money backed project slated for the same ground. Also, how could he possibly come up with the cash to finance this if he didn't trust banks and foreigners."

"Did he say that much?" she asked to clarify Mr. P.'s words from my interpretations.

"Yes, he said specifically that borrowing money from foreigners would only keep Russia held back and that the banks would only steal the land from him eventually," I blurted out.

"Was it specifically about the land? Was he not talking about the hotel project?" she asked again a pinpointed question.

"No, he was talking about the land rights or land purchase. There was a question of leasing or owning," I remembered.

Del nodded his head. "That's correct. A renewable ninety-nine-year lease or outright purchase. The laws are being changed right now. We don't know what the final bill will allow."

All of a sudden, my mental dam broke! "He said his father had left him some money that he would purchase the LAND with! That was the last thing he said to me before he rolled up the plans and kicked me out. He didn't even shake hands, he just tossed me out."

"Well done, Peter." Els looked at Del with an expression that asked a show of appreciation for her assistance.

"Well done, Els!" Del chirped.

Els stood up and looked at us both and asked, "Something to drink, boys?"

After cold bottles of Pepsi were passed around and opened, we sat in the living in the room and the interrogations continued.

"What do you think he meant about his father leaving him money?" I asked Del. "From my understanding, there was no such thing as an inheritance in the Soviet Union. Everything belonged to the state and you couldn't pass down property or assets to your family because it wasn't yours to keep. The state was there to take care of orphans and widows, in theory, and therefore inheritance wasn't allowed."

"True, but that changed in about 1989 when the good citizens could start making profits and buying property and foreign investors could buy shares in state enterprises. Owning property did become legal, and now we're a few years later as well. It's possible his father was also a government crony and privatized some state assets into his name, like Gazprom for example. Maybe his father got rich overnight and left him shares in a privatized state enterprise...or stashed in a foreign bank," Del speculated.

"No, he said his father was an engineer and lived here in Nizhniy Novgorod," I discounted Del's theory with more information from my interview.

"Did he tell you that, too?" Els jumped all over this new revelation.

"Well, it was part of his story. That's how he learned to be mechanical with the cars. His father studied and worked in East Germany for some time. They would speak German together when nobody else was around. That's how he could negotiate in Germany so well, he said," I explained.

"Kid, you know what Nizhniy produces right? You know why the city has so many engineers and engineering schools, right?" Del asked rhetorically.

"Yes, the GAZ factory is just down the street from my place: cars, boats, trains, airplanes, and whatnot," I proudly answered.

"MIGs, kid, MIGs," Del spelled it out for me. "The Soviets closed the place because this was their center of excellence for fighter planes, military aviation, not GAZ built troop transports."

"Do you remember anything he said about aviation?" Els asked me again looking me square in the face.

"No, I had it my head from his story that his father was an automobile engineer. That's how Mr. P. got the idea and his start at the car parts factory. His father has a dacha where he kept the inventory, and he drove his father's car once a week to pick up a new load of spare parts. In my mind's eye, I imagined his father to be an automotive engineer," I explained.

"Nothing at all that would tie him to airplanes, aviation, radar technology?" Del continued with the questions.

I hesitated with my answer as I felt like I was being treated as a hostile witness now and I gave them both a very unsure look. This wasn't about the hotel anymore. Something had shifted in the discussion and I couldn't figure out exactly what.

"We're just trying to figure out if his claims of having money left from his father are viable enough to make us worry about his bidding for the ground, that's all," Els reassured me with a smile.

"The only mention of the word 'airplanes' was that he rented an unused warehouse from an aircraft parts manufacturer that was short on orders and supply. He stored his car parts there when they branched out to other car models and needed more space," I revealed.

"There it is!" Del slapped his knee and stood up and paced around the room.

"Did I miss something?" I queried looking back and forth between the two of them.

After a few moments of talking to himself and staring at a blank wall, Del asked me, "Kid, you understand don't you, why he wants to set up a casino?"

"He says it's to bring money and jobs to Nizhniy. He wants to make Nizhniy a Las Vegas type of city, God willing," I answered.

Del explained, "Kid, you said you had the impression that the guy wasn't more than a crook with honor maybe, but make no mistake about it: the casino will be there to launder money, white wash it and put into foreign reserve banks, out of the hands of the Russian government and tax collectors. The little shark has to get his money out of the country before a bigger shark comes and eats him and his territory up, or as Mr. P. might put it, take over his market share.

"It sounds like Mr. P. has tapped a vein of wealth and is getting ready in the next year or two to make his big move and is setting up the needed infrastructure to move his money around Russian banks to someplace else. I think you found your perfect example to prove your model for your paper, but he is still perhaps too small of a fish for you to recognize it at this point. He's just about to make his move into the major leagues with the casino plans. No doubt about it. It's a perverted 'rags to riches' bonanza!"

I laid awake that night in my room until late thinking about the last few days and all the information I had learned and processed. It was enough to leave me suspicious of everybody and anybody. The evening with the Sannings had left me very unsettled. From the steel door to the panic button and the nonchalant way that both Del and Els took the break-in and the threats, to the professional interrogation that Els put me through to pull information from me about their business competitor. I had felt a palpable shift in the intensity of their interest when Mr. P's father was being discussed. I began to suspect that Del and Els had a shadow agenda that they were also keeping from me. After all the warnings that Els gave me about looking into peoples' motives and being careful with my choice of research methods, she lulled me into a sense of security to trust her, to trust Del with everything that I heard and learned during my studies and interactions with people in the city. Perhaps it was time to be less forthcoming with them about what I was learning. Maybe I needed to start asking them the questions that would fill in my gaps instead of me being used for the information I had gathered through my investigations and research. I felt that I was starting to be carried along by deep currents of other people's agendas which were becoming frighteningly obvious; violence, corruption, industrial espionage.

Perhaps it was time to be very, very cautious. Perhaps it was time to walk away...

19. British Knights

Hans had a new girlfriend without whom he could go nowhere. Not even our Saturday afternoon fried chicken lunch was sacred anymore. She held his leash very tightly. Tamara was as beautiful as any fabled Russian girl, and for that Hans could be forgiven for falling head over heels in love. Most likely it was lust, but at twenty-three years old, who really knows the difference? She was indeed beautiful and most likely a gold-digger looking for a foreign boyfriend to take her far away from the poverty, snow, and ice. Unfortunately, her brains did not match her beauty.

"Just look at what that tramp is wearing! Look at her hair and look at her fat backside, she needs to wear some heals to flatten that out!" was Tamara's critique of nearly every female that entered our favorite eating establishment that day.

I rolled my eyes at Hans while Tamara poured scorn on what I thought were some very attractive young ladies. Hans gave an apologetic look back, but he was hardly sincere in his shameful looks. It was tragic to watch and hear.

"Why can't these Russian girls see that their boyfriends are ugly dogs? Russian men look like cavemen! They all look like gorillas the way they walk. And why don't they wear any colors? I can't stand the black leather jacket look." She clucked on while I silently devoured chicken thighs and drumsticks. Tamara ate nothing. I assumed it was to keep her fabulous figure from developing fatal flaws.

Those who have the impression that Russia is a gray, colorless place obviously have not visited the country in the spring, because when the weather is warm the streets are awash in all the colors possible under the sun. The wearing of bright, brash, and clashing colors by the ladies is almost an expression of the freedom of the body liberated finally from the black, gray, and navy wool overcoats and fur hats. Young college girls wear the shortest skirts, the sheerest blouses and the tallest heels they can without breaking an ankle. The young men wear the same in their own right—tight silk button downs or the t-shirts of their younger, much smaller brothers with their new denim jeans.

Wild flowers grow from any unpaved patch of dirt, springing up from between the cracks in the pavements and walls, in the brightest, happiest colors. This spring ritual of promenading without much on in Russia is undoubtedly a back lash from the months of not being able to feel attractive under the heavy winter clothes that one must wear to keep warm, indoors and out. In the warming weather people have a need to be noticed by those around them as opposed to everybody looking the same wrapped from head to toe to the point that even gender is sometimes not discernible through the layers. Gordost that afternoon was full with young couples enjoying the late April sunshine and making Russia look all the better for it! Only Tamara didn't see it that way. Hans didn't see anybody but Tamara.

"And just look at this gangster-looking thug walking in. He drives a black Lada, he wears a black shirt and black leather jacket, black denim pants and what does he wear on his feet? British Knights trainers whiter than new snow! Where did he find those? First time wearing them. Just look how clean they are. They must glow in the dark. Why can't Russian men get a hairstyle? You think they all just came from the army." I feared what she might say about my worn-out style of mismatched jackets and dirty blue jeans I couldn't quite get clean for the last four months.

"They wear their hair that short so nobody can pull their hair in a fight, and the police can't grab them by it," Hans commented to her, somehow instantly knowledgeable about gangster fashion.

"Don't encourage it, Hans," I said dryly to him across the table in English. This woman was thoroughly ruining my weekly ritual. I quickly checked my own reflection in the plate glass window. My hair looked horrible and I had thinned out considerably.

"Hans, how did your presentation go last week? Did your master's topic get approved by the panel?" I asked him, trying to infuse some intelligence into our conversation.

"Yes, the panel approved. So, I will start my formal research now and then come back in September for one more year," he cheerfully replied.

"Hans is taking me to Germany for the summer break, right Hans?" Tamara added.

"Is that even possible, Hans?" I queried with irony. He kicked me under the table.

"How is your research coming along, Peter?" Hans was trying to change the subject quickly.

"Swimmingly, thanks!" I was very amused at the perturbed look Tamara had on her face at the thought that a girlfriend visa was not a valid travel document. I took a swig from my Pepsi bottle trying not to laugh at the world of trouble Hans was in now.

"Sweetheart, you told me it was possible for me to stay with you this summer in Germany," was the most intelligent comment she could make, not picking up on the real motivation in this faux relationship.

"It should be fine. Peter is doing the same with his girlfriend and it's harder to get a visa for America than for Germany." He was surprisingly very good at lying.

"Oh yes!" I put down my bottle and played along for Hans' sake. "I will go to the American Embassy in June with our papers to prove that we are a serious couple and tell the consular that it's time that she meets my parents. They'll stamp the paperwork without further question."

Hans kicked me under the table again.

Looking at my watch I stood up and declared, "I have an appointment at two o'clock, so I need to get going." I left my plate of chicken bones for Hans to clean up, gave Tamara a peck on the cheek and a wink to Hans and was out the door to meet Misha for another round of apartment viewing.

Misha and I agreed to meet just off Bolshaya Pokrovka Street at the cross street of Oktyabraskaya for two or three viewings. As I was running a bit late I decided to forego walking the usual scenic route and headed out through the narrow residential streets, heading up Nesterova Street, past the hospital on the left and crossing the busy Vavarksaya Street. When I stopped to wait for the light on Vavarskaya Street, a very long legged young lady in a yellow sun dress waiting to cross on the opposite side caught my eye and kept my attention. I shamelessly watched her walk towards me. I walked as slowly as possible toward her. As we met in the middle of the crosswalk I turned to see her from behind as she passed me. To my surprise just a few steps behind me was the fellow that Tamara had spotted at Gordost; short cropped hair, all black clothing except for the snow-white trainers with the British Knights logo on the side. He too was looking back, watching the swaying skirt and hips. Before he noticed me looking at him I snapped my head around to walk forward, now at a faster clip.

"Is he following me?" was my first thought. "No, he's just heading to Pokrovka as well, don't be so paranoid. Who wouldn't go to Gordost first and then walk to Pokrovka? It's Saturday. This is the fastest route."

I did keep an eye on him in the store front window panes, just in case, as I walked on. When I stopped at the corner where I was to meet Misha at five minutes to two, the British Knights walked on and turned left up Pokrovka as casually as anybody.

Misha arrived right on time again and seemed to emerge from another dimension, as one minute he wasn't there and the next he was right in front of me.

"How do you do that?" I asked him, startled.

"Do what?" he was unaware he was doing anything odd.

"Nothing, nothing. I just didn't see you until . . . nothing, nothing." I was flustered.

"Are you okay today? You seem nervous," he observed.

"I was just watching the girls and not watching out for you," I lied.

"Oh, yes, it's that season again isn't it? May holidays coming next week. All the girls out today in their short skirts, are they?" He took a quick glance around. "Okay, let's go."

We walked on along Oktybraskaya opposite the tram tracks on the pavement behind all the parked cars. We continued past the junction, to the left up Dobrolyubova Street until we came to a red brick apartment block, maybe twelve stories tall directly opposite a dingy gray church that was just starting its renovation. On the ground-floor there was a small shopping complex with the usual boutiques selling cheap imported cosmetics and pantyhose as well as a green grocers and bakery. We entered on the ground floor and took the lift to the eighth floor.

After seeing two different apartments in the same building, which were less than optimal for our desired clientele, we exited the building onto Sergiyevskaya Street on the other side of the building and walked down the incline to the intersection with Dobrolubova Street to turn right and back toward Pokrovka. As we turned right, I glanced instinctively left to check oncoming traffic and saw, leaned up against the scaffoldings built up around the church, the glowing white British Knights of a young man dressed in black, smoking a cigarette. He was looking at his wrist watch and watching the entrance where Misha and I had entered the building. He was following me!

"Misha, we're being followed," I muttered to my colleague.

"I know. I spotted him already on Pokrovka. He was walking behind you from Vavarskaya and fell in behind us when we met and started walking. What an idiot wearing those shoes to be a tail." Misha didn't break his stride and kept on walking. When we reached the tram stop, we jumped on board and watched out the back window to see our tail still standing in the shade of the scaffolding, his plume of cigarette smoke and his shoes giving him away. He hadn't seen us climb aboard and we rolled away with a sense of relief.

"You know that Del's apartment was broken into?" Misha asked.

"Yes, I was there last night. I heard the whole story," I answered.

"Something is going on. Not too sure what it is, but they sure are a bunch of amateurs, especially that guy!" he said, motioning over his shoulder out the back window.

When we came back to Pokrovka I moved toward the doors but Misha motioned that I stay on the street car. I didn't question his judgment as he seemed to know better what he was doing than I did. We stayed on the street car until we came close to Senaya Square via Bolshaya Pecherskaya, which ran parallel to Minin Street. We stepped off at Frunze Street. Misha thought it important to inform Del that I had been followed. I decided to walk back to Gordost and get a good look at the fellow when we came back to pick up his car that he had left parked on the Upper Embankment Street. Misha didn't think that was a good idea and went to find Del to consult with him about how to proceed. When I arrived at the restaurant to spot the driver of the black Lada, it was not where I watched the same fellow park it. I decided to walk on toward Minin Square and down the grand stairs to the waterfront and to the River Station bus stop. It was time to leave the old city today and spend some time at home. My face had become too well known in the old city.

I phoned Yulia from the Moscow Station and asked if she wanted to go for a stroll along the Oka River with me. After forty-five minutes, she emerged from the metro station where I was warily waiting, making sure nobody had tailed me again. We went for a walk up the bank of the Oka River, arm in arm, past the Yarmarka and the Alexander Nevsky cathedral and enjoyed the sunshine. I told her nothing of the morning's intrigue with the British Knight. We spoke of the coming May holidays and what each of us would do with two weeks free from school. I told her about Hans's new girlfriend. She was just as put out as I was. She said she never wanted to meet her. I described her as a gold-digger. Yulia used a different word.

When I finally arrived back at my apartment, Babushka was sitting outside with her friends and acquaintances peeling potatoes into small tin pots with red embroidered cloths over their laps and with their summer headscarves on. All the old ladies greeted me politely, and I them in return. Before I could pass to go into the building, Babushka told me that some of my friends had just been there to ask for me. As I had just been with Yulia and I knew Hans would be very busy with his young beauty that evening, I couldn't think of who it could have been.

"Had you seen them before?" I asked Natasha.

"Nyet. Two boys in a car. I've never seen your student friends in cars before."

"A black car?" I pressed.

"Yes. Do you know them?'

"No, they are not my friends. What did you tell them?" I pressed further.

"Luba there told them that you don't live here anymore." She giggled with her lady friends who were masters of neighborhood misinformation. "And that you had moved to the student dormitories."

"Many thanks, ladies!" I looked each of them in the face and gave them a smile.

"Hooligans!" Luba replied. "Just hooligans. They think they can drive right up to our door and demand information from us like they are the KGB! Fu fu fu. The youth of today. We weren't like that in my day. We were polite and respectful to the grandmothers in the village."

I spent the evening at home with the curtains closed and kept my light off, spending time talking with Raiya and Babuska in the kitchen as we cooked and ate a late dinner together for the first time since I had come to live there. I felt for the first time that these were my true friends, the simple people of the town without a hidden agenda, who I could trust to protect and help me as needed. I had to be careful not to put them in harm's way when it came looking out for me again.

I spent most of Sunday indoors with my curtains closed and spent the day reading in English to distract me from the growing commotion surrounding my research and Del's hotel and apartments project. I wrote a letter home but only mentioned that I had seen old friends on the river boats and that Yulia and I may go for a voyage again at the start of the summer holidays in July. I mentioned that I was busy with a research project but didn't mention any details. I was becoming suspicious of who was reading and listening to all my correspondences. I kept the letter short and vague.

Around four-thirty that afternoon while I was cooking in the kitchen, the doorbell rang. Babushka toddled into the kitchen to ask if I was expecting any company, Yulia maybe? I confirmed that I was not waiting for guests. She said it was better that she go to the door.

"Nobody will hurt an old grandma," she said and cackled as she waddled again to the door. The bell rang again with impatience. I stirred the vegetables in my fry pan.

After a few moments, I heard raised voices come down the hallway that could be heard over my stir-frying dinner. I turned off the gas and walked with care and concern into the hallway to see Natasha with her back to the door pushing it closed while a foot was keeping it open and somebody was pushing on the other side. Babushka was yelling for them to go away, to leave and that nobody else was in the apartment. She motioned for me to get out of sight and continued to push on the door with her old, bent back. The shouting from outside grew louder and the door started to open further. Babushka was too small and frail to get the door on the latch.

With my kitchen knife in my right hand, I pulled Babushka out of the way of the door and let it fling open. I met the assailant on the other side with my lunging stiff arm to his chest, palm thrust onto his sternum pushing him back out the doorway and in the stairwell. With a raised kitchen knife over my head in my right hand I was yelling and demanding that they leave. There were two others behind the man whose raised arm I was about to slash with my knife.

"Stop, police!" the front man shouted at me.

I stayed my arm and lowered the knife, but not my hand on his chest, palm open, pushing him out still across the threshold of the apartment.

"You show me your documents now or leave!" I yelled at him, adrenaline pumping through my arms with each heartbeat, I raised the knife higher.

"We are the police, we are all detectives!" the third man screamed at me.

All three revealed their concealed badges from their suit coat pockets and then let into me with a verbal barrage of accusations and questions. Babushka started crying in the hallway. The lead detective yelled at her like he was yelling at a whining dog to shut up and go to her room. She obeyed and disappeared into her bedroom.

"What do you guys want? Pushing in like this and frightening old ladies?" I spoke to them in a way that one would speak to somebody angrily on the street or the market, not as one would speak to police officers.

"You will call me, Sir! You will call him Sir and him Sir!" The senior officer pointed to each one of his colleagues, in turn, to make it clear that my near attack on them and my lack of respect was weighing quickly on their patience.

"We have shown you our documents, we now demand to see yours," was the command from the detective.

I produced my passport and visa from my jacket hanging in the corner and waited silently for their verdict.

"American citizen, student visa, registered in Nizhniy Novgorod," he spoke to his colleagues so it was clear who and what I was.

"What are you studying, young man?" the questions were short and exact.

"History and linguistics, sir." I found my polite voice as the adrenaline was subsiding.

"Do you have proof of this?" he asked again quickly with suspicion.

I found my student card in my book bag and handed it over calmly.

"Seems to be in order," was his commentary as he handed the documents to his partners for a confirmation of his conclusion.

"Do you usually greet people at your door with a knife?" there was an inference in his question.

"I apologize. My babushka has been harassed yesterday by hooligans. I thought they had come back to rob the place now that it's getting dark," I said demurely.

"Did you report this to the local police?" he asked dryly without any intended irony.

"No, sir. I was not here to witness anything. She only told me about it and asked me to stay home tonight in case there were further problems. I was cooking in the kitchen when the bell rang," I lied.

"You know that I could arrest you right now for assaulting a police officer?" he was trying to scare me, and it was working

"As I said, I did not know you were police officers. None of you are in uniform. I could not see any markings. I stopped when your colleague identified himself," I replied humbly.

The other two detectives were looking around my room as I was held captive to the questioning of the lead officer. I was conscious of them while not looking away from the interrogator. Luckily, I had sealed the letter to my mother and put it in my school bag and my notes on Mr. P. were in the same bag zipped up by the door, not on my desk where the police were looking. On the head of my bed was a novel by Maxim Gorkiy with a bookmark somewhere in the middle pages. A large Russian-English dictionary was open on my table with last week's translation work next to it. In my window sill were a few English books I had brought with me from the States. There was a growing stack of *The Economist* magazines in the corner of the table with highlights around every article about Russia's transition economy and mixed with that my printed articles from the American library. My shortwave radio and cassette player stood quietly next to the wall with a Russian group in the breach. It looked like the room of a studious student.

"You do not drink? You do not smoke?" the third officer inquired with a scowl on his face.

I looked sheepishly at the questioning officer and gave no answer.

The questions and answers went back and forth like a tennis match.

"Where in the city do your attend lectures?"

"Linguistics school on Minin Street, history department, Minin Square and literature on Gagarin Street in the foreign students' division."

"Who are you advisors there?"

"Mrs. Valentina Petrovna, Lyudmilla Daskova and Dean Karamzin, and sometimes Professor Strelyenko."

"Do you study there every day?"

"Most days, yes sir."

"Do you have contact with other foreigners in the city?"

"Mostly just the other students from other countries each week, sir."

"You are not involved with other foreign businesses in the city?"

"I am acquainted with a business man from America who my university advisor introduced me to. We share dinner every other week when he is not traveling."

"Why do you not live in the dormitories with other students?"

"Honestly, because I want to learn Russian, not speak English with other foreign students."

"Do you rent this room?"

"Yes, for twenty dollars per month."

"We are here looking for the owner of this apartment, your landlord. Do you know where he lives?"

"No sir, I have only met him once in January. He doesn't even come for his rent money. You can see that I have put three twenty-dollar bills in an envelope in my cupboard with his name on it. There, just open that door."

The second detective opened the cabinet door and found the envelope with the rent money in it from February, March, and April. It wasn't May yet. He counted the bills and nodded to his boss.

"It's the only money I keep in the apartment. I called him February and told him he is free to pick up his money anytime he is in the neighborhood. I don't have a telephone in this apartment so I said he could just use his keys to come in and find the money when he needed it even when I am at lectures or the library," I explained.

"Your landlord is sought on charges of tax evasion. We need to know where to find him," the detective demanded from me.

"I only have his telephone number. I can give that to you if you wish," I offered helpfully.

"Yes, please."

I reached into my bookshelf to find my address book and showed the officer the number scratched into the front cover. He took it from me and noted the number in his own notebook and then continued to look through my contacts. The addresses were from all over Russia: Moscow, Voronezh, Kazan, Ryzan, Samara and a number from Kyiv as well as a Belorussian from Brest. I waited for his further questions.

"You have many friends in Russia. Have you traveled to all these places?"

"No sir, we all met on a river cruise last summer. We send letters and photographs to each other," I answered truthfully.

"Please remember that you are not authorized to travel without permission from the police outside this province. Do not leave Nizhniy Novgorod without informing the police. If we are not able to find you, you could be arrested when you return and be fined and then deported. Is that clear?" he threatened.

"Yes, sir!"

The lead detective gave a nod to his colleagues and they filed to the hallway and out the door. I closed it behind them and latched every latch without bidding them good evening. I went to my bed and nearly passed out, shaking and cold. Babushka stayed in her room for the rest of the evening but Raiya knocked softly on my door after fifteen minutes, took a seat at my table and started to ask even more questions than the police did. "That was horrible with all that shouting! Was nobody in uniform?"

I was laying on my bed with my arm over my eyes. I shook my head in the negative, not raising it from the pillow.

"The law says that if a plain clothes detective comes to the door they must have a uniformed officer with them. You were completely right to push them out! Did they ask you for any money?" she asked.

I shook my head again.

"What did they want?" she wouldn't stop.

They wanted Roman, my landlord.

"Roman has never lived here. His aunt died and left this apartment to him," Raiya revealed.

On this news, I sat up and looked at Raiya, "Say that again, please?"

"It's true. Roman, he's a dirty snake. He never lived here. His old aunt, who he never took care of, died last year in February and the apartment has been closed up since then. He never registered the apartment in his name nor ever lived here. He just rents it out illegally," she embellished.

"There you have the argument for tax evasion..." I dropped my head back on the pillow.

"Did you read their police identifications?" Raiya insisted.

"Yes, I looked at them but didn't get time to take notes," I moaned in annoyance. "For all I know they could have been fake."

"Did they read 'Militia' or 'FSB?" she continued to push for details.

"FSB, why?" I answered.

"Well, because FSB is not the local police that would investigate a man for hitting his wife or a fight at the bar or a stolen car or arrest hooligans at the train station. The FSB are the officers that only go after spies from other countries and make sure spies aren't in our own country. I can't imagine that they would pursue someone not paying local property taxes on a little room. It doesn't sound right. You should report this to the local militia office. It's very irregular," she cautioned me.

"And what good would that do when I am a foreigner? Maybe they came to make sure that I am not a spy. Did you think about that, Raiya?" I was getting very weary of her talking and decided to go for an evening walk to clear my head. I got up to put on my coat and hat.

"You are going to go out? What if they are watching you still?" She was more paranoid than I was.

"Then they will watch me take a walk! I'm not going to call anybody or pass secrets. I'm just going for a walk," I said defiantly.

"If I was you I would stay indoors until tomorrow and do your normal things. They won't just go away. I can bet you somebody is outside now watching the doors, smoking a cigarette under a tree or sitting in a car with the lights off." She was serious.

I put my hat and coat back on the rack and sat at the table opposite her and listened.

"When the Chechens started the fighting last year, the FSB was watching all the different Muslim men in the city. My brother was harassed almost every day. They searched him every day, questioned him about where he was going every day. Followed him and searched his house when he was at work. They had a guy watching him all the time so they knew when they could go into house and when he was home. It was horrible. So, he went to Kazan and left his wife and kids here in Nizhniy for a few months until the harassment stopped. They didn't trust the Tatars because of what the Chechens did. Tatars are good Soviets, too, we are just Muslims by heritage, but nobody seemed to care. Natasha even has a medal from the Red Army for her service in the great patriotic war against the Nazis, but you saw how that officer treated babushka. It's not fair what they do to us after our men died next to theirs in the war." Raiya had a deeper story than I had ever suspected.

"What did babushka do doing the war to earn a medal?" I asked in sincere curiosity, having calmed down again.

"She worked in the uniform and boot factory for the entire war. Her fiancé volunteered after the first invasion by the fascists and she volunteered in the uniform and boot factory because she couldn't go with him of course. Only the men could serve in the ranks. She was an overseer of a huge work group in the factory until it was all over. For that they gave her a medal. They say her factory made the best boots of the entire country and soldiers would fight to get her boots!" Raiya was beaming with a bit of pride.

"What happened to baba's fiancé? Did they marry? They didn't, did they. She doesn't have children," I concluded.

"He died in Smolensk and is buried there," was the sad news from the front. "Natasha will be getting another medal next week in the anniversary celebrations of fifty years of victory. She is also one of the last survivors of the ladies that worked in the factory with her, so she and another friend will be recognized by the mayor in a ceremony."

I sat and pondered on this for a few moments, thinking about babushka trying to push the police out of the apartment thinking she was protecting me from hooligans.

"I would like to be there for that. Do you think anybody would mind if I attended?" I asked.

"Of course, you will be there. It's a big public ceremony on Minin Square on May the ninth," the pride in her voice was audible.

"I won't miss it," I confirmed.

I bid Raiya good night and she went back to her shared bedroom and locked the door behind her. I didn't sleep well that night. Every shadow passing by my veiled window was an assailant and every noise in the stairwell a break-in.

06

20. Exposed

I dragged myself out of bed at nine o'clock knowing immediately that I had missed my morning lectures. The sunshine was trying desperately to get through my curtains and my eyelids, which were all still closed tight due to the weekend excitement. I shuffled down the hall towards the bath with the hope that some cold water over my head would help me to wake up enough to be able to make something of the day after not having slept much. As I was moving down the hallway, Raiya bid me good morning as she was heading for the open market up the street for groceries.

Being alone in the apartment that morning after bathing, I decided to forego dressing in the bathroom, wrapped a towel around myself and headed down to my room to get dressed. On entering my own room, which was closest to the outside door, I noticed that Raiya had left behind her rolling shopping cart in the apartment, with her keys in the bottom of it. I decided that I would get dressed quickly and see if I could catch her at the market and do some shopping for supplies myself. But, as I entered my room I could see the shadow of a woman standing in front of my window as if waiting for me to come to the window—perhaps trying to get my attention. As the curtains were still closed I could see a shadow where a torso of a woman blocked the sun's morning rays. Thinking it was Raiya trying to get my attention to open the door so she could get her keys and bag, I stepped quickly to the window and opened the curtains to let her know that I would open the door for her.

I was shocked to find that the woman standing outside my window was not Raiya. There I stood, with only a pane of glass and a towel between my naked self and a woman who I did not at first recognize, who was standing squarely in front of my window, staring straight in. After I got over the moment of shock that it was not my house mate but a stranger standing so obtrusively close to my window and unabashedly peering at me just out of the bath, I realized it was the obtuse lady with the dog who I usually saw at seven o'clock outside my window every morning, when I was eating breakfast, before leaving for lectures. The first thought that went through my head was . . . how funny that she is walking her dog again at nine-thirty, just as I am getting ready to leave . . . what are the chances?

No sooner had I asked myself the question, alarms went off in my head. Every morning and evening as long as I could remember since living in that apartment I saw this woman and her dog outside of my room enjoying the grass, trees and the easy view into my room. She wasn't walking her dog, even though she had a dog with her. She was watching me!

I never once suspected or even noticed the woman watching me because she had been there since the first day I had been there. I figured simply that, with me as the new comer, I was observing her routine that she undoubtedly kept for months, if not years before I arrived. But this morning she was not on schedule, but was doing the same thing at the same time that I was doing my same thing—just two hours later. It was brilliant of the authorities to assign such a person to monitor me. I had never suspected the ugly woman with the stupid expression on her face until I caught her in the act of spying on me. It had only taken a few seconds for my brain to connect all the dots and put the entire story together. I wanted to let her know that I now knew what she was and what she was doing. I looked her square in the face, standing there in just my towel, and opened the first pane of the double paned windows and shouted as loud as I could.

"Come on in? Should I heat up some tea for us? I can tell you what I told your bosses last night."

She disappeared quickly from in front of my window without calling her dog this time, leaving him to roam between the trees. I got myself quickly dressed and headed up to the market.

It was no great surprise to me when I stepped off the bus on Gorkiy Square on Tuesday morning to see who now I referred to as my 'British Knight' in spanking white trainers, smoking on the street corner, pretending he was waiting for a mini-bus. As I was on my way to classes I didn't pay him any attention and continued up towards the Gagarin Street campus. Perhaps he would join us for a lecture on Dostoyevsky? It would probably do him some good. He did not enter the building but I saw him duck into a student café across the street from the main building. He could spend his whole day smoking and waiting for all I cared.

Before the class was to begin, Valentina Petrovna stepped out of her office and asked me to step in for a few minutes.

"It will be fine to be a few minutes late for the lecture, Mr. Turner. It's rather urgent." She was speaking English, so I knew it wasn't a social visit. "How are your studies progressing, Peter? You had some very encouraging mid-term evaluations from your professors, but as we go into the May holidays we need to make sure you are on course to finish at the end of June at the right level. Do you feel that you are still moving forward?"

"Yes ma'am," I replied politely, not wanting to shove a stick in the hornets' nest that was buzzing all around me the last few days. "I feel I am progressing with my translation courses both written and verbally, but I still feel weak in Russian composition. Reading is going very well and I believe my conversational skills, both comprehension and speaking, have improved greatly these four months and my vocabulary and use of idioms and expressions I believe are much improved."

"Very good. I am pleased to hear this. You do seem very comfortable and sharp when I speak Russian with you. The university is pleased to see your progress," she said with no sincerity.

"Thank you, ma'am." I sat still looking straight ahead adding nothing more.

"Professor Dashvokva also feels that you are making great progress in all areas but is concerned that you are picking up too much street language, perhaps from your housemates. I understood that they are Tatars?" Her question perked my ears. I had never told anybody about my housemates.

"Ma'am I believe the street language has been picked up from socializing with other students on Friday afternoons. They have taught me to curse quite well. This is all they do when they hang about smoking and drinking on the weekends," I parried her implications.

"Yes, that is very true. I sometimes too get red in the face when I hear their conversations," Valentina admitted.

"I believe I learn more civilized and proper language from my housemates than I would in the dormitories, and I believe my conversations are more widely varied speaking and listening to people of different ages and taking care of my own household needs. You know I even have to pay the gas and water bill myself at the district offices. It's quite the experience looking at it as a whole." I had gone on the offensive in the conversation.

"Yes, perhaps you are correct," Valentina had to concede. "How then are your history studies progressing? I understood that the dean had asked you to prepare an article for his annual journal. Have you made progress on a topic to research?" She was now getting the heart of the matter.

"Yes, ma'am. I have and I am making good progress and finding materials to support my academic format." I was being very vague on purpose.

"Are you getting the needed support from the faculty there as needed?" she advanced again.

"Yes, ma'am. Both the dean and other professors are very accessible for me," I stalled.

"What is it you are researching, may I ask?" she wouldn't stop kicking the hornets' nest.

"I am researching and writing about the current privatization process of state enterprises. I have held interviews at the World Bank office, visited a privatization auction, and Dean Karamzin is trying to set up an interview with Governor Nemtsov, but he seems to be a very busy man, and the Sannings are also a great resource as they give perspective to the foreign investment aspect of joint venture companies." I was not lying, just avoiding telling the entire truth.

"It does sound very interesting. I will look forward to reviewing your paper before you publish it." Was Valentina telling me that she was required to censor my research? "Will you be interviewing local businessmen for this research as well?" I sensed that the hornets had already been stirred.

"I am not well acquainted with private entrepreneurs in the city. If you know of any that would be appropriate I would love to meet and interview some," I was on the edge of untruth.

"Peter, it has come to my attention that you have been researching some very sensitive topics and that you have been using the university's database at the American library to support your thesis." Valentina was now setting herself up directly against me and my efforts.

"Yes, ma'am. Why shouldn't I be allowed to research using the university's resources? I paid my tuition in cash, in dollars for that privilege. Arkadiy was my witness, remember?" I remained on the offensive.

Valentina paused to consider her next move in our cerebral game of chess and looked at me to see if I was threatening her in any way. We both knew what I was referring to. I looked her square in the face without blinking and with no expression on mine.

"It is the university's request that you refrain from any further research into local activities and concentrate on the political and policy developments of your topic," was Valentina's measured retort.

"I have done nothing but look at political and policy developments, and the best examples of how to avoid the problems of the last few years with privatization are happening right here in Nizhniy Novgorod. How can I ignore the local developments when all of Russia is focused on what is happening here in Nizhniy?" After this Valentina had only one further move—pulling rank.

"Mr. Turner, the university will not be put at risk by reckless academics. I have allowed you considerable leeway to live out of the dormitories and to allow you to study history and politics with Dean Karamzin, which was not a part of your application to study with us at this school. You are a student of linguistics and literature, not politics. If you will not refrain from questioning respected businessmen in accusatory tones then your credentials will be revoked and you will be asked to leave immediately." She had shown her hand and she wasn't bluffing anymore.

"I'm sorry. What are you referring to? Who did I interview in accusatory tones?" I was thoroughly annoyed.

"Mr. P. is a respected businessman in Nizhniy Novgorod and is a friend, patron, and sponsor of this university. You are not to pursue any of the points in your discussion with him in your research or your article for the school journal. Is that clear?" Valentina was getting a bit red in the face.

"I would be very interested to learn what part of our discussion was accusatory at all. I was very professional. I listened, took notes and he sang like a canary. I only had to ask him maybe three questions and I got his life story. Accusations? There were no accusations, Valentina," I was adamant. "If there is anybody in Nizhniy Novgorod that is active with the whole privatization process it is Mr. P.! Of course, I should interview him. He is the city's go-to man for efforts to privatize many types of businesses," I insisted.

"Mr. P. demands that on no account should any parts of his interview with you be published in your paper. Is that clear, Mr. Turner?" Valentina had put her foot down.

"Dean Karamzin is fully supportive of my research and is overseeing my thesis. He has given full academic freedom in this paper. His quote was 'Stalin has been dead a very long time.'" I was now pulling as many stripes off the dean's sleeve as possible to keep from being censored. "If I am not allowed to continue under the dean's guidance without interference then I will not continue at this university next term, and my fifteen-hundred dollars in cash tuition money will not be at your disposal." My threats were no longer veiled.

"Publishing your research with the name of Mr. P. or any of his associates will be dangerous to this university, your fellow foreign students, and for yourself. Under no conditions can you use the information that you learned from your interview with him. Is that clear?" She was yelling now and slapping her hand on her desk. "You will turn into me any and all notes that you took during that interview."

I took my notebook out containing all the notes about Mr. P. and ripped out the pages and left them on her desk.

"Read them! You will see for yourself there was nothing at all accusatory in the questions of mine that implied anything but being interested in how he began his growing private enterprises as an entrepreneur. I cannot imagine what he understood to be compromising. There is nothing in those notes that should make anybody worry about anything. In fact, I thought his ability to grow a business in these times to be rather clever and was going to write it just like that. Anyhow, there you have all my notes about Mr. P. Burn them if you want to."

I stormed out of Valentina's office and left the building altogether in a rage. As I crossed the street to the bus stop heading back to Gorkiy Square, I had forgotten about my tail until I saw him throw away his cigarette and stamp it out with his gleaming white shoes. "What an idiot!" I thought to myself. He came and stood near to me to wait for the same bus. I paid him still no attention and did not try to elude him at all. My movements through the city were hardly a state secret. I was headed to Minin Square to speak with the dean, as this had all been his idea to begin with.

I arrived at Minin Square to see tall risers and stages being put into place for the viewing of the parades of workers, trucks, cannons, and tanks that would be held there. The red flag of the Soviet Union was hung on every street corner, the yellow hammer and sickle visible in the breeze. The university buildings were draped in banners and flags with the emblems of the different branches of the armed forces. The square itself had been cleared up as well. Rubbish bins had been emptied and painted in the city's coat of arms. The gutters had been swept and washed and the flower beds were all teaming with newly planted pansies and red geraniums. The grass areas were cordoned off to protect them from being trampled by the crowds that would assemble. It had never looked more pleasant.

Billboards were being renewed with nostalgic propaganda posters of the Red Army from 1944 and 1945, calling attention to their heroic efforts fighting back the Nazis. The posters reminded us again not to be chatty on the telephone as you never know who was listening! We were encouraged to contribute to the war effort by foregoing luxuries and sending any extra socks or boots to soldiers on the front line. My favorite was a young man in a stormtrooper's uniform, carrying a rifle and with an enthusiastic smile who was waving his comrades forward with the tagline: "All the way to Berlin, boys!" How glorious they made it all look.

I decided to take a breather before I stormed into the dean's office and made a fool of myself. I strolled the square out to the Chkalov Monument and looked down the grand staircase to the Volga. The hydrofoils were speeding down the middle of the river, running circles around the barges and the cruise boats. The river was blue and calm, like the vast sky to the north and west. It was a beautiful day, it had just started out poorly. After taking a few deep breaths, I turned to head back to the history department building and there across the street was my personal shadow pretending to talk on the public telephone. "What a dope!" I said to myself and paid him no attention as I entered from the street into the building.

The dean offered me a chair as he finished his telephone conversation. Luckily the office window looked directly onto the square where the 'British Knight' had taken a seat and was smoking another cigarette and watching the door with one eye and the passing university girls with his other eye.

"Mr. Turner!" the dean said, putting down the handset. "We have not spoken since your interview. How did it go? I am very anxious to hear the details."

"Good morning, sir. I am afraid that Mr. P. did not find the interview very ingratiating. He has somehow got a hold of Valentina Petrovna who has confiscated my notes from the interview and has forbidden me from writing about anything I learned in that interview in my paper," I whined.

"That old cow! Don't pay her any attention. She is an overcautious old lady. We must go forward with the project." Dean Karamzin was very dismissive of the morning's events. "You can still remember what you spoke about, yes? Just rewrite your notes and everybody will be happy. Mr. P. thinks he killed the story, Valentina Petrovna can tell the university director she stopped it and we will still publish your article. Everybody wins!"

"Valentina says that such an action would be dangerous for me personally," I retorted.

"She has such an imagination! What does she think, we live in Moscow or something? To my knowledge we don't have a single Chechen in our city," he continued his rant.

"Might it be possible to write this paper anyhow without using this example? Even without a name? I was able to get a picture of how funding from a small operation of theft and smuggling grows into a larger operation that then moves to legitimize their operations with the local government's blessing. Perhaps we can find some more and make a composite picture instead of focusing on this specific local example, and then everybody wins!" I smiled with irony on my lips.

"Young man! We do not need another academic paper without specifics. If we are going to flush this pheasant from the underbrush we need to use the dogs!" he bellowed.

"Why is it your goal to name your friend and client? Wouldn't that be bad for your business?" I challenged.

Dean Karamzin leaned back in his chair, a bit pensive and spoke quietly, "Mr. Turner, I know for a fact that the politicians of this city are in direct cooperation with the criminal elements to make themselves rich. They use their positions of power to make themselves rich and not care for the people of this great city that fought and worked hard to preserve the independence of our country from occupation. My father, my uncles! These criminal elements are quietly and secretly setting the policy agenda for the future of our country. I know you feel the same way I do regarding the way that these opportunists are robbing Russia blind. If you say you have the information that we can substantiate as criminal, I can bring you into contact with people who can tell you how that money is corrupting city council decisions."

"And do you think people will really care? Aren't they just resigned to the fact that Russian civil servants are only there for themselves and their own profit?" I replied.

"The governor will care! He has already been fighting the corruption and making more and more of what happens in Nizhniy more transparent. If we can show that the criminals of Nizhniy are in bed with the city administration, we might get some change here, very soon; but we have to act quickly as Nemtsov is being courted by Yeltsin's people and could in the next year go to work in Moscow with the national government," he appealed to me.

"I am sorry, but I don't have anything that I can substantiate as criminal. The way he tells his story it all sounds plausibly legal, especially during the Perestroika period. Nobody really knew what was legal and what wasn't. Did he steal car parts just because nobody knew how to price them? I would have to do a lot of inference to turn shady entrepreneurialism into criminal. Inference is not an academic tool last time I checked." I thought I had the dean in check.

"This is why you must continue to research what you learned about his past and future plans. Perhaps you can pin him down squarely on criminal activities and then we can connect that black money to city hall. You must keep digging away in that database and find proof, find some documentation of his activities. We need to find the link!" He was almost desperate.

"Sir, I need to let you know that I am being actively watched and followed. I had a visit from the FSB to my apartment on Sunday evening for a short interrogation and to give me a warning. All this started after my interview with Mr. P.," I confided.

"I think you are imaging things." he insisted.

I motioned to the window. "Please tell me if a young man, about my age, dressed all in black except for his white shoes, is still sitting on the bench in the square, smoking and watching the door of this building."

Dean Karamzin stood and looked out the window. To his surprise he saw exactly what I described would be outside his window.

"For how long has this been going on?" he queried.

"Since Saturday afternoon. Today is Tuesday. He goes everywhere I go when I'm on this side of the river. When I am in Zarechnaya there is an ugly woman and a dog that keep watch over my apartment. That young man knew my home address and went there after I was able to shake him on Saturday afternoon in the old city. He drives a black Lada and has a partner."

"Ah yes! A black Lada has just pulled up and they are speaking through the window," the Dean blurted, surprised.

"Voila!" I breathed out in French.

"I will speak with the governor and have this stopped immediately!" he declared to me.

"No, please don't! They don't know yet that I know I am being followed. I need them to keep using the idiot on the bench in the white shoes so I know I can lose them when I need to, and know that I have truly lost them. I am not doing anything different than before so I have nothing to hide from them. It's just to show you that if I go any further and make people mad they'll know exactly where to find me should they want to 'persuade' me with something more than words and threats," I calmly explained.

"You say the FSB came to your apartment?" he queried again, watching out the window with his back to me.

"Yes, Sunday night around dinner time. They did not come with a police officer in uniform either," I offered to get his response.

"They can't do that! That means they are working without orders. Who are they working for? You didn't tell them anything, did you?" He seemed genuinely concerned now.

"I gave them truthful answers to everything they asked me, of course. I was terrified!" I exclaimed.

"Why? What right did they have to take you anywhere?" he remarked with doubt in his voice.

"I threatened one of them with a knife...." I confessed.

"What? Why?" he turned to look at me with wide eyes.

"We thought they were the hooligans trying to break into our apartment," was my apology.

"Did they take anything from you?" he asked the same question that Raiya had.

"No, I think they had Valentina Petrovna do that this morning to keep it from escalating or making me..." I paused briefly and corrected my thoughts, "make us suspect that they have a direct connection to Mr. P."

"What connection could they have to Mr. P.? FSB is involved in state security, not local criminal activities." The Dean slowly took his chair again as he expressed his amazement at this information.

"Are you sure you want me to keep looking for that missing link, sir?" I gave him a look filled with sarcasm and second guessing.

"Perhaps we should take a break for the May holidays and see where things are after that. I did not think that Igor was capable of getting involved in high crimes and treason. He never even seemed capable of signing his own name to a confession." The dean sounded a bit spooked.

"Perhaps I will head back to the library and refocus my research this week so that I can still make a paper about the privatization process of the factories and focus on the foreign investors. This way, everybody will clearly see that we didn't use the local materials, and we can all walk out of this with our legs unbroken," I proposed.

"I think that this might be a smart course of action, Peter, just until we can find our feet again," was the dean's reserved response after he had regained his composure.

"Dean, you might think I have a big imagination, but, do you have a back door to this place?" I asked carefully.

The dean walked with me to the concierge's room on the ground floor and spoke to him in a low voice that I couldn't understand and pointed to me a few times. The old man took a bushel of keys from his drawer and without speaking a word motioned for me to follow him. Before we reached the exit to the courtyard and then the street, we turned left down a corridor with a door which was always locked. He deftly picked a single key from the mess of metal and with it opened the door and ushered me through it and locked it behind us.

We walked down a dimly lit, narrow concrete staircase into the basement of the building. It was dank and dark, and I could smell that we were underground. The old man led me through a maze of small corridors and past many locked storage rooms, hot water pipes with insulation hanging from steaming pipes. Dim light bulbs lit the way through the labyrinth, left, right, straight on. After passing through this subterranean maze we ascended another similar staircase to the one we descended from the history department.

When we emerged again at ground level, we were in the lobby of the medical school on the same block but kitty-corner to each other, not back to back. The lobby of the building opened up on the upper embankment street near the Chkalov monument and the grand stair case. I thanked my guide and darted out the door and down the stairs as fast as my legs would carry me. I caught a bus at the River Station to the metro at the Moscow Station; no sign of the 'British Knight' following on my heels.

21. Exit Strategy

Upon arriving at the train station, I stopped at the public phones to see if I could reach Yulia to ask if I could stop by to collect my money and plane ticket that I had left in her apartment just in case I needed to think about a quick exit from the city. Perhaps I was being a bit too paranoid? The phone at Yulia's apartment was not answered. She must have still been at school. As I hung up the telephone I saw through the blurry, scratched glass of the phone booth a familiar figure step out of a taxi. She wasn't Russian, that was for sure, but I couldn't place her for a split second.

"Els? Els is that you?" I called out to her still on the curb.

Just then, Del stepped out from around the other side of the taxi and was fishing in the trunk of the car to retrieve their travel cases.

"Del! Els!" I called out again. This time they heard me and looked my way, but didn't see me immediately. I stepped up closer. "It's me, Peter." I removed my cap so they could see my face.

"Oh, Peter! What a coincidence. What are you doing here in the middle of the day? Shouldn't you be in lectures?" Els asked me.

"Yes, I should be, but some difficulties have arisen. I am just on my way back to my place on the metro line." I tried to keep my answer vague and untroubled. "Where are you heading?"

"We're catching the two o'clock to Moscow. We have some business to take care of there," Del replied.

I was startled to hear that they were leaving and feared that they may not be coming back.

"Peter, what is wrong?" Els asked, "And don't lie to me!"

"Is it that obvious?" I asked.

"You can't fool this one, Peter. She can read everybody like a book," Del conceded.

"Are you coming back?" I asked with concern in my voice.

"We'll be back next Thursday. We just have a few meetings over the next week with different people," Del informed me. "Heard that you have had some troubles since the weekend."

"You aren't leaving because Misha and I were followed and you all had the apartment broken into and all?" I asked a bit relieved.

"Kid, let's step inside where we can have a private word," Del said as he turned to pay the waiting taxi driver. "It's not good to speak about such things where everybody can hear us."

I helped carry their bags into the train station and the three of us found a table in corner of the station restaurant where we spoke in quiet tones. Del sat with his back to the wall so he could keep a full view of the people in the restaurant.

"Kid, since our chat on Friday night we have been able to uncover a bit of information that you should probably know about." Del spoke to me but never looked me in the face, his eyes scanning the dining room and the door. "It turns out that in fact Mr. P.'s plans are real and he is planning to officially submit his application for a building permit during the May holidays so that nobody from the steering committee is around to prepare any resistance. Technically, the mayor's office is open these weeks even though all of his staff will be on holiday. Citizens are therefore able to submit requests per legal procedures. The mayor, of course, will stay in the city for the Victory Day ceremonies so business can be done 'legally' but under the radar."

"Who told you this? How did you find out?" I was puzzled.

"Everybody has a price, kid. Problem is that I can't act on it without jeopardizing my information source for the future. Past info has also proven to be correct, so I believe it's very credible," he said, avoiding answering my direct question.

"Why does this concern me?" I protested, not wanting to hear Mr. P.'s name again that day.

"Because he is at a critical phase of planning and it would be a good idea if you stopped stirring the pot for a while. The word is out that Mr. P. is having somebody followed to make sure that they don't cause any further trouble for him. I can only guess that what he told you was not meant to be in the open before the tenth of May," Del speculated.

"What's so important about the tenth of May?" I asked.

"He has an appointment with the mayor that afternoon when he will submit the application for what we understand will be a quick approval process with different witnesses to the process," he answered.

"But what about your project?" I protested. "They can't just set your project aside."

"Listen kid, it gets better. You know our little side hustle of searching for apartments for expats? Well, a councilman, also on the city's steering committee, evidently had the same idea. So, we have some competition," Del confided.

"Well, I wish them all the luck in the world. They won't find the types of apartments that will fill the bill." I puffed with resentment.

"They are going about it all a bit differently. He and his 'investors' have bought up a small apartment building in the old town and are, as we speak, renovating the entire building up to standard. There will be a compound with full security and full lock down capabilities. They will provide cars and drivers for the residents, one driver and car for each three apartments. It sounds like they've got the right idea. Just don't know from where they are getting the financing," Del speculated.

"Del, there is so much black money flowing under this city, I'm surprised it hasn't come up through the toilets and the plumbing yet," I hissed emphatically over the table.

"Keep your shirt on, kid, keep your shirt on." Del didn't want our conversation to look too secret. He scanned the hall for people standing about looking our direction. Not finding any his eyes came back to me. "It's important that you and Misha stop looking for any further apartments until I get back from Moscow next Thursday night. If you are being followed, somebody will get word that the two of you, known to be associated with me, are searching for apartments. It could set off alarm bells. Until I know who is financing those apartments we had better keep our heads down. Get it?"

"Is it time for me to get out of town, Del?" I asked concerned.

"Not unless you want to. Just be a student having fun during the holidays and don't give anybody a reason to think you're researching anything further from your interview with Mr. P. It could be real trouble for you if you do. It goes deeper than you think," he warned.

"Yes, I figured that out with the FSB showed up on Sunday night at my door," I offered.

"What? Did you say KGB at your door? Why? What did they want?" Del was taken off guard by this revelation. He gave Els a concerned look. She looked at me.

"They said they wanted my landlord for questioning. Tax evasion," I replied.

"That's bullshit, kid. That was a recon visit. They were establishing that you were still living in that apartment and you can bet that they are watching your every move. Do you think you were followed here?" Del's eyes starting darting around the train station again and he sat up straight in his chair startled at this news.

"No, I lost my tag in the old city by sneaking out of the faculty through the basement. They have an idiot following me in white sneakers. He's an idiot." I brushed off the idea that I had been followed to the station.

"No kid, that's Mr. P.'s goon. Counter intelligence in this country doesn't work like that. They have radios and people all over town watching in traffic check points and whatnot. You lose one and they will see you seven minutes later at a different location. Never the same person for more than five minutes. You'll never know you're being watched if they don't want you to know it. They're really good! It's just about as good as a helicopter in the sky," he chided me for my ignorance.

"Either way, they think I'm still in lectures as I left by a completely different entrance and nobody knows I am on the move." I tried to sound smart but knew I was in over my head.

"Not so sure about that, kid," Del said looking over my shoulder again, "but I think it's time for me and Els to be on a train.

"Should Peter not come with us now to Moscow?" Els suggested. Del chewed on this question for a few moments, shifting his jaw back and forth.

"We would need a good cover story if we did that. We aren't prepared for it. It would create a dangerous situation for everybody, especially if he is being watched by two groups. Somebody will sound the alarm that he is gone," Del concluded.

"Kid, you need to start getting real obvious. Do very obvious things that make it look like you are preparing to leave. Pack up your apartment real slow so that anybody watching or letting themselves in on a regular basis can see you are slowly, deliberately getting ready to leave. Go to the Aeroflot office in town and book a ticket back to the States. Make sure everybody knows about it. Don't do anything too fast or somebody will swoop in and grab you. Understood? Don't do anything dumb and don't try to lose your tag again. Keep everything you do visible. You need to make sure everybody stays bored by you being very predictable.

"Yes, I like boring at this point!" I agreed.

On Wednesday, I wore a bright orange rain jacket to protect me from a rainy day and to make sure that everybody who wanted to follow me could spot me a mile away. I went to all my lectures that day and walked between the lectures via Pokrovka, stopping along the way to purchase lavash, waiting in line with the 'British Knight' four people behind me in the line at the hole in the wall. I bought a bottle of Pepsi from a café and sat and drank it in the sun as the clouds started to dissipate around lunch time. I stopped and chatted up some girls I knew well. I could see that my shadow was getting very bored and was starting to lose interest in my movements.

After my literature lecture with Professor Dashkova, I went back to the Telephone and Telegraph building on Gorkiy Square and scheduled a telephone call home to the United States. It was the very early morning at my parents' home. I woke them up with some alarm and went on to tell them that I was just having a very difficult time in Nizhniy and was thinking about coming home in a week or two. My father sounded more concerned than I had hoped to make him. I tried to reassure him it was just a matter of being tired and a bit lonely, maybe some culture fatigue, but nothing to worry about. I put on some false emotion for those who were listening to my call. I hoped that my parents would go back to sleep and forget I even called, but I had to go on record with the FSB as actively planning to leave soon and this was the best way to make it public knowledge.

After I finished upsetting my parents at four in the morning, I stepped outside to the bank of public telephones on the porch of the Post Office and called Yulia's home. This time she picked up the phone.

"Hi, it's Peter!" I announced in Russian this time.

"Where are you?" Yulia seemed taken aback. I always spoke English with her on the phone.

"I'm on Pokrovka. Just finished speaking with my parents in America." I was speaking loudly.

"Are they alright? Why would you call them in the middle of the night there?" she was very puzzled.

"Listen, I need to come by and pick up my plane ticket from you. I need to schedule my flight to the USA for the summer break." I continued to be as obvious as possible.

"I thought we would go on the trip together, remember?" she was getting worried at this point.

"Can I come by on my way home for tea and get my ticket, please?" I continued with my story line.

"Yes, of course. We can talk when you are here. See you soon." She hung up the telephone.

As I got on the bus at Gorkiy Square to head across the Oka to the Zarechnaya district, I noticed that the 'British Knight' didn't get on the bus with me. Instead, he stepped into a car, one I didn't recognize, and they drove off in another direction down Gorkiy Street and out of sight. Perhaps they figured that I couldn't do any harm at home since I didn't have a telephone in my apartment and nobody of any consequence lived on that side of the city.

After I dragged myself to the top of the five flights of stairs to Yulia's door, I paused a moment to catch my breath. I debated for a split second whether I should tell her everything that was going on. It has been almost six weeks since I had actually told the truth about anything I was up to. Our discussions had only been light, based on fairy-tales about the coming summer cruise, last summer and her graduating from her college in June. I had revealed nothing about my conversations with Del, my work with Misha, the interview with Mr. P., the people following me, the FSB. I decided it was all too much to put on her.

I knocked on the steel door. Gung, gung, gung.

"What's going on? Are you okay? Why are you calling your parents on a Wednesday in the middle of the night? Why do you need your place ticket? Are you ill?" Yulia peppered me with questions as we sat in the living room.

"Well I, uhhh, I am, uhhhh, I don't know. I think I'm in some trouble and I don't know what to do," I blurted out.

"Is it at the university? Did you have a conflict with a professor or that old witch Valentina Petrovna?" she scowled when she said Valentina's name.

"Yes, yes, and yes and then some more." I nodded deliberately but not explaining any further.

"Well, at least we have the holidays coming up and you can take a two-week break. The weather is supposed to be really nice next week! Would you like to go to Moscow with me and mama? We are going to visit my aunt for a few days. The Victory Parade in Moscow is always the best. And do you remember the fireworks from last year in Moscow? They don't do them any better anyplace else." She thankfully forgot about my troubles, or perhaps didn't really want to hear about them. Ignorance can be bliss.

"No, I'm afraid I don't have the needed permission to leave Nizhniy Novgorod. I still have to ask for a travel visa for our voyage in July." I told the truth but had no intention of staying through July. I was ready to get out as quickly as I could without looking like I was running.

"OK, but what about this plane ticket for the summer? I thought we agreed to do the cruise again this summer." She put on a sad face.

"Of course, we'll do the cruise, but after that I will go home for a month. After being away for seven months, my parents said that they would like to see me for a bit before the fall term begins. My father said he would buy me a new round-trip ticket if I came home in August," I lied. My fibs seemed to satisfy Yulia and she happily went to retrieve my money belt from her bedroom. I unzipped it to see the ticket jacket and a stack of twenty and fifty-dollar bills.

"I'll go apply for a travel visa tomorrow for July and August so we're ready to sail the Volga again." I smiled.

Yulia served some tea and biscuits and we chatted further about something that I cannot remember as all I could think about was escape, and how to avoid looking like I was trying to be clandestine at the same time. It was a fine balancing act that drained me mentally and emotionally.

When I arrived home that evening to my apartment, I left the drapes wide open and sat at my desk with books open and a pen in my hand. I had the look of a studious academic, but I was scribbling in a stream of consciousness all my fears and worries, all the possibilities and variables I could anticipate during my secret retreat: first to Moscow, then the airport, and if I could make it past the passport control, maybe I could make it home.

As I thought and wrote in my shorthand, I obsessed on one thing that could be a hang-up. Even if I made it past the customs agents and boarded the aircraft, I would be flying on a Russian registered aircraft which could be forced to surrender me before the doors closed, or even return to the gate after being cleared for takeoff. A foreign registered aircraft, perhaps from Switzerland or France would not have to hand me over at the last minute to any border patrol. Once on board a foreign registered aircraft, it would be almost as if I was in their embassy. Upon arrival in Zurich or Paris, I could claim some sort of asylum or protection while they considered any request to send me back.

The thought also crossed my mind that perhaps, if I could make it to Moscow, maybe on an overnight train when everybody would think I was sleeping, perhaps I could appeal for protection at the US embassy there. Maybe they would be watching for me boarding any trains in the next few days.

I was probably already on a watch list. I thought deeply and carefully about how my next steps and went to soak my worried body in a hot bathtub. Tomorrow I would go about my normal business and act as if I was not suspicious nor aware of any of the people watching and following me. I would act completely normal.

The doubts and fears swirled in a mess of fear and adrenaline. The slightest noise would have sent me sprinting. I drifted off to sleep in a whirl of intrigue and insecurity feeling that I would soon be swallowed up by a world that would not stop for me to catch my breath. I felt that I would simply be stamped out. Then, almost suddenly, I realized I was dreaming and felt my tension dissolve into sleep.

06

22. Expelled

On Thursday morning, I returned to Valentina's office and apologized to her for my behavior on Tuesday morning. She responded as well in a professional manner. I thought for a moment that maybe I had misread everything and began to be hopeful again that things could normalize.

"Mr. Turner, I understand your reaction although I cannot approve of it. You are a serious student and everybody at the school appreciates your hard, academic work, and we understand you are not happy to give up your research and your months of work, but, this is still Russia and you must respect that you do not understand the different elements in our society as a foreigner," she lectured.

"Yes, I have thought about it for the last few days and I recognize that I have been reckless and should think more about my fellow students instead of my hope for glory in print," I offered my contrition. "Perhaps I can still use the base of my research at the end of next term to write a paper that the dean will still publish."

Valentina Petrovna gloated silently in a smug, superior manner and couldn't have been more pleased to hear this admission of guilt and contrition. "I'm sure that you will check with me in the future to avoid these problems and circumstances," she said in a self-righteous tone that made me want to jump over the desk and strangle her.

I wondered who had gotten to her to force her to quash my project. Was she directly linked to Mr. P., or was somebody else putting pressure on her to be able to stay in the shadows? I looked through her with daggers in my eyes.

I rode the trolley bus from Gagarin Street down to Senaya Square and walked the rest of the way to the linguistics school for my one lecture that morning. I had decided that I would keep my usual schedule and on Thursday, which meant that I would spend some time on the database in the American library so as not deviate from my usual activities. As I approached the building I was forced to step off the pavement and walk in the street as there were several cars parked on the sidewalk just before the entrance stairs to the school: two black Volga sedans with a burgundy Mercedes sandwiched between them. I gave them no thought, as there were no designated parking areas anywhere in the city, and the drivers would just jump the curbs and park where they wished. Train stations and airports seemed also to have no parking policy nor enforcement. I skirted the delinquent parkers by walking into oncoming traffic. Horns blared. I was in no mood for it and gave the driver a gesture that warranted another from him back. That conflict quickly settled, I bounded up the stairs and into the school.

Following the lecture, as planned, I settled into my usual corner in the computer lab and set up my usual stack of notebooks and logged into my computer. My username had not been changed on that terminal by any other researchers for almost four months. Everybody knew it was my spot. On occasion, I would recognize a few faces but for the most part, the students used the resources casually, for a rare reference in a research paper, but there had not been anybody up this point who made research and exploration a discipline as I had. Hence, my complete astonishment when my password was not accepted by the system, blocking me out of my account. I retyped my user name and password three times out of disbelief. There had never been any problems before!

I stood up from my work station and approached the librarian's desk.

"Pardon me please, Olya Sergeyevna, but I am not able to access the computers. Has the system been reset? Do I need a renewed password to log on?" I politely inquired.

"I am sorry, young man, may I please see your student credentials?" the librarian asked me in a very formal manner.

"Olya, you know who I am and you very well that I am a student here. What's all this about?" I protested.

"May I please see your student card, young man?" she repeated without acknowledging me.

I walked back to my workstation and rummaged about in my book bag and returned to the service desk. I ceremoniously handed the student pass to this suddenly cold and formal librarian with whom I had spent hours upon hours over the last four months behind these barred windows under the buzzing fluorescent lights. This had become my home away from home. How could she need to see my student card?

"*Mr. Tournaire*, I am afraid that you are not entitled to use these computers at this location," Olya replied after inspecting my credentials.

"I'm sorry, what do you say, ma'am?" I replied, not believing my ears.

"You do not have a right to use these computers in this facility," she repeated without looking me in the eyes.

"Can you explain to me why this has changed since last week?" I pleaded.

"I can only tell you that only those studying economics can use these computers, as they are part of the economics department. Your student card says that you are studying linguistics and literature, not economics," she stated coldly with no emotion and went back to making notations in a notebook.

"Olya Sergeyevna, please explain to me what has happened here. I have been here for four months now using these computers and the database with the permission of Dean Karamzin, who signed the permission for me to research here. I gave that paper to you in January and you created the account for me!" I was getting rather worked up at this point. "And further, I am the only regular student that uses these resources. Can you seriously tell me that you see any students, let alone students from the economics faculty here searching for information? I am the only person in this school with English good enough to utilize what is stored on these disks." I angrily roared as I motioned toward the wall of CDROMs in their racks covering a full wall of the library.

The librarian did not look up from her writing. She was trying very hard not to speak back to me or let any emotion show, but just before she did look up and bid me a good day she slid a paper toward me and turned it right side up for me to read.

"I wish you a good day, *Mr. Tournaire*. Now leave!" she said in an angrily to me, but her eyes motioned to the paper she held in her hands.

The scrap of paper read, 'THEY ARE STILL HERE WATCHING. GO!' Reading this warning from Olya, I stomped back to my workstation and continued to spout off angry words at her while I walked away.

"I will go to the dean and to Valentina Petrovna and I will be back today to get my access back. I can't believe that this has happened!" I was now acting to be angry at my friend.

Just as I stepped to the door and opened it to exit the library, I stopped and looked back quickly and gave the librarian an acknowledging nod of appreciative thanks. She replied with her eyes to hurry away. I darted out into the street to catch a departing trolley-bus.

As I burst through the front doors of the school on to Minin Street and directly into the closing doors of the back of the bus, I saw in the corner of my eyes a startled fellow in bright white trainers smoking around the corner of the building to the right as I exited. He didn't have the time to jump on the bus with me as I barely made it through with the doors closing on my book bag, and I was away. I hadn't seen him earlier in the morning on Gagarin Street, but as this Thursday lecture was part of my weekly routine it was no surprise to see him here again. I continued to watch him out of the back of the bus and noticed that he stepped into one of the black Volga sedans that were parked on the sidewalk that I had to walk around earlier this morning.

As I watched my tag jump into the passenger seat of the lead car, I suddenly recognized the cavalcade of black Volgas, the burgundy Mercedes with blackened, bulletproof windows. It was the same group of cars that had delivered Mr. P. to the Yarmarka for the city auction. Those same cars had nearly run me down there in front of the exhibition hall. This was undoubtedly who Olya Sergeyevna was warning me about.

The lead car jumped off the curb and accelerated quickly to catch up with the trolley-bus. I pretended not to notice them and turned forward on the bus until I reached Gorkiy Square again. I was heading back to Gagarin Street to speak with Valentina Petrovna again about the library privileges. To go anyplace else, I reasoned would not have been predictable. To have acknowledged the presence of my persecutors would have given them reason to make direct contact with me, to stop me from exposing the obvious. I needed to pretend still that I was not aware of their shadowy actions in order to keep them in my shadows. I needed it to remain passive and keep it at an arm's length for just a few more days, but with each escalation of their activity toward me, how much more determined I was to expose their oppressions.

I walked from Gorkiy Square back to Gagarin Street to give my pursuers the chance to catch up with me. The black Volga drove past me and parked just beyond the main entrance of the university building. I could feel their eyes on me from the rearview mirrors as I turned right and entered through the iron gates of the school gardens.

I stormed into the offices of the foreign students and found Arkadiy busily typing away on his word processor. He looked up and greeted me in his always cool, aloof way. It seemed that he was never aware of the stresses of the people around him. He was clueless to the storm clouds gathering around me.

"How can I help you, Peter?" was his cheerful greeting.

"I need to speak with Valentina Petrovna immediately," I replied to him in English.

"Well, I'm afraid she is in a private meeting. I cannot interrupt her. She will be another twenty or thirty minutes. The meeting just started." He smiled his apology and went back to his word processor.

"OK. Arkadiy, Can I leave my book bag here for fifteen minutes, please? I would like to go across the street for a drink in the student café," I asked.

"That's no problem, Peter," he replied as chipper as he could be.

"Can I borrow your overcoat?" I asked.

"No problem, Peter." he couldn't be distracted from what he was typing.

I stuffed by cap into my book bag, then I pulled on Arkadiy's black thigh length overcoat as I slipped out the door. I walked right out the front entrance of the university and crossed the street to the café opposite where a number of students were gathered smoking and drinking soft drinks at stand tables. From the front window, I watched for any movement in or out of the black Volga. Everything was still. After ten minutes I stepped outside again, passed the other students and jogged across the street again and through the gates a second time, just in time to see the burgundy Mercedes and the second black Volga pull up and park behind the first. I did not stay on the street to watch and learn what they were doing there. I figured I already knew.

Valentina's office door was open when I came back to the foreign students' office. I stepped in without waiting for an invitation and let right into her.

"Valentina Petrovna, when I arrived at the American Library today, the head librarian informed me that my privileges for using those computers and the database had been rescinded," I explained.

"Peter, I thought that you told me this morning that you would not continue your research into this topic," she rebutted.

"Valentina, yes, that is what we agreed. Do you expect me to stop all research on any topic? That database has information about all sorts of different topics about Russia. It has nothing to do with my research about the new class entrepreneurs," I pleaded.

"Please then explain to me what the topic your research will be and I will see what we can do to restore your research abilities," she demanded.

Not having had time to consider a new topic yet, I decided to throw a curve ball at Valentina and see what reaction this might elicit from her. "I am planning to research the government's current decision for the privatization of the aerospace factories here in Nizhniy Novgorod."

With no warning, Valentina stood straight up out her chair and in an outraged voice yelled, "Mr. Turner, I will not stand for this any longer! I have explicitly instructed you to stop researching any areas of politics and economics that have anything to do with Mr. P. and his interests. To continue to do so will see your student status revoked and you will be sent home." Valentina was almost foaming at the mouth.

I sat quietly and blinked at her in disbelief. I did not say another word for maybe thirty seconds until Valentina had regained her composure and had retaken her seat. She had almost immediately realized that she had just overplayed her hand and let slip information that I had not yet uncovered myself.

"Please excuse me, that was very inappropriate of me. Mr. Turner, I think it would be best if you handed over to me all of your research materials now and ceased from all forms of research into the current economic and political situation in this country. I am afraid that you asking any further questions will create an incident with the university and the local government that we will not be able to repair. I cannot permit to have any research privileges any longer. You are welcome to continue your studies in linguistics and literature, for which you have been invited to study at our school. Any further meddling in the government's economic reforms will not be tolerated. Is that clear, young man?" She held tight to her regained composure, but it wasn't convincing.

"Very, very clear, Valentina Petrovna," I muttered with my eyes locked on her in a cold stare.

"Please then, give me all your notes and materials now and I will have them destroyed," she insisted.

"Yes of course ma'am. Only I do not have them with me. There is too much material for me to carry around with me each day. I have them in my room in Zarachenaya in two folders," I volunteered innocently, but defiantly.

"Then you will go get them and bring them to me at once. At once, Mr. Turner!" She stomped her foot under the desk.

"Would it be allowed for me to bring them tomorrow morning first thing? It would take another two or three hours to make the whole trip. I will be here for early Friday lectures tomorrow morning and I will bring you all that I have, I promise," I requested deliberately.

"That will be fine. Tomorrow morning at eight-thirty," she ordered.

"Very good. I will see you tomorrow then," I stood up and excused myself from her office.

"Mr. Turner, it would be a good idea if you took the next two weeks of holidays to reevaluate your standing at this university and be prepared when we reconvene to stay focused on your language exams for the MGU. Perhaps you would be happier studying in Moscow than our small provincial city." She was not making a suggestion. This was my expulsion notice.

"I will certainly do my best to score a high mark on the exam, ma'am. Guaranteed!" I affirmed.

The parade of cars that were tracking me that morning had thinned out to just one black Volga, with the other two vehicles no longer to be seen up or down the street. Perhaps they had heard the entire exchange with Valentina Petrovna? What Valentina had just revealed to me by accident was more than I was ever meant to know, and remembering Del's interest to make a link between Mr. P. and the aerospace industry, I had now a very frightened feeling that I had just stepped over a line that would be impossible to get back over. I was desperate to find Del and get out of Nizhniy Novgorod as quickly as possible.

"Who's there?" to my relief it was Misha asking his usual gruff questions.

"Hello, can we meet please?" I pleaded into the telephone.

"Nyet, that is not possible," was Misha's simple answer.

"It's very important," I argued.

Misha paused and covered the mouthpiece on his handset.

"OK, when?" He had changed his mind.

"Four o'clock, Gorky Square. In front of the Telephone and Telegraph building," I ordered.

"Too visible!" he protested.

"Sorry I have no other choice. I'll be at the bus stop. Just come ride a bus with me," I commanded.

"OK, but no talking until we're on the bus," was his condition.

"Agreed." I hung up my phone and sat down on a bench to take it all in until our meeting in ninety minutes.

I sat on the bench in the sunshine trying to anchor my racing thoughts after the revelation that Mr. P. was indeed linked somehow to the aviation industry in the city, just like Del and Els had been trying to establish. What did Valentina already know, but more importantly why? I could not make the connection between Mr. P. and Valentina that would put such an inconsequential person in a position to know the current or future business dealings of the head of a criminal organization. It is not often that academia and the mob mix company. The two trades seem diametrically opposed to each other. The academics try to establish and measure truth while the criminal does his best to obscure the truth from any form of daylight.

The question played over and over in my head. Had she reacted purely on the point that I wanted to continue to research and observe the privatization process further? Did it really have anything to do with Mr. P. and his future ventures? The aviation industry could in no way be compared to the market for automobile spare parts. Each part for an aircraft must have a verifiable pedigree in order to be installed in an aircraft. A cheap knock-off spare part in an airplane that costs forty-five million dollars brings the whole investment into risk. No reasonable manager or engineer of an aircraft fleet would ever accept a part they couldn't verify. It seemed to me that Mr. P. was neither clever nor connected enough to be able to launder aircraft parts or forge their authenticity. The producers of such are too few and far between to make bombastic claims that you have taken over the distribution of their spare and repair parts. It didn't make any sense to me. Was I reading too much into it? Somehow, I knew that if I could share this information with Del that he would be able to shed more light on it. Why I needed that light shined on it was another internal struggle I sat and wrestled with, waiting to meet Misha and hopefully learn how to contact Del in Moscow.

With just a few minutes until my rendezvous with Misha on the bus, I looked for my personal shadow to set him up, in order to lose him. He was taking it easy today riding around in the black Lada and smoking with the window down just out of my sight—if I wasn't looking for him—parked in a small service driveway by the T&T building. I hung back a bit out of his sight for a moment as I noticed Misha come from their direction and stand to wait for the next yellow bus to pull up. Misha did not look around for me. He stood with his back to me. He probably already knew where I was and had already anticipated my plan. He seemed very disinterested with the people around him. As the exiting passengers stampeded out of the doors of the arriving bus to the curb, I quickly stepped out from the corner of the building, using the commuters as camouflage, like a fish swimming against the current, and slipped into the middle doors of the bus without the 'British Knight' even stirring from his bucket seat. Misha had stepped in through the rear doors. The bus pulled away from the curb leaving a rank cloud of unrefined diesel fumes. Misha and I met in the back and looked out the back window while holding on the poles and railings so as to not topple over as the bus circled through the roundabout.

"You're still being followed," Misha said in a very business-like manner.

"Yes, not a day has gone by without the idiot in the white shoes," I replied with sarcasm.

"Seems you've gotten pretty good at slipping away from them. That was well timed," he complimented.

"Why thank you very much. I will treasure the compliment from a professional," I answered with some pride in my voice.

"So, what is so important?" Misha asked, turning to look me in the face.

"I need to contact Del. I have some important information he needs to know," I muttered in a low tone. "Do you know how I can reach him wherever he is?"

"No, I'm sorry. He contacts me daily but never tells me where he is. He calls at different times of the day as well," was Misha's honest reply.

"Do you have any idea where he could be? Someplace that you know he stays regularly while in Moscow?" I was searching for any leads.

"Yes, he regularly stays at the Slavyanskaya Hotel, but not always. He moves around also during his stays in Moscow. Never more than two nights in one hotel," Misha confessed.

"What is it with this guy, Misha? There is something more to him than his hotel project, isn't there," I mused.

"I don't ask. He pays me to run his business here in Nizhniy and keep his information safe and legal. He pays on time and he pays well. The rest doesn't interest me," Misha mumbled while looking disinterested out the window. "Doing this type of big ticket, highly visible business in Russia is not safe. He's probably smart to keep moving around. Somebody always wants to steal what you've built."

"Do you have a telephone number of that hotel?" I asked with hope.

"No, sorry I don't. He usually calls me. I only know this information because I see his invoices that he keeps for tax deductions."

"Would a receipt have a telephone number on it?" I was searching for hope.

"No, maybe in Germany or America, but not in Russia. They don't want you calling them!" He looked at me with irony in his eyes.

"Ah yes, Russian customer service." I sighed.

"The Slavyanskaya is near the Kyivskiy Railway Station. Do you know it?" Misha asked.

"Yes, I do," I was in thought, trying to picture the skyline. "It's just opposite the Supreme Soviet, correct?"

"The Russian White House, yes," Misha confirmed.

The next morning, the final day of lectures before the spring break, I arrived at Valentina's office at eight-thirty to surrender all my notes and research materials. I found her office dark and locked. I also found Arkadiy behind his desk typing his eternal letter. He was as upbeat as ever.

"Can I help you, Peter?" Arkadiy chirped.

"Valentina Petrovna? Is she not coming to school today?" I inquired.

"No, she has been called away. Can I help you with something?" he asked.

"No, thank you. I think it would be better if I give these materials directly to her," I said, puzzled.

"I will tell her that you came by this morning. Is it something urgent?" Arkadiy never looked up from his screen but just kept typing.

"No, but it's..." my voice trailed off as I had become distracted, "...important. When will she be back?"

"Not until after the holidays I'm afraid." Arkadiy looked up finally just as I was exiting the office.

I returned to my apartment with my bag filled with notes, articles, and interviews. I did not want to be out and about with this trove of information around my neck. It was not only heavy but very exposing should I be found with it. Better to keep it at home under my table if Valentina was not available to take custody of it. I thought about destroying it but figured that Valentina would not believe that I had done so and expel me from the university. I had to turn the notes over to her even if it was after the May break. I then spent five straight days at home avoiding the old city in order to avoid any trouble.

With my research privileges revoked by Valentina and whoever was pulling her strings, and with no lectures to attend, perhaps the urgency of tracking my every movement would diminish and in mid-May, I could go back to life as normal. I spent the my days reading on my bed with the windows open to catch the warming spring breezes and tried unsuccessfully not to worry about the world around me.

06

23. Fifty Years Victory

On the morning of May 9th, the apartment was a flurry of activity with Natasha and Raiya preparing for the Victory Day celebrations and presentations. Natasha was to receive a medal and recognition from the mayor and she was as nervous as a prima donna going on stage on opening night. The ladies had pulled their Sunday best from the closet and were fussing about hair or headscarves. Babushka chose a rich red and paisley headscarf. She was beaming that morning. I slipped out the door before her family arrived and purchased her a small bouquet of roses, red roses for the Red Army hero, which she carried with pride with her up the old city to watch the parade and air show and be ready for the presentations.

I accompanied the family up to Minin Square but did my best to keep out of the family discussions. I was present but kept a low profile. We rode the bus to Gorkiy Square where the bus stopped as the city center was closed down for only pedestrian and parade traffic. We strolled down Bolshaya Pakrovskaya to Minin Square where the festivities and ceremony would be held.

Knowing that Del had returned to the city on Thursday night, I was very anxious to speak with him. I brought with me my book bag with the two folders of research materials hoping that together, before I had to surrender them to Valentina Petrovna, Del could help me complete my model of a small criminal organization, the little shark, growing into a great white shark with teeth that take huge chunks of capital and lifeblood out of a country with one big bite. Even if I was not going to be able to publish the research in Nizhniy Novgorod, I had decided that I was going to process the information as deeply as I could before the materials were confiscated so that I could reconstruct it once I was free again to research and write what I wished, in an environment of academic freedom. Valentina would not be able to expunge the information in my head once she shredded my materials. I was determined not to let the investment I had made come to nothing.

Minin Square was filled with spectators both old and young alike. Banners proclaiming 50 Years Victory hung from every lamp post and flagpole. The square was awash in red flags. There were groups of veterans, seventy years old and a bit, marching in columns in their war time dress uniforms. Their shrinking frames and growing bellies made the jackets difficult to button. Their gray hair and gold teeth shone in the May sunshine. Medals hung from their chests: The Battle of Moscow, The Battle for Leningrad, the capture of Berlin! They were cheered as they marched as proud as the day they returned from saving the Motherland from the fascists. Military transport trucks, some modern, some dated, towing artillery pieces rolled down Minin Street and across the square. Small children on the shoulders of their fathers waved to the young soldiers in dress uniform, faces stern and turned, saluting the crowd, ceremonial rifles on their left shoulders. The crowd cheered the local brigades and they trooped through with their local colors.

As the last of the parade marchers passed over the square, a faint pulsing could be heard in the distance: dug, dug, dug, dug, dug. It grew louder. As it grew louder the heads of the people in the crowds looked up, looked left and looked right. A squadron of attack helicopters had announced its arrival and they flew up from the river over the kremlin and then directly overhead above the square and were launching fireworks from rocket launchers. The deep pulsing vibrations of the rotors shook our soft abdomens. The squadron split into different directions with a bit of acrobatic flying, causing the crowd to applaud and cheer with surprise. Young children cowered and cried.

As the reverberations of the helicopters faded, there was a rush up the river valley, like rushing wind, or rushing water. The crowd turned forty-five degrees to the north to watch six military jets, MIGs, flying low over the water in a tight formation, pull up and ascend into the air at a steep incline and then branch out from each other like a blooming flower, petals peeling off in six different directions with afterburners thrusting them into the atmosphere before arching upside down and eventually back toward the earth. As they looped around and toward each other, they too launched fireworks in a celebratory dogfight. As the MIGs swooped out of sight around the river bend, a large formation of larger transport aircraft, propellers grinding through the air, buzzed the river bluff tipping their wings back and forth—a pilot's wave. The crowd was electric and the cheers spontaneous!

As the parade and the airshow eventually subsided, the crowd milled about and welcomed the veteran soldiers into the crowd with handshakes and salutes. A color guard emerged from the kremlin gates and marched through the crowd to the stage and risers where the government officials overseeing the festivities were gathering and shaking hands with the military colonels and generals that were there to issue the 50 YEARS medals to those who served and had survived. The loud speakers were switched on with a squelch and a deep man's voice grumbling, "test, test" into a live microphone.

"Ladies and gentlemen, behold our honored veterans! Glory to the heroes of the Soviet Union!" came from the loud speakers.

The crowd answered, "GLORY to our HEROES!"

"GLORY!" again from the speakers.

"GLORY!" the crowd answered back again and a loud cheer arose from the crowd as a division of the old generation who had won the war for their children and grandchildren climbed the stairs to the raised stage waving and smiling to their families.

A barrel-chested officer with his own left breast covered in his own heroism presented and pinned a 50 YEARs medal to the coat of each of the men who were well enough still to stand at attention. Each was saluted for his valor and returned the salute with his chest out and head high. The crowd applauded with appreciation for each in the unit. Bouquets of flowers were brought up from the crowd and given to each of the heroes. A few of the old men began weeping and wiping tears from their faces with their rough hands and wrinkled fingers. They all waved to the crowd one last time before stepping off the stage on the side opposite they ascended.

Raiya started to poke me in the ribs and pointed to the stage now where Babushka and her group of female heroes were now being signaled to come on stage for their presentation.

"Quick, take some photos!" Raiya demanded of me.

The loud speakers boomed again.

"Ladies and gentlemen, behold your heroes of the Red Army!"

The crowd answered again as in a type of religious ceremony, the priest an officer, the sacrament the sacrifice of years given in service. "Glory!"

I struggled to pull my camera from my book bag and had to put it on the ground between my feet before I could pull it out from between my folders of papers. I was able to still find Natasha in my view finder and snap a few photos of her standing at attention while the medals were presented in long dark boxes, opened for viewing and presentation. In good taste, the General had not been tasked with pinning the medals on the ladies' chests, but handed them over ceremoniously with a formal hand shake. No salute.

Babushka beamed on stage with the other few ladies that had survived another fifty years. The applause and the pageantry were less than with the soldiers who had fought and bled, but the ladies looked just as proud as they received their medals and flowers for their service in the clothing and boot factories that kept the boys warm and well healed on their march to Berlin. Then the ladies filed off after their soldiers with waves and blowing kisses.

"Ladies and gentlemen, honored veterans and heroes! Today we make a special presentation to a local hero of the Red Army who we have not forgotten! It is my privilege to present the next medal of appreciation to a man who did not fight in the war against the Germans but who, from his laboratory here in Nizhniy Novgorod, worked tirelessly to preserve the motherland from the western imperialists. For his work and accomplishments in the important field of military aviation, we present this posthumous medal to Ivan Sergeyevich S. Mr. S. died late last year while in the line of duty in Tajikistan doing his part to protect mother Russia from terrorists. Here to accept this medal on behalf of his father, is his son Igor Ivanovich S." A polite applause came up from the crowd. My jaw dropped as I watched Mr. P. accept the highest honor the Russian army could give to a civilian, in the place of his father, for his work in advancing the supremacy of Soviet military aviation.

Taken completely off guard by the obscene spectacle of Mr. P. receiving his father's award, I didn't notice until it was too late that somebody had snatched my bag from between my feet and was hurrying away behind me, pushing spectators violently out of his way. Without thinking, without considering who it was and why that bag was the target of the thief running away through the crowd, I gave chase.

Getting to the edge of the crowd I watched the bag snatcher sprint away from festivities and run up an alleyway just past the Pedagogical school and toward Sverdlov Park. As I chased him up the alleyway through the series of small parking lots behind the school buildings, I watched him disappear around several different corners, and then I turned that corner just in time to see him turn the next corner. As we reached the open areas of the city park in front of the Conservatory, we both broke into a full sprint again. On that open ground running between the trees, my legs and lungs started to burn. I thought for a split moment to give up.

Then, imagining who would be reading the contents of that bag if I gave up, a shot of adrenaline went to my heart and muscles. I started gaining on the punk. When he was four yards ahead of me I could feel him coming back to me as he was also tiring. We crossed from the grass and uneven ground onto paving stones as we were nearing the Piskunova Street entrance to the park. I could hear his heavy breathing in front of me.

I was reaching my arm out to grab his collar or sleeve. As he turned the corner of the Conservatory and bounded up a small stairway of five steps, I was just a step behind him. I saw the open street just in front of us. If I could just stretch! As I reached, his collar in my grasp, I was dropped to the pavement with a violent fall, skidding and rolling a good distance before coming to a stop. My legs were still churning as I was doubled over on my side, eyes bulging with my lungs spasming without breath. I could not see or perceive what I had run into or what had hit me. I tried desperately to breathe, gasping without result for breath. I thought for those seconds that I was going to die. Then, as quickly as it left, air flowed back into my lungs with raspy gasps. I would live! Who was that standing over me?

Another sharp blow was landed on my lower back causing me to scream in pain. My back arched reflexively with that blow exposing my belly and chest to another blow by a foot to my gut. After what seemed fifteen minutes but was only fifteen seconds, my attacker crouched down and pressed the temple of my head with what felt like cold metal held in his left hand. A pistol. I could smell the gun metal. In his right hand a metal baton club, the kind the real riot police use was laid across his squatting lap. I could now see his bright white trainers.

"If you try to follow us again, I will kill you. Understand that, you stupid Yankee?!" he muttered to me in a put-on sophisticated meanness, as if he'd watched too many television shows of hitmen who kill for fun.

He gave me another kick to the gut, but it landed on my arms and hands that were instinctively folded in for protection as I lay doubled over. I watched his white shoes step over me and yell to his brother in crime "Poshlee!" or "We're out a' here!" and I listened to their fleeing footsteps turn an unseen corner and then they were gone, vanishing in the back alleys of the old city.

I laid still there at the corner of the Conservatory building alone. Breathing normally but with some pain still, I pulled myself up into a sitting position against the wall and started to survey the damage. My palms and knuckles on both hands were skinned and bleeding, one pant leg ripped open at the knee, and the left sleeve of my jacket was ripped and stained with blood. My shoes were scuffed but intact.

I took a deep breath and exhaled and looked around me to see if anybody had been witness to the assault and threats. The park was empty and the trees shielding any view from bedroom windows four and five stories high across the street. I was on my own. I got to my feet and walked out toward Piskunova Street and sat down on a bench and rubbed my knees aching from the impact with concrete. I held my left side where the initial blow from the baton had first knocked me down. Deep breaths made me wince. I worried my ribs on that side had been broken. I didn't dare look under my shirt. I sat still and closed my eyes and took several slow deep breaths to see if the sharp pains would subside.

With my notes and research materials now stolen and, I could only assume, in the hands of a criminal who decidedly would use violence to reach his objectives, I felt the ill-boding of fate descend on me. In a way, I was relieved. Maybe now this would all end. If they were going to kill me, if that had been their design, they could very well have beaten me further there in the secluded park. Would this escalate if they read and understood my articles and notes? I could only hope now that Mr. P. or his operatives couldn't read English well enough nor discern my shorthand writing to understand how far, or how close I was to what I had just learned about Mr. P's father. Perhaps what eluded me in those flow charts and diagrams would be obvious to somebody with the missing piece of knowledge. Maybe they would just burn everything. Maybe they would still come after me.

I had a distinct feeling that this was not yet over. I resolved to get to the Sannings' place for some first aid and to tell Del about what I had learned about Mr. P.'s father, Mr. P.'s real family name, and to ask for their help to get me out of Nizhniy as quickly as possible. Everything was now out in the open. The dance of masks had turned violent, and I needed to leave the party.

I limped and shuffled from Piskunova Street to Bolshaya Pecherskaya where I waited for the tram to come past instead of walking a painful five blocks to Frunze Street. Crossing Minin Street on foot after a short ride on the street car, I looked around to make sure there were no black Volgas or black Ladas or armed thugs wearing white trainers still following me. I continued around the back of the building to the parking lots and entrance to the building. By the last stairwell entrance, I noticed with a panic and shock two police cars keeping guard, backed up against the cinderblock wall. I did my best to walk calmly towards the entrance door but my approach triggered two policemen to step out of the cars and stand behind the open car doors, hands on their weapons. I stopped and held up my hands at chest level to show I had nothing. I was carrying nothing. One guard told me to stand still. I obeyed. They came close to ask my business and my name. They looked over my bloody hands and ripped clothes and growing blood stain at my elbow.

"Did you have an accident?" one asked me gruffly.

"No, I was robbed and threatened with a gun," I admitted.

"Do you want to make a report? Do you know who it was?" the other officer interrogated.

"I only saw the backs of their heads," I lied.

"Why are you here?" asked the first again.

"I have come to speak with Mr. Sanning on important business," was my honest answer.

"Your name, please?" demanded the second officer as he reached for his radio.

I was permitted to go upstairs.

"Peter, what happened to you?" was Els' shocked reaction. She began fluttering around looking for bandages and disinfectant from the first aid box.

"Do I look that bad, Del?" I turned to his concerned face.

"Do you know who did it, Peter?" he asked solemnly.

"Exactly who," I said with resignation.

"Well, I guess it's time to stop before it happens again," he instructed.

"I already have stopped. I told the university as much and besides that, they revoked my research privileges so that I can't do anymore. I think as well that they will cancel my student status so that I have to leave, which at this point won't be such a bad thing," I complained.

"Peter, you need to take off that jacket and let's look at the gash on your elbow," Els instructed like an instinctive nurse.

I removed the jacket and could see that the dark green shirt I was wearing had turned black and was soaked through with blood. "That doesn't even hurt!" I said.

"That's a bad sign," muttered Del. "Get that shirt off so we can take a look at the wound."

I winced from pain in my ribs as I took off my button-down shirt. Del recognized the hesitation as I slowly peeled my arm free of my left sleeve.

"You get hit in the ribs too, kid?" he correctly questioned.

I nodded with a grimace as the shirt finally came free. Del took a look under my t-shirt at the left side and winced himself.

"Kid, that looks bad. You're going to want to wrap those up tight. That's going to hurt for several days. It looks you got kicked by a mule," he confirmed.

The split in the left tricep was still bleeding. We wrapped it tightly with gauze and bandages. Del gave me a sweatshirt to wear.

Del sat down opposite me as I gingerly reclined the uninjured right side against the arm of the couch and asked, "What kind of trouble are you in, Peter?"

"I have evidently hit a nerve in Mr. P.'s organization. The university suspended my research privileges, I have been followed and watched for about two weeks now, my notes from my meeting with Mr. P. were confiscated by Valentina Petrovna, and now the rest of the materials have been stolen. I've been beaten by mafia goons and had my life threatened this morning. So, yeah, I'm in pretty deep." I smiled a resigned grimace.

"It's time for you to walk away, kid. It's time for you to walk away now!" he said seriously.

"Yes, that has been obvious now to me for about a week and I've been trying to make it obvious to everybody that is interested, that I have stopped my research and writing. I suppose they are now making it clear that I need to keep my mouth shut and leave town," I confirmed.

"I told you that these types have long memories, and once you cross them they don't just let it go. You really need to walk away now. I can't stress it enough, Peter." Del remained very serious. "Listen, we have been able to put some pieces together as well since we left town last week that make this whole scenario a bit more dangerous for us all."

"I have some new information as well that you'll want to hear," I added.

"OK, great, but let me tell you first what we learned about the arrangements for Mr. P.'s hotel plans. The meeting for Monday or Tuesday next week will go through and there isn't much we can do to stop what is going to happen. So, we are resigned that we will lose the hotel site through a collusion of the mayor's staff and Mr. P.'s organization. Evidently, the financials are being fictionalized to make his plan look more advantageous for the city and province than it really is. Once the place is built of course, they can't turn back the clock. Evidently, Mr. P. has made a deal with the devil and will take on partners for the hotel. The deal is that he, as a local in the region, will acquire the land and submit the project plans while it is almost fully financed by a larger mafia operation, a nation-wide group that is really known for its viciousness. It is believed that many former KGB agents are involved with this group giving it exotic expertise. So, Mr. P. is more or less merging his operations and inviting the big sharks to share his territory in Nizhniy Novgorod," Del revealed.

"So, his entrance fee is to acquire the land, get approval for the casino and hotels; and it turns into another money laundering base of a more or less legitimate local entrepreneur with the regional government's blessing. They certainly have covered their bases!" I mustered all the outrage I could without hurting my ribs.

"Yes, and so Mr. P. evidently is hoping to contract my employer to build his hotel for his own consortium. So, this is why he has been muscling in on me a bit to learn how to get in contact with my chain of command and make an offer around me, since I won't cooperate with the overtures from his organization. I didn't realize that this fellow was behind the proposal until you pointed it out to me, but now we've been able to put all the pieces together," Del concluded.

"Del, I really should tell you the rest," I tried to interrupt.

"Just wait. Here is where it gets sticky. A city councilman has hired Mr. P.'s thugs to go and visit the few expats that are already here for the different projects, and do their best to scare them into the housing project that they are now renovating. They think then if they can get me and two or three others to endorse it, after being chased out of our current housing situations, that they can get the big corporate contracts for any other foreign companies trying to set up new operations in town. They want to corner the market on expat housing and earn some fat profits. Not a bad plan. So, before Mr. Z. from the city council figures out that I am also looking to provide him competition and he sends his blokes with batons and pistols, as you see they are ready to do," Del motioned towards me and my broken ribs, "I have also decided to stop my project. I have already instructed Misha to wrap up the property management activities and cancel all tentative agreements. This little project is not worth getting our throats cut by the little sharks in town," he wisely concluded.

I nodded in agreement.

"So, kid, get your ticket and get out as soon as you can. So, what else did you need to tell me?" he finally asked.

I sat up straight the best I could. "Del, before I tell you what I think you want to know, I have a question first for you, and I need a straight answer," I said seriously.

"Sure, kid. What is it?" he was curious.

"Can you get me out of Nizhniy tonight if I tell you what I've learned? I have the feeling that you are more than just a project manager for a construction company or a hotel chain. You have connections and knowledge that a project manager wouldn't have. I've listened to you and Els the last few months and there is something that you are not telling me. If I give you this piece of information that you are looking for, for the reason that I think you are looking for it, I am going to need help to get out of town tonight. Can you help me with this?" I looked him straight in the eyes.

After a long pause with much consternation from Del and Els alike, Del shifted in his chair, sat on the edge of it and looked me straight back in the eyes.

"Kid, you're as sharp as they come. We saw that after our first meeting. There is little fooling you despite some initial naivety on your part. But you're young and untrained, so that should be expected. There are things I am not allowed to tell you, but it seems you have filled in the details yourself, so I am pretty sure that you don't need a confirmation from me. Let's leave it at that for now. Until I hear what further information you have, I can't promise anything, so it's best you tell me and then we'll figure out what it means." He had never sounded so serious.

"Ok, thanks for the straight answer. I wouldn't have accepted a B.S. answer from you at this point. So here it is. During our last discussion, you were desperate to make a link between Mr. P. and the aviation sector here in Nizhniy Novgorod. We were puzzled by what Mr. P. said about his father leaving him some money to purchase the land of the hotel with. Do you remember? Well, two things. First, when I was trying to direct my research in a new direction away from Mr. P. as the university demanded, I mentioned then that I would like to study the government's plans for privatizing the aviation factories here in town. Valentina went into a rage! She was foaming at the mouth and spitting on me, she was so mad, and more or less told me no, because that was a current or future interest of Mr. P.'s entrepreneurial activities. She knew she had slipped up and she knew that I knew she had let too much be known. I think that is why the problems haven't stopped for me. Second, and this is something I should have remembered from my meeting with the dean: P. is not Mr. P. 's birth name. He changed his name when he was released from prison. His real family name is S. His father Ivan Sergeyevich S. just received a posthumous medal from the Red Army for his contribution to Russia's military aviation development. Mr. P. accepted the medal for his father just before my bag got stolen. I was there and heard it with my own ears and saw him shake hands with the mayor in front of the whole crowd!" I revealed.

"What did you say the engineer's name was?" Del jumped.

I repeated the name clearly, slowly.

"Do you know anything more about him?" he demanded from me.

"Only what I told you, and that he died in Tajikistan last year," I was cut off by Del.

"In Bishkek? Did he die in Bishkek?" Del was now adding information that I couldn't confirm.

"Do you still have the articles you showed me about the arms shows last year in Kirgizia and Tajikistan?" Del pushed.

"Sorry, Del. Everything I had worth keeping for my case studies was just stolen. All of it!" I said with resignation. "That article though came from an issue of *The Economist* in late January, I think. Have you kept the copies I brought you each week?"

Del sprung from his chair and went to his office and came back with a small stack of magazines and quickly found the editions from January. Del leafed through them until he came to the article I was referring to. He read silently while moving his lips in inaudible whispers.

Del was silent as he paced the living room again as he did when he learned of Mr. P.'s hotel plans and inheritance. He stopped and stared out the window onto the city skyline. He spoke with his back still to me.

"Peter, it will be very important that you are out of town by Monday morning. You need to pack up and get gone. As you will understand, if I am seen helping you leave Nizhniy, it could put you at more risk than you are leaving on your own. Mr. P. wants you gone, he isn't going to stop you from going. The FSB will, however, will try to stop you if you are traveling with me and Els. We can't be seen together. You already gave your name to the cops downstairs so we can't have any more contact. You'll need to get your things as soon as possible and hop on a train to Moscow and fly away. Got it?" As he finished his thinking and speaking he turned to see my reaction.

I was silent. I was doing everything I could to hold back tears.

"Are you able to get back to your apartment and get some clean clothes, get fixed up, and leave tomorrow morning? Take as little as possible with you. Don't get delayed and bogged down by your luggage. Just go as quick as you can," he instructed again.

I nodded and started to get up slowly from the couch. The pain in my ribs was now acute and laming. I straightened up stiffly and offered a hand shake to Del. He then handed me a business card from his shirt pocket.

"Kid, when you get back to the States, please call this number and leave me a message that you arrived in the States, or wherever you land, and that you are safe. Leave a number on the message machine and we'll be in touch after some time. Understood? Do not call the apartment phone any longer and don't come back here again." His instruction seemed well rehearsed.

I nodded again and put his card in my pocket after glancing it over. I had no more questions and I couldn't think of anything else to say and headed for the door. I collected my blood-stained jacket with my passport and wallet in it.

"Kid, don't tell anybody where you're going. Just go!" Del opened the door and I slipped out and onto the street. With my bones and joints aching, I decided to hail a cab for the first time in Nizhniy. I did not speak to the cab driver. Twenty minutes later I was let out at the Proletarskaya Metro Station and twenty steps from my door.

06

24. Yankee Go Home!

The apartment was quiet. Raiya and Natasha were still visiting with family further up the street. The apartment was dark when I entered and seemed colder than usual. Maybe they had left the kitchen vents open. I fumbled for my keys in the dark with my uninjured right arm. Bending to pick them up was painful. Finally, I got the key into the lock and turned it. I was met by a stiff breeze rushing from my room into the hallway. I was very confused and disoriented by the rush of the air. Something was not right! I flipped on the light.

The curtains were wide open and flapping in the wind. A pane of glass was broken and lay in pieces on the floor inside the apartment. The other windows had been left wide open. No effort was taken to conceal the crime. The room had been turned upside down. Every book had been shaken and thrown on the floor and their spines were broken. My table was on its side and the chairs smashed. My shortwave radio lay smashed in pieces on the floor. All my clothes were thrown out of the wardrobe and my bed was ripped apart. All the drawers were pulled out and overturned as well as the cabinet doors in the hutch. Everything I owned had been pulled out and strewn on the floor. For owning so little it had made a tremendous mess.

The timeline of the day's events became clear as I stood there gaping at this violent scene of recent intrusion; not having found my research notes in my apartment the intruders stole my bag from my person. Mr. P. had to be sure before Monday's meeting that I had no more materials and notes in my possession to potentially use to interrupt his hotel project, a project that would bring the big sharks to Nizhniy Novgorod and raise the bar of illegal and violent crime in the city. All the loose ends were being cleaned up now. Had Valentina been just a loose end, too? I sat down on the couch and cried quietly a few tears of fright and helplessness.

After a few moments of despair, I dried my eyes and gathered up some clothes into a backpack. I changed from my ripped slacks into denim jeans, put on a new shirt and my orange rain coat and found my gray cap in the mess. I found my black shapka near the door and my address book among the broken books and stuffed them as well into my bag. I took my passport and wallet as well out of my bloodstained jacket and then threw it on the floor with the rest of the mess for dramatic effect. Taking mental stock of the scene, I retreated to the bathroom that seemed to have been untouched by the burglars. Being injured I took a stool from the kitchen—instead of climbing on the edge of the bathtub—and pushed on a small panel in the ceiling open to find my money belt and airplane ticket that I had hidden there a few weeks earlier, after retrieving them from Yulia's apartment.

I thought about writing a note for my housemates, but had second thoughts of involving them any further. l closed the double paned windows tight, the broken pane on the street side. I pulled the curtains closed, turned out the light and just before I locked the door behind me, I remembered the card Del gave me just before we parted. I found my slacks in the pile of clothes and took the card and put it in the jacket of my passport for safe keeping. Out of habit I locked the doors and took my keys with me, but knew I would not be returning.

When I left the apartment again only fifteen minutes had passed, but in that quarter hour, a resolve had developed in my core that I knew exactly what I needed to do. I was determined to make the evening train to Moscow. From there I would take a taxi directly from Kazanksiy Station to the airport and catch the first flight out of Russia, using my Aeroflot ticket, or if necessary, winging it to any safe European capital and from there back to the United States. I was determined not to spend more than one more night in Russia.

The Moskovskiy Station was all but empty at nine o'clock that evening. Only a few travelers were crossing the dusty granite floors and just a few taxi drivers were waiting for a fare. The city was still celebrating tonight in concerts and festivals in the old city. Nobody was traveling.

A feeling of despair and panic rushed through me when I found the ticket window closed for the holiday. The trains were idle for the fifty years anniversary. There were no departures listed for that night. I turned and looked again at the empty hall.

My ribs throbbed, and in the gash on my left arm I could feel every beat of my racing heart and my head was spinning as I hadn't eaten all day. My thoughts raced with all the horror scenarios that could happen in the next forty-eight hours if I wasn't on an airplane by Monday morning. Del had told me specifically to be gone by Monday morning. Why? What was going to happen on Monday morning? Was Del going to try to stop Mr. P.'s meeting with the mayor by exposing them both? The next train to Moscow wouldn't be until Sunday evening at ten o'clock. Where could I hide out for the twenty-four hours? I couldn't call Del anymore. Returning to and sleeping in my apartment was only asking for trouble; if they wanted to find me again I would be an easy target. I needed to stay hidden. Yulia was away in Moscow. Staying in a hotel would be just as unsafe as sleeping in my own apartment. Nothing happens in the hotels without the police and mafia goons knowing about it before it happens. Then my thoughts caught a flash of hope: Hans! Where was Hans tonight? Hans should be at home! I stepped quickly to the taxi stand.

I asked the taxi driver to take me only as far as Senaya Square via the lower embankment and the Kazanskiy Syezd so that if later questioned by any operatives of Mr. P., they would think of and look first at Del's apartment and not a few blocks further up at Hans's apartment on Proviantaksaya Street. The walk was a little too much for me with my entire body aching. I stopped several times and sat on benches near bus stops and in the occasional courtyard of another apartment building. I used this as a chance to see if I was possibly being followed by anybody. I highly doubted that anybody would have had the chance to follow me as I had moved quickly from my apartment to the train station by metro and then by taxi to the old city again. As the taxi driver hadn't sent nor received any radio messages while I was in his cab, not even to radio his destination for his dispatch coordinator, I was pretty confident that nobody who might have been watching for me would have had the chance to be in place at Senaya Square where I exited the taxi.

I walked along Bolshaya Pecherskaya instead of Minin Street down to Hans's street. If I had been tasked with keeping an eye for myself, Minin Street is where I would have been waiting, and so I stayed in the twilight shadows a street over instead of walking right past the American Library again. There was nobody on this street: no automobiles, no footsteps, no street cars. There was not a single soul visible up and down the street as far as I could see. I needed to hurry.

Following a young family through the ground floor entrance of the building and off the street as they returned home from the festivities on Minin Square, I felt already a bit safer. At least, if needed, I could hide anonymously in this random stairwell if Hans wasn't at home. Not wanting to sound and look panicked, I waited a few moments until the adrenaline subsided and I caught my breath again before I headed up the stairs to Hans's door. The building and the stairwell were quiet, the street even more so.

I rang Hans's bell and waited to hear movement behind the door. I rang the bell again and then a third time in short bursts. This time somebody inside was stirring and padding quickly to the door. From the peephole a flash of pinpoint light pricked the darkness of the landing. The spy glass went dark. I could feel Hans blinking at me. I removed my cap and waved at him. The latches eventually were opened after a moment of hesitation and the door opened letting light spill from the apartment's hallway on to my feet and legs. Hans stood shirtless behind the door, poking his head into the gap between door and door jam.

Hans was annoyed. "Peter, this really isn't a good time." He was giving signals with his face and head movements that I had buzzed him at just the wrong moment. He seemed to be in earnest.

"Hans, I really need to sleep here for the night," I whispered from the shadow on the landing. "I'm in serious trouble and have no place else to go."

"Not now! Really, not now. Please just come back in two hours..." he was insistent.

From behind him I heard a woman's voice call out from the living room.

"Who's there, Hansy?" it was Tamara.

"Nobody, Mein Schatz, just a drunk guy looking for his keys," Hans replied and moved to close the door.

Without thinking I put my foot between the open door and the door frame before Hans could get the door on the latch. His reaction was one of shock and disbelief. His face took on a concerned look and he peered past me further into the dark stairwell.

"Hans, I really need your help! Please don't close the door," I said firmly. I didn't push the door any further, but I did not remove my foot.

Our eyes met and we strained at each other's glare for a few tense moments. To my relief his resistance gave way and the door opened a bit further. Hans waved me in with a defeated drop of his head and closed the door behind me. I glanced at

Tamara's bare legs and backside in the dark living room as she was picking up her clothes and dashed into the bedroom and slammed the door behind her.

"Peter, this had better be good!" He wheezed at me not wanting to raise his voice.

"Hans, thanks for letting me in. I'm sorry to interrupt, but I have no other safe place to hold up." I calmly explained to my friend, grateful that he didn't send me away. "Listen, I was robbed, beaten, threatened with a pistol, and had my apartment broken into and ransacked. I'm trying to get out of town but there is no train to Moscow tonight. I have to be out of Nizhniy by Monday morning so don't worry, tomorrow I will be gone."

"Why do you have to leave Nizhniy by Monday?" Hans was now looking worried.

"Listen, I don't want to involve you any further than letting me sleep here tonight. Tomorrow I will be gone, by Monday I'll fly away to the USA and won't bother you anymore," I explained.

"Look, Peter, you're not a bother. It was just a bad moment. Come in. Do you need some tea?" he offered.

"I haven't eaten all day. Do you have something I could eat, too?" I had no pride left.

I woke with a start. The room was dark. I could hear a terrible commotion on the streets outside with blue lights flashing and reflecting off the glass of all the windows up and down the buildings on Minin Street. I panicked and rushed to pull my shoes on. In the dark, I stumbled over the coffee table and landed hard on the floor on my left side and let out a yelp of pain. My eyes were pulsing in the dark searching for the shadows coming to deliver more blows as I struggled to get up. How did they find me? I was so careful! Holding my wounded left arm against my ribs I stood up again from a kneeling position and moved clumsily to the hallway. Hans stepped out and turned on the hallway light.

"Quick, turn those off!" I rasped at him emphatically.

The hall was quickly dark again.

"Hans, I'm sorry, I'm so sorry. I'll get out before they figure out which apartment I am in. I won't let them know where I was hiding!" I whispered in the dark.

"Peter, there's a fire up the street. They aren't coming to find you. Look, you can see the smoke and the fire from my bedroom window," he said, standing in his bedroom door.

I stood paralyzed with fear but felt the relief come quickly. My legs became limp and I felt that I would faint. I braced myself against a wall to catch my breath and equilibrium.

"Peter, go lay down. Everything is okay," Hans sympathetically ordered.

The sirens of the fire trucks came wailing under our third-floor balcony as we stood in the warm night and watched the black smoke billowing up over the block. Down below the street was filling with students from the technical school dormitory across the street.

Hans yelled down to them. "Guys, guys! What's burning?"

"The university building is burning! Come with us to help the fire fighters!" was the cry back from the group of students moving quickly together toward Minin Street.

Hans turned to go back in the apartment to find his clothes and shoes to go watch, if not help. As he stepped from the balcony into the living room, the pieces came together in my mind.

"Hans!" I called out. "It's the Linguistics School. It's the American Library! They've set fire to the American Library!" I felt my stomach sink. Guilt and shame came over me because of what I had brought on everybody due to my recklessness. How could I face the world again? Oh, God! Please don't let there be any victims in this fire, I prayed in my sick, churning gut.

"You'd better stay here then, Peter! I'll go check it out," he yelled back to me from inside the apartment.

"No Hans! I'd better go before they find me here," I cried.

"Sit your ass down! And don't go anywhere until I get back!" he ordered me. I sat on the couch and cried quietly in fear and despair. How could I have let it get so far? What had I done? Why hadn't I walked away earlier? The regrets and guilt piled on me like heavy bags of concrete. I hid my face in the couch and curled up, frightened for my life.

Hans woke me with a shake to my shoulders as the first daylight was just visible through the balcony door. It was four-thirty. I had slept for about two hours.

"Peter, you were right. Somebody threw a Molotov cocktail through each window of the university building. It wasn't an accidental fire."

"It just couldn't have been anything else!" I said, blinking sleep from my eyes. I seemed to be in my right mind now after a night of hysterics. My eyes stung with fatigue and tears.

"Peter, you need to get out of town," Hans confirmed what I already knew.

"Why? What has convinced you?" I pushed.

"On the front of the building they sprayed: Yankee Go Home!" Hans was embarrassed to tell me.

"Do you know if anybody was hurt?" I carefully asked.

"No, the place was empty. Nobody was found inside," Hans confirmed.

"Oh good. That's a huge load off my mind." I sighed.

"They think the fire was done for political reasons..." he reported.

"No, it's not! They did it to destroy the CD database because they saw all the materials I was able to find out about them in just a few months. They are very, very nervous!" I felt the panic coming up again into my throat and my heart was thumping quickly again. I wanted to run!

"You gotta get out of here, Peter!" Hans reconfirmed.

"OK, I'll get going, friend. Can you do one last favor for me, please? Will you go check up and down Minin Street to see if you can spot a black Lada with two goons sitting inside smoking?"

"There are so many people still in the street that I wouldn't be able to tell who is who," Hans commented.

"OK, I'll just go quickly across Minin and head down the Upper Embankment toward the stairs and I'll catch a cab from the river station to the train station. Maybe it's too early for anybody else to be out and about." I was lacing up my shoes as I was talking.

I gave Hans a firm, thankful handshake, picked up my backpack and bade him farewell and slipped out the door and on to the street. The air was rank with smoke and vapors. My nose and lungs burned and I jogged down the street and sprinted through the intersection at Minin Street toward the river. I didn't stop to look to see if the 'British Knight' was loitering around with his driver. I passed by Mr. P.'s residence at number eleven on the far side of the street; to my relief nothing more than the lights from his security office on the ground floor were burning. The house was still.

As I started gingerly down the river bluff stairs under the Chkalov monument, I heard a car pull up behind me and glimpsed quickly the lights of the black Lada. I ducked down so my head wasn't visible from above and crouched as I continued down the stairs, now at a quick clip trotting as fast as my ribs would allow. I heard the car rev its motor in the morning silence, spin around and head quickly down Georgiyevskiy Syezd to the lower river embankment. Luckily that road was in the opposite direction of where I was headed before it switched back in the direction of the River Station. I had a few minutes to hide myself in the alleyways of the lower old city or in the shadows of the kremlin walls.

Halfway down the stairs I veered left instead of descending the entire staircase which intersects with the lower embankment boulevard, and jogged a bit toward the Conception Tower of the kremlin to stand behind the ramparts and watch the black Lada race by. As I reached the tower I heard the frantic motor of the small car zip by below behind the trees. For now, I had eluded them.

I continued walking along the wall of the kremlin between the Conception Tower and St. John's tower in view of the chapel of St. John the Baptist. From there I could see the River Station in the morning sunshine at the junction with the Oka River. I stopped with the realization that I wouldn't be able to make it to the train station and if I did, they would be waiting for me there, anticipating that I would run, as I wasn't in my apartment.

I stood still and watched the few cars down below the slope zipping around the squares and alleys. I was frozen with fear and could feel the net closing in around me. I slowly descended the stairs rounding St. John's Tower and was resigned that if I ran, they would catch me. If I stayed still, they would eventually find me. I was hungry and I hurt all over after the running and the jarring on the stairs. I just wanted to lay down and let whatever was going to happen, just happen. I sauntered further down gradual slopes of Ivanovskiy Syezd, having given up. I walked casually through the intersection and headed toward the river bank where I knew I could at least be hidden from the street above as I slowly made my way toward the bus stop in front of the River Station.

As I emerged from the buildings I glanced left and saw the tail lights of a lone black Lada waiting in front of the River Station five blocks further up. I walked out from the buildings and crossed the street as if I was in no hurry, showing no intent to hide myself from anybody. The brake lights went out and the Lada lurched forward to make a u-turn and head in my direction. I did not hurry my pace. I reached the riverside and trotted down the embankment stairs to the mooring berths for the river boats and began walking toward the station. I could hear my pursuers up above speeding toward me but I could no longer see them, and they couldn't see me.

As I paced myself up the moorings and along the boats tied up for the overnight stay in Nizhniy, I could hear the crews cooking below decks preparing breakfast and an officer giving orders above deck to prepare for departure. As I passed the Pushkin, a long, low sitting boat that was half the size of what I had become used to the summer before, I noticed another. Just as one would bump into an old friend and not recognize her for a split second, there was the Giorgiy Zhukov sitting in the water right behind the Pushkin, tied up and quietly bobbing up and down with the river's current. How many times I had been so happy to see this noble boat after a long, scary day in Moscow, or after my harrowing visit to the hospital in Kazan! Now again the relief was immediate as I knew that I had friends and refuge in sight. Without any hurry or rush I sauntered down the gangplank and stepped on board, like I had arrived home.

I ducked inside the open door of the upper deck dining room and hid myself behind the bulkhead of the boat where no windows would betray me. Just sitting down was relief enough. Here I would be safe and could find the rest and refuge I needed with people I trusted with my life.

06

25. Stowaway

After two hours, the lights of the ship's dining room were switched on at seven o'clock. I woke from my half sleeping state, groggy and exhausted from very little sleep and too much excitement. I was immediately aware of the pain all over my body. Feeling that enough time had passed to have certainly eluded the henchmen trying to catch me, I slipped below deck to find Nikolai before the crew found me stowed away in the dining room. I headed straight to the bar. Before I could make my way to the bow of the vessel I saw him standing alone on the water side railing enjoying his breakfast of a cigarette and orange juice, gazing at the morning sun on the river's current.

As I opened the door from the broad stairwell he turned to greet who he thought would be a fellow smoker. When he realized it was me, he nearly dropped his glass into the water. He gave me a warm man hug and a kiss on both cheeks while exhaling smoke out of his nose. His bristly, unshaven cheeks didn't make it any more enjoyable.

"Peter, what a huge surprise! Nobody told me that you would be joining us so early. I thought you would join us in July!" He was sincerely pleased to see me.

"Well, if I'm welcome to join you all this week, while the school holidays are still on, then I'd be happy to sail with you this week." I tried to hide my desperate situation from him, at least for some time.

"We just completed the ship's manifest last night and submitted it to the river authority, but I am pretty sure that Irina could amend it with the captain this morning. I just don't know if we have a spare cabin." He was all business.

"Friend, can I ask you not to report me as a passenger on the ship please?" I looked him in the eyes with a pleading gaze.

"Is there something wrong? You know that if you aren't on the passenger manifest that they could take you off the boat at any port. You know this." Nikolai began to suspect something was wrong.

"I know, I know, but, I am....I am in a very difficult situation right now. I am in some trouble and I need to vanish for a few days and not be on any manifests. I can stay on the boat without going ashore if we see that a river authority is going to tick the boxes anywhere. We both know how to get around that anyway, right?" I proffered.

"What is so bad, Peter? Why do you have to hide? What's happened?" Nikolai pressed me for details.

"Let's just say I got on the bad side of a local criminal group. They are determined to close my mouth one way or another. I have to get out of Nizhniy and to Moscow without being noticed, and I can't take the train or a taxi in town without somebody snitching on me," I confessed to my friend.

"Peter, this sounds very serious. Have you gone to the police?" he asked.

"Nikolai, that's pretty rich coming from a guy like you!" I quipped. He chuckled at the irony. "I can't go to the police because the mayor is also involved...and the FSB. I am sure that all three groups are looking for me right now." I added the last bit quickly so as not to call too much attention to this latter fact.

Nikolai nearly swallowed his cigarette. "What in the name of the Virgin Mary have you been doing?" He coughed while exhaling.

"My friend, it's a very long, complicated story," I said heavily while leaning over the railing to gaze at the Volga. I didn't want to look my friend in the eye and admit that tomorrow I could be floating face down in the river.

"Well, I'm glad you used your time well, Peter. But the FSB just doesn't turn up for no reason," he said sarcastically and turned to watch the rising sun with me.

"I know. I know. This little circle of friends I've discovered is somehow connected to military aviation and I think that is why the spooks are involved. Can you keep me hidden on board until we reach Moscow? After that I'll slip away on the buses to the airport," I said calmly, already having made a plan.

"That would be fine, my friend, but we're heading the other direction, to Volgograd on this voyage. We've just come from Moscow, and you know in Moscow that they always tick the boxes on the manifest when we arrive," he warned me.

"Volgograd, eh? Is that a ten-day round trip then?" I asked.

"Eleven days this time. I don't know why." Nikolai clarified, "But we'll back to Nizhniy in one week. We'll dock here again next Sunday morning, wait a day before sailing back up the river."

"Can you keep me on board until we get back to Nizhniy next week?" I asked again.

After a thoughtful pause and a long gaze over the river and a long drag on his second cigarette, he said without looking at me, "We'll do our best." He flicked the smoking butt into the water. "Let's go find Irina. Can't keep her in the dark. You'll need her help."

Irina was shocked to see me. Not because I was unexpectedly on board her boat but because I was so pale, looked so tired, and couldn't stand up straight. I was listing left.

"Peter, what has happened to you?" she asked with concern.

After Nikolai told her an edited story of my situation, she scolded me. "I thought we taught you how to avoid these situations! You're not supposed to take the bull head-on with these types! You need to stay with us and we'll get you fixed up." She saw the desperation in my eyes and didn't make me ask to sail with the group for the next week.

"We will register you on board as a crew member. This way, you can't be considered a stowaway, and the authorities never check the crew manifests. The harbor masters are only after the extra fees that the passengers can pay when something irregular is discovered."

I was given a cabin to myself which seemed like too much space for me and my one backpack. Once I was alone in my cabin I passed out on the lower bunk and slept soundly until the early afternoon. I hadn't had a more comfortable and cleaner bed for over five months. The tiny closet shower felt like a rushing waterfall after having nothing other than a broken bathtub to bathe in for months, and I felt like I been welcomed to the Ritz Hotel with the fresh white towels. In Russia, there was no better way to spend a holiday than on these floating hotels.

After a shower, I felt many times better, even though the gash on my arm didn't look good and my rib cage was badly bruised with deep splotches of purple and pink. I avoided looking at myself shirtless in the mirror. It was too much for me to look at. Not looking helped me to deny the worst part of what happened in the last twenty-four hours.

By the time I was cleaned up and looked half presentable, the boat had long left the quays at Nizhniy Novgorod and was sailing southeast toward Kazan. I just glimpsed the tall bluff of the old city off the stern of the boat as we passed the river island near Kstovo, a wretched little suburb of Nizhniy filled with country dachas and broken industrial estates. Seeing Nizhniy disappear behind the bend I felt that I could relax. I knew that those looking for me had no idea how I vanished into thin air when they were so close to nabbing me. I imagined what the 'British Knight' was telling the chief henchman at this point. I chuckled aloud at my luck. My ribs reminded me that the score was one to one and that the match was not over yet.

Irina found me on deck watching Nizhniy disappear around the bend and commented from behind me before I sensed her presence. "I imagine that this is a big relief to you to get away for a week to let things calm down."

"Yes, very much so!" I said with relief. I turned to her familiar voice and face. "I don't think I can go back, Irina. In fact, I know I can't."

"You must have made somebody very angry with you," she commented but didn't want to know more. "Peter, I have spoken with the ship's nurse. I told her that you are a crew member for this voyage, a translator, and asked her to look at your injuries."

"That was very kind of you, Irina, but I don't want to be a burden," I apologized.

"Nonsense. You get patched up and get some lunch and I will make you work for every crumb and bandage. We can use you on this voyage." She smiled and then went off with her usual long, purposeful strides to help smooth out another problem another passenger was having. She was always on high receive and understood how to make her guests comfortable.

I found the nurses station on the lower deck at the front of the boat. It was simply a double size cabin with a stock of first-aid supplies and local elixirs for different common ailments for passengers not accustomed to living on a boat. I knocked politely and waited for the nurse to answer. There was no answer. I expected that she had waddled herself above deck in her sterile white orthopedic shoes and tunic and was taking the blood pressure of another geriatric American who was worked by a bit of indigestion. As I turned to leave, the cabin door opened and a doll faced, rosy-cheeked, slender young woman in a gauzy blouse and black slacks cinched tight at her waist asked how she could help me. I stood transfixed and couldn't speak.

"I, I, I am Peter. Irina sent me," I stammered, trying to find room in my mouth for my tongue between all my teeth. "Are you the nurse?"

"Yes. Please come in. I was expecting you a little earlier, but I guess you had just arrived and needed to sleep a bit." She was as sweet as morning sunshine! "What happened to you?"

"I fell running for the bus to get to the boat on time," I lied and looked away.

"Can you show me the injuries please?" she asked in a clinical way.

I pointed like an idiot to my upper left arm above my elbow, under my shirt without saying anything.

"Will you please remove your shirt so I can see what it looks like?" she said again as a matter of routine.

I unbuttoned my shirt and while trying to take my left arm out of the sleeve the nurse noticed the wincing and the slow stretch backward. I showed her the unwrapped gash from twenty-four hours earlier. It wasn't bleeding anymore, but it was undressed after my shower and was deeply bruised.

"Are you sure you fell?" she looked at me with doubt in her eyes.

"I was mugged," I reluctantly admitted with a bit of shame in my voice.

"Did they hit you with a metal baton?" she asked specifically looking at the shape of the bruising.

"Yes, I think so," I admitted again with a whisper. "and then kicked me a few times."

"Will you please show me your ribs? Are they as bad as your arm?" she ventured.

"Yes, very bad." I lifted up my t-shirt to expose the bruises. She winced but looked carefully.

"I see that you were hit at least twice in the ribs with that baton. So, I would count three hits in total. Did he hit you anyplace else?" She lifted the back of the shirt up to see a bruise but not as dramatic as the others. "That looks to be a bit different, less severe."

The nurse wrapped my torso tight with broad bandages to support the ribs and treated the gash with iodine that made my eyes water.

"Can't you all find something other than iodine in this modern age?" I squealed as she dabbed into the wound to disinfect it. My lower arm was streaked brown.

"I'm sorry, can you say that again? I don't speak English," she replied to my outburst.

"All is normal. It just hurt, that's all," I replied through my clenched teeth.

"I will give you some tablets for the pain. But you should rest for the next three days. No more running for buses!" she commented sarcastically.

"No more buses..." I repeated with a bit of relief in my voice.

"Did they steal something important from you?" she asked with sympathy as she wrapped the wound with clean bandages.

"Yes, but it wasn't mine to keep. So, I don't have to worry about getting it back. I just made them very angry that I had it," I commented.

"Oh, so they knew you had it and wanted it returned?" she asked further.

"Well, it was never theirs to begin with, but they didn't want me to have it," I confirmed.

"And how did they know you had it?" she was a bit confused.

"It's a long story. Maybe I could tell you another time." I stood up and put my shirt back on.

"Sure. Another time then." She handed me a box of pain killers and held up two fingers, tapped her wrist watch and held up four fingers.

"Two, every four hours," I confirmed my understanding.

She nodded yes and motioned for me to back up toward the cabin door with her sweet dark hazel almond shaped eyes and perfectly arched eye brows. I extended my right hand to thank her for her care. As she took my hand to shake it I felt her pale soft slender fingers in mine and a zing of electricity up my neck.

"And your name is?" I left the question hanging.

"Lara. My name is Lara," she affirmed and opened the door and waved me out with a smile.

Being on board the Zhukov again was like being on a different planet. The news of the outside world didn't reach the cabins and decks of the ship. The days spent on board were a blissful journey over a plane of ignorance. Only when one was able to turn on a television in a hotel suite was there a connection to the outside world. The world could go to war and for six and a half days and those on the Volga could sail on, not knowing who had been shot or bombed. I kept a low profile for my first evening on board not wanting to get into too many involved conversations. I felt still that I would be safer if I could keep my misadventures to myself. No need to raise suspicions and questions where they didn't already exist. It was for me the perfect place to hide for a week until I could formulate a new plan for getting to Moscow and on board a departing airplane.

I sat with Nikolai in a corner of the dining room gingerly spooning a delicious borscht into my mouth with my right hand while holding a chunk of black bread in my left hand. Nikolai sat across the table from me drinking a steaming cup of coffee after his dinner. We were speaking in low voices when the ship's nurse, Lara, took a seat across the table next to Nikolai and looked me up and down.

"I am happy to see you have an appetite. That means you are resting well," Lara said with a serious face.

"Yes, thank you. The tablets," I held up two fingers, followed by four fingers, "have helped me very much. Thank you for your care." I smiled as charmingly as possible.

"So, Kolya here told me that you have been to Kazan before....?" she insinuated.

"Oh, Kolya has been telling you stories has he?" I glared at Nikolai with accusative eyes. He just shrugged back at me and sipped his coffee casually.

"He says that you seem to have a habit of getting very injured. Should we be watching out for you with extra care to make sure you don't fall again?" Lara was poking a bit of fun and her eyes told me she was enjoying it.

"So, what exactly did Kolya-cuddly-bear here tell you about what happened last year?" I said in a mocking voice directed at my good friend who still showed no embarrassment or discomfort as he sat relaxed in his dining chair, "because I never fell down."

"What he told me was that you were taken away in an ambulance one morning in Kazan and that you weren't quite the same after that," she said in a curious but serious manner.

I had resumed eating my soup and bread and was chewing a bite when she mentioned the medics in Kazan. I stopped chewing and looked at Nikolai again with an annoyed look. I swallowed my bite and put my spoon down on the saucer under the bowl and folded my hands, resting my forearms and elbows flat on the edge of the table and leaned into the table a bit.

"Yes, it's true. I was taken to the hospital in Kazan due to complications from a head injury," I stated officially. Lara gasped and sat up a bit straighter in her chair.

"That must have been horrible!" she peeped.

"Which part? The head injury, the hospital, or the fact that it all happened in Kazan?" I asked with some impertinence in my questioning.

"What happened?" Lara asked again.

I told her the harrowing story as the dining room slowly emptied of passengers.

"On the second night of a ten-day voyage to Volgograd, much like this one, I hit my head on the staircase on the low overhang that leads up to the auditorium where they hold concerts and lectures."

Lara nodded, "Yes I know it."

I continued. "I didn't lose consciousness, and luckily I did NOT fall down the stairs after I hit my head. In fact, I was carrying a large speaker in my arms for that night's entertainment and was still able to finish climbing to the top and set it down. About fifteen minutes later I was a bit sleepy and dizzy and went to lay down in my cabin and I guess I slept the whole night."

"That is so dangerous!" Lara declared, knowing from her training the signs of a concussion.

"The next morning, I felt like I had a sack of rice or flour on my head. It felt like it would push my neck down. I couldn't wake up and I couldn't remember clearly what had happened. It was rather scary not to be able to remember. So, I asked somebody to ask the ship's nurse to come to my cabin and she was immediately very worried. She scolded me for not having called her the night before. She said I had a huge welt on the top of my head, larger than she was comfortable to treat, and she told me I should be in the hospital for observation for a few days," I continued.

"How horrible!" Lara remarked again, but very eager for me to continue.

"As it turned out every time I would fall asleep, and I guess with a bad concussion it's hard to even stay awake, that I couldn't remember anything that happened thirty or forty-five minutes before I fell asleep. As the boat was always sailing down river, each morning I would have to work to help myself remember things." I paused for a dramatic effect. "Many mornings I would find hand written notes to myself reminding me of where I had been when I went to sleep and where the boat should be when I woke up. The notes would help remember where I was and what was happening, but I could never remember writing the notes the next morning."

"This was a very serious injury!" Lara covered her mouth with her hands in fright.

"Yes, we had figured that point out, but the thought of spending two weeks alone in a Russian hospital with my short-term memory frightened me more than anything else. I insisted that there was nothing more that the doctors of a hospital could do for me than what the ship's doctor was already doing. The doctor was very nervous and checked on me every few hours to make sure that I was still lucid. She told me that any digression would mean that she would have me removed by Captain's orders and hospitalized." I looked to Nikolai for corroboration.

"One hundred percent right! Why were you so stubborn? You were in real danger!" Lara seemed more worried a year later than the treating doctor at the time.

"By the time we reached Nizhniy Novgorod, I had begun feeling much better and the doctor had said that the bruising on the top of my head looked better and the swelling had decreased." I rubbed the top of my head for effect. "She allowed me to leave the boat for fresh air and thought that being on shore would help me get my sense of equilibrium back. I spent that afternoon strolling the riverfront at Nizhniy Novgorod. The afternoon onshore had improved my mood and my stamina and as the doctor had thought it might. We decided that I could return to work after another day or two when we reached Kazan.

"When we arrived in Kazan, I went ashore in the early morning to shake hands with the local guides and drivers that were already waiting for us at the docks. While I was discussing schedules and procedures with the drivers, I began to get real dizzy and felt my left knee buckle. My right leg began to tremble, too. One of the bus drivers reached out and caught me and helped me to sit down on the pier before I collapsed." I felt out of breath telling so her so much.

"If you had hit your head again, the results could have been fatal! It sounds like you were still very unstable." Lara's eyes were as large as saucers as she listened and diagnosed my condition.

I went on trying to generate a sympathy effect from her. "The ship's doctor insisted that I go to the hospital to be looked at by specialists. I was petrified to go alone! We agreed that one of our ship's tour guides would accompany me to the hospital, to be there in case things got worse with me, but she didn't want to go with me because of it being Kazan and all. She was afraid that the Mongols were still there ravishing all the blond Russian women in town or something. She was just as nervous as I was."

"I would be nervous, too!" Lara declared.

"Well, I can say that I have never met a more hospitable group than the Tatars. I think that Russians are just prejudiced against them. I found them to be very professional. The medic that came with the ambulance, Vasily, was definitely a Tatar. He was very confident in his job and helped me calm down. He asked questions like he already knew the answers. He was good. He knew what he was doing and he did it well. My blood pressure was erratic and my heart was racing. I did not have a temperature, but I was noticeably sweating, even though my face was faint and pail. My legs were numb and I could not walk on my own power. Vasiliy spared me the humiliation of being carried off of the boat on a stretcher with all the tourists watching from the shore. They more or less carried me standing upright down the gangplank with a medic under each arm. I just tried to look like I was waking," I said, giving Lara sad eyes.

"They took me to the Kazan regional hospital and they reassured us, Valya and I, that I would be in good hands, as it was the newest and most modern of hospitals in the province. But when we arrived I had to climb out of the ambulance and hop down from the bumper and then walk down a flight of stairs to reach the trauma ward. Luckily I had help!" I was really playing it up now, although every word was true. She was eating out of my hands.

"The hospital itself was so new that it had yet to be finished. There were piles of rubble, garbage, and concrete from the buildings they demolished to build the new hospital. A jack hammer crew was busy pulverizing the old foundations of the old buildings. The clouds of dust this caused coated the outside of the building, and was everywhere inside too, on tables, sinks, light fixtures in the beds and the floors. It was filthy!" I went on and on.

"Yes, our hospitals in Russia are horrible places!" Lara agreed with professional embarrassment.

"They finally laid me on a wobbly gurney and wheeled me from room to room instead of having me get up off the examination tables in each room. This would have been better than walking, had the safety engineers not built speed bumps in every doorway. Yes, each doorway came complete with a raised threshold to keep out winter drafts. It made moving from room to room very jarring. Before going through a doorway, I had to lift my injured neck and head off of the pillow, otherwise I would get whiplash. I have great sympathy for those who arrive the victims of a hit and run, or who come with a broken leg or a broken back. Given the chance, I would choose to die on the street where I had been run down, because the hospital is hardly a place of comfort and reassurance for the injured citizen. Better to just stay away!" I thought I had gone too far with that reference, but Lara agreed whole heartedly.

"Yes, this is what patients tell our doctors as well, that they would rather die at home than be put in the hospital." Lara seemed ashamed.

"The doctors were looking for signs of hemorrhaging either in my head or in my spinal column. The results were inconclusive, so they put me in a room, in a bed, while they debated the issue. When the decision was made to keep me in the hospital overnight for observation and more tests I had no more energy to argue. Valya, who had accompanied me to the hospital, was growing concerned about the time of day and told she was afraid to be left in Kazan, so she headed back to the boat, but promised to send others back to help me, or if necessary somebody who could come and stay with me." I pouted a lonely pout.

"You poor thing!" Lara seemed to be on the verge of tears.

"There was thick dust everywhere: on the floor, window sills. There was fuzzy mold along the floor boards and in the refrigerator. My pillow case had been blood stained in the past, the toilet smelled of undiluted ammonia. I did my best to close my eyes and rest while I waited for my colleagues to arrive, but even laying in the bed was impossible because a spring had broken through the top of the mattress and was poking me in the small of my back. I laid on my side on the edge of the bed facing the door and watched and hoped for somebody to come save me!" I told her every gory detail until even Nikolai was looking worried.

"I woke up to a knock on the door and was so happy as I thought it was Irina come to rescue me. But it was a group of three doctors. They came to announce their decision. One of them tried to explain it to me in English but it was so poor that I asked them to repeat it in Russian. Instead they handed me a medical book, in English, and asked me to read it. The procedure was called Lumbar Puncture. As I read further through the narration to the dramatic pictures of needles, poking between some poor guy's vertebrae and muscles, I freaked out! They wanted to perform a spinal tap on me!"

"Bozhe Moi! Did you let them do the test?" Lara blurted in horror.

"No, no way! Absolutely no! Even the book said that the chance of death was high in a sterile environment. Seeing that the hospital was so filthy, there was no way I could trust those doctors to stick a needle, even if they had a clean needle, into my spine. If I didn't have meningitis before they did, I most certainly would afterwards! No, I refused the procedure and made it very clear the answer was no, no, no!" I insisted.

"Did the boat leave without you? Did you have to stay in Kazan?" Lara was very nervous for me.

"No. Soon after that Irina and Richard arrived and convinced the doctors to release me to them and they would take responsibility for my health. The chief doctor made me sign a paper that said that I was taking full responsibility for my own health as they believed I could die before I made it back to Moscow if I was moved. They warned me that flying would further weaken the blood vessels in my head and I could easily die on an airplane with such a head injury. I didn't care! I signed the document and we caught a taxi back to the boat. Luckily, I didn't die," I said as matter of factly as I could and started eating my soup and bread again.

"And so now you thought you could tempt fate and piss off mob bosses," Nikolai said as dry as ordering bread and cheese at the grocers. "That's a good plan!"

"Is that who beat you and stole from you?" Lara quickly connected the dots and was shocked.

I held up two fingers, tapped my wrist and then held up four fingers and finished munching my black bread silently with an admitting look on my face as Lara seemed to fume at this revelation. What did she care anyway?

06

26. On the River

The weather as the boat approached Kazan had quickly turned hot and dry. The warm air coming up the river valley from the southern regions of the steppe was having the effect of a blow dryer on my hair when I stood on the forward deck enjoying the view of Kazan's white walled kremlin come into view. This warm air made the mornings and evening very pleasant to be on deck and out of doors but made the afternoons almost too warm. I had only brought a few pieces of clothing with me from my ransacked apartment when I fled on Friday night and I had taken the wrong things with me. Why did I grab my shapka? It seemed I had clothes for being outside in March, not May. The plan was to be somewhere over Greenland on Monday morning not on the river, not still in Russia. I needed something else to wear and to have my hair cut as we were heading toward the southern steppes where May and June are already too warm for those used to snow and ice only six weeks earlier.

As I was not assigned a tour group by Irina, but just worked as an interpreter for passengers while on board, I took a stroll through Kazan after we docked, while the groups boarded busses and went to see churches and mosques. Once in the center of the old city, I visited the barber and did some shopping at the bazaar for the basics that I had left behind in Nizhniy. While the choice of clothes, shoes, and sandals was almost endless, the quality was pitiful. I could have bought an entirely new wardrobe for the prices being asked, but walked away with some locally made slacks and a few button-down shirts of both light materials and light colors. I purchased a single disposable razor and a small bar of shaving soap, a toothbrush, a small sampler tube of toothpaste labeled fully in German, and a bottle of shampoo. I looked for deodorant but there just wasn't any to be found. With my hair so short a basic comb was all I needed. I bought a cheap backpack to carry it all in and then strolled through the town that I had missed last year due to my medical misadventures. The city was being restored after decades of neglect. Scaffolding and street works were ubiquitous. There was a distinctly different feeling in this city than other Volga towns. While I couldn't quite put my finger on it, it felt like Kazan was perhaps just a bit more 'free' than Nizhniy and Moscow. How exactly I couldn't tell. Maybe it was all in my head. Maybe I was feeling liberated in the warm sunshine, my hair buzzed off, away from my studies and the mess I had made for myself in that icy cold apartment on Prospect Lenina. It was good to be on the river again.

As it was Monday morning I was glad I was out of Nizhniy and was safe. I thought about calling Yulia. I decided it was best not to call as who knows who would be listening. Surely the FSB had her phone tapped by now and were waiting for me to make contact again. Were Mr. P.'s goons camped out in front of my apartment window, harassing Babushka and Raiya every day? For all they knew I was still hiding out in Nizhniy. They were probably watching Hans's apartment too. I felt guilty for bringing this on my friends. I wanted to fix it somehow instead of running away and hiding. As I walked through Kazan back to the River Station, I thought about how I might be able to get in contact with everybody to let them know I was safe without revealing where I was and without putting them in any further danger. Perhaps I could send a postcard? I would be long gone from that town before it reached them. Perhaps I could even be out of Russia before anybody could intercept it. Why take the risk? Perhaps it was just better to call once I was out of Russia. I vacillated back and forth about what to do. My thoughts weighed me down as I boarded the trusted Zhukov again in the early afternoon. I sat alone on the deck in the sunshine in my new clothes and enjoyed the warm, dry breeze. The boat was deserted except for the crew.

"Pyotr? Is that you? I didn't recognize you dressed like a Russian man."

I pulled my cap off from over my eyes and face that was shielding them from the bright sun as I lazed on deck. Lara was standing above me in her working uniform. I smiled a lazy smile and put the hat back on my face. The sun was brilliant that afternoon. Her blouse ruffled in the warm breeze.

"And what did you do to your hair?" she sounded horrified.

I sat up and put the cap on my head.

She was dumbfounded. "You look completely different. I only recognized you because of the bandage on your arm."

"Sorry, but I hadn't brought the right clothes with me on the trip. I bought some new threads at the bazaar," I explained.

"Yes, it certainly looks that way." She chuckled, referring with amusement to the poor quality of the vestments. "Why did you cut your beautiful hair?" she asked again.

"Did you like it the other way? I thought boys in Russia shouldn't have long hair..." I was teasing her a bit.

"Well, yes, but you're not Russian. It looked wonderful on you." She was being sincere.

"I thought so too, but it was too hot. Needed a summer style." I grinned and removed the cap to show her my bristly head again.

"You look like a soldier," she puffed and sat down on a deck chair opposite me in a bit of disgust.

"Do I really look that different?" I asked again, getting an idea.

"I would have walked right past you had I not see that bandage there under your short sleeve," she affirmed. "All that is missing is a cheap wrist watch."

"I can get one!" I said triumphantly.

She waved her hands at me in disgust and muttered, "Phoo! Phoo!" as Russians do to their dogs when they are misbehaving. After a short pause in the conversation, she asked directly, "Why did you not pack the right clothes, Pyotr?"

"Dear doctor, I am not supposed to be on this boat. I am actually hiding on this boat from the people who robbed me, beat me, broke into and destroyed my apartment, and fire bombed a university building, all to keep me quiet," I explained in an overdone gracious voice. I then switched to a more serious tone. "So, I grabbed a few things and I ran. Luckily, the Zhukov was in port when I was running away from the fellow who beat me the first time. I had not planned to be here. I planned to be in the United States by now, but couldn't make it to the train station without getting caught. I don't know what they'll do to me if they catch me again."

"Kolya was serious then. You did get beaten by thugs," she concluded.

"Yes. And I don't think they'll stop looking for me. So, I have to get out of Russia as soon as I can," I admitted with defeat in my voice. "I can't go back to Nizhniy."

"Do you live there, in Nizhniy Novgorod?" she asked surprised.

"Yes, I am a student there," I affirmed.

"I also finished nursing school at NGU," she announced. "I live there with my grandmother."

I had another idea come to my head, but I sat and listened patiently to her story.

For the next few days I didn't shave my face. Even though I had purchased a razor and shaving soap in Kazan, looking in the mirror at the three days of growth on my chin and jaw on Tuesday morning, I decided to let it grow. It was growing in as a red beard even though my hair was a dark brown. Maybe it was the full warm sun for several days in a row that gave it a tinge. It was certainly the sun that had given my face and neck a good tan. I had spent several days on the deck of the boat taking in as much sunshine as possible. The white, pasty, winter look was gone and I was turning rather brown in my face and arms. I continued to let the beard grow.

During our day stop in Samara I snuck off to the bazaar or street side markets during the guided tours and bought myself a track suit, flip flop sandals, and a pair of classless sunglasses. A simple silver wire frame with shades. In Saratov, I didn't have to look far as vendors came to the River Station to sell their wares to the tourists and I was able to buy a cheap gold wrist watch with a white face, gold hands and no numbers, and an old soldier's field glasses. The watch had to be wound each day to tell time twenty-four hours later and the lenses of the binoculars were heavily scratched. By the time we arrived into Volgograd it was nearly impossible to tell me apart from the other local punks loitering around the docks in multi-colored, jerry-rigged Ladas smoking cigarettes and drinking cheap beer from chunky brown glass bottles with no labels. My transformation had been complete, except for my body language.

Where the Volga river spills out onto the southern Russia steppes is one of the most beautiful places I have ever seen. One is not quite sure where the earth and the river meet as the high steep banks melt away after the city of Saratov, and there is nothing but arid rolling plains and dramatic skies filled with tall white clouds. One can literally watch a thunderstorm roll in, roll over and roll out and disappear over the horizon. There is nothing on the land to obscure one's view of the horizon—nor anything on it. The weather in Volgograd is warm and arid, and in the summer time only warm breezes blow. Along the banks of the river, tall, slim poplar trees sway in the warm breezes from the steppe and make a calming, gentle rustling noise that sweeps up and down the river. The mornings are bright, clear, and fresh, and the morning sun quickly heats the stones on the river, welcoming the afternoon strollers and sun worshipers. On the riverbank the men strip to the waist and lay on the grassy banks of the Mother Volga and the young women stroll in wispy sundresses that flutter around their bare legs in the warm breeze.

In Volgograd after a warm day of bus tours, we bid farewell to one batch of tourists in the afternoon and had the night off, until ten in the morning to relax and rest until the next group arrived for their voyage from Volgograd to Moscow, via Nizhniy Novgorod. After a few shots of vodka, Nikolai was loose enough to help me perfect the walk, the squat, and the deep guttural talk of the street punk. After a few more shots we were strolling around the bar, bow legged, to the hysterical laughter of our colleagues as we perfected the lazy drawl, the long O's of the Volga vagrant and sitting on chairs with our legs wide open, slouched with a look of complete incredulousness on our faces, not caring if Tsar Nicholas himself had just been raised from the dead. Between shots of Pepsi and vodka I practiced squatting in the corner for twenty minutes at a time until my knees went numb or until Kolya fell over half drunk laughing his head off. My beard had fully grown in and was as red as an Irishman's.

That evening before bed, like I always did, I took a stroll along the entire railing of the top deck. It was a calming practice I had picked up the summer prior and it felt natural to do it again. I padded around the deck in my gangster flip flops and track suit; slap, swish, slap, swish. While I rounded the stern of the boat, I noticed Lara staring out across the water into the city lights. A warm breeze was blowing through her shoulder length sandy brown hair. She was off duty like the rest of us for a shore-visit or other horseplay.

I greeted her in proper Russian, not in the street slang I was practicing in the bar, "Good evening, doctor."

"Good evening, Pyotr." She looked briefly at me and then looked away.

"We missed you tonight. Did you go for dinner in the city?" I inquired.

"No, I don't know anybody here. This is only my second voyage," she replied in a business-like way.

"OK. Would you like to join me for a nightcap in the bar?" I invited.

"No thank you. I don't like sharing a drink with a street urchin." She glanced me up and down. I reached to zip up the track suit jacket and hide the undershirt. I stood quietly for a moment.

"Pytor. Do you think I'm a fool? Do you not think that I know what you're doing? And don't you realize how stupid and dangerous it is?" she blurted out with no warning.

"Lara, I'm not asking you to do anything. Why are you so upset?" I protested.

"You're asking me to stand by and watch you get picked up by those thugs again and get beaten so nobody can recognize your face anymore! You won't fool people for long, you know!" She was rather emotional and turned away.

"I only have to fool them for maybe four or five hours until I can get on a train and make it to Moscow. I'm not going back to my apartment. I won't be going back to school. I just have to blend in long enough to get from the River Station into the train station without somebody recognizing Peter Turner. That's it!" I explained. "I'm very confident it will work!"

"Why don't you just get on a flight from Volgograd and go direct to Moscow? That way you don't have to go back to Nizhniy at all," she proffered.

"I've thought about that. But the one place that they will check my passport and visa will be at the airports. I don't have permission to be on this boat, I don't have permission to be in Volgograd. I don't have permission to even be out of the Nizhegorodskiy Province. If I tried to get on a plane here, in Volgograd, they'd collar me so fast. I know, almost for sure, that my name is already on an FSB watch list. If any border guard sees my visa, that it's not in order, and checks his latest national alerts, they'll have me either way. At least sneaking through Nizhniy, I have a chance to make it to Moscow without getting picked up," I explained earnestly.

"How will I know..." she stopped herself short. "How will we know if you've made it?"

"Lara, I'm sorry. I didn't know you were this concerned about me. I can always send you a postcard or call your grandmother from Moscow to let you know," I offered.

"Maybe I could come with you, just to make sure?" she half whispered looking me in the face.

"Don't be silly. Why would a beautiful woman like you be walking arm in arm with a street punk? That would only call attention to me, just as if I put on my orange rain coat again. If I don't go as a street punk they will recognize me from a hundred meters away. There is no other option," I rebutted.

"Is there any way I can help you? I could not bear it to think of you being beaten again. What they did to you the first time without even trying was horrible!" She shuddered.

"Well, if you really want to help me..." I left the possibility hanging in the air. Lara turned to me to hear my suggestion. "Will you have your grandmother call a few people for me in Nizhniy and give them a message from me?" I asked skeptically.

"I can ask her. I will talk to her tomorrow morning from the captain's telephone on the bridge before we depart tomorrow afternoon. Please let me know who you need to call and what the message is," she replied resolutely.

"Thank you, this will help me greatly. I am sure there are people worried about me. I left without a word," I said with gratitude.

Lara took me by the right arm and walked with me toward the staircase. "Come, let's have that drink..." She tipped her head against my shoulder as my sandals said: slap, swish, slap swish across the smooth deck. "...and please take off those stupid sandals!" She laughed.

As the turbines revved up to push us northward from the moorings at Kazan on Saturday night, my heart jumped. The bow was pointed north and the next stop, my last stop, would be Nizhniy Novgorod. It was a late Saturday evening and the sun and clouds had made a brilliant sunset in the east. Heading indoors was the last thing on my mind. Sleep, I knew, would not be possible that night. After eight days, the stiffness and pain from my bruised ribs were gone, even though the bruises still hurt when poked. Lara had dressed them just that morning again and told me for sure that nothing had been broken. The gash in my arm was closed up and getting ready to leave a manly scar. I had eaten well this last week and felt confident and ready to make the dash to the train station.

I packed my new Russian rucksack with my new clothes and my black shapka; I couldn't be parted from it. I left my other clothes and shoes with Nikolai. Maybe his brother could use the blue jeans and shoes this fall. My beard after a week and a day looked perfect. My hair was just a bit longer, but still cropped close. With the sunglasses on, the open track suit, an unlit cigarette in my mouth, my own mother wouldn't have recognized me. I could hardly believe the mirror myself. I was ready. There was a knock at my door. I took off the glasses and hid the cigarette, as I hoped it was Lara. It was.

"I don't know if I will get a chance to see you in the morning before you disembark. I just wanted to wish you good luck.

Please don't forget to call from Moscow. I have the next week off of work and will be home. My grandmother is almost always home. You can leave a message..." she was pining.

"Thank you. Did you get a chance to call home before we left Kazan port?" I queried.

"Yes, Grandmother spoke to the people you wanted to give messages to. She says they were all very relieved to hear you were safe. Yulia wanted to know where to find you. Baba didn't know so she couldn't tell her. That's all. The man she phoned, she couldn't understand him but he understood the message," she reported.

"Thank you very much!" I leaned over and gave her a bristly peck on the cheek. "That's fantastic news!"

"No thanks needed," she replied surprised.

"Say, I don't plan to sleep tonight. I'm too crazy. I was going to watch the stars tonight off the stern. Would you like to join me?" I invited.

"Only if we can sit out of the wind," was her only condition.

Wrapped in the blankets from the two bunks in my cabin and with warm tea in hand, we sat on the deck and watched the villages and other boats pass in the night. There was no moon that night so the stars were more brilliant than usual. It felt like we could pluck the stars from the sky if we stood up and reached out for them. They sat as low as the horizon and reflected on the water in the wider stretches of the river. We watched the river locks close behind us and lift us to a new level, and we watched again as the red and green flashing lights of the river's bulwark faded behind us and around a black bend in the night. The night was all shadows and stars.

"What will you do with the information once you arrive in the USA?" she asked me serenely with her head on my shoulder.

"I suppose it's nothing that other people don't already know, but because it's original material I'm sure I can use it for a thesis to finish my degree. Nobody here wants it!" I speculated.

"Why didn't you stop when you knew it was getting dangerous?" she pushed.

"The momentum just carried me through. Every way I turned, it was just in front of me. This one mobster dominates the business community, legal and illegal. I tried to stop, but nobody would believe that I had stopped," I explained.

"And now look at you. You've gone from an intelligent academic to a street urchin with a barge puller's accent. You could fool your own mother now," she admitted.

"You know, I was just thinking the same thing before you knocked on my door," I said with glee.

"So, you're having fun now?" She slapped my arm.

"Thanks for staying with me tonight. I'd be too nervous to sit alone in my cabin and watch the shadows on the water. It would have driven me crazy," I said quietly.

"No thanks needed." She rested her head on my shoulder again.

It was three-thirty when we saw the first hint of dawn on the eastern horizon. Lara took that as her signal to head for her cabin and get a few hours of sleep. As she stood to leave, she bent over and kissed my lips softly, looked me in the eyes, said nothing more, and disappeared below deck. I felt that I would never see her again, and let her go without protest.

06

27. Blood in the Water

At five-thirty in the morning the Zhukov chugged into her home port and docked at the Nizhniy Novgorod river front, very near the station house as the berths were mostly empty that morning. As the boat cleared the bluff with the old city perched on top, I was on the top deck viewing the river front through the old military binoculars I had bought in Saratov. From my vantage point I could see the lower embankment street fairly well. The only part of the boulevard I couldn't see was directly behind the River Station's passenger terminal, but, I figured, they wouldn't park there as it gives no overview of an area. If someone was watching they would want to sit and be able to see the lower promenade where passengers disembark. I saw no black Lada loitering in the morning sun. I saw no duo of thugs hanging about on benches or under lamp posts. The river front seemed rather deserted except for the tourist buses that were pulling in on schedule to carry the boat's passengers around town that day. I sighed with relief but still kept watching until the boat was tied up to the docks and the turbines shut down.

The first train from Nizhniy to Moscow was at two o'clock that afternoon. The second would be the night train leaving at ten-thirty in the evening. I had hoped to get the two o'clock and then overnight in Moscow wherever I could get a room. By Monday afternoon I planned again to be in the air. As the Zhukov had docked so early I had some time to kill. Breakfast would be at seven o'clock, the tours would start at nine o'clock. If I remembered right, a crew shift should happen at around eleven o'clock. The sailors who had just worked for ten straight days would get ten days off and a new crew would arrive and take over their duties. I would depart the boat at eleven as the young and middle-aged men in working clothes would move as a group to the bus stop, and I would blend in with them and walk past any henchman sent to watch the river front for my reappearance. I did not go below deck for breakfast but held my solitary watch, too nervous to eat.

I watched the tourists disembark, mill about on the pier, and then be led like sheep by their tour guides from the waterfront into waiting buses. They filed away in an orderly manner and the buses, once full, departed leaving just a plume of diesel fumes. I scanned the street and the cross streets again with my binoculars and still noticed nothing usual; nobody loitering, no police cars on a stakeout up and down the entire water front. Everything was going to plan. I rechecked my bag to make sure my passport, money, and plane ticket were still there and easy to reach. I made sure my visa was still tucked safely in the jacket of my passport. Everything was ready. I paced the deck in my track suit and sun glasses and killed another ninety-minutes until I began to see more and more people arriving, being dropped in cars, stepping off the buses and moving toward the boat. Here came the crew change!

Twenty to thirty young men with crew cuts, most wearing track suits, some wearing locally made denim and t-shirts starting milling about on the pier, smoking lazily while they waited for their counterparts to make room for them in the crew quarters and head home for a well-deserved rest. They carried with them clothes and supplies for ten days of sailing in cheaply made plastic carryalls, with zippers that split after three months of use. I slipped downstairs to the boat's main passenger door and stepped to the shore and mixed with the newcomers. As more exited the boat and walked to the bus stops in small groups, I walked in the middle of them wishing them all a good break, wishing them good weather, hoping their girlfriends would treat them well. The little crowd at the bus stop thinned as different buses passed the station coming and going in different directions. It was my turn to step onto the bus headed to the Moscovskiy Station and Zarechnaya. I waved my temporary comrades goodbye still in character and boarded my bus. I sat alone, sprawled over two seats with my sunglasses on and a cigarette behind my ear. Nobody paid me any attention. The bus was nearly empty. I watched out the back window for signs of anybody scrambling to a car, running with a message. No cars fell in behind the bus to follow it. I let out a sigh of relief and rested the back of my head against the grimy window behind me. "I could just possibly pull this off!" I said to myself. But then the critical voice in my head made me remember that there had been nobody watching. "You haven't passed any test yet!" was my own response.

As the bus pulled up to the train station, I could see again that it had not been a busy morning, but that activity was picking up. More people were flowing out of the metro station carrying bags of merchandise to set up a makeshift Sunday bazaar. That was a good sign. The more people around the better; I would have more people to blend in with. I stepped off the bus and stood by the public telephones near the taxi stand and pretended to call somebody. I used the time to scan the area again for anybody else who was standing around, loitering, doing nothing, sitting in a car and going no place. I talked to myself on the telephone which was now giving me the signal tone to hang up the handset and try again. I thought about punching in Yulia's number, but knew it was too long until the train departed. I had ninety minutes still to kill and didn't want to alert anybody who was potentially listening to her phone to know that I was nearby. Surely, I would be putting everybody into further danger should I have called her.

I hung up the telephone, collected my bag, and sauntered into the station's hall and up to the ticket window with a walk that told people who may have been watching that I didn't have any place to be, and I didn't give a damn about what you think about me. I had gotten good at the walk and thought I was doing it quite well behind my sunglasses and week-old beard. On the inside, I was shaking like a leaf. I feared if I received any resistance I would crack and start crying a guilty confession. I waited in line impatiently behind two others at the ticket window. Finally, my turn.

"Third class on the afternoon train to Moscow please," I muttered half eating my words like I had practiced.

There was no response from the ticket window. A small digital sign of greenish number flashed behind the thick plastic barrier. I shoved my money under the window in wads, nothing too neat and tidy and out of character. In return, I got a third-class ticket to Moscow for two o'clock departure that same day. I couldn't believe my luck! Such a wave of relief went through me that I almost said "thank you" to the woman behind the window, but caught myself and walked away like I was disappointed that I hadn't been upgraded for free to first class.

It was imperative that I stayed in character as I hadn't yet had time to scan the passengers' hall for any risks. I loped over to the perimeter of the hall, next to the newsstand and tobacconist kiosk, took off my sunglasses, and leaned my back up against the wall. I watched those passing by, and those waiting, like me, for a train to go when I realized that I should probably be smoking, not watching everybody like a hawk. I reached for the smoke behind my ear only to find it missing. I cursed under my breath, afraid I was missing a vital piece of my disguise.

I quickly stepped up to the kiosk next to me to buy a pack of cigarettes for the first time in my life, but before I could even point to what I should have already decided was my favorite brand of smokes, there was Mr. P.'s face right in front of me! My heart jumped out of my chest and my mouth turned completely dry. I picked a newspaper from the top of the pile and read the headline above his picture: "Local businessman murdered in Nizhniy Novgorod!"

"Hey, punk, you gonna pay for that?" bellowed the salesman. "Can you even read?"

I looked up at him and blinked and asked with a blank expression of amazement, "He's dead?"

"Yes, why? Was he your boss? You here to collect his money for him? Well he's dead today and I ain't payin' no more!" the newspaper man continued. I handed the man five hundred rubles and wandered back to the wall where I had been standing and read the article slowly.

The newspaper was short on speculation and told only the facts. What was very clear was that he had been shot at a very close range in the side of his head while sitting in the driver's seat of his Mercedes. The window had been down, the motor still idling when he was found. He was found on the edge of town on the river bank, but the article didn't say exactly where. He had not been robbed, therefore the police suspected an underworld liquidation similar to what was going on in Moscow and Vladivostok in recent months.

Reading this news sent electricity through my system. I was almost elated to see his face and death on the front page of the newspaper. Could it be that all my troubles had been resolved in a split-second flash of gunpowder, brass, and lead? The circumstance of Mr. P.'s death, his murder, didn't concern me even though the gruesomeness, the cold-blooded element should have chilled my blood. The man had ordered his thugs to rob me, beat me as necessary, break in and destroy my home, set fire to my school, and if they had caught me again last week I could have be the one floating face down in the river. I needed friends to celebrate with! I needed a pretty girl to kiss! I wanted to cry with the release of my worry and anxiety. I had been given a second chance. What was I going to do with it?

I found my address book in a backpack and quickly stepped outside again to the public pay phones. I found Lara's telephone number. Yes, she should have been home already. The dial on the phone took an eternity to stop its ticking and clicking to connect us.

"Halloa?" her sweet voice was music to my ears.

"Hello—this is Pyotr!" I said with great anticipation.

"Pyotr? Are you in Moscow already?" she sounded surprisingly relieved.

"No, no. Lara, did you hear the news this morning? Did you read the newspapers?" I couldn't help but want to shout the news to her.

"No, Pyotr. I just arrived home from the boat. What is happening?" she sounded worried again.

"He's dead, Lara! He's dead! Somebody shot him on Friday night," I was hissing into the telephone with my hand over my mouth and the mouthpiece, unable to contain my excitement.

"Who? Who is dead?" she was understandably confused at my delight at such a horrible crime.

"Him! The one I was running from! The mobster boss!" I reiterated.

"What? Really? Are you serious? How could that happen?" She was taken fully off guard.

"I don't know, but it's all over the newspaper," I reconfirmed slapping my folded-up copy in my hands like an over enthusiastic Bible thumping preacher.

"Pyotr, where are you?" she asked cautiously.

"Moscovskiy Station. I am thinking that I might go back to my apartment and carefully slip into my normal life again. Can I come see you tonight?" I was elated at the thought of seeing her again after already reconciling myself that we would never meet again.

"Pyotr, No! Please don't be foolish and reckless. Go to Moscow and wait there. Call me soon and I will try to keep you informed of the news here locally. Maybe you can work on the Zhukov again with your friends if this is all over, but please don't go back to your apartment. Remember that they burned down your school. Why couldn't they throw a Molotov cocktail through your window too?" she pleaded.

"OK, you're right. I will go to Moscow on the train now and will call you tomorrow from there. Talk soon!" I hung up and moved to the departure platforms to board the train.

In the excitement of the news and the chance I saw of getting my life back to normal, I forgot to act the role of an apathetic street punk and nearly sprinted across the hall to the platforms with excitement in my smile. As I waited in a short line to have my ticket and documents checked, I looked behind me into the nearly vacant hall and pledged in my thoughts that I would be back again soon and the story about Lara would have a sequel. Perhaps all the pain and worry would pay off for me. I just had to go lay low for another week in Moscow and I could come back quietly in time for the language exams. Maybe I could go back to work on the river for the summer as Lara had suggested.

28. Caged Canary

"Documents!" snapped the officer at the control station.

I handed the blue uniformed agent my train ticket and passport with my student visa and student card. He looked at the photos of me and looked at me again and did a double take. Of course, I had completely changed my appearance in the last week. My hair was short, my beard thicker every day. I was dressed like a street urchin, as Lara called it. I removed my sunglasses so he could see my eyes. The eyes always matter! I smiled. He looked down to his hidden desktop and looked over a secret list that all of us hope and never expect to be on. With nothing more than a grunt, he handed all the papers back to me and waved me through to the platforms with a nod of his head. I tucked my documents away in my backpack and passed through to the waiting train.

The conductors were busy preparing to open the doors of the third-class compartments, checking lists and handing papers back and forth to each other. I stood away from the gathering throngs waiting to board. I had learned that waiting in a line in Russia can be a long wait for usually nothing and so I avoided them as a matter of habit. I stood back and watched the old ladies elbow their way forward to be able to board first. The prerogative of a grandmother, I observed. As the carriage doors opened and the conductor's shrill whistle blew to alert the waiting crowds that their cars were now open, I felt something strike the back of my knees and launch me falling forwards to my knees.

I watched my backpack skid out in front of me, sliding quickly from my shoulder to the floor as my hands instinctively moved to brace my fall. As I fell to my hands and knees, just stopping short of planting my face on the station floor, I looked behind me to see the rushing, clumsy traveler who had hit with a baggage cart in the rush to get a seat in the third-class carriage. Expecting to find an old man with thick glasses and a deeply wrinkled face I was surprised to get hit again across the top of my back with a tommy club by a man in a tacky polyester suit. My face hit the concrete floor. I could smell the grime and grease next to my nose. Before I could catch my breath and gather my wits, I had a knee in my back and my arms and hands were being pulled behind me. A hard edge of metal slapped on each wrist that gave way but circled back again to pinch painfully the bones on both arms. Handcuffs!

I was yanked from the floor to my knees, gasping for air with my eyes bulging and searching for the face of my assailant. Before I could turn my head to look at the police officer, a black cloth hood was thrown over my head and synched at the neck. I could see only small dots of light through the woven threads but no detail of people or objects in front of me as I was forcefully removed from the train station by two men, each holding me by my shackled wrists and upper arms on each side. A third man was giving orders and opening doors.

We exited the platform through a narrow service access door. A hand then pushed my head down and pushed me forward and onto the backseat of a car. I heard the other three men climb into the car as well and all three doors slam closed. The car bounced on its springs. As the motor started up I could hear the faulty muffler with its high-pitched sputtering that was indicative of a Volga sedan. I didn't speak a word. They had quickly beaten the struggle out of me. I sat still and leaned up against the far-left door with my shoulder and tried to keep the handcuffs from digging too deep into my wrists.

I listened carefully to every word the men spoke to try to understand who they were, which group they were acting for and what was probably waiting for me when we arrived at the mystery destination. I was having trouble controlling my bowels and bladder. I was scared to the most inner part of my organs. How I regretted making that phone call to Lara!

I felt the car head over the bridge to the old city and climb the steep bluff. We must have passed through Minin Square and shot up Bolshaya Percheskaya as I felt the tires of the car slip over the smooth iron street car tracks in the middle of the road.

"Oh shit!" I said to myself. "We're headed to The Monastery." The regrets of my stupidity in twenty-three short years piled on my heart. I wouldn't even get the chance to say goodbye to my mother! Tears were streaking down my face as I held in the sobs, trying to maintain some sort of dignity. It simply seemed pointless to beg these guys. They were obviously working on orders and had no sympathy for me.

The car was steered roughly around a corner, but it was the wrong direction to go to The Monastery if I was right about our location. That was enough to give me hope! Curiosity dried my tears and I became once again more aware of the entire situation. The men were professionally silent. Nobody was smoking. The car was being driven fast, but the driver seemed to be in good control of the vehicle. The thought started small and grew until I was almost sure that these were professional security officers, not henchmen of the late Mr. P. This offered me some relief and I tried hard to regain my composure. I tried sitting up straight in my seat with some success, but the handcuffs made it difficult.

The car stopped abruptly and my covered head and face lunged into the back of the seat in front of me. Three doors opened simultaneously. My door opened with a violent pull. I made it easy for them to pull me from the back bench but struggled to keep my feet under me as I tripped over a curb and steps leading up to a door. I could feel the sun on my hood before we entered the cavernous dark of a stairwell. I heard the empty echo of a wooden door slamming behind us and the footsteps of their heeled shoes on the rough concrete floor.

I smelled the stench of stale cigarette smoke and the urine of drunks. I heard an elevator sliding down its shaft to us. The doors of the same slid open with a stutter. My handlers pushed me face first into the back wall of the narrow elevator cabin. With a jerk, the elevator pulled us up five floors, hesitating and restarting in a slip second as it passed each set of doors on each floor: one, two, three, four, open. Keys were jingled. A door opened, light flooded through the pores of my mask. Door closed. An inlaid wooden floor squeaked under my feet. An apartment? A safe house!

"Sit down!" came the first words from my captors. "Sit down!"

I hesitated not being able to see nor feel anything to sit on. I turned my head indicating I was looking for something to sit on. A chair was shoved into the back of my knees. I collapsed abruptly with a thump on my back side on to a wooden chair, my hands still uncomfortably pinned behind me. I still said nothing. I was scared for my life.

The room's blinds were pulled and the dots of light in my hood dimmed considerably. I was not supposed to know where I was. I felt hands around my neck, nothing threatening. The hood was yanked off with one tug from the top. When my eyes could focus in the room none of the three tried to hide their faces, nor did they shine a bright light on my face. One stood behind me ready to grab me should I try to make a break for it. One sat on a hard-backed chair almost directly in front of me and the third on a sofa with an ashtray balanced on his knee. He was just lighting up a cigarette at that moment. The tip of the paper glowed red, and then smoke came out his nostrils. He flicked his lighter closed and set it on the side table next to him.

All were dressed in gray and brown suits with dingy white shirts and tasteless neckties. The one smoking had a belly. Too much alcohol, potatoes, and smoking, no doubt. All at once I recognized the fat one smoking. This was the same FSB agent I had threatened with my kitchen knife, who asked me all sorts of questions about my stay in Nizhniy, while the others looked around and inspected my apartment. I couldn't remember what the other two had looked like. I said nothing and waited.

My backpack was opened up and all the clothes pulled out of it. I saw my passport flip by and onto the floor. My plane ticket and visa as well. For some odd reason, I was relieved to see those. My address book flittered past as well. I thought of Lara for a split second. Every pocket of the bag was searched. Every pocket of the pants and shirts was searched. I had no idea what they were looking for. I knew that there was nothing in that bag that mattered so I chose not to stress about it and watched with a curious look on my face.

"Mr. Turner. We can do this easily and quickly if you will simply tell us where the disc is," the fat one said, blowing smoke out the side of his mouth.

"As you can see, I don't have any disc with me," I replied like an idiot.

"You need to tell us then where you have hidden it or who has it, and we will see you on the next flight to the USA," he stated very politely.

"I don't have any disc. I don't have a computer to use a disc in. I have no disc and I am not hiding any disc," I answered as resolutely as possible, trying hard to keep my voice from cracking and wobbling.

The man sitting directly in front of me slapped me hard across the face with the back of his right hand, spinning my head the other direction. The blow came so unexpectedly that I felt my eyes would fly out of their sockets. I tried to close the eye lids but instead, I just watched the room blur in front of me as my head whipped around. I waited with my face turned the other direction for a second blow. No second blow came. The left side of my face burned and ached at once.

The fat one began again, "Mr. Turner, we are professionals and will get what we want from an inexperienced goat like you. Let's save us all a lot of time and money and in your case, teeth, and you tell us where you have hidden the disc or to whom you have sent it and we will all go together to retrieve it and you'll be on your way. We have no interest in you for the murder. We just need the disc back."

I could not believe what I was hearing. A murder? Not interested in me for THE murder? What murder? I didn't kill anybody!

"I didn't kill anybody. What are you talking about?" I asked like a mouse with his lower half caught in the vice of a trap.

"Mr. Turner. We don't have time for games and a long interrogation. The longer that disc is unguarded, the more people's lives are in danger, good Russian lives. If you will not help us now to recover this data then we will not stop until you do. We have our orders," he said, leaning forward from the couch to make sure his words made it to my ears.

"If I had a disc, believe me, I would have given it to you already," I replied looking at the floor.

"Then you will need to help us to locate Mr. Sanning before we can let you go. If you do not have the disc, I'm sure that he will be so pleased with you for turning him over to us that your organization will do worse things to you than we could. It always hurts more when it comes from your own side. The shame will hurt more than our fists," he said in a flippant, offhand manner as the agent across from me punched my face as hard as he could, lifting his backside off his chair to use his weight behind the fist. I felt the blood in my nose fill my nostrils and trickle down to my lips. I started to cry.

"Mr. Turner, you will lead us to Mr. Sanning as quickly as possible or this will continue all day long. I have two men who can hit you until tomorrow morning, taking turns for smoking breaks. It will be much easier if you give us what we need and we can all be home for dinner with the kids before the school holidays are over tomorrow!" he said again in a more vicious tone.

"Del Sanning lives just around the corner from here on Frunze Street. He's not hard to find," I said, trying to lick blood from my lips and speak coherently.

Another blow to my face knocked me off my chair to the floor. I laid helpless on the floor bleeding on the rug. I couldn't get myself up because of the handcuffs still holding my hands behind my back. The agent standing behind me picked me up and put me back in the chair. I was sobbing now trying to hold in the sounds of my crying. Sniffing only filled my mouth with blood. I swallowed it to try to save some dignity of spitting blood on the floor.

"Mr. Sanning disappeared from Nizhniy on the same day you disappeared. His apartment is also empty of any helpful information. He was the smart one to stay hidden. Maybe he took a private car to Moscow and is back to Virginia already and left you here take his punishments. You go underground, change your appearance, change your clothes, and then you put your head above water again showing your passport after the murder and think you can just slip out of the city? I have never seen a more unprofessional operation in all my years," he said with disgust and dismissal.

"I wasn't hiding from the police! I was hiding from Mr. P.'s thugs. Those guys don't check passports. The clothes and the hair were to keep them from spotting me while I left town," I sputtered.

"Why would you be hiding from Mr. P.'s thugs then, because they think you killed him?" he questioned.

"I didn't kill anybody! I just read about that an hour ago in the newspaper!" I protested, looking straight at my interrogator with desperation. "I was running from him because he was trying to kill me! You know the fire bomb on Minin Street at the university? That was to get to me, to keep me quiet. He smashed up my apartment and beat me on the street on Victory Day because I found out too much information about him! When I disappeared from Nizhniy last week it was because I was running from his henchmen who were trying to pick me up again. That was last Saturday morning early. I jumped on board a boat, the Zhukov, and sailed back and forth to Volgograd. I just got back into port today at five-thirty and went straight to the train station with what was in my backpack. I didn't know he was dead until after I had already bought my train ticket. I read it in the newspaper." I paused my plea and took a breath, my captors seemed to be considering my story. "How could a student like me get close enough to Mr. P. without his bodyguard to shoot him at point blank when he was the one looking to do me in? Why would I even hang around? It doesn't make any sense!"

I braced myself for another punch to the face by turning and lifting my shoulder as high as possible to shield my nose and cheek bone. There was no attempt made. I opened my eyes again and looked carefully at the leader of the three to see if the reprieve was just a whim.

"What is your relationship with Mr. Sanning?" was the short, searching question.

"No relationship. I was doing some ad-hoc work for him, looking for apartments for expats, but that project didn't go well. We had stopped in April," I confessed.

"Why did you stop?" he questioned further.

"Because somebody on the city council was doing something similar and had hired his own thugs to stop Del from doing the same. It's how Russians deal with competition best. They literally cut the throat of the competition. Del told me to stop searching for apartments to rent for his and my safety." I was singing like a canary. I thought it was a useless detail but it seemed to be very interesting to them.

"Did Sanning talk to you about Mr. P. at all?" they pressed further.

"No, I was the one who was talking with him. I was doing research on Mr. P. for my studies and would talk to Del about what I learned. Del has more experience in Russian business and he was able to help me understand what I was learning. I am the one who told him all about his hotel plans, his protection rackets, his car smuggling, and his father!" I spilled it all out hoping to avoid a fourth hit to my aching, bleeding face.

"How is this possible? How could Sanning not have known about Mr. P.?" a real question was asked, nothing implied, while the interrogator looked to his colleagues.

"Del always said that so many people have shadow lives and hidden agendas that they don't just volunteer information. I learned about him from my professor and went to interview him for an academic project. That is when all my trouble started with him. He told me too much information about his financial plans for his hotel and thought he needed to shut me up. I told Del all about Mr. P. He didn't even know who he was until I went to the night club one night." If I was telling too much I didn't care. I just wanted to get out alive.

"Surely Sanning was sent to Nizhniy because of Mr. P.!" the fat one said again in a bit of disbelief.

"I don't understand," I mumbled, not understanding who would have sent Del anywhere.

"How did Sanning know how to contact Mr. P. and kill him and steal the data?" I was asked.

"I don't know. The last thing I learned about Mr. P. is that his real family name was S., not P. Del seemed to make some sort of connection when I told him that. He didn't explain anything to me. That's when he said I had to get out of Nizhniy as fast as I could. He said I wasn't safe anymore. I tried to get out, but Mr.

P.'s men were after me and I couldn't get to the train. So, I asked if I could stow away on the Zhukov with my friends until I found another way out!" I was so relieved not to be being punched any longer that I would have told them every thought in my head.

The lead agent sat and scratched his chin in thought. He gave a signal to one of the junior officers who stood me up and removed my handcuffs. My wrists ached more out than in them for the first few minutes. I sat in my chair like an attentive school boy rubbing my wrists and arms waiting for the next list of exam questions.

I volunteered the next bit of information. "I thought I was only helping Del protect his hotel project by giving him this information. Del knew so much about the mafia activity in Moscow so I would tell him what Mr. P. was up to and Del would help me understand the illegal activities it was hiding. I didn't know about any data or secrets that could be stolen. I thought I had already given Del information about all the secrets that Mr. P. was hiding about his money, his family connections, his hotel plans, and the rest. I don't know about any disc or about who murdered Mr. P."

More thoughtful looks from my interrogator and then he said softly, offhandedly, "Go clean yourself up. You look horrible," as if it was my fault I was bleeding all over myself.

One of the henchmen showed me to the washroom but stood nearby in case I thought about bolting. Cold water on my face first stung in the cuts on my left cheek but soon it numbed the pains. Blood and water mixed and swirled down the drain. I didn't dare look in the mirror.

While I was checking to make sure all my teeth were still in my mouth, I overheard my kidnappers talking over the information I had just shared with them. I continued running cold water trying to get my nose to stop bleeding but listened with one ear.

"How could Sanning not know it was P.? Certainly, the agency sent him here because of this family connection. How could the CIA have missed that family connection to Mr. S.? Either the kid is lying to us or the agency doesn't have good data on people outside of the Moscow circles," said one voice.

"Perhaps Sanning was here talking with a go between and that man was making the deals with P.?" the second voice postulated. "Perhaps keeping Sanning in the dark about the source."

"Who then? We know everybody that is operating in Nizhniy. There are no Chechens here, no Uzbeks, and certainly the Pakistanis and Chinese haven't gotten this far out of the capital.

We would have discovered them before the handover on Friday night," said the first voice again.

"I still think the kid knows more than he is telling us about Sanning," the second voice concluded.

My guard switched off the light in the washroom and told me breaktime was over and I should return to my chair. I had no towel so I dried my face on my undershirt and was followed back into the living room of the apartment turned jail cell. The men were going through the contents of my backpack again, doing a more thorough search than the last time, finding nothing new.

"Please sit down," the chief politely requested. "We have been watching you for many months and we know all of your movements except for the last week when you disappeared. You are a known associate of a foreign agent operating in the Russian Federation and for that, we could have you charged with espionage and for the procurement and transporting of state secrets compromising state security. We know of your dispute with Mr. P. and what his people did to you and your apartment, so we can establish motive and opportunity. With that and your change of appearance and trying to leave Nizhniy the day after P.'s murder, we have enough to take you to the local police and have you arrested on suspicion of his murder, at the least. The rest of the evidence we can take care of. You see, Mr. Turner, you are in a very, very difficult situation. Espionage and murder charges are very serious. That is easily thirty years in a Siberian prison. Effectively a death sentence. The inmates do not tolerate traitors to Russia in prison with them. What do you have to say for yourself?"

"I have told you everything I know and what I have been doing in Nizhniy. I told you where I have been the last week and why I changed my clothes and hair and face. If you don't believe me, I don't know what else I can do to convince you," I pleaded.

"Do you have any stamps in your passport of your stay someplace else? Do you have a ticket from the boat you say you were traveling on? Do you have any photographs, any souvenirs, anything to prove your whereabouts for the last week as well as the night from Friday to Saturday?" he asked me rhetorically.

"No, I don't," I whimpered.

"Do you have any witnesses that you were with who can witness that you were with them and not shooting Mr. P. on early Saturday morning, by the way, with an American made handgun?" my interrogator had turned prosecutor.

I thought quickly about how to get in touch with the Zhukov crew. I had no phone number of how to reach Irina or Nikolai. I remembered that I had Lara's telephone number in my book and nearly blurted it out—but decided to hold my tongue and keep her out of all this. In five minutes, they could stitch her up for trying to assassinate Boris Yeltsin.

"No, no I don't." I sighed.

"Your only option then, Mr. Turner, is to cooperate with us to help us find Sanning and recover the data disc that he murdered Mr. P. for," was the ultimatum given by the head officer.

I looked at the floor in dejection with mixed and raging emotions. I knew I was completely innocent of all their made-up charges and knew I was being used. I was angry with Del for having used me for information to further his hidden agenda without informing me. I didn't even know if Del had been in Nizhniy to build a hotel or not at this point. I understood then that Del also had layers of a shadow life too. Was he even from Wyoming? Was Els his partner or his spouse? I was very confused.

"Well, Mr. Turner. Are you going to cooperate or do we turn you over to the local Militia, who by the way were on the payroll of Mr. P. and will only be more than happy to capture his killer? The killer who had disrupted a very nice flow of benefits to the chief of police and his lieutenants," was the agent's final proposition.

I nodded my head in despair and surrendered to his demands. I felt like a traitor even though I had no allegiance to any side in this fight. I listened to the demands on me.

"It is a simple order. You will use all of your connections and knowledge of Sanning to help us locate him and recover the stolen data. You will disclose to nobody that you are in our custody or working with us. While you cooperate, we will protect you from any revenge actions from Mr. P.'s organization or his associates by keeping you hidden and watching you if it is necessary for you to leave this apartment to accomplish your orders. Is that understood?" The agent spoke this to me as if had been reading a sentence from the bench of a court room.

"Yes, it's clear, but it may not be easy," I muttered.

"You will have all the resources you need to get the job done. Just ask," he replied with a polite and ironic smile.

"And what do I get in return?" I asked with some defiance.

"Mr. Turner. I already told you: protection from Mr. P.'s organization, freedom from arrest and prosecution by the local police for murder, and if you help us recover the disc, freedom from arrest and prosecution for espionage. What more could a man ask for? You certainly aren't hoping for a cash reward! That would be very greedy, young man." The condescension in his voice was ripe.

"I just want my passport and plane ticket back when I succeed. That's all I ask," I added.

"And so it shall be. As a show of good will..." he reached for my documents from the table next to him and gave them to me. "Here, you keep them so you have no reason not to trust us."

"I will need my address book," I commented.

"No, we will keep that for security purposes. You just concentrate on finding Sanning," was the agent's curt response.

"I need the address book to phone him," I stated bluntly with an angry stare at him.

This revelation stunned the agent and he looked again disapprovingly at his colleagues as if they had missed something so simple and vital in the book.

"Please explain," he said, looking back at me with just a bit more respect.

"When Del told me to get out of Russia, right after I told him that Mr. P. was the son of Mr. S., Del gave me a business card with a telephone number on it. The business card had only the name of a Swedish construction company and its telephone numbers. He told me to leave a message on the machine to let him know that I had made it back to the USA safely. He said I wouldn't get a call back, but he would know that I was safe," I explained.

"We did not find this business card in your belongings," he stated.

"I know you didn't. I wrote the number in the address book," I retorted.

"We found nothing," he rebutted again.

"Did you call every number?" I asked with some sarcasm and a hint of ridicule.

I got no response from anybody in the room.

"I disguised Del's number under an entry of my real Swedish friends. You see an address, you see Sweden and a phone number listed under that. It is not the phone number of my friends. I only write letters with them. I didn't call them from the USA. We are poor students. It's too expensive. That is the number to Del's answering machine where I am supposed to leave a message for him. If you will give me the book, I will call and leave a message right now on any phone you can provide me," I offered.

The agent threw the book at me with a look of surprise and compliment in his eyes and motioned with his head to one of his colleagues to show me to the telephone.

I was shown into one of the bedrooms that had been converted into a field station office. All the blinds were drawn tight and no light from outside could be seen through the darkening drapes, closed off from all prying eyes and curious neighbors. The wall was covered in a map of the city with what looked to be random pins and post-it notes. A few photographs lined the perimeter. Without pausing and looking too curious I did spot what I thought was my apartment with a flag on it. I wondered what Babushka and Raiya were thinking as I never returned after the Victory Day celebrations with them. For them, I had just simply vanished from one moment to the next.

"I will dial the number for you," I was told by the second agent, the one who hadn't punched me repeatedly.

We first had to call the local operator to provide us an international line. I let my host do the talking. After the line was procured, the second agent read the number to the operator. We heard the whirling and clicking of the phone line connecting to the Swedish line, seven hundred kilometers away. It took a few minutes before the line starting ringing. Then, an answer, in Swedish. The agent listened on an earpiece while I used the handset.

"Tack for att du ringde Sver-Invest konstruktion. Vara kontor ar for närvarande stängd. Lamna ditt meddelande och lamplig officer kommer tillbaka ditt samtal sa snart som mojligt. For English press two."

I pressed the two-button on the telephone, but instead of the needed tone, the telephone pulsed twice with two quick ticks in my ear. The Russian phone system was still using pulses and dials instead of tones. I rolled my eyes with impatience.

The tone to leave a message sounded before any English explanation was given. I was taken a bit off guard.

"Hello, my name is Peter Turner. My message is for Del Sanning. Please call me back at..." I stopped. I looked over at my clueless guard who obviously didn't understand what was said in either Swedish or English, and asked in Russian, "How can he call me back?"

The guard stopped the call abruptly and hung up my hand set.

"Sergey, come in here," he shouted to his boss. Sergey quickly appeared in the door way of the office.

"How can Sanning contact the kid? What is the number of this telephone?" he asked in an unconcerned way.

"That's not possible. Please hang up the telephones," Sergey huffed. "Blyat! We'll have to find another place to be able to be contacted. We cannot give this number to a known foreign agent. We'd get shot, you idiot!"

"The number works," I reported, sitting studiously and thoughtfully at the desk.

"Get out of my chair, punk." Sergey hit the back of my head and picked up by my collar and pushed me into the living room again.

We sat in a stalemate in the living room with Sergey, the chief agent, pacing the floor thinking. The two other agents looked rather sheepish and unsure about how to proceed and exchanged glances at each other every few moments for moral support. Everybody was at once very tense and unsure. Somehow, I felt I had the upper hand in this situation. Without me, they had no way to find Del, or else they would have been looking for him already someplace else instead of having waited for me to pop my head up again in Nizhniy.

It slowly dawned on me as I watched the two agents and their superior officer scramble to get back on top of their strategy that perhaps this was not an official operation. Otherwise, why didn't they have further resources at hand to track down state secrets? Why were they relying on a student and giving him so much influence? This wasn't about the murder of Mr. P. This was about recovering the disc without letting their superiors in on the fact that they had lost track of it and it was in the open. They were in damage control and to ask for further resources would be to have to admit that they had lost their mark. I sat quietly observing their silent panic. I felt a bit of hope creep up in me.

Sergey abruptly ended the silence, "We will move to the hotel, and Sanning can call the kid back there."

With this command, the other two quickly stood and moved toward me with hostile body language as if I had made a break for an open window. These men were attack dogs and all they knew how to do was bite! Their handler called them off.

"That's not needed. The kid will have to check himself into the hotel without a bag over his head. I'm sure he is going to be very cooperative as he has no way around us." Turning to me said in a grave tone, "Am I right, young man?"

I nodded in agreement, ready to take any olive branch of non-violence towards me that was being given, no matter how short or thin it was.

"Excuse me, sir," I addressed Sergey politely, "I cannot check into a hotel wearing this, with blood all over my shirt. I have my own clean clothes in my apartment. Will you take me there and let me gather up the things I need to make this operation believable? Nor can I meet Sanning looking like this. He'll see me and know to disappear again knowing exactly who is handling me. I must look myself or you won't get your disc back

286

and I'll go to jail for murder and espionage. Something I know I don't want."

Sergey gave an understanding and agreeing nod.

We headed down the elevator and out to the waiting black Volga and sped through town, dodging street cars and old ladies crossing the road.

"I assume I don't have to tell you my home address..." I muttered with some irony from the back seat squished between Sergey and the second agent who enjoyed punching people in the face. No response from the three, humorless counter-intelligence officers in the car. They all looked straight ahead. I found the comment rather humorous and felt my wits coming back to me after taking a beating and bleeding from Brutus, sitting left of me.

06

29. Setting the Trap

It wasn't dark at all at seven-thirty when we arrived at Prolataraskaya Metro Station. The car was parked a distance from my apartment and Sergey and I walked together to my apartment. I had zipped up my jacket to hide the blood-stained undershirt. The left side of my face was swollen and aching, but luckily my eye hadn't become swollen. I could see fine. As it was evening already the old ladies had gone inside to roost. Any earlier and they would have been outside still peeling potatoes and cutting vegetables outside chirping away like barnyard chickens. The Sunday evening was still and warm.

Through the familiar dark entrance, up a half flight of stairs, directly into the right dark corner of the landing I found my door by touch alone. It was dark enough for me maybe to make a dash for the door, but I knew that I couldn't stay hidden long from the long arm of the secret police. They had patience and means longer than I could hold my breath. My keys slid into the locks. One, two times around, click, clunk. The door popped open a crack, released from the grasp of its deadbolt and I put my shoulder into it and leaned to push it open. The apartment was dark and quiet. How I hoped nobody would be there.

I stepped to my door and spun the cylinder deftly and pushed the door wide open. Sergey stepped in behind me and guarded the door. The apartment was just as I had left it. Bloody jacket, ripped slacks and scuffed dress shoes atop the clothes that were strewn around the room. The broken windows closed but the room was drafter than normal, the table on its side, chairs broken in pieces, books with broken backs. I found my blue jeans and a few shirts, my felt cap and some lace up shoes, pajama pants and a t-shirt. I motioned to Sergey that I needed to move down the hall to the bathroom to collect my shaving kit. As

I shuffled passed Natasha's room in my sandals she opened the door with a start to see the back of me enter the bathroom.

"Pyotr, Pyotr. Is that you? Have you finally come home? Are you healthy?" her voice sounded worried and relieved as she entered the hallway to follow me to the bathroom. She did not notice Sergey standing silently at the end of the corridor guarding the front door behind her.

"Yes, Baba, it's me. But I cannot stay. I must go back to America," I replied from in the bathroom.

I found my bag of toiletries and put it in my backpack. As I turned to face her she froze in horror to see my face swollen up.

"Pyotr! Who did this to you? You must let me put ice on this. You come sit down in the kitchen!" She pulled me by the arm, with her back still toward Sergey in the hall. I looked to my guard with a question on my face. He gave a flick of his head to say, 'Go with her, don't cause alarm, the fewer people who know about this the better.' I followed Natasha into the kitchen and sat on her stool. She pulled a frozen, wrapped piece of meat from her tiny ice box and held it against my face.

"Do you need some tea? Why are you dressed so funny? I'm glad to see you cut your long hair. Boys shouldn't have long hair. Where have you been? Why did you leave without telling us? Yulia has been looking for you and is very worried," she chirped and whirred through the kitchen.

"Baba, please, I cannot stay. I have to go back to America. My colleagues are waiting to take me to the train station in their car. I'm sorry but I don't have time for tea." I handed the frozen chicken breast back to her and smiled.

"You will be coming back, right? You'll send us the photos from the award ceremony, right?" She did not want to hear that I was going.

"I'm sorry, but my camera was stolen. I don't have the photos any longer. The people who stole my camera are the ones who did this to me." I motioned circles in the air around my swollen face. "They are very powerful people and I need to leave so you and Yulia are not in danger." As I said 'Yulia,' I looked Natasha straight in the eyes, hoping she would understand to tell Yulia that I had shown up alive and was returning to America. "Please tell Yulia I will call her from America as soon as I can."

Babushka started to cry.

"Give Raiya my best. But I have to go now." With a quick embrace, I hurried past her and quickly out the door. I tossed my keys onto the floor of my room, pulled the door closed and slipped out the front door behind Sergey.

My three new friends set up camp in my hotel room at the Rossiya overlooking the river without my invitation. On my request, Sergey sent Brutus to buy some fried chicken from Gordost just up the street. While we waited for the food, Sergey wrote down the telephone numbers for Del to use to call me back, if he ever would, and insisted I call again and leave a message.

The same recording in Swedish played. The message was clear: I had reached Swed-Invest Construction, leave my name and number, beeeeeep!

"Hello, my name is Peter Turner. This message is for Mr. Del Sanning. Would ask for a return call at the following number. The matter is very urgent." I read the sequence of digits Sergey had prepared. "I am in room 375...with a great view of the Volga." I hoped Del would catch the message of which hotel I was held up in by the remarks about the river. Sergey wasn't amused.

"If you do that again I will shoot off a toe," he muttered at me angrily. "You say only the very minimum information on the telephone. Is that clear?"

"Listen!" I snapped back at Sergey, "Del and I talk to each other in a certain way. If I don't sound myself, he won't call back. I need him to call back so I can go home. If Del is a secret agent, he didn't tell me about it and I am not working for him. I don't even expect he will call back. I'm not on a mission for him. He has no responsibility for me. So, I'm going to do everything I can to get him to call me back, otherwise, you will see that I go to Siberia. I don't like that idea. I don't work for Del or his government. I don't work for you and your government. I just want to get out of this alive. Got it?" I was up in his face from across the table where he sat listening to my call.

"You will say only what I say you are allowed to say," Sergey repeated slowly, alliterating his words carefully.

"Tell me then! What do I say to Sanning when he calls me back?" I hissed through my teeth.

"You tell him that you have to meet him as soon as possible," Sergey commanded impatiently.

"Why, then? Because I miss him?" I shot back sarcastically. "I have no reason, I have no more business with Sanning. He doesn't know that I know that he shot a man and stole a disc. How do I introduce the subject?"

Sergey did not have an immediate response and looked angrily into my eyes.

"Like I said, Sergey, I want to get out of this as much as you want to get Sanning. It has to sound right, so let me do the talking. Are we going to trust each other?" I pleaded with him.

The evening dragged on late into the night. Sergey slept by the door in a chair. Brutus in a chair by the window, and I got the bed that they made me pay for. I was not sleeping and neither was agent number one who had guard duty. From my perch on the bed, I watched the moon rise over the river at about one in the morning and shimmer on the river's current. I watched a number of barges pass by quietly below. I thought back just twenty-four hours earlier with Lara on the back of the Zhukov watching the stars spin around the pole star, sitting next to her curled up in the blankets from my cabin. What a difference twenty-four hours can make! Talking with her I was sure my plan would work. Now, my only hope was for that telephone to ring. I wasn't sure it would.

At around five o'clock, the phone on the table buzzed and choked instead of rang. It was a ghastly noise that woke up those not on guard duty. We all counted to three...

"Hello, this is Peter," I mumbled with sleep in my breath.

"Peter? Where are you, kid?" It was Del, but he was smart enough not to say so on the phone. I didn't repeat his name.

"I'm in a hotel in Nizhniy center." I kept it short and exact.

"What happened? I thought you were gone." He left out details.

"I was running from the same people and took a cruise to get away. Sailed with old friends who kept me safe for a week or so." I watched Sergey's face. He didn't disapprove.

"Are you safe now?" he asked.

"Yes, but I need your help to get out of Russia." I was not lying.

"Can you get to Moscow on your own?" he asked me. I didn't ask if he was there.

"Yes. Something awful happened and so they aren't looking for me anymore...I think," I speculated.

"Can you meet me at Kyivskiy Station in Moscow this afternoon?" he proposed.

"No, sorry, I can only get the two o'clock from Nizhniy to Moscow later today." I didn't know any other way.

"Ok, meet me on Wednesday afternoon, twelve-thirty at the taxi stand at Kyivskiy Station. I'll find you. We'll do our best to help you get out quickly," Del assured.

"Ok, thanks. See you then." We hung up our telephones.

I flopped on the bed relieved and exhausted with my ears pounding with the sound of adrenaline in my blood stream. My hands and armpits had been sweating and I could feel their cold dampness against the rest of my hot skin. After half a minute, I sighed a huge sigh of relief and then sat up and looked to Sergey for his next instructions.

As if it was déjà vu, I found myself back at the Moscovskiy Station just like twenty-four hours earlier at eleven-thirty buying a train ticket to Moscow, but this time I was not in disguise and I was buying a first-class ticket and traveling with three colleagues in a private compartment. We made an unsightly quartet.

Sergey had insisted that I arrive on the train from Nizhniy as I had told Del on the telephone. He was certain that somebody other than Del would be watching for me at the Kazanskiy Station where the train would arrive. If I arrived in Moscow without having arrived on the train from Nizhniy, then perhaps the meeting would fall through. Sergey also mentioned that if I arrived at Kyivksiy Station with the same people around or anywhere near me that stepped out of the train at Kazanskiy, then the entire operation would be blown.

About one hour away from Moscow, Sergey gave me very exact instructions about how to proceed once I stepped off the train. I was to leave the train and the station alone and take the Moscow metro from Kazanskiy to Kyivskaya. From Kievskaya Metro Station I should cross the street and take the room at the Slavayanskaya Hotel that had been reserved for me. He and his agents would meet me in my room later that night. It was imperative that it appear that I was alone as Del would certainly have a team following me to watch and see who was already potentially following me.

"Sergey warned me that other FSB agents that I did not know and would not recognize would be following me from Kazanskiy Station to make sure I didn't make a change at Byelosrusskaya and head for the airport. If by chance I managed to make it as far as Sheremyetovo Airport, my name had already been alerted to border officials and I would be detained anyway while I tried to board a flight. He assured me again that he was in his control and trying to flee Moscow would be futile.

I believed him and was spooked to the point that I decided to follow all his mysterious, nuanced instructions. I thought that this intrigue, cloak and dagger, had all ended at the same time as the Cold War. The words that my half-drunk friend Olya said, back at the disco night at The Monastery rang in my ears. "You think that all departments of KGB just stopped existing? They changed the name to FSB and kept their jobs. That's it. We still do the exact same thing, Peter." How right she was.

After the instructions and warnings from my handlers, the three agents somehow evaporated into the Moscow evening. One by one they simply slipped out of our train compartment and before I realized it, I was alone in the cabin, standing in front of the window watching the Moscow suburbs roll slowly by. I let out a huge sigh of relief that they had left me alone for a while, even though I knew that they weren't far off.

30. Moscow

The sun was obviously in the western sky but was still bright and warm. In this pseudo summer warmth and yellow evening light, even the run down concrete apartment blocks on the city's outskirts looked slightly romantic. The tangle of iron rails and switches on the ground mirrored the tangle of overhead electricity lines as we glided along the shifting metal roadway. The train's passengers jolted with every pass over a switch which led us closer to that city center, filled with breathtaking cityscapes of both the magnificent and the repugnant.

There is no place in the world I love and hate more than the city of Moscow, and Mother Russia for that matter. Both are filled with the contradictions and contrasts of the Russian soul that can be sincere, compassionate and heartfelt; yet at the same time callous and unmoved by the cruelties which the reality of modern society imposes with indifference to life and decency. There is for me, even as a foreigner, always something very nostalgic about summer evenings in Moscow, even during my first summer in the city before I had memories to even long for. Yet, I, too, felt that special longing for a more peaceful, stable time that those around me on the deck of the Zhukov remembered and shed tears for when we all sang Moscow's unofficial anthem while docked up at the northern river station.

In the evenings, it seems that one can sense the vastness of Russia and its sky better than during a summer day when the sun is as much a tyrant as was Stalin, and the humidity smothering. Muscovites, as well, are civilized and gracious people, proud of their city, proud of their culture; yet they are the first to tell you everything that is wrong with it, with a sense of shame and helplessness to do anything about it. Moscow, it seems, has a life of its own. It does not draw its energy from united communities of good people but does its best to grind them into the ground every day of their lives. To survive Moscow is to survive anything heaven and hell can conjure up to thwart one's happiness. It draws in those from the surrounding land yet repels those it has held close to its bosom from childhood. A perfect Moscow evening is to be with friends and remember it the way it was before it became the way it is.

The skyline became more familiar as we came closer to the Kazanskiy Station, and the nostalgia was quickly replaced by the anxiety and fear that my short life could still come to a sudden end, even if I was able to succeed in helping the secret police apprehend my friend. Would they really just let me walk away knowing what I already had learned? Would they not just make us both disappear? I tried to push out the image of a bullet in my head, but somehow, I could feel it already lodged in my skull. I unconsciously rubbed the back of my head as I watched the rail lines spread out in preparation to line up next to waiting platforms. The speakers in the corridors of the train car squelched and demanded that all passengers prepare to disembark. Kazanskiy Station was the end of the line.

Stepping down from the train car I hesitated for two seconds to glance left to make an inventory of those who would be walking behind me as I turned right and headed for the hall of the station. The crowd bumped and jostled like only crowds in capital cities do. Nobody was really from the capital so nobody really knew each other, and they cared even less about who they might offend. Those commuting wanted only to get in and get out as quickly as possible. I felt like a rat fleeing a burning building as we all pushed closer together to fit simultaneously through the exit doors from the platform to the street, circumventing the hall altogether.

If anybody from Del's team had been there to watch for me and to put a tail on me, as Sergey has suggested, I wished them the best of luck for even spotting me in the mosh of heads and shoulders. Somehow though in the crowd I felt safer. I felt less exposed. Maybe in Moscow, I could simply disappear and not be found. As the rush of bodies spilled out onto the pavement in front of Kazanskiy Station I gasped for air, stepped quickly to the curb, and turned to watch the crowd behind me. I looked to see who might also pause next to a wall, look the other way, tie a shoe or otherwise try to look as if they were paying me no attention. I scanned the faces and shoes of anybody who looked to be a credible tail for my trek across the wide city center. Nobody stood out. Not a soul stopped to look at me, nobody hesitated. The crowd, like a cloud burst of rain, flowed quickly to the gutters and out from under my feet.

Soon I was alone with millions of other Muscovites on Komsomolskaya Square, facing the Yarolsavskiy Station opposite, looking over the din and chaos of the evening commute. How my stomach growled at me. How dry my throat was! How I wished this all to be just a dream. How I just wanted to sit down for a moment. I pushed on to the metro station.

Instead of taking the longer ring route around the city as Sergey prescribed I do, I decided to travel right under the Kremlin and Red Square to reach the other side of the city and then one stop further to Kyivskaya. I was curious to understand from any reaction that Sergey might give at the hotel about my choice of metro lines, to signal if I was really being followed by another colleague agent of his, or if these three were really working outside of official orders. From the platform of the ring route, or the brown line, I could just see the platform for the red line down a small flight of stairs that would take me to the same place, but perhaps without an FSB tail. As I saw the wind of the approaching train begin to blow the hair of the travelers standing on the platform below me, I quickly darted down the half flight of stairs and stood at the bottom to see who else might come down them to follow me. I waited for the exiting crowds to pass to the exit tunnels and then slipped in-between closing doors of the red line cars. I watched the platform behind me to see if anybody would appear looking on helplessly as the train pulled away. Nobody appeared. Either I was quick enough to shake the FSB tail, or there was nobody following me through the underground tunnels that evening and Sergey was spinning tales—I wasn't yet sure which.

I waited patiently in my hotel room in the Slavanskaya Hotel watching both local and international news on the television. Not having watched television for nearly five months I felt like a kid again flipping through the different channels. I stopped on a random news report from the BBC. How professional the newsroom looked! How rich and clean London looked! After an hour, I took a shower and dressed again. I didn't dare leave the room until I had made contact again with Sergey, so I ordered a late dinner from the room service menu. I fidgeted and paced the room waiting for my food. Sitting still seemed impossible. Being alone with my thoughts and the possibilities of the next day was frightening. I tried to watch a report on international cricket matches. I surfed channels on the television. At eleven o'clock Sergey let himself into the room. I didn't ask how he had a key. It didn't interest me. We looked at each other with suspicion.

Sergey broke our mutual silence, "Good to see you kept our agreement." I nodded without speaking. I kept my eyes on him.

"We have about twelve hours until you meet Sanning across the street. Until then you must stay in this room until I come back tomorrow morning at ten o'clock. You may not use the telephone. Watch as much television as you like. Please, relax, and enjoy some good American food tonight. The service in this hotel is better than any Russian hotel," Sergey commented in a patronizing way.

I nodded again without speaking. I was waiting for any comment from him about my stunt in the metro earlier. If he knew about it, it didn't seem to bother him. I had to know.

"Sorry about getting the metro lines wrong. I misread the signs. I was nervous and took the wrong line," I lied.

"You know your way around Moscow, do you? You seemed pretty confident when you lost our tail at Komsomolskaya, yet arrived here right on time," he said with a smile. "Just don't try something like that again tomorrow. Tomorrow we will shoot you if we need to. Don't test me again," Sergey retorted.

I nodded again submissively without offering excuses. He knew what I was doing, and we both understood that he had underestimated my familiarity with Moscow. Sergey left the room with visible displeasure. I bolted and chained the door as he left and collapsed on the bed and fell asleep, exhausted both physically and mentally from the intensity of last forty-eight hours.

I slept until the sun of the following morning woke me around eight o'clock. I woke with a start and jumped to the window to try to remember where I was. As I pulled open the drapes the sunshine flooded in. Below me, I could see the snaking Moscow River and just across that the menacing skyscraper that houses the Russian Ministry of Foreign Affairs that stood at the foot of the famous Arbat Street. I could see the map in my head. We were just a mile or two from Red Square and the Kremlin. The Supreme Soviet building was just across the river to the north of the hotel and the American Embassy sat just behind that. If I started running I could be there in fifteen minutes, if my legs would hold out and if my handlers didn't spot me, catch me, and beat me first. It was all too risky so I did my best to put the panic of out my head. I sat down on the bed again and waited for Sergey and ten o'clock.

The chance that Del would have already anticipated this entire situation and had a plan was the only sliver of hope that I felt I had. I certainly wasn't going to be able to slip away with guards in the hallways and the next room. I would have to wait until I was out in the open again with some distance between me and them. I turned it all over in my head again.

Would they move quickly to apprehend Del? Would they really just let me go? Wouldn't they just take us both and dump us on the edge of town in a shallow grave? Would Del have the data with him? We didn't talk about him bringing any data with him. Surely, if he had what the FSB was after he was keeping it someplace safe. If he really was an agent of the CIA, this information was already in the Embassy, or already long ago moved out of the country in a diplomatic pouch. What was Sergey really after? Why would Del stick his neck out for me if he even suspected I was being handled and managed by the FSB to get him to show his face? The questions were endless and they played on a loop in my head making me nervous and fidgety. At precisely ten o'clock there was a knock on the door.

Об

31. The Deceit of Riches

At a quarter past twelve, I was standing in front of the Kyivskiy Station facing Europa Square and looking again directly over the river to the same skyscraper I could see out my hotel window. It loomed large on the skyline, making it look deceptively close. Having walked most of Moscow the year prior, I understood that sprinting to a landmark in the distance in this city scape could easily turn into a marathon. Russia is a broad country and nothing is as close as it seems.

While I stood waiting at the taxi stand to be found by Del, Sergey and his men sat in three different types of cars in the chaotically designed parking and waiting area. Each was accompanied by a local Moscow agent. With no perceivable order to the way cars and taxis should park, there was no way for the untrained eye to spot these tails as being focused on me and whoever should approach me. Even those local operatives who stood outside their cars and leaned casually against a fender, arms folded over pot bellies, seemed to fit right in. I worried that Del would not spot the trap. Another part of me hoped he wouldn't. Del showing up meant a chance for my escape.

Despite my familiarity with Moscow, it was still difficult for me to blend into a crowd of locals. My face, my hair, my clothes were always going to be different and the locals could sense it. While I waited on the curb I was approached by several cabbies asking for a fare. They would repeat poorly memorized phrases in English to attract my attention. Most would take me any place in Moscow for twenty US dollars. I thanked them all and brushed them off. I told them I was waiting for a friend to collect me from the curb. I waited and watched glued to that spot on the sidewalk to see Del emerge from the greenery in the park along the river, or out of the train station, and walk up behind me. I looked for an Embassy vehicle with diplomatic plates...and immunity! Instead, another taxi driver, unkempt, but courteous, approached me with his eyes downcast offering to take me any place in Moscow for seventy-six US dollars. My ears perked up. I spoke back in English.

"Did you say seventy-six dollars?" I asked alertly.

"Yes. That is correct. Seventy-six dollars. I take you anywhere in the city of Moscow for seventy-six dollars," he repeated in a thick guttural accent, but in English.

"Where would you take me for seventy-six dollars?" I asked again.

"I know good place where friend is waiting for you," he replied without naming names.

"Ok, I'll pay you seventy-six dollars to take me there," I confirmed.

"Please follow me to car." He offered to take my backpack but I refused and carried it myself.

As I stepped off the curb with the cabbie from 1776, the agents watching me stood at alert. Walking just a step behind my guide I gave a very small nod to Sergey in the white Lada closest to me to let him know that this cabbie was my contact and he would be taking me to Del. Sergey's eyes told me he understood.

The cabbie put me in the front seat of his light blue Volga sedan, an older model. The muffler sputtered on contact and all through second gear as we pulled out of the parking area and onto the Borodinskiy bridge over the river, and directly toward that ever-visible monolith skyscraper. A little further up Smolenskaya Street the cabbie pulled over right in front of the Foreign Affairs ministry and motioned for me to step out. I was confused. There was no way I was about to walk right into that building and report myself as a spy! I looked back at him for further instructions.

"You walk up Arbat Street. Go to the Losev House. Have coffee across from Losev House. Your friend will find you. No cars on Arbat allowed. Your friends who follow us cannot drive there," he clearly instructed.

"OK, I get it. Thanks," I replied and with that stepped out of the taxi and walked toward and up the Arbat Sreet. I did not run, but strolled up the Arbat slowly and obviously so that Sergey or one of his team had time to also follow me up the street about half a kilometer.

The Arbat Street is a pedestrian zone filled with street artists, theatres, sidewalk cafés and tourist curiosities, and new hip restaurants. Apart from Red Square and the gardens around the outside of the kremlin walls, it was the only place I knew of in

Moscow where cars are not allowed to drive. Del had anticipated that I would be followed and made it so that my handlers would have to step out of their cars, be on foot and be visible. With all the narrow one-way streets intersecting with and ending at the Arbat Street, it would be difficult for the unprepared to position a car nearby. My steps began to grow in confidence as I approached the actors' guild theater building on my right. As I came to the Losev House I stood and turned a full circle looking for a coffee shop. Before I found what I was looking for, I heard a familiar voice call to me.

"Kid, hey kid! Over here," Del shouted to me. He was sitting at an outdoor café table under a parasol, enjoying something cold and tall in his glass. He looked very relaxed. I was immediately annoyed.

"Come on over. What can I get you?" He offered me a chair and a drink. "How the hell are ya', kid?"

"I've had better weeks," I admitted with a stunned expression on my face.

Now quieter, Del asked directly, "Are they following you?"

I nodded.

"Good, let them see us, and talk loud," he ordered and then started again in his loud American voice. "Can I get you a beer?"

I screwed up my face. "Not a Russian beer, please," I said, holding up my hands. "Does this place serve Pepsi with ice?"

"Waiter!" Del bellowed. A sheepish young man shuffled over with a look of boredom on his face. "Can you bring a Pepsi Cola with lots of ice for my friend, please?"

The young man looked blankly at Del. I ordered the same in Russian to make it clear. He came back with a cold bottle of Pepsi and a glass but without any ice.

"Would you like some lunch?" Del turned to the waiter again. "Lunch menu, please?"

This was such strange behavior for Del that I was beginning to get worried that in fact he didn't understand what was going on and didn't have a plan.

After lunch was ordered, Del began to behave a bit more like himself now that everybody who was following me had taken up their positions on the street and were waiting to pounce on him, and me.

"So kid, I got your message from an old lady who phoned me last week. It was cryptic, but she said you were safe, but in Russia. I guess she was lying," he said casually sipping his beer.

"No, she told you the truth. When she phoned you, I was in Volgograd and was very safe," I replied.

Nearly choking on his beer, Del sat up straight in his chair. "Volgograd? What on earth were you doing in Volgograd?"

"I was hiding on a river boat with some old friends of mine. It took me out of Nizhniy Novgorod for a week while I was being chased down by Mr. P.'s men," I replied defensively.

"That was very resourceful. How did you swing that?" he asked with a bit of admiration

"Don't know really. Just was in the right place at the right time. The boat I mean. I was in the completely wrong place!" I confessed.

"Good for you, kid." He held up his glass to toast me. We touched glasses lightly over the table. "So, tell me, what's the problem now?" he inquired with an amused look on his face.

"This may be funny to you, friend, but I am...we are...you are in big trouble!" I said confrontationally.

"Keep your shirt on, kid. You don't even know what is going on. Let me explain the situation and you may see things a bit differently." Del seemed somehow in his element.

"Del there isn't time for an explanation, nor lunch." I was starting to panic.

"Kid, if you move from this table, it's all over. You understand?" he said firmly. "If you leave this table somebody is going to throw you in the back of a car with a gun in your side and you'll be floating downstream tonight. The only chance you have is to sit here, eat lunch with me, and then walk away with me. If you get up and run, you'll be dead before you make it to the metro station. Am I clear?"

"Why did you get me into all this mess, Del?" I asked desperately.

"Me? I didn't get you into anything. You got yourself into this one, kid! The sharks have been feeding for years over the spoils of the Soviet Union, carving up Moscow, carving up Prague and Budapest and all the oil in Siberia; and then you came along and dove head first into the shark tank of Nizhniy Novgorod when there was already blood in the water. All I could do was try to pull you out before you lost your legs, but you were having so much fun snapping pictures of the sharks that you couldn't see their teeth coming right for you. I told you to walk away to get out as quickly as you could, but here we sit in the most densely infested depths that is modern Moscow, and I'm trying to save your hide again. You just won't get out of the water! It's you who kept coming back and feeding me the information that I was paying other people to provide." Del was right.

"So, you are a CIA agent?" I asked in an accusative tone.

"You know I can't confirm that, so don't ask again," he snapped.

"So, what is stopping me from getting up and walking away, then?" I demanded.

"The cross hairs of a trigger-happy fellow from Bishkek who expects you to hand me a disc of data at any moment, that's what." Del sipped his beer again. I looked at him incredulous that he would threaten me so blatantly and so casually.

"Kid, he's not under my orders. He's an independent contractor and is waiting to deposit twenty million dollars in a Swiss bank account of my choice as soon as I have the package from you," he clarified.

"I don't have any package for you, no disc. In fact, the people following me think you have a disc that they say they need to have. I am supposed to signal to them when I know that you have it with you," I countered his advance.

"I know you don't have anything for me, but the only reason you are alive is that my friend from Kyrgyzstan, working for the Iranians, believes that you do have it and will surrender it to me today," he explained further.

"You set me up?" My trust in my friend was growing thin.

"Kid, you know enough to be killed by three different groups. If I played an open hand with all the powers that want this data and told them that you are clean, you would have been dead yesterday. The only reason you are alive is that the Iranians believe you are transporting the disc for me from Nizhniy." Del's eyes had grown very serious. The tension gathered around the table as I listened to the twisted fairy tale of intrigue.

"The FSB believes that you have the disc," I challenged.

"Only after they caught you and you convinced them that you don't have it, that's why I'm still a free man. They heard about you from my customer, I'm sure, and came after you," he countered. "You see, the FSB agents and I are being paid by the same intermediary to get the data that was in play. Both the Kyrgyz, Chechens, and the FSB were looking for you during your river excursion. I told them you had the disc and would on my orders pop up again soon and meet me right here," he said, boasting his bluff.

"What's on the disc?" I asked defiantly.

"Well, that's a bit of a story. A story that you, by the way, helped to unravel. As you know, Mr. Ivan Sergeyevich S., or as you know him, Mr. P.'s father, was somewhat of a genius when it came to radar and tracking technology. Working on the MIGs for the Sokol development department there in Nizhniy Novgorod he designed what is most likely the most sophisticated missile guidance systems ever known to man, adaptable to all sizes of projectiles, whether it was ground fired, surface to air, air to surface, air to air, you name it. This system is able to guide a Tomahawk cruise missile through a circus master's hula hoop, after passing through the big tent doors without knocking the hat off the monkey turning the organ grinder. We have never seen anything like it. The Chinese have never seen anything like it, the Russians went crazy when it worked in a test in 1993 and even more so in the spring of 1994 when it did even better. The Iranians are jumping up and down to get it and are willing to fork over an oil well to get it." Del was rather worked up.

"What does Iran want it for?" I asked naively.

"Kid, if you're sittin' on the beach of the Strait of Hormuz with your binoculars and a cup of mint tea and you see the USS Nimitz passing by with impunity, making waves in your tidal pool, you'd give twenty million dollars to be able to put a missile through the gap of the front teeth of the captain on deck lookin' right back at ya with his binoculars thinking he runs those waters. Don't mistake it kid, the indignity they feel watching the Great Satan's Man-of-Wars float by every day has really got them indignant." Del explained his cowboy politics in a unique way; I wished I had been recording him. "If one of our fighter pilots so much as turns on a cockpit light to read his pre-flight checklist, the guidance system can latch on to the electric pulse and pick it off the deck of the aircraft carrier before he's been cleared for takeoff. It's that sensitive!"

"So, how does Mr. P. get involved in all of this? How did he wind up with this technology? I can't believe security is so bad at a top-secret facility that he could just waltz in and burn a disc for himself," I queried.

"We believe that Mr. P. had his father killed to obtain the disc in order to sell it himself. Mr. S. was in Bishkek last year officially helping with an FSB sting to help stop the smuggling of Russian technology to the highest bidders, in that case, it was the Chechens. Those arms shows throughout the central Asian republics of the USSR are deadly places for innocence! The materials one can buy there, Oohhhwee! Deadly, deadly. Mr. S. had that program with him in Bishkek for some reason. We know because we were watching there too, thinking he was meeting somebody to sell it himself. The meeting we anticipated didn't happen. S. never showed up. He was dead in his hotel room. Strangled the night before by a prostitute," Del expounded.

"Did you kill Mr. P. then to get the disc?" I asked again with accusation in my voice.

"No, I did not kill Mr. P., but I did get the disc in the end," Del confirmed. "There were enough people willing to knock Mr. P. off that wanted his organization, that it didn't take long to find somebody willing to do it for me. They did a great job to make it look like a mafia hit. His own second in command shot him in his own driveway and then drove his car to the place where Mr. P. was supposed to meet another contact of my Kyrgizian friend to make the swap. Mr. P. planned to use the money from the sale to buy the land from the city for his casino hotel which would have gotten him into the big game with the big sharks. From there it would be arms smuggling and oil deals instead of pimping and racketeering.

"It's the timeless deceit of riches that nobody can resist, not Mr. S., not Mr. P., not Mr. P.'s second in command, and not the KGB boys! They believe that the money will make them immortal somehow. They think that they can outrun the grim reaper and get away with more than their fair share, but in the end, it just makes them all dead. Too many people without enough imagination chasing and killing each other for it. The siren's song luring them all straight to ruin."

"The FSB agents holding my leash are accusing me of the murder and say they have enough to turn me over to the local police in Nizhniy to have me locked up for thirty years. I need to know who pulled the trigger, Del," I demanded.

"Kid, the FSB agents jerking you around are all working off the books. They are as corrupt as Yeltsin's cabinet and their hands just as dirty. They aren't trying to protect any state secrets. They're looking to score big by being the ones to sell the S.'s software to the Iranians and as soon as they do, they'll retire to the French Riviera or buy a villa on Cyprus and keep their money in Switzerland. Yes, sir, they're out for their piece of the pie. You don't have to worry about them turning you over to anybody. They'll shoot you first," Del clarified.

"My signal to the spooks around the corner is to stand up and walk away. That will mean to them that you have the disc," I threatened.

"And if I get up and walk away that means that you've turned over the package to me and Mr. Bishkek will let it fly. As I said, you know too much," Del gave me an ice-cold stare. "You see kid, it's a stalemate. The FSB is well aware that if they were to jump all over us like circus monkeys right now that Mr. Bishkek, who they are now trying to double cross, would simply pick them off right now to protect his package. If Mr. Bishkek were to step out of his sheltered position right now and grab your backpack, the six FSB agents watching us would apprehend him thinking that he was trying to grab the disc and disappear and then they could turn him in for espionage. So as long as we sit right here, and leave together in a civilized way after our lunch is finished, we may both get out of this with all our limbs attached. If we split up, you're dead before morning. Got it?" Del was dead serious.

"Got it," I said in a defeated and terrified whimper.

"Good, let's eat!" Del smiled and bit into his club sandwich.

With his mouth half full, still chewing, Del spoke again. "Kid, you've got some great skills. You should think seriously about using them to help keep the world safe. The skills set that you have could help us keep this post-Cold-War world from coming apart at the seams. I haven't had an official field agent work for me that showed more competence than you have. Your ability to research and make connections to the real world is impressive. Your raw talent for this work can be honed to craftsman level if you'd allow yourself to be trained. That is why I am still here, to get you out. The disc has already been destroyed. The mission is over. We want you to come work with us."

"Oh, that's comforting. I thought you called me back because we're friends, and that's what friends do for each other," I said, wiping mustard from my lip with a waxy napkin.

"Don't make it personal, kid. I have always told you that you need to be able to walk away when it goes wrong. Don't get into it so deep that you can't walk yourself backward out of it. I'm just doing my job," Del said, chiding me.

"Del! Shove it up your..." I blurted but then stopped short.

"Woah, take it easy!" Del was adamant. "You are one of the sharpest students I've met. You have adaptive skills. You're sociable. People tell you things off hand that I can't pay for! You're actually the one who helped me make the link between Mr. P. and his father Mr. S. I was still paying too many people in the city for the information you volunteered last week. Without the information you provided, we'd all still be in Nizhniy on a fishing expedition. Kid, I don't think you could have done better work if I had been paying you."

"Like you paid Valentina Petrovna? She was playing you and Mr. P. and that's why you didn't know anything about him. It's just like you taught me, Del, everybody has a shadow agenda," I muttered, trying to hurt his pride.

"Yes, that's why we spread the net as wide as possible," he countered and finished his beer with a swig and a gulp. "Just think about it, kid. You could do a lot of good in this crazy world if you applied your skills the right way."

"I'm optimistic that things will work out without having to kill anybody," I said with a sarcastic smile as I washed down my last bite with the rest of the Pepsi in my glass.

"Good then. Shall we go take in some nice artwork? Have you ever seen the Tretyakov Gallery?" Del said, standing up from his chair. "What'ya got in the backpack, kid?"

Об

32. The Tretyakov Gallery

We strolled slowly down the Arbat Street back to Smolenskaya Boulevard in order to prevent any sudden actions from those who were watching and waiting for their respective signals to pounce, to shoot. Del seemed to be sincerely enjoying the nice spring weather and couldn't be less concerned with the scramble of secret police agents going on behind us, but yet, nobody touched us just as Del had predicted. Del was firmly in charge of the situation.

We waited for four or five minutes for the same taxi and driver who had found me at the Kyivskiy Station, to pick us up in front of the Ministry of Foreign Affairs. We waited there idling in the car for another four or five minutes and then the driver slowly drove us south on the ring road along Smolenskaya Boulevard toward the next bend in the serpentine Moscow River. As we ascended the Krymskiy bridge over the water, the towers and walls of the Kremlin appeared out on the left, white and gold against the blue sky. On the other side of the river, we passed the majestic gates to the famous Gorkiy Park on the right that extended up and down the river bank as far as the next bends in both directions. After turning north off the broad boulevard, we headed up into the old city of Moscow on a narrow one-way street, Pyatnitskaya Street, in between low built buildings, some in stone, some in wood, all in different states of dilapidation or restoration, in light pastels or drab colors, some grand and some very humble. The street was in need of repaving.

The car slowed and pulled up to park on the curb in front of a faded, crumbling old red church with scaffoldings holding it up. Del climbed out of the car and gave me a signal to follow him. We stood and admired the church being restored like curious tourists.

"Del, why are we standing here like idiots?" I complained.

"Because this is one of Moscow's busiest foot passages, well, besides around Red Square, and the tourists and the families and kids all walk past here. Nobody will pull a gun or kidnap you or me here. Too many good citizens as witnesses," he explained while pointing to the church tower having a new bell installed. "We want everybody to see and follow us into the museum, Peter. We can't outrun these people. They have guns and radios, they have cars, they have jet planes and helicopters. We have to outsmart them, not outrun them. Have some patience and enjoy the sights." He seemed perturbed at my lack of perspective.

After a few moments of sightseeing, we strolled lazily down Klimentovskiy Lane, a pedestrian street, following the signs to the Tretyakov Gallery. We wove in and out between groups of tourists who were following an umbrella or an orange flag on a pole, moving to and from the museum. As we approached the gallery's ornate orange and white brick facade, there was a long line for tickets and entrance to the museum stretching nearly to the end the street. Del was very concerned when we saw the long line.

"We'll be sitting ducks in that line. They will use local police to pick us out without causing any commotion from the onlookers. Too risky," Del observed.

"I'll go find us a guide for the museum," I responded.

"Kid, we're not here to see the paintings," he retorted.

"Del, the guides have special passes. They can cut in line and can get us in faster," I appealed.

"OK, great idea, but make sure she speaks English!" he agreed.

I found Del again and introduced him to Tatyana, a middle-aged English instructor with hair dyed orange against the gray roots, tied up in a flyaway bun on the top of her head. She was moonlighting as a guide for the recent influx of American and English tourists to the city. For twenty dollars she would take us to the front of the line past the tourists with guidebooks and tell us all about the history of the Tretyakov family, the mansion that houses the collections, and of course, the paintings.

Del asked her immediately, "I am very interested to see The Execution of the Streltsiy; I understand that it is in this museum. Can you guide us to that room when we get inside?"

"Oh yes, I know that painting. It's very powerful. We can go now," Tatyana answered and motioned for us to follow her away from the main entrance and through a hidden door that was reserved only for guided groups. Tatyana showed her museum credentials to the guard and we were waved through to a staircase which descended half a floor where we merged with the rest of the tourists in the basement wardrobe and checked luggage room.

"It is not allowed to carry bags in the museum, young man. You will need to check your travel bag," Tatyana said to me sweetly.

I gave Del a bit of a panicked look when I heard I had to leave my bag in the basement, knowing that indeed we weren't there to see the paintings and was afraid that I wouldn't get it back if we had to make an emergency exit.

Tatyana tried to reassure me, "No, no, everything will be fine. These ladies are as faithful as any guard dogs. Nobody will be able to take your bag while it's stored here. Nobody can take your bag as long as you have your claim tab. These ladies are professionals and they take their work very seriously and they have a police officer here with them if anybody other than you tries to take your bag." Indeed, there was a uniformed police officer standing nearby keeping a watchful eye on the wardrobe.

I slipped my folded plane ticket and passport into the front pocket of my pants just in case. I then reluctantly turned my bag over to the stone-faced, middle-aged ladies on the other side of the counter and received in return a red triangular claim tab made of hard plastic with the number 375 engraved in white digits on it which I could redeem again for my personal belongings. I had a strange feeling that I would never see the bag and its contents again. As soon as I returned to my small group, Tatyana stepped out in front of me and Del and led us through the corridors to the main exhibitions and up a wooden staircase to the third floor. As we climbed the stairs, Del held his hand out to me and looked me in the face without speaking. I did not understand what his open hand was waiting for.

"The claim tab. I'm going to need it," was all he said.

I slipped it to him, quickly sensing that this was something that should be done discretely but unsure what was going to happen.

We passed by the museum visitors and through the gallery halls, quickly passing some of Russia's most famous and most precious cultural treasures. After a number of turns, we took a long walk down corridors and rooms painted in varying shades of dark and light greens lined with framed paintings both large and small, as well as sculptures and antique furniture. We then came to a large open hall with white walls and a large skylight in the ceiling. The floor throughout was the classical white birch inlaid pattern found in most formal or official buildings in Russia.

Tatyana ushered us into the room that Del had specifically requested and started to explain the significance and relationship of the paintings that hung here. On the three complete walls of the hall hung three very large framed paintings, all dramatic and highly detailed. Between them were rows of smaller studies and portraits and small antique display cases with fragile etchings or sketches on centuries' old brittle paper. The room was full of visitors two or three rows deep in front of each of the paintings, all entranced with the sheer scale of the paintings as well as the emotional detail with which each had been rendered.

The painting of The Morning of the Execution of the Streltsiy is a dramatic scene of chaos and grief expressed as another mutineer is led away by a guard in a black dress uniform with a long, shining sabre in his right hand to the gallows towering visibly behind the crowd of people gathered to say goodbye and mourn the loss of the mutinous regiment. All this is staged in front of St. Basil's Cathedral and the Moscow Kremlin walls with regents, boyars, and priests looking on haughtily from horseback and a royal carriage. I could feel the mud of Red Square under my feet and hear the wailing of a grieving wife and son, widow and orphan to be. I couldn't help but be moved by it even though my own fate could possibly be that of the mutineers if my own situation didn't resolve itself soon. Del stood entranced as he listened to Tatyana and asked questions, completely detached from the reality that the dragnet was closing in around us quickly.

After a few minutes, the crowd in front of the painting thinned out and the three of us stood directly in front of this tragic rendering, Tatyana between me and Del, pretending that this painting was the reason for our visit to the gallery. In my feeling of impatience and vulnerability I looked about the room to see how easily trapped we would be should Sergey and his team close in on us. Over my right shoulder, I recognized one of the FSB team waiting by the wider of the two exits but couldn't see another one directly. I put my attention back on the painting and held my breath.

Another small group came to stand with us in front of the scene of execution to the left of Del and began snapping photographs of each of them with the painting as a dramatic background. The last of the four to pose fumbled with his camera, dropping a number of items, sending them skidding across the floor in front of us. The man looked embarrassed and apologized in a language that I didn't recognize as he bent down to collect this hotel room key, loose change, and his own red triangular claim tab. Del bent down to assist the man as a few of the items slid to lay directly at his shoe tips. Tatyana scolded them in Russian and they all looked sheepishly ashamed. In just the blink of an eye, I watched Del's fingers deftly swap my claim tab with that of the clumsy tourist in a slight of hand that called to it absolutely no attention. Adrenaline flooded my blood stream and I felt the pupils in my eyes expand. My body tensed up, my heart began to race, and my stomach and throat synched up ready for the threat that I felt closing in on us. I was ready to fight or flee.

From over my right shoulder a commotion rose that I didn't comprehend quickly enough, nor did I anticipate. With my back to the room and my attention theatrically fixed on the painting and Del's switch of claim tags with the clumsy tourist, I couldn't find the presence of mind to break my act to turn to see what it was tens of others in the room were moving quickly away from.

Just as I was able to shake myself out of my adrenaline induced paralysis and turn my head to see what was happening behind me, I was struck with a force that spun me around and into Tatyana who let out a scream just as I toppled over on top of her to the hardwood floor. I couldn't breathe. Each second was a struggle to live. As my lungs finally filled again it felt as if my whole right side had been sheared off. It felt as if the endings of all the nerves in my right side were being rubbed with sand paper. I couldn't even scream the pain was so overwhelming. I wretched and gasped face down on the floor.

As Tatyana struggled to get out from under the deadweight of my body, more gunshots rang out from the left and the right. In the immediate shock and haze of my own pain, it seemed that everybody at the museum had opened fire on the person next to them. I tried hard to stay oriented. I rolled over onto my back with my neck propped up against the wall under the frame of the painting. My right shoulder felt as if it was on fire! Confusion reigned. Next to Tatyana, who was now laying on her side, curled up in a ball screaming in horror with her hands and arms over her head and ears, I saw the bulging eyes of the clumsy tourist to whom Del had given my claim tab with blood running out of the corner of his mouth. The dead man's friends had, out of thin air, produced hand held sub-machine guns and were spraying the room with bullets. I could see Del hiding behind an overturned red velvet bench. I couldn't see if he had a gun or not. I couldn't imagine how he had gotten over there so fast.

As the gunmen in the corner stopped to reload their weapons, two single shots from different guns flashed at the other end of the hall and hit their marks, dropping two men efficiently to the ground. Just as the second of the shots had been loosed, the third machine gunner opened another volley at the FSB agents in a sweeping motion from left to right, piercing the walls and splintering the moldings of the door frames penetrating through the walls on both sides of the doorway. The thud of bodies was heard dropping to the floor on the other side of the wall. A pistol slid across the floor and came to rest in the door way just out of reach of the hand of the dead FSB agent sprawled face down on the floor.

Around the corner of the second exit, a pistol and the right side of Sergey's face appeared to take aim at the last machine gunner. I saw Sergey at the same moment as the gunman. As quickly as my eyes could move right to left again, he tugged on the uzi's trigger again and spat out a burst of twenty bullets, splintering the woodwork along the door frame that Sergey was sheltering behind, just as Sergey's bullet found the forehead of his own assassin. Both men flopped violently, simultaneously to the floor.

Del sprang from his flimsy cover behind the overturned bench and snatched up one of the miniature machine guns and covered the room. He kicked the other uzis out of the reach from the other dead shooters, a habit of professional precaution.

"Kid, kid! You awake? You alive?" Del called out to me.

I moaned an answer that was not quite a word, yet just enough to acknowledge I was alive. Tatyana was still screaming in terror but was otherwise uninjured. Del moved quickly to help Tatyana to her feet and pulled her behind him and pushed her out of the hall through an external fire exit. Bodies of tourists lay scattered across the floor. Some obviously dead, others crying for help. Sirens of the museum's emergency alarm echoed through the still halls around us. Instructions to calmly leave the gallery blared from intercom speakers. Nobody else around me moved.

I closed my eyes to concentrate on moving a wave of pain through my body. Del crouched over me and lifted my shoulder from the floor and put his hand under me. I felt my whole body involuntary recoil in pain from Del's probing of the wound and I screamed in agony and surprise. I felt like I was going to pass out. His hands were red with my blood.

"Kid, you'll be okay. It passed through your shoulder," he said, trying to reassure me.

He took off his light jacket and placed it under my shoulder and laid me directly on top of it, tightly packed. He then removed his own button-down shirt, his muscular shoulders and biceps visible under his t-shirt, and wadded it up in my hand and told me to hold it tightly with my left hand over the exit wound. The pressure was initially sharp and painful, then finally soothing. I tried to breathe normally through my clenched teeth. I closed my eyes to concentrate and when I opened them again, Del was gone.

I lifted my neck to look for him performing triage on other wounded tourists, but didn't see him anymore. I looked back to the dead gunmen to my right and into the open eyes and hand of the clumsy tourist. Where Tatyana had been lying next to me I saw the claim tab Del had taken from me at the wardrobe. Pulling my left arm over my body I rolled and stretched with all my might, causing horrible pain in my right arm and shoulder, but was able to snatch the plastic triangle and tuck it into my pants' pocket.

The next movement I heard and saw was that of heavily armed police agents wearing helmets, bullet proof vests moving in assault formation through the adjacent hall towards me. They shouted to each other and other colleagues behind them "CHIESTIY!" or "clear," and then more and more footsteps. Voices and cries for help were heard from the injured nearby. As the armed squad entered the room where I laid bleeding and sweating, I felt a wave of pain-free relief pass over me and watched the room spin and go black.

33. Dobrynin & Yeltsin

It was dark outside my window, but the hall from the nurses' station glowed fluorescent through the observation window's thin drapes. I could sense somebody in the room with me but was still too groggy to be alert enough to track him or her. My eyes fluttered open like I was waking from a light sleep. They then rolled back up in my head again and I slept for another few hours.

When I gained consciousness again the sky was lighter but the sun had not yet risen. My shoulder felt heavier than lead. I didn't dare try to move my right arm. I twitched my fingers out of concern. I moved my head to see my fingers move. I was awake.

A soft feminine voice to my left whispered, "Good morning. How do you feel?"

I slowly turned my head to see a woman, a nurse, changing a fluids bag over my bed. Its tube undoubtedly was inserted someplace into my body. I twitched my left hand and felt the needle in the back of it. Found it.

"May I have a drink of water, please?" I rasped back in English, barely audible.

"Once again?" She hadn't understood me.

"Water? Give me please some water to drink," I repeated, but this time in Russian. She returned to the bedside with a cup of water and put a straw in my mouth. It was cold and refreshing. I drank the cup dry.

"Thank you," I said, clearing my throat. Just that small action caused my whole torso to scream at me to "Hold still!"

She left the room again to take away the cup and straw but re-entered and came to stand at my bedside. She waited to see that she had my attention.

"Do you know where you are?" she asked kindly.

"In a hospital," I responded with a whisper.

"Do you know why?" she continued.

"No," I lied and closed my eyes and pretended to need to sleep more.

"Do you know that you are being guarded?" she whispered.

My eyes opened again with a bit of alarm, "By who?"

"You are in the TsKB, The Kremlin Hospital in Moscow under the guard of the FSO," she confirmed.

"Not the FSB?" I asked.

"No, the Federal Security Guards," she confirmed.

I smiled with relief and asked if I could sleep a while longer. She left the room, closing the door quietly behind her. I watched her pass the observation window and disappear out of sight.

I was woken again by a knock at the door. This time I woke easily as the room was full of light from the sunshine. Out my window I saw acres of nature: woods, grass, walking paths, and an endless Russian sky with bright morning clouds. I figured I was about four stories up. The door opened and a doctor in a white coat entered, followed by another man in his mid-thirties, trim and trained, looking bright in the eyes, healthy and robust. He was wearing a sharp dark suit and a conservative dark tie. He came across very formal. He spoke English perfectly. The doctor stood by to observe his patient's condition.

"Mr. Turner, good morning. I am glad to see you conscious. My name is Major Dobrynin of the FSO. The nurse tells me that she informed you about where you are," he said to me formally.

"Yes, she told me some things, but to be honest I don't know what it means," I admitted honestly.

"What did she tell you, exactly?" the officer asked kindly.

Switching to Russian I repeated as carefully, word for word what the nurse told me.

"Yes, that is correct, you are in the Central Clinical Hospital in the Kuntsevo district of Moscow. This hospital is under the guard of the president's security guards. All the living victims from the museum shooting on Wednesday have been brought here and will be questioned and protected as witnesses to those events. When you are feeling well enough, I will come again and take your statement about what happened. Do you understand?" His tone was explanatory, not accusatory.

I nodded and asked, "What day is today?"

"It is Friday," he replied matter of factly. "Do you want to ask your doctor for anything while he is here?"

"No, thank you. I'm fine for now," I answered.

As they turned to leave the room I asked the major, "Am I under arrest, sir?"

The major stopped and turned again to the bed to speak directly to me. "No, you are not under arrest, but you are in protective custody for your own safety."

"Protection from who, can I ask?"

His reply turned my blood cold. "You witnessed a violent attack by one of Moscow's most violent mafia groups which killed six FSB agents and thirteen civilians including several foreign nationals. Your safety is being safeguarded from both the mafia gang involved and the FSB, as the agents killed were not acting under official orders at the time. We expect both groups to try to influence your statement and eventual testimony, and you are therefore being kept here in this secure location as a matter of both personal and state security."

I said nothing in return but nodded my head and looked straight ahead to the wall in front of me.

"Does my government know that I am here? Has anybody contacted the American Embassy?" I asked after a brief pause to take in the weight of the situation.

"Yes, a consular has already applied to visit you. We are formalizing his visit as quickly as possible." And with that reply, he turned and left my room. The doctor looked at me, nodded and closed the door behind him.

Alone again I started to cry. It started deep down in my loins and moved up my abdomen and convulsed my entire body until I was wailing in despair, crying from pain, shedding tears of relief and joy all at the same time. The last ten days had been the making of nightmares and to have survived one mafia group and one round of FSB agents, I was now a target all over again. I feared for my freedom and my life as I laid in my hospital bed alone and cried into my pillow.

"The doctor says it would be very good if you could get up and walk a bit," the nurse said as she was busy changing the dressings on my shoulder.

"I will give it my best try," I said as she pulled the bandages tight across the wound. I winced. I remember Lara having done the same with my battered ribs to offer support to the bruised muscles.

"Sister? Did the police leave any of my belongings?" I asked quietly.

"You can call me Nelya. Yes, they are in your bedside drawer," she said in a friendly way and reached to open the drawer for me.

I saw immediately my passport, plane ticket, wallet, and wrist watch. I wondered about the claim tab.

"I had a bag checked at the museum and had a claim tab. Do you maybe know where that tab is?" I inquired with concern.

"No, I am sorry. Your clothes are in the closet, but you will need new shirts as they were blood soaked and had holes in them" She looked at me with pity.

"Would you maybe ask the right people? I had an address book in that bag that I need. I have some people to inform," I politely asked.

"I'm sorry, but you are not allowed to contact anybody. I cannot let you use a telephone or have any communication that you are alive. It's for your security," she apologized.

I stood up from the bed slowly with the help of my left hand to steady myself when I got to my feet. The room tilted just a little bit. I stumbled half a step backward. Nelya caught me with a hand on the small of my back and helped to steady me. After a few shuffles across the floor, my balance came quickly. The dressing the nurse had prepared stabilized the wounded shoulder and with that, I was able to move rather well.

Nelya accompanied me downstairs to walk in the gardens for ten minutes through the pine groves and past flower beds and ponds. I was in wonder that such a calm, peaceful place so isolated from the din of the city could exist anywhere near Moscow. What a far cry these grounds were from the building site of the Kazan Regional Hospital I had experienced a year earlier. I felt somewhat ashamed of myself for enjoying the luxury and individual attention I was receiving from nurse Nelya as I remembered the old man bleeding from his head, begging for a simple pillow while he lay dying in the corridor. The disparity of privilege between citizens of the same city seemed to me repulsive and evil.

Upon returning to my room, Nelya and I were met by two men waiting with the door open. On our entry, they both stood up from their chairs and greeted us with smiles and nods. Nelya helped me back into the bed and exited quickly without speaking. Both men were dressed alike in light colored wool suits with brilliant white shirts and silk ties, tightly cinched at the neck. They wore decorated wing tips and carried leather-cased notebooks. They didn't have to open their mouths for me to understand that they were from the American Embassy.

"Hello, gentlemen. Thank you for coming to see me," I said politely. "I assume you know my name already."

"Yes, we are happy to see you up and about, Mr. Turner. My name is Brett Richardson from the US State Department. I am the consular for citizen services here in Moscow," the first man

318

introduced himself and approached to shake my hand, "and this is the embassy's chief of security, Ben Arkadin."

Ben nodded from his chair, seeing that shaking hands was not a pleasant experience for me with my right arm wrapped up tight against my chest.

"Mr. Turner, we are of course very sorry that you got caught in the crossfire of that horrible attack on Wednesday, and we are here to help you in any way we can," Mr. Richardson pledged.

"Again, thanks for coming to see me. Can you give me any idea of when I will be released so I can go home?" I asked directly.

"We understand that that is a matter for the Russian police and the prosecutor's office. Once they are satisfied with your statement, we understand they will allow you to leave. They may ask you to testify as a witness in an inquest, but that is not even for sure. You are just one witness of many," Richardson replied, but actually told me nothing.

Mr. Arkadin addressed me with a different sharpness from his chair. "Mr. Turner, we've come about a different matter. We hope that you might be able to clear up a few questions for us today. Our security personnel photographed you on Wednesday afternoon lunching on the Arbat Street with a person named Delmore Santander who is a mercenary and arms dealer to the world's regimes who are, let's say, not friends of the United States of America, and certainly not to our mission here in Russia. Can you explain to us how you know this man and what your meeting was about?"

I could not believe what I was hearing. My mouth went suddenly very dry and I stammered my surprise and disbelief at what I was hearing.

"I don't know anybody by that name," I answered, half choking.

"Do you recognize these photographs? This is you in the photo, correct?" Arkadin handed me a photograph taken from behind where Del and I were sitting at the open café eating lunch, trying to navigate our way through mafia and FSB dragnets.

"Yes, that is me with Mr. Del Sanning of the CIA. You could say he was trying to recruit me to work for the agency. I told him to shove it where the sun doesn't shine," I said, handing the photograph back to Mr. Arkadin.

"How did you come into contact with him, if I may ask?" Mr. Richardson asked.

"I became acquainted with him many months ago during my studies in Nizhniy Novgorod. He was there as a businessman with the agency, trying to build a hotel. He only told me the truth when we met for lunch here in Moscow. I didn't know before that," I answered truthfully.

"Mr. Turner, what is your purpose for being in Russia?" Mr. Arkadin asked in a suspicious tone.

"I am studying history, language and literature," I answered innocently.

"What was the reason for your visit to Moscow then?" he questioned further.

"A cultural excursion to the Tretyakov gallery. Mr. Sanning invited me for lunch when I told him I would be in Moscow at the same time as him," I was now lying but hid my discomfort under the pain of my wound.

"Do you know where this man is now?" pointing to the photograph.

"No sorry. He was traveling on business and I didn't know the rest of his plans," I improvised.

"Are you aware of any dealings he may have had with arms producers while in Nizhniy Novgorod? You understand the significance that this city has for Russia's aviation sector," he asked and implied in one sentence.

"No, not really. I am just studying linguistics," I lied again.

"Why do you believe Mr. Santandar works for the CIA and was trying to recruit you?" Arkadin pushed.

"He said my language skills were some of the best he had seen, above that of American agents, and thought I could be trained to best serve our country with that skill." I wasn't lying this time.

"Did he tell you that he works for the CIA?" Richardson interrupted to ask.

I paused to reflect for a moment. "No, he never confirmed that. I even asked him straight-up, but he told me that he was not free to confirm such an answer to me. It sounded plausible to me," I said honestly, shrugging my left shoulder.

"If you have any further contact with him, you should inform us immediately," Arkadin insisted.

"I can't imagine that I will ever see him again. He doesn't have any of my contact details in the USA where I will be going as soon when I am free to leave," I affirmed.

"Do you need any travel documents, Mr. Turner, or other support to leave Russia?" Richardson inquired.

"No, I have my passport with me and a valid return ticket. I'm good. I just need to get healthy enough to travel," I answered.

"We will be able to help you leave with a government airplane as soon as the police release you to go. It could take you weeks to be ready to fly commercially. We feel it is important to get you home as quickly as possible," Richardson added. "Please call me at this number directly when you are cleared to leave. We'll arrange an embassy car to take you to the airport and fly you to D.C."

"Thanks for the offer. I'll certainly call you when I'm released." I took his offered card and put it on the bedside table with no intention to contact him voluntarily. The men excused themselves and said they would look in on me again in a few days to see how I was healing.

As the door closed behind the Americans, I felt my gut sink and my face turn pale. I gazed out the window with tears blurring my vision. I cursed again the day that I first arrived in Russia. I cursed the years of studying the language, Pushkin, and Dostoyevsky. I cursed both Lenin and Yeltsin for both the hope and the upheavals that they ushered in. I cursed my idealism and swore in my fear that once gone, I would never come back! An uncontrollable urge to flee rose up in my limbs. I started from my bed and removed the hospital scrubs and slippers I had borrowed and began to put on my own denim jeans. The white hospital t-shirt would have to do.

As I sat in my chair struggling to put on socks and shoes with one hand, the door to my room opened without warning. I looked up with exasperation and impatience to see two guards in suits and ties barge in. They opened all my cupboards and closets, looked under the bed and inspected the lavatory. I was instructed to stand. One guard frisked me from head to toe and between my legs while the other stood by to watch. What were they looking for?

"Please sit on the bed and do not move!" I was instructed.

I sat on the bed without argument while the two guards stood at attention between the window and my bed, leaving the door wide open and nothing stopping me from exiting the room in my bare feet. I looked again at the twin guards and gave a questioning look. One motioned for me to stay put on the bed but did not speak again.

From the corridor, a commotion was heading toward my door. A group of five people, all of them speaking busily with each other in excitement, appeared at the door. I feared that I was going to be arraigned and charged with espionage by Major Dobrynin. If the Americans had photos of me with Del on the Arbat Street, then they had already figured out that I was with him at the museum, too. My nerves were completely shot. Horrible visions of a trial, prison, and firing squad rushed through the neurons and synapses of my brain at light speed. I closed my eyes and tried to breathe slowly and push out the visions of doom swirling behind my eyes. The group entered my room.

A cameraman with a large television camera on his shoulder walked cautiously backward toward me and then around the foot of my bed. Just behind him, a woman with a microphone on a wire connected to the television camera also walked backward into the room. To my disbelief, the next figure who strode into my room was a tall, barrel-chested, silver-haired man, in a sharp blue wool suit with the flag of the Russian Federation pinned to his lapel.

President Yeltsin looked serious yet he smiled as he approached my bed and held out his hand to me. I timidly offered my left hand and he shook heartily with both of his. Photographers behind him took pictures of our handshake. Shutters flickered like hummingbird wings. They called for turned heads and an extended handshake.

"We are very sorry for your distress!" the president said to me in a clear, slow baritone voice.

"Thank you very much, Mr. President," I replied demurely, nodding my head in deference.

"We will find those responsible for this terrible attack on innocent people and punish them!" he bellowed for the camera, looking at me.

I thanked him again and withdrew my hand.

"Will you be going home soon?" he questioned.

"I hope so! The doctors and nurse are taking good care of me," I offered.

"Yes, they are the best in Russia. I wish you a quick recovery," he replied and then clasped my left shoulder and looked me in the face with a sincere expression of concern. The photographers were rabid for this photo and Yeltsin stood still for another five seconds letting the press satiate itself.

As quickly as the guards and the entourage had entered, they left my room and went next door where another victim of the shooting was convalescing. I listened to the president bellow the same deliberate words of canned comfort to the woman in the next room who was obviously sobbing and blubbering something back to him. She would surely make the seven o'clock news!

Nelya came quickly to see if the commotion had disturbed me and to help me get comfortable again.

"Why are you dressed?" she demanded and picked up the scrubs on the floor behind my bed and demanded to help me change again. "You know that you can't leave. So please stay comfortable and rest. It is almost time for dinner."

The following morning at ten o'clock sharp, Major Dobrynin came into the room together with my nurse and asked to take a seat. He greeted me with a nod and a smile on his tanned face. He had the face of a stern man, but he had kind eyes and moved in a non-aggressive manner.

"I've asked the nurse to stay with us for this discussion in order to help you stay comfortable and bring anything you might need while we speak," he explained without any hesitation. He had come for a specific purpose and was prepared to see it though.

"I understand our president came to visit you yesterday evening," he said in a friendly manner.

I nodded without a word.

"You should be honored. He's a good man who has Russia's best interest in mind. I'd take a bullet for him!" he affirmed with pride.

"Were you with him in 1992?" I asked politely.

"Yes, but I was not with him that day when he stood on the tanks. Wish I could have seen it!" He was obviously a great admirer of the man who he had sworn to protect. Changing tones suddenly, Dobrynin started the official business, "Mr. Turner, I have a number of questions that I need for you to answer with as much detail as you can recall about the shootings in the museum on Wednesday afternoon."

"I will do my best to remember," I assured him.

"Please start by relating to me what you saw and experienced in the museum that day," he instructed.

I didn't know how to start the story. I hesitated and looked at him and then at Nelya. I knew if I started such an interrogation with a lie that it would only be bad for me. There was no way that I could construct a story other than the truth to explain why I was in Moscow, what I was doing at the gallery, and why the FSB agents were present. After my interview and questions from the embassy staff the day before, I was careful to anticipate that they already knew half the story. They had probably already spoken with Tatyana, the guide who I fell on and who Del lead out of the exposition hall with a machine gun in hand. They'd want to know who had packed my wound and from whom I had taken a shirt from to stop the bleeding on my shoulder. I knew that the physical evidence and the other eye witnesses would contradict any story I could create. I stalled.

"I'm sorry, I don't know if I'm ready yet to talk about this. It's all so fresh," I bluffed.

"I understand, but it is very important that we speak now before you start to forget," Dobrynin insisted.

I took a deep breath. "Major, how much time do you have?" My voice shook from nerves.

"That depends on what you have to tell me, Mr. Turner," he said, putting away his pen and closing his notepad. He looked through me and leaned towards me in his chair.

"Sir, what kind of protection can you offer me if I tell you everything I know?" I asked emphatically.

"You are in one of the country's most secure facilities," he offered.

"After this interview can you help me leave Russia very quickly?" I pushed him.

"If you have committed no crimes, then you will be free to leave Russia as soon as your doctor gives his consent." His voice stayed calm and said nothing rash.

"That's not good enough, Major. Can you get me out tonight if I tell you what happened there Wednesday?" I was emphatic.

"You first tell me everything that happened as you know it, and I will judge what type of protection you might need," Dobrynin assured.

I took another deep breath. "I was the reason that both the FSB agents and the Chechens were in the gallery that day. I am the reason that they were all gathered around the one painting. I was shot by an FSB agent and now—because I was being followed and watched—now how many people are dead? Twenty-three or twenty-four in total?" I confessed, "It's not my fault, but it is because of me."

"That's a big claim for a young student, Mr. Turner. You may be feeling like you were a target because you were shot in the chaos, but I can assure you that they were not there for you," Dobrynin said, dismissing what he thought was the confession of a survivor's guilt.

I doubled down, "Major, I was there in the company of a man who is either a CIA agent or an international terrorist, if I am to believe the officials from my embassy." I insisted, "We know each other from Nizhniy Novgorod where I am a student and he was involved in the theft of Russian military secrets. The FSB was in pursuit of me because they believed I was transporting the disc or discs for him from Nizhniy to Moscow. The gallery was agreed to be the place of the handover, but I was carrying nothing for him. He was bluffing the Chechens. Either he still has the disc or he destroyed it like he claimed."

The Major held up his hand to stop me and asked for the nurse to excuse us. Nelya protested, telling Dobrynin that she had security clearance as hospital staff. He politely acknowledged that fact but explained that it was above her clearance level. She complied with his request and exited quickly without further discussion.

I continued, "I was shot when Sanning handed one of the men my claim tab from the wardrobe. I guess he had agreed to make the swap in this way so that nobody would see any goods trading hands. As soon as the FSB agents saw the handover, I believe they drew on the Chechens. I didn't see anything before I got shot and then all hell broke loose. I saw the last gunmen shoot and kill three of the FSB agents at the same time he got a bullet to the forehead."

"Mr. Turner, will you be willing to sign a statement to this effect?" he asked solemnly.

"If I can leave here tomorrow, yes!" I blurted out.

"Can you tell me how your associate acquired the military secrets you believe he was smuggling?" he asked with some doubt.

"He murdered, or had murdered, a local mafia boss in Nizhniy Novgorod, Mr. P. who was the son the famous Ivan Sergeyevich S., a top aviation engineer at the Sokol research facility for the MIG aircraft. I understand that Mr. P. was trying to sell the military secrets to a man from Kyrgyzstan who would sell them through to Iran. That is the story that Sanning told me at the least," I proffered the theory with fluency.

"Can you offer any proof about these events?" Dobrynin emphasized his disbelief.

"Last weekend, Mr. P. was murdered; that is really all I can prove. The American Embassy has photos of me meeting Sanning in the city on Wednesday just before we went to the gallery. I don't know if they will show those photos to you. My guide at the museum can verify I was with him. The rest are dead. Del has disappeared. The only other proof I can offer is in the address book in my bag that I checked at the gallery," I conceded.

"What role did the FSB agents have in these events?" Dobrynin began taking notes.

"They arrested me in Nizhniy Novgorod. As I know Sanning well and did some ad-hoc work for him, they believed I was involved with Del's espionage work. I helped them to make contact with him again via a telephone number in Sweden after they lost track of him. They brought me to Moscow and followed us from the Arbat meeting to the gallery. Del was very careful to make sure they followed us. It seems to me he set the whole thing up and knew that the FSB and those wanting the disc would shoot each other for it," I explained.

"And where is this person now?" the Major asked.

"Sanning? The last I saw him he helped our tour guide leave the gallery room where all the shooting happened. He packed my wound, gave me his shirt to put pressure on it, and while I had my eyes closed he just disappeared into the crowds I guess," I speculated.

"Mr. Turner. I will ask you not to repeat this information to any other police officer or investigator. If what you tell me is true, we want to keep this as quiet as possible while I make unofficial inquiries. If any FSB officials hear of this, your life could be in further danger. The agents that arrested you and brought you to Moscow, were they the same that we found dead at the museum?" Dobrynin was very serious.

"Yes, at least three of them. The other three I didn't see until I was in Moscow already," I confirmed.

"Peter, if I am able to substantiate any part of this story it will be difficult for me to release you to the American Embassy officials as you will be critical to our investigation and apprehension of the criminals," he explained with an apology.

"I can't see how I can help any further. I wasn't involved in the data theft. I have no idea who it was who wanted to buy it. My research and information were about the local mafia boss and what he planned to do with his money, that was evidently to come from selling the information. It was Del who knew that somehow there was somebody looking to sell and buy the weapons data. I didn't know anything about that until the FSB arrested me," I pleaded.

"Do you know what type of weapons?" Dobrynin caught every new clue in my explanation.

"It is a very accurate missile guidance program," I revealed.

Dobrynin closed his notebook, thanked me for this statement, stood and turned to leave. Just before he opened the door he turned to me again and said, "Peter, thank you for telling me this information first. It would have been very bad for you if I had to come back and ask you about it myself. You are now on the right side of the law. In Russia, one does not want to be on the wrong side of the law. The consequences of that get quickly out of control." He left without waiting for a response.

That same afternoon I received another visit from the embassy staff. Mr. Richardson did not come this time, but Arkadin the security chief, and another embassy officer accompanied him. I invited the men to walk with me on the grounds instead of sitting in the stuffy hospital room. My stamina was improving and I was no longer struggling to catch my breath after short strolls. Once we were out of ear shot, Arkadin started the interrogation while we walked.

"Mr. Turner, we need to better understand your relationship to Santander as we don't believe you have been forthcoming with the information we asked for," Arkadin grumbled.

"What is not clear, sir?" I asked with fake deference.

"We believe that you accompanied Santander to the gallery where you were shot. We don't believe that your meeting was just a chance meeting in Moscow. We have reason to believe that he was with you and may have been involved in the gun fight in the museum." Arkadin was probing for information.

"Let me guess, you have more photos?" I remarked offhand.

"There is a term that we use in our business, Mr. Turner, it's called 'chatter,' and since Thursday the network has been replete with chatter about what happened at the museum. We know that Santander was there. We believe he was there to turn over data, Russian military data, to a wider terrorist network. Do you have any knowledge about the whereabouts of that data?" Arkadin stopped and looked me in the eyes. He was an open book. He had no shadow agenda and hid nothing. The USA wanted that data and saw me as their only way to get close to it.

"No, sir. I do not know where that data is," I replied directly.

"Do you know the whereabouts of Santander?" he asked point blank.

"As I told you yesterday, sir, I do not know where the man is or where he was going," I reiterated.

"How did you arrange your meeting on Wednesday?" He was getting aggressive.

"What's in the data that the United States wants so badly?" I questioned back.

"We want to prevent this from getting into the wrong hands!" he emphasized.

"How did you find out about it?" I asked naively.

"Mr. Turner, the United States has the most powerful intelligence gathering tools in the entire world. We are professional security and intelligence officers. There is very little in the world that happens that we don't know about first." Arkadin was clearly annoyed at my amateur status. "Now tell me, how did you arrange your meeting on Wednesday?"

"By telephone," I answered with an obvious irony.

"He just called you on the telephone, in Russia, and set up a meeting to hand over highly classified military secrets?" Arkadin was getting frustrated.

"No, for lunch. I met him for lunch on the Arbat, just like you saw. He called and asked me to meet him at twelve-thirty." I was answering the man truthfully but he thought I was evading an answer.

"Mr. Turner! You are testing my patience and when that runs out the embassy services will be closed to you. Do you understand me?" he muttered through clenched teeth.

"I'm sorry but I am telling you the truth. I can't make it like in the movies with secret passwords and computer chips in my brain. He called me on the telephone. Told me where to meet him. We had lunch, we talked, we went to the museum. I got shot. Here I am. Here you are. I was not involved in any transfer of military secrets to terrorists. I am a student. Sanning, or Santander, was posing as a business man, we got to be friends, he helped me with some school projects, he tried to recruit me for what I thought was CIA work," I bellowed at Arkadin and finished by looking at his silent colleague with a look of exasperation. He stood as still as a statue without a wince, not a drop of sweat on his brow in the warm afternoon sun and Moscow humidity, and then he spoke.

"Mr. Turner, I am Special Agent Jones. I have clearance to take you out of Russia today if you can help us contact Mr. Santander. Do you have any contact channels with him?" was the direct, uncluttered offer and question from the secret agent.

Arkadin turned a bit flustered and glared at his colleague for his interruption.

"I had a number to call. It's a Swedish telephone number. I no longer have that number. If I can get my bag from the museum that was checked there in the wardrobe, I could possibly supply you with that number. Can you get me that bag, sir? It was checked under number 375," I replied calmly and businesslike.

"We trust we will find you here again later tonight?" the special agent asked.

"They have me under guard. I'm not going anywhere," I confirmed.

They both turned and walked away to the exit, leaving me in the garden alone. I sat down on a bench and gave a huge sigh of relief when they were out of sight. I felt my shoulder ache from the deep breath.

I felt a twinge of anger at Del for getting me shot, but also a twinge of relief that he did what he did to get me out of the hands of the FSB. Was I ready to turn him in? Did I even have the ability to turn him in? I figured he would already be two steps ahead of me, the Americans, and the Russians, and wouldn't reply again to a call to his Swedish answering machine.

With that, I resolved to turn over everything I had to Arkadin and Jones and use the get-out-of-jail-free-card that they were offering.

06

34. Jailbreak

Just after finishing my dinner alone in my room, listening to a classical music radio station, Nelya, who should have been off duty, entered my room in a hurried manner and started quickly emptying my drawer with an urgency I hadn't before seen in her. For the few days that she had been caring for me she was always very deliberate, never rash.

"Nelya! What are you doing? What's going on?" I asked in a growing sense of panic. I watched the door as she demanded I get dressed. She would help me put on shoes and socks. I obeyed. Once I had my blue jeans on she quickly slid my socks over my feet and wiggled my shoes onto my feet and tied the laces.

"You'll need a shirt!" She noticed I still had on surgical scrubs with my right arm immobilized under the loose-fitting top. She ran out of the room and ten seconds later came back with a light jacket, put my left arm through a sleeve, draped it over the right shoulder and zipped it up for me, leaving me looking like an amputee, right sleeve hanging empty and limp.

"Will you please tell me what is going on?" I demanded as she walked me down the corridor to the elevators.

"Dobrynin phoned me. He is coming to collect you now." She was out of breath and had to inhale quick breaths before finishing her message. "Somebody just made an attempt on his life and he is afraid that they will be coming for you next. He will take you someplace safe."

"I thought I was safe here!" I protested, running my left hand through my short hair and looking instinctively for a hiding place in the hospital department. The doors to the elevator opened before I was able to decide on any alternate course. I followed the nurse instead into the elevator with my heart in my throat pounding with a refreshed burst of adrenaline that I seemed to have become used to after the last two weeks.

When the elevator doors opened on the ground floor, to my surprise Nelya did not rush us out into the lobby and out the front doors. She calmly brushed her hair into place and took me by the arm to give an appearance of a nurse aiding a patient to take a walk. We did not try to leave the secured zone but lingered inside by the exit to the gardens and patios. We found a bench in the relief of the corridor, just out of sight from the elevators and the security check point at the entrance to the hospital.

"We must wait here for Major Dobrynin. So now we just wait," she whispered and patted my good arm that she was still holding.

After a few minutes of restless sitting and shifting my backside on the hard marble bench, I tried to stand up, but Nelya pulled me back to the bench.

She hissed in a whisper, "Do not stand up. If you stand they can see you from the elevator and the doors!" I sat down again.

"Who? Who can see me?" I asked in dismay, seeing nobody paying us any attention.

Before Nelya could answer, three cars pulled into the circular drive. Screeching tires came to sudden stops from high speed. The troika took up defensive positions in front of the main entrance-exit of the hospital, parking at angles to block a possible pursuit of the lead, or maybe a getaway car, parked a length ahead of the other two.

The cars were black, late model Mercedes sedans, with all the windows blacked out. Blue lights flickered from the front and back windows and grills from all three cars. This was an official convoy. Had they come for me? One of the sedans had the passenger door dented and the wing mirror hanging like a lame appendage. The damage looked recent, the mirror hanging by wires.

Nobody at the security station seemed to stir. They seemed to be used to seeing high-speed convoys pull in and out of this complex carrying VIPs, heads of State, and ministers of government. There seemed to be no alarm in the security staff.

A door of each car opened simultaneously, and from the protection of the bulletproof steel and glass three men stood and trained their handguns on the guards over the roofs of their cars and demanded that they drop their service weapons. Having been drawn on unsuspectingly, the guards put their hands on their heads and followed orders to lay down on the paving stones of the walkway leading to the hospital entrance. With the first guards neutralized and covered, Major Dobrynin stepped out of the passenger door of the last car with the collision damage closest to the entrance doors of the facility. Two guards from the other cars followed closely behind him acting as his rearguard. With weapons drawn and plenty of shouting, the three men moved in precision to disarm the guards at the metal detector. From that position, a call was heard in English.

"Peter Turner, please come to me now!" Dobrynin shouted, "Quickly!"

Nelya pushed me up and without a word of goodbye or even turning to thank her for the risk she had taken, I walked calmly but quickly to Dobrynin who was covering a guard with his pistol. He motioned for me to walk through the metal detector and outside. As I passed him he followed me, walking backward and very deliberately keeping his weapon trained on the hall guards. As he passed his colleagues, he tapped each on the shoulder and they too started to fall back, guns still trained on the sentries who looked stunned and confused.

As the other two guards covered his back again, Dobrynin grabbed me firmly by the left arm and walked me directly to the lead car and put me in the backseat on the passenger side. He climbed in on the other side. After a three second delay to wait for all the agents to return to their cars, the troika sped away with the renewed screeching of tires and strained motors as they sped for the main road.

The troika reached the main boulevard, the Rubleskoye Highway. The car Dobyrinin and I were riding in turned right and was followed closely by one of the cars. The third car turned left and accelerated in the opposite direction with great speed. We sped past a highway patrol station of the MVD on the left, but they paid us no attention and had no hope of catching this high-performance cavalcade in their standard Lada patrol cars. The patrol officers standing on the side of the road with their striped batons watched helplessly as our cars ripped past them already at one-hundred kilometers per hour. I started searching for a seat belt with my left arm. Dobrynin had to lean across and help me fasten it.

"Good idea!" he said as he reached for his as well.

"Major, can you tell me what is happening, please?" I asked, trying to sound as calm as possible.

"I'm very sorry to have to make such a dramatic scene, but I believe that the FSB would soon be at the hospital to try to assassinate you," he said with more than a twinge of stress in his voice. "I started an unofficial inquiry into the details that you told me about stolen military plans and the FSB's involvement."

Dobrynin broke off his story to give instructions to the driver and the car behind him with the radio phone. "Pull in front of us!" he hollered into the radio. On that instruction, a burst of speed sounded from behind us and passing on the left side of the car, an identical Mercedes passed us at two hundred kilometers per hour and pulled in front of us. Both cars continued their trajectory at one hundred sixty kilometers per hour.

"Do we have to go so fast?" I appealed.

"It's standard procedure! Anybody else driving this fast to keep up with us will be seen immediately and be assessed as a risk!" Dobrynin replied, looking over his shoulder out the back window.

He continued his explanation: "I spoke with only one man, my direct superior, about the details you provided yesterday. He listened carefully and then told me to drop it and not take it any further. He told me that the official investigation of the shooting had concluded—that it was a terrorist action from the Chechen army, and the FSB had been tailing them, and then as you say... all hell broke loose," he recounted as he watched in three directions at once for any pursuit vehicles.

He spoke into the radiophone again, "Vnukovo!" and said to our driver, "American Embassy!"

As the cars neared the interchange of the Kutuzovsky Avenue, our driver pulled again in front of our twin escort and sped off under the overpass of the crossing highway, while the other car, now suddenly behind us, took an unexpected right turn to exit and head southwest to the Vnukovo Airport. My head was spinning at the speed with which we were passing other cars and trucks on the road.

"I sent my car to Sheremetyevo Airport and the other car is now heading to the Vvukovo Airport to act as decoys while I deliver you to the American Embassy. I can't trust any Russian security services with your safety," he said much more calmly. Our car took a hard right as well on the highway exit to change direction and merge with the Kutuzovsky Avenue that would take us directly into central Moscow, and almost to the doorstep of the American Embassy. The driver did not temper his speed as he flashed his headlights at slower cars in the far-left lane to move right, with several near misses.

"On my way back from the Tretyakov, after having told my superior officer about your theory, I was chased by two cars from the FSB. They rammed my car and shot at my driver, to no effect. One of them wound up in the Moscow River, right off the ring road bridge by the Sparrow Hills, and the other driver we were able to out maneuver and lose. They were obviously alerted by somebody in the FSO, which means that you were not safe in the TsKB."

Our driver was starting to slow down now that we were approaching the city and had crossed the third ring road. We could see the pearly white Supreme Soviet out the left window slowly passing by across the river. Just behind that was the American Embassy. Between us and safety, though, was another ubiquitous bend of the Moscow River that first had to be crossed.

Dobrynin continued, "There are so many criminal elements inside the law enforcement agencies, that entire cases are kept in the shadows. With so many profiteers busy inside the government itself, our central command isn't even able to assess the risks and threats before state assets are stolen and sold. Russia is short of patriots! If what you have told me is true, Russia will need your help to recover the data that is going to market, but Russia's traitors that are now in charge of our security services are not willing to help you. Can I count on you to follow through with your contacts at the embassy to try to recover this? Either destroy it or bring it back to us."

I sat silently listening to this man, risking his career and life to ask me to help him help his country. I was overwhelmed. My look back was fearful and uncertain.

"Do what you can!" Dobrynin replied and from his suit pocket he produced my address book and handed it to me across the backseat. I was stunned.

"How did you find it?" I asked with my jaw slack from surprise.

Before he could answer me, the driver indicated that a car had just fallen in behind us as we crossed the bridge and was keeping pace on the bumper.

"Hold the course, Major?" he asked for confirmation.

"Hold the course, Dima!" the Major replied with confidence in his capable brother in arms as he checked his service weapon and removed the safety. I held my breath and felt my legs go slightly numb.

As the car crossed the bridge, we entered into a wide intersection with lanes branching out in multiple directions at varying angles. Our driver, Dimitri, veered slightly left, off of the New Arbat Street, ignoring all oncoming traffic and traffic lights and flung us through a near miss with an oncoming Volvo. He accelerated again through the broad plaza of chaotic cross traffic and with great skill and precision sped up Konyushkovskaya Street, right past the huge white building of the Russian parliament on our left again.

Without warning or slowing, the car veered hard right and fish-tailed as the driver moved us down a side street just in view of an American flag billowing behind the embassy's compound wall. Accelerating at full RPMs, the driver was determined to out maneuver the Volga sedan tailing us in order to give me time to safely enter the embassy.

In the blink of an eye, there was a second vehicle that had pulled out in front of us from a side street on the right, blocking the road. I expected our driver to slow down, but instead, he gunned the engine to a frenzied pitch and bore down on his steering wheel. Just before impact, Dmitri pumped his brakes and then released them again.

The energy of the accelerating car was thrown into his bumpers and fenders and it nearly flung the blocking car parallel to us and nearly let us pass. I could see the stunned driver and passenger out my window, the driver pinned inside his car by our right fender and passenger door. The only thing between me and him was the safety glass, tinted and bulletproof. The driver's airbag had deployed and the windshield had become a shattered web from the high-speed impact.

Major Dobrynin jumped out of the car and opened fire on the two FSB agents in the car that tried to block us, hitting them quickly. I watched as they both flailed and jerked with the second bullets from Dobrynin's pistol. The Major motioned for me to quickly follow him out of the door. Dmitri also had his door open by now and was staggering out. Behind us, the black Volga that followed us over the bridge was heading up the street toward us now at a quick pace. Dobrynin pushed me behind the open car door and also took up position behind it.

"Peter, you run to the guards at the embassy! Go now and use the Mercedes for cover. Keep your head down!"

On his command, I turned and ran to the uniformed American guards that were taking up a defensive position at their gates, alerted by the collision and the gun shots on the street just outside. The Russian police agents tasked with guarding the embassy's exterior, having seen the collision of an official FSO car, were moving to assist the major and Dimitri who were now in a standoff with the driver and passenger of the unmarked black Volga sedan, guns drawn, taking cover behind the smashed and steaming Mercedes. I sheltered myself behind a brick pillar of the embassy's perimeter wall and looked back to the smashed cars and the two dead FSB agents, and waited to see what would happen. Major Dobrynin looked back to see if I had made it safely into the embassy. As he turned to look at me, a second black car was heading down towards us from the other end of the street.

"Peter, get inside now!" he yelled and kept his gun trained on the fast approaching car.

I darted from my cover behind the brick pillar and ran toward the American marines as fast as my injured body would take me.

One of the soldiers ordered me to stop. "Halt, stay still or we will shoot!" he commanded with his own weapon drawn.

As I tried to stop my momentum and stop in my tracks, the third car coming toward us from the other direction also stopped at the same moment with the skidding of tires and blocked the entire street, stopping diagonally across both narrow lanes just short of the other side of the embassy's guard post. The driver stepped out with his weapon drawn and aimed it at me while the passenger from behind his open door did the same. Shots rang out again.

I flinched, expecting to feel another bullet enter my body. A million thoughts ran through my mind in a tenth of a second. Instead of feeling the sledge hammer hitting my chest I watched the driver jerk violently and fall backward out of sight behind his car. I turned to see Dobrynin taking aim on the passenger and open fire on him, with three shots, hitting the heavy steel doors of the Volga.

"Peter, go now!" Dobrynin yelled again to me to run.

I advanced toward the marines again. One of them now had his own weapon trained on the passenger hiding behind his car door, and the other on me, and both were retreating behind the steel plated gates of the embassy compound, watching me carefully as I walked quickly with my one good hand raised with nothing in it. As I stepped behind the closing gate, Dobrynin loosed three more shots into the door of the car to keep the FSB agent's head down and his gun from being raised. As the gate closed shut with a deep metallic thud, I let out a huge sigh of relief. Police sirens from the surface streets were approaching from different directions. We could hear a car backing up quickly and leaving the street, while voices were shouting instructions and urgent commands to each other.

"Stand still!" commanded one of the marines with a pistol pointed directly at me. "Keep your hands where I can see them!"

"I only have one good one!" I explained while it was high above my head. "My passport is in my back pocket." I turned myself around facing away from them. I felt a hand in my pocket take both my wallet and passport, and before I could turn around the guard frisked me from shoulders to toe. I flinched when he patted down my wounded shoulder.

"What happen to you?" the guard asked.

"I was shot through the shoulder!" I confirmed with a grunt. He gave no response and asked no further questions.

"He's legit," the one guard said to the other and with that assurance the pistol aimed at me was holstered.

"Please come with us," I was instructed and walked between the otherwise silent guards into the main embassy building and was shown into a security office and turned over to a civilian embassy officer. The guards passed my wallet and passport to the embassy officer, turned, and without further ceremony, returned to their guard posts while sirens and commotion happened just outside the gates.

"Are you the cause of all the commotion out back?" the officer commented as he looked over my passport, and then quickly looked up at me with a start. "Was Mr. Arkadin expecting you?"

"No. I'm sure he wasn't. I didn't even know I was coming until about ten minutes ago," I replied with a shaky voice not even recognizable to myself.

"You'll need to wait for Mr. Arkadin to return for a debriefing, young man," the officer confirmed.

"Do you think I could sit down? I'm not feeling too well," I heard myself say as the room spun and went dark.

When I came to, the fluorescent white lights of the embassy clinic were buzzing in the ceiling. I felt the wax paper covering the examination table crinkle under my legs as I shifted them to sit up. The stolen jacket from the TsKB was gone as well as the scrubs. The bandages around my shoulder stained with blood again from the inside. The nurse on hearing me stir stood up from her desk and entered the examination room.

"How do you feel now?" she asked in a sterile way.

"Hungry, very, very hungry," I replied with a bit of dismay at myself.

"We will need to change that dressing before we get you something to eat," she replied. With all the supplies laid out on a rolling tray table, she began to cut away the gauze and bandages.

"Can you tell me what the wound is?" the nurse asked.

"Gunshot," I revealed.

"Was this dressed in a Russian hospital?" she asked with caution.

"It's okay. I was treated at the Kremlin Clinic. The place was up to standard. No worries," I replied as if it was just everyday business to have been shot and treated at the most elite hospital in the country.

"Well, I've been instructed not to discuss things with you until you've been debriefed by our security chief, so we'll leave it at that," she was warming up a bit.

After the wound was cleaned and the dressing restored, the nurse made sure that my arm could be free to get dressed before she secured it with a sling. She brought me a sweatshirt from Georgetown University to wear, as the scrubs from the TsKB were also somewhat blood stained after all the action of the evening.

"It looks good on you. You should think of enrolling," she joked as she secured a sling for my right arm. "I will let Mr. Arkadin know that you are ready to talk with him."

"Ma'am, what time is it, please?" I asked in a pitiful voice.

"Two o'clock in the morning," she answered and left the room.

I was taken to an interview room by a guard and after a few moments, a very tired looking Arkadin came in with a cup of coffee in his hands. His five o'clock shadow was coming in well. He looked like he had been sleeping at his desk.

"I've asked the guard to bring you a sandwich and a Coke," Arkadin muttered warmly, quite out of character. I thanked him.

"Peter, I don't like it when I get called at ten o'clock at night and I'm told that there has been a good old fashioned international incident outside my embassy gates. Nobody here witnessed a thing and further, nobody can put the pieces together to make any sense of it. The Russian's foreign minister is saying it is an internal affair and is being tight lipped about it. What they don't know is that you emerged from the crossfire without warning.

"Now, why would a bunch of Russian cops start shooting each other up outside the American embassy gates, and how the hell did you get in the middle of it all? I don't think it was coincidence. Please, I'm all ears." He slowly sipped on his mug of steaming black coffee, but then stopped and added, "And please, Peter, don't shovel me any bullshit. It's too late, or too early for that. Just tell me everything I want to know."

"The police officers outside your gates tonight were from two different divisions. I saw six agents from the FSB. They were after me and the major from the FSO who had just grabbed me from the TsKB in a raid with guns and speeding cars. Major Dobrynin was the officer in charge of investigating the shooting at the Tretyakov Gallery on Wednesday, where I, as you know, was shot. I know that three FSB agents were shot and killed by Major Dobrynin. As we didn't hear any more shots fired after I got inside the compound gates, I don't think anybody else was killed," I explained.

"Peter?" Arkadin said from inside his coffee mug and gave me a look that said, 'Go on.'

"Major Dobrynin had started an informal investigation regarding the missing data disc that you are also looking for, which Sanning stole from a now dead mafia boss in Nizhniy Novgorod. After that discussion with his superior officer, the FSB tried to run him and his driver into the Moscow River. He then came straight to the hospital to get me because he rightfully feared that the corrupt agents at the FSB would try to get to me at the hospital with help from his own chain of command in the FSO." I paused and looked at Arkadin to see if it was enough yet.

"Can you tell me why the FSB has your name? Should I be worried about your allegiance, Mr. Turner?" Arkadin remarked with a raised eyebrow.

"The FSB kidnapped me from Nizhniy, thinking as you do, that I know how to contact Sanning after he made off with the disc that they were wanting to lift from the middle man. They brought me to Moscow after I had set up the meeting that your team photographed on the Arbat Street," I confessed.

"Do you have the disc?" he asked, more alert this time.

"No, sir. Sanning said he destroyed it. He used the gallery meeting to bluff the Chechens. Make them think it was a real drop. He was very careful to make sure the FSB agents were able to follow us easily. I figure he knew that when he passed the claim tab from the wardrobe to the Chechens at the gallery that the FSB would go after them, leaving me to walk away. Instead, everybody got killed, Sanning disappeared, I went to hospital and have been in police custody since," I finished with a deep breath.

"And you have been cooperating with the FSO, Major Dobrynin?" he queried with some irritation in his voice.

"I had no choice, sir. He already had so much circumstantial evidence on me that I couldn't not tell him the whole story. It was that or be treated as a suspect," I pleaded.

"So, you would happily cooperate with a Russian intelligence officer instead of aiding representatives from your own country? Is that how we should understand this?" He poised his questions so loaded that only one answer was possible to keep on the good side the line. I did not answer his questions immediately but thought pensively for a moment.

"Mr. Arkadin, sir, do you know what is on that data disc that you are searching for?" I asked, suspecting they weren't sure why they wanted it.

"We have our suspicions," he replied evasively.

"The technology on the disc was developed by Ivan Sergeyevich S., an aviation engineer from the Sokol research and development plant in Nizhniy Novgorod. It is the state property of the Russian Federation. It is not, nor ever has been, property of the United States of America. If I was to help you find this disc and export it to the USA, I would then be a co-conspirator in espionage against the Russian state, and then they could lock me up. At this point, I have still done nothing against the law for which I could be legally detained. Helping the Russian police establish motive for mass murder in a public place of innocent tourists and six state security agents by giving a statement to the investigating police is not a crime punishable by our laws either. I have been caught up in this involuntarily and plan to keep my hands clean," I declared.

"Fair enough. Fair enough," Arkadin conceded. "What more can you tell me about the technology we're looking for?"

"While I'm still in Russia? Absolutely not another word," I admitted.

Arkadin chewed on his lower lip for a moment in thought and then spoke again. "We were not able to retrieve the backpack you said you had checked in the museum's left luggage area. Our contact told us that it had already been seized as evidence. Information about the disc without any connection to Santander leaves you in a poor position for withholding any information, Mr. Turner."

"I have been able to recover the telephone number with the help of the FSO. Dobrynin returned my address book to me on the ride over here." I reached in my front pants pocket and laid it on the table. Arkadin looked at it, picked it up, and flipped through the pages and then tossed it back to me.

"Would we even know if we called the right number if we called every number in that book?" he asked the right question.

"Nope!" I looked at him with a slight gloating in my face, but handed him immediately an olive branch. "As soon as you have me back in the USA, out of the reach of the Russian police and FSB, I will provide you with a full description of the technology that is on the disc and I will even help you to recover it using my connections with Sanning."

Arkadin stood up slowly from the table and stretched his legs and then grumbled to me, "Go get some sleep, kid. It's a long flight back to Washington. I'll make the arrangements for tomorrow afternoon. The nurse has prepared a cot for you in the infirmary." He turned and shuffled out of the room.

"Good night, sir," I called after him.

He answered with just a tired wave above his head as the door closed behind him. He knew he'd been checkmated.

06

35. Two Years Later

For the last few days, my hands had been shaking with nerves and my heart raced every time I turned the small, thin key of my mailbox. I had waited already what seemed like an eternity to receive the evaluation of my thesis defense. Today, my heart stopped for a few beats and legs fell slightly weak as the first envelope I pulled from my post box bore the university logo in two bold letters: GW. This was not a tuition bill as it was from the Elliot School of International Affairs.

I had no patience to wait and open this in ceremonial fashion with my family and my girlfriend in an upscale restaurant with drinks and hors d'oeuvres. With my hands visibly shaking and my heart now beating in my ears, I ripped the envelope open with the blunt notches of my apartment key. I had envisioned the moment already many times behind my desk where I had written the thesis, with a sharp letter opener and wearing white gloves. Nobody in the room would be allowed to breathe. Instead I stood there in the stairwell of the Washington, DC apartment building, struggling to pull a one-page letter from a paper envelope, cursing under my breath as I dropped my keys on the floor. The letter finally unfolded, I turned to the dim light in the entryway. My eyes quickly scanned the letter, skipping the niceties and greetings of a formal letter. Had I been successful?

"Dear Mr. Peter Turner...We are pleased to inform you... Master thesis defense...Organized Crime in the Former Soviet Republics: the USA's most pertinent security risk.... successful... We congratulate you...award you with a Master of Science degree...."

The rest of the letter was irrelevant. I had done it! I let out a "Hoop!" of joy that echoed up the stairwell. As I bent down to pick up my keys, I bumped my head on the sharp edge of the open post box door as I stood up. I cursed under my breath and slammed the door out of disgust. The flimsy metal door bounced open and as the door swung open again, it pulled with it a postcard that landed face down on the floor at my feet.

Latching the post box door closed this time, I bent down a second time to pick up the postcard on the ground. I flipped it over in my fingers as I stood up, and as I was able to make out the chaotic scene of the picture, my blood froze. I stood paralyzed as I looked at the tragic scene of the Morning of the Execution of the Streltsiy in miniature, printed on glossy card stock. I instinctively flipped the card over. It read:

"Hey Kid, Congrats on the thesis! Need a job? Ray's Steak House, Arlington 19:00."

The elation of the moment of achievement turned to horror as I looked again at the dramatic scene on Red Square on the postcard and remembered the terror of being shot and witnessing six others lose their lives in front of my horrified eyes. I felt that I needed to run.

I tucked both my letter from the university and the postcard into my book bag and exited the apartment building on to F Street and turned right on 18th Street and at the corner of H Street. I walked straight into the Hampton Inn and booked a room for the night. I paid in cash.

I plopped down in an easy chair and pulled the telephone onto my lap. From my book bag, I took an address book, worn and battered but filled with names, numbers, and email addresses of my contacts around the world. Finding the phone number I needed, a Virginia area code, I dialed and waited for an answer.

"How can I direct your call?" a nondescript operator's voice asked.

"Special Agent Hal Parker," I replied with no niceties or greetings.

"Connecting you now," the operator answered flatly.

After a few rings of an extension telephone I didn't know the number to, I heard the agent answer.

"Please identify yourself," the man's voice said.

"Turner, Peter, 52-48-76," I revealed.

A moment passed.

"Mr. Turner, this is Special Agent Parker. What is your status?" the contact questioned.

"Santander has made contact. Will meet tonight at 19:00 in Arlington. Please advise instructions." I waited for a response.

"Are you positive?" Parker questioned in a bit of disbelief.

"Absolutely. No one else could have known the details but him," I confirmed.

"No updates. Proceed with caution. No wires, no surveillance. Make contact and try to ascertain where he is staying. Call back no more than sixty minutes after the meeting," were Parker's instructions.

"Understood," I confirmed and hung up the telephone.

I took a cab from downtown across the river on the Roosevelt bridge and up Wilson Boulevard until just past the Court House Metro Station. The cab dropped me across the street. Not wanting to create any suspicion on Del's part, I did not hesitate to cross the street and darted out in front of the oncoming traffic and lighted the curb and sidewalk in front of Ray's Steak House. I walked right in at seven o'clock and looked about the waiting area. Empty. I approached the hostess at her podium and stood without knowing what to ask.

"I am here to meet my party. Sanning?" I propositioned, not sure if he would use a name he had already been known by.

The cute blonde in her server's uniform looked over her reservations lists and shook her head with an apologetic look on her face. He blonde bob shook from side to side with her head. "Are you sure it's tonight?" she asked back.

"Oh, I'm sorry, it's not Sanning, it is Streltsiy. Can you check again, please?" I tried to sound forgetful and a bit spacey as if I met people every day at upscale steak houses as a habit.

"Oh, yes, Mr. Streltsiy has arrived and is waiting for you. Please follow me." She smiled and showed me to the back of the restaurant, which wasn't full, but was certainly far from empty... and then I saw him with a beer in hand, sipping carefully from a full mug. When he saw me, his face lit up and he quickly stood up from his chair.

"How the hell are ya, kid?" he bellowed and gave me a manly bear hug. I can't say I wasn't pleased to see him again. "How's the shoulder? Kid, you look great! You look smarter than when I last saw you! You got your color back!"

"Del, the last time you saw me I was on the floor of the Tretyakov Gallery bleeding out!" I reminded him. "Of course I'm going to look a little bit better."

"C'mon sit down. I understand celebrations are in order! Heard you passed your thesis off for a degree." He snapped his fingers for the waitress and ordered me a tall Pepsi with lots of ice. I chuckled remembering the fuss he made in Moscow two years ago about ice with the clueless waiter.

"Del," I started, "of course nothing I learn about you will ever surprise me again, but how do you know that I passed my thesis defense, and how did you get my home address?"

"How do I know about your thesis? Who doesn't know about your paper? The whole community has been talking about it. It's making the circles and you are going to be a very hot asset in the intelligence community as soon as that diploma is placed in your hands. I thought I'd try to be the first to get an offer in!" he said as a matter of simple business. "Are you hungry?"

"Sure, why not? I'll call my father after I've celebrated with you," I said with some sarcasm and opened the menu.

"So, kid. I had to lay pretty low after the shootout at the Tretyakov. I heard about a week later that you had made it stateside again but you didn't leave any details on the answering machine. What happened with you? How did you get on?" Del asked.

"Well, it wasn't anything crazy. Woke up in the hospital with big Bertha as a nurse. The embassy helped me get a plane ticket booked and I flew home maybe ten days later. Thank God, there was no more drama! I couldn't have handled it," I fibbed.

"That's funny. Could have sworn I saw you on TV shaking hands with Boris Yeltsin at the Kremlin Hospital. You looked pretty shell shocked," he said with a wink at me as he sipped his beer again.

"Jeez, that's right. Yeltsin! I forgot about that. Sure wish I had a picture of that." I put on a bit of a show, trying to figure out how much he knew and how much info he was fishing for.

"So, I assume having been treated at the TsKB that you were under guard. That place is more a fortress than the Kremlin is, but doesn't let in tourists!" he attested.

"Yes, I was kept under guard, they took a statement from me and then turned me over to the embassy. From there they booked me a flight home," I extrapolated.

"And you had nothing to do with the shootout at the American Embassy that made the international headlines," he probed.

"Nope! Just one shootout a week for me, please! One bullet wound in my life time is enough for me, Del," I lied.

"Funny, because I thought I saw a one-armed fellow that looked like you run from a crashed car into the embassy gates with two marines with pistols drawn," he said with a cold stare on his face.

I balked, "C'mon, Del. What don't you know? Why are you playing games with me?"

"I just wanted to see your face when I know you are lying to me. It helps me get a baseline for the rest of the conversation I want to have with you tonight. Does the bureau have you on a leash? Did you already call them to let them know that I contacted you?" Del wasn't guessing. I nodded my head in defeat as I sipped my tall glass of frosty cola.

"Was your call from Washington two years ago under duress as well?" he continued to shoot holes in every cover that was contrived for me to bring him in close enough to get him.

I didn't even bother answering him anymore; he obviously knew all the procedures and tricks that all the world's intelligence and counter intelligence agencies use.

"Have they compensated you well? You certainly have enough experience and knowledge at this point to have started with them at a rather high level. No bachelor's degree entry level position for you, I'm sure. Did they pay for your degree as well?" Del saw straight through the details of the last twenty-four months.

I piped up in my own defense. "You didn't leave me many choices, Del. It was either full cooperation or be charged with aiding a terrorist organization or conspiring with them as a foreign agent. It was the fry pan in the States or the fire in Russia. Thought I might at least get some good education out of it instead of thirty years in Siberia. You would have done the same!"

"Absolutely, kid, absolutely," Del agreed. "I'm glad it worked out for you. It's like I said to you in Moscow, you've got skills and they needed some honing. I'm glad to hear you took the chance to get that training. Did they give you any security clearances for your research for the thesis? The material you've been able to dig up was not stuff you read in *The Economist.*" Just then the waiter brought our dinners and placed them in front of us both during an awkward silence.

"Tell you what, Del, I'm just going to eat this nice juicy steak and these perfectly browned potato wedges, and you can tell me MY life's story while I listen. Geez! If you already know everything why do you invite me for a chat?" I griped at him as I sawed vigorously into the meat on my platter, crammed a chunk of beef in my mouth, and chewed with a look of defiance on my face.

"Kid, you gotta understand something about yourself. You're a boy scout. You're an idealist. If you had grown up in California you might even have become an activist with a granola smell to you. You can't keep working for the Americans in the capacity you are now. Once you understand the depth of their corruption, you'll think the Russians still have the training wheels on. The folks you are working for don't even know who they are serving and whose agenda they are forwarding," Del expounded.

"Hmmm..." I answered chewing another piece of my steak while I crammed in potato wedge showing little interest in his lecture.

Del could see that his tactic wasn't working and put his utensils down. He came down off his own high horse and said with a stone-cold face, "Kid, we're going after Zlobin and his entire network. We're going to bring them down." Del said this with no inflection or emotion. He was done trying to sell anything to me. I stopped chewing the meat in my mouth and looked him straight in the eyes. I swallowed the half-masticated bite of meat and gristle with a bit of a gulp. I had to wash it down with a sip from my glass.

"Zlobin? You're going after Zlobin and his entire empire?" I stammered in disbelief, stunned. Del only nodded back, void of any bravado and swagger. His eyes showed he was serious, but worried at the same time.

"I assume you know what you're getting into, Del. This isn't just some provincial gangster like Mr. P. who couldn't keep his mouth shut. This is the most sophisticated, the most educated, and arguably the most vicious group of criminals that have ever existed in the modern history of civilization. They have no rules! They are into everything. I estimate his network alone is siphoning at least a quarter of Ukraine's state revenues into their own network. They pretty much own anything that is shipping to, from, in, and out of any Black Sea port. Their network is massive!"

Del nodded again and said quietly, "We've done our homework."

"Del, you just can't show up one day with a cover story on your own and slip this guy a pill in his glass. I don't think anybody outside of the most inner circle has actually even been able to specifically identify who Zlobin is! There are at least four different descriptions of the man, and they don't trust anybody from outside their own circles. You won't even get close to him!" I explained in earnest, trying to convince him of the fool's errand he was starting off on.

"Kid, we know we can't get close to him, and assassination is not our goal. We want to slowly pick apart his different networks, expose the local corruption to local authorities, and whittle him down, revenue stream by revenue stream. We hope to get through all the tangled webs that protect him from prosecution and let the Ukrainian authorities finally get him on their own terms. We are just going to work in the shadows on this one," he said with an honest twinge of humility.

"Del, who are 'we'? Who do you work for?" I asked again with a bit of defiance.

"I don't work for anybody. I work with a network, and we receive support from different intelligence agencies around the world to work on projects that they know they don't have the resources or expertise to do themselves.

"We don't have a name. We don't have a list of operatives, and we don't have a pension plan," he said with a sarcastic smile on his face, "and I am asking you now if you are interested in really making an impact, or are you satisfied with just making a difference?"

"I need to know what kind of impact you're talking about Del," I insisted. "Impact can go both ways. I need to know that I would be supporting the rule of law and not helping to create chaos and conflict."

"Kid, tell me, is the bureau still looking for that disc I took from Mr. P., the one with the radar tracking technology I explained to you about in Moscow?" Del asked, changing the subject. "Do they still harass you to find me and try to get that disc for them?"

"Yes, that's why I'm still on their payroll," I admitted.

"Well, then you've got job security. As I told you in Moscow, the disc was destroyed. Nobody gets it. Somebody in the future might invent something just as useful to the rogue elements in the world, and we will steal it again and destroy it again. We don't trust anybody with something so attractive. Somebody somewhere will always want to get their sticky fingers on it. It may be a measly twenty million dollars in the big picture of national defense budgets, but for one man, that's a life of luxury, leisure, and power. Most people can't resist that temptation. The FBI and CIA can keep searching for the disc from the Sokol plant, but I promise you, it will never be found." Del was adamant.

"Del, why me?" I asked.

"Kid, are you so conceited that I have to tell it to you again so you get a big head about it? You're an idealist and you've got the skills we need for this task. That's all I'm going to say about it." He was slightly annoyed at my youthful need for encouragement, unable to believe that I had something special in myself.

"What kind of protections are there?" I asked, realizing that they worked off the grid.

"None! In fact, you'll be hunted by the same people next year that pay you to do a project this year," he said as a matter of fact.

"Can I get out when I want to and need to?" I asked with reservations.

"As long as you don't get your hands on the dirty money and think you can walk away with the spoils of a defeated target," he replied in an accommodating voice.

"What do I tell the FBI?" I asked with some trepidation.

"Anything you want to. Tell them you're going on vacation. Tell them you're taking a different job, but don't worry, they'll have a very hard time finding you if you come along for the ride," Del reassured me. "We have a client who will fund us for three years to bring down Zlobin. They're offering all sorts of support that we've never had on a project before as they have also recognized these groups to be their largest security problem, just as you outlined in your thesis. This could very well create the momentum we need to put the internationals out of business and help the national agencies get control again and start to stamp out those cockroaches. This could be the beginning of the end for them."

I sat without further questions of Del, just doubts about myself. I looked away as my thoughts raced in circles around my head. I reflected on my newly finished degree. What was I going to do with it? What kind of difference was I really going to make? Was the world really any safer because I wrote a paper?

I thought of Dean Karamzin's urgency to expose the local corruption. I thought of Yulia and her hope to continue Bolshakov's work. I reflected of Major Dobrynin and his determination to do the right thing regardless of the consequences. I remembered the old lady on the bus in Nizhniy Novgorod whose grandson was going off to fight in Chechnya for nothing of value, nothing noble, but to extend corruption's long arm of cruelty.

Del spoke again, bringing me back to the present moment, "Kid! Are you in?"

Made in the USA
San Bernardino, CA
16 June 2019